Watch for More Novels by Robert N. Chan
from *Indigo Sea Press*

indigoseapress.com

Girl

By

Robert N. Chan

Deep Indigo Books
Published by Indigo Sea Press, LLC.
Winston-Salem

Deep Indigo Books
Indigo Sea Press, LLC
302 Ricks Drive
Winston-Salem, NC 27103

First Deep Indigo Books edition published
January, 2016
Deep Indigo Books, Moon Sailor and all production design are trademarks of Indigo Sea Press, used under license.

For information regarding bulk purchases of this book, digital purchase and special discounts, please contact the publisher at indigoseapress.com

Cover design by Pan Morelli

Manufactured in the United States of America
ISBN 978-1-63066-381-0

"To my wife Amy and our son Adam, now 18 and off to college. *What hath God wrought?*"

I

Sleep Tight, Ya Morons

"Are you too busy *again* to come with us, Hannah?" Deborah asked as they left school.

"I'm afraid I have to pass up the thrill of going three blocks out of my way to watch the boys leaving the *yeshiva*," Hannah said. "Not that I don't enjoy seeing you and the others peek through your fingers and giggle and gossip about your marriage prospects."

"*Forgive me*. I should've known the *rebbetzin*-in-training would have no time for fun." Of course Hannah wanted to be a *rebbetzin*. What girl didn't? As a rabbi's wife, perhaps the wife of a famous one, she'd have unlimited opportunities to perform *tikkun olam*, helping to repair the world, an obligation she considered to be Judaism's most sacred. Rav Moscovitz would've been outraged had she told him her opinion, but she'd never do that. She listened to Rav Moscovitz, didn't speak to him.

Deborah tucked an errant hair under her headscarf and pulled up her shapeless wool coat to cover her neck. Lips moving, she swayed back and forth as if *davening* in prayer. Hannah didn't mind her friends teasing her for following God's commandments. Having recently turned fifteen, soon to be introduced to her future husband, she had every reason to hope for the best as long as her sterling reputation remained untarnished.

It seemed to her that everyone, not just her friends, made fun of her. Just this morning at breakfast, she'd said, "God must love gentiles very much, He made so many of them." Her father called her *my little philosopher*; and her mother sat with her elbow on her knee, fist under her chin, mimicking a famous statue. When she played with them, Hannah's younger sisters,

Robert N. Chan

Rivka, Sarah and Rebekah, and her younger brother, Isaac, enjoyed laughing at her silliness. Maybe in part because she herself came from such a small family, Hannah thought five children would be the proper number for a *rebbetzin* who'd need time to help the members of the community and maybe even engage with the outside world.

In spite of their teasing, Hannah knew her parents loved her and liked it when she expressed her own thoughts...as long as she didn't go too far. While there were many unbendable rules, the basic ones were clear and simple: to follow the Torah, put the needs of the community before her own desires and honor her father, mother, and Rav Moscovitz.

Leaving Deborah, Hannah headed home through familiar streets. So far the winter of 1990 had been cold and wet. Today was no exception. She pulled her headscarf tight against the wind-driven drizzle and realized she'd been singing to herself, "The morning stars sang together, and all the sons of God shouted for joy," a Yiddish lullaby she'd sung yesterday to Rivka as she tucked her in for her nap.

A man came from the other direction. She sensed him look at her. Lately men seemed to be staring at her all the time, probably her overactive imagination. She focused her gaze on the sidewalk, but not before noticing that, although he wore a yarmulke, the man didn't have a full beard. Her father disliked the modern orthodox almost as much as he disliked reformed and conservative Jews, whom he called *minim*, heretics. The way he would spit out the word communicated that he considered them even worse than the Christian or atheist *goyim*. "We don't dislike other people," her mother had explained. "Our traditions and our community keep us safe and make us who we are. Those people who think it's okay for men and women to touch in public or turn on lights on *Shabbos* compromise with the word of God." She didn't need to remind Hannah of God's feelings about such compromisers and doubters.

Hannah had never had a conversation of more than a few dozen words with someone who wasn't *haredi*, ultra-orthodox.

2

But under the covers with a flashlight while her family slept, she would read decidedly un-orthodox books, even essays by Emma Goldman, a distant relative whom her family referred to rarely and then only in angry whispers. But what she wrote made sense: "The most violent element in society is ignorance." And she could be funny: "Every society has the criminals it deserves."

As she walked, Hannah delighted in the tiny droplets of rain that hit her face with cold little hellos, like angels brushing their wings against her skin. The sky darkened and the droplets became full-fledged raindrops. The butcher, Mordechai Kaplan, stood in the doorway of his shop, looking out on the street, now deserted except for Hannah. His stomach seemed about to burst through his blood-splattered apron. Blood? Only small spots, but there shouldn't have been any by the time the meat arrived at his store. The *shochet* must drain all blood from the carcass.

Although she'd known him for four years—a relative newcomer to the community, he'd arrived from upstate when the community's previous butcher died—Hannah averted her eyes, as she would with any man outside her home. But it wasn't just that, the way he always stared at her while he spoke to her mother seemed creepy. Yet another example of the overactive imagination Mother chided her about.

A puddle forced her to step closer to the shop, close enough to smell the rotten egg stink of bad chicken.

"Come in; warm up," the butcher said.

She'd never do such a thing.

He stepped into the rain and looked up and down the street. Then he grabbed her wrist. Yanked her inside.

Hannah screamed. He slapped her.

"Shut your mouth!"

Squeezing her wrist so hard she thought he would break it, he locked the door with his free hand and shut the lights off in the front. He dragged her past the counter and into the back room, her rubber heels squeaking along the floor. She squirmed but couldn't escape his grip. He slammed the heavy wooden door, trapping her in the place where he cut the meat. A single bulb hanging from a frayed cord did little to illuminate the room. Cold mist wafted from the adjoining meat locker's ajar steel door.

Her stomach clenched. She was too scared to scream, only a soft high-pitched mewl. Was he going to hang her on a hook like a side of beef?

Her gaze fixed on the knives and cleavers arrayed along the pitted wooden table and the splattered circles, oblongs and tears of blood . Dead eyes stared from a severed chicken head.

Everything went fuzzy.

He let go of her. His hands went to his belt.

She darted toward the door.

He grabbed her arm. Spun her around. Slapped her face.

"Stand still!"

"Wha-what are you going to—?"

"I said, shut up."

He took a long glittery knife from the table and held it in front of her face. Would he slice her throat in a single motion like a *schochet* slaughtering an animal?

He touched the point of the knife to her neck. She trembled.

"Take off your coat."

She shook her head. The knife-point cut her.

Still holding the knife to her neck, he unbuttoned her coat and pulled it open so it fell to the floor.

"Now your blouse."

She couldn't move except to shiver like on the coldest day ever.

He stuck the blade between her neck and the fabric. She felt its tip in her backbone, a tiny disgusting mouse running up and down her spine.

"Are you going to take it off, or should I cut it off?"

What would Mother say if she came home with her nice new shirt cut to ribbons?

Her hands shook. She couldn't undo the buttons.

He slapped her. Her face felt as if it were on fire. She tasted blood. He hit her again. He stared into her eyes.

4

Girl

"I'm sorry I hit you, Hannah," he said, his voice soft like her uncle's. "I don't want to hurt you. Just do what I say and everything will be fine." He brought the knife back to her neck, almost gentle now, like Abraham and Isaac on Mt. Moriah. "Please don't make me hurt you."

She undid the top button, then the next.

She didn't want to die. She whispered, "*Sh'ma Yisrael Adonai Eloheinu Adonai Eḥad.*" "Hear, O Israel: the Lord is our God, the Lord is One." The prayer a distant relative had said while being burned at the stake for refusing to renounce his religion. She took a deep breath. She had to do something, couldn't just let him...

Hannah hit him. He laughed. She tried to scratch his face. He grabbed her hand and pushed back until her wrist started to crack. Then he punched her stomach. She doubled up. Taking a handful of her hair, he pulled her into a standing position. She shook all over.

The light from the single bulb that had seemed dim before now burned her eyes.

He held the knife an inch from her right eye.

"If you want to be able to see, you'll take your clothes off. Now!"

Tears streaming down her cheeks, she took off her blouse, then let her skirt drop to the floor. She tried to cover her chest and down there.

"Stand straight. Hands at your side. Don't make me tell you again."

Her teeth chattered. She had to calm herself. She tried to count the tiles on the floor, couldn't get beyond two.

"Take off your underwear."

She shook her head.

"Take it off!"

"I...ca-can't."

He nodded as if he understood, then cut her underclothes. Not all the way. Enough so they drifted to the floor like dead leaves.

"Because you've been good, you can leave on your shoes

5

and knee socks."

He untied his apron. Undid his pants.

She whimpered.

The knives! She feinted toward the door. Pants around his ankles, he blocked her way. She darted toward the table.

He grabbed her hair, then yanked it so hard she fell to the floor. He kicked her, knocking the air out of her. He pulled her to her feet by her hair.

"Try to run or fight me, and I'll really hurt you." He slapped her again.

Through tear-clouded eyes, she again looked at the knives on the table. Too far.

"Lie down."

She didn't move. He shoved her. She fell. Her head bonked on the floor. The butcher flopped on top of her. She bucked, not even moving him an inch. He held her shoulder and forced her legs apart. Then...

The butcher got up. Turning his side to her as if to shield his nakedness, he pulled up his pants and straightened his clothes. Hannah didn't move. The pain seemed to be coming from far away. From somewhere above, she saw herself lying there, naked, bleeding, whimpering.

"Get dressed and stop that blubbering."

He pulled her to her feet.

His grip loosened and she fell. He looked at her as if she were a large clump of grease.

She couldn't move, couldn't even cover herself with her hands. Her life had ended. If only her brain would stop thinking. If only she could forget what happened, forget what it had been like to be Hannah.

He again pulled her to her feet, this time spreading her legs so they'd support her. She didn't care whether she stood or fell. The shame of her nakedness enveloped her, but putting on clothes wouldn't change that.

He picked up her underpants and brassiere with the tips of

his fingers and tossed them to her.

Her hands shook so much she dropped them. He hit her again. She felt nothing beyond the awful wetness between her legs, his yuck slithering down her inner thigh.

He threw her blouse and skirt at her. Acting out of vague and distant habit, she held them to her front, covering what she could as she reached for her torn underclothes. Although he'd already seen *everything*, she turned her back to him. By tying a knot, she made her underpants stay in place. She pulled on her skirt and buttoned her blouse. She tried to straighten her clothes. She kept trying, brushing them with her hands, smoothing the wrinkles, pulling at the hem. They felt like they belonged to another girl. A nice girl, one who hadn't been...

She had to go home. What would she say to her mother? What could she say? Her eyes wanted to cry. Her stomach wanted to vomit. She couldn't do either.

He grabbed her shoulder and turned her toward him. Hand under her chin, he gently raised her head. Unable to avert her eyes, she stared into his face, the beard black with strands of white, the nose spider-webbed with broken blood vessels, the hate-filled eyes the color of boiled beef.

"No one is to know," he said. "No one would believe you anyway. I've never before been with a girl from the community, so my reputation is spotless and the word of a girl..."

She held back the tears, her entire being filled with shame.

The butcher opened the door and stuck his head out. The bright light blinded her. He looked both ways, then shoved her. She skidded onto the sidewalk. The door slammed behind her, sounding angry at her for having crossed its threshold.

She couldn't restrain her sobs. Her legs wobbled. Two steps and she collapsed. She couldn't move a muscle. The sky darkened. The air cooled; the rain became a drizzle. She lay where she'd fallen.

"Can I help?" A deep, kind voice.

She looked up. Oh, no! The homeless *schvartze* who'd been

begging on their streets for the past few weeks. As a colored person, he didn't belong in their neighborhood. Hands under her armpits, he gently helped her to her feet. She'd resisted, or at least tried to, when the butcher grabbed her; but now she felt as limp as a rag doll.

Her coat had a big dirty gray streak from the sidewalk. Mommy would kill her.

"You're shivering."

He took off his jacket—leather, one sleeve torn, a pocket ripped—and put it around Hannah's shoulders. She told herself she should give it back to him. But she'd stopped shivering, and anyway her arms weren't working right.

"What happened to you?"

She bit her lip, shook her head.

"Are you hurt?"

Hannah didn't respond. *Hurt? That's almost funny. No, Mr. Black Man. I'm dead. Well, not dead but not alive.*

"Where do you live?" His right eye twitched. The left one had a bright red spot.

She pointed.

"Come on. One step after another." Voice deep but soft, almost the way God would speak to a child. "You'll feel better when you get home."

Moving her legs caused pain...down there. When he directed her, arm around her waist, she didn't resist. Even with her life having ended, she knew it was a sin to let a man touch her. She would never ever be able to explain why she had permitted it.

They passed women, two, four, more; Hannah didn't know. They gave her well-deserved nasty looks but avoided looking at the *schvartze*.

Someone, Reuben the plumber maybe—her brain had ceased to function—knocked away the man's arm with a hard swat. The plumber spat out his words with such hate that Hannah didn't understand them. Maybe if her brain were clearer... The *schvartze* seemed to shrink. He shuffled two steps back. The plumber blew his nose on a twenty-dollar bill, then tossed it at

8

the man's feet.

"Take this and don't *ever* come back here! Understand?" He turned to Hannah. "Go straight home."

One step. Okay. Now another. I can make it.

The two blocks to her house felt like ten.

Her hands shook so much she couldn't fit her key into the lock. When Mommy opened the door, Hannah fell forward sobbing. Her mother held her at arms' length.

"You let a man touch you, a *schvartze* yet." She slapped her across the face, something she'd never done. "I've heard from three people already."

"He was nice," Hannah said through tears. "He helped me after—"

"*Nice?*"

"Please, Mommy, please."

"Please, what?" Voice cold as summer borscht.

Hannah shook her head. She understood that having been seen being touched by any man in public, particularly *that man*, would lead to this sort of reaction. She had to explain.

"Yes?" Her mother thrust her jaw forward. "I'm waiting."

How could she say it?

"The butcher…" Her voice turned hoarse. "Mr. Kaplan, the butcher…attacked me. He…" Hannah took a deep breath.

Mommy did the same.

Hannah pointed to the rip in her blouse.

"Why would Mordechai Kaplan do that?" Mommy's face sagged for a second; then her eyes narrowed. "The *schvartze* had his arm around you. You're wearing his jacket!"

Hannah had forgotten she had it on. She knocked it off with two violent shrugs.

Her mother had a confused look: anger, sadness, maybe pity too. Hannah had sinned.

Shouldn't Mommy have asked me to explain about the butcher? She must see how awful I look. No, it's better this way. I couldn't tell her, can't tell anyone.

"Go to your room," Mommy's calm, take-charge voice.

"Change your clothes, wash your face and hands, and pray. I'll call your father. He'll call Rav Moscovitz. I sent your brother and sisters to my parents so we won't be disturbed."

Rav Moscovitz? Hannah bit her lip.

"You're going to have to tell Rav Moscovitz the truth," Mother said.

Tell the truth? How?

As Hannah climbed the stairs, some part of herself left her body—like a soul departing a corpse—and looked down at her. She watched herself take step after step and felt only pity and not much of that.

Hannah prayed with greater intensity than she'd ever prayed before. There had to be a reason God had allowed the butcher to do what he'd done and let the *schvartze* touch her. Perhaps He was testing her to see if she'd take the easy path, if she knew that to lie would disrespect Him. She asked one thing of Him: to make her brave and give her tongue the power to tell Rav Moscovitz what had happened—everything, even what Mordechai Kaplan had done when he got on top of her. Rav Moscovitz would make it right. Well, not *right*, nothing could do that, but better. He'd make sure Mordechai Kaplan was punished.

After what seemed like hours, but had only been twenty minutes on the clock by her bed, Mother called her to come downstairs.

She continued to pray as she descended the stairs.

Rav Moscovitz sprawled across the living room couch. The last time he came to their house, over a year ago, mother had cleaned the house like it was the week before Passover. Now she hadn't even straightened the rug. He was more than the leader of the community, far more. His grandfather had had a vision just thirty-six days before the Nazis invaded. A week later he led their congregation out of Poland, all 198 of them. Their four-year harrowing journey took them, on foot, across Russia, through war-torn China to Shanghai, then huddled together in the cargo hold of a freighter first to Panama, then to Cuba. Only half the original unwanted-by-anyone group made it to Crown Heights. Now the congregation numbered well over 400, all living within five blocks of each other, scrupulously following the same traditions, rules, and rituals they had in Poland.

Home an hour earlier than usual, her father sat straight and stiff in the armchair. Her mother stood in her proper place behind him. With a languid flick of his wrist, Rav Moscovitz directed Hannah to stand in the center of the rug. She obeyed, her scarf-covered head bent.

"Hannah, you allowed a man to put his arm around your waist and drape his jacket over your shoulders." His tone conveyed on-high authority, like God speaking to her in a dream. Not like the black man's kindly God voice, more like "I, the Lord your God, am a jealous God, punishing the children for the sin of the fathers to the third and fourth generation."

"He helped me." Hannah's voice sounded not quite like her own but not like anyone else's either. "Mordechai Kaplan had just done...that very most terrible thing to me. I was dazed, hurt. I didn't know what the man was doing, only that he was helping me."

She could hardly believe how clearly and honestly she was explaining why she'd been lying in the street, unable to make herself move and what the butcher had done. God heard her prayer.

"How could you not know what he was doing?" Rav Moscovitz asked, voice now so quiet she could hardly hear him.

Please God help me explain.

"Mordechai Kaplan had pulled me into his back room and..." her lips continued to move; but sounds stopped passing through them. Even with God's help, she couldn't say more.

While she spoke, Father had shifted in his chair, face getting redder and redder. When she finished, he turned to Rav Moscovitz, "If Mordechai did that—"

Rav Moscovitz cut him off with a raised palm. Father had squeezed his lips so tight they disappeared, replaced by a thin dark line. His eyes bulged.

"Perhaps, Hannah, the *vagrant* did that to you," Rav Moscovitz said. From the corner of her eye—she would never look directly at him—Hannah saw him stroke his long white beard. She felt the stare from his dark, furious eyes bore into her. "And your brain couldn't acknowledge that you had been *attacked* by a *schvartze*. Mordechai's shop was nearby. Maybe you'd just seen him standing in the doorway, and your mind convinced itself that Mordechai—"

"No. I told you the truth, here before God. The butcher did that horrible thing to me." Hannah would never have believed she'd disagree with Rav Moscovitz.

He emitted a little sigh. He looked older than he had a few minutes earlier. Mother's eyes were wide with shock. Father started toward Hannah, his hand raised ready to slap her. Rav Moscovitz shook his head. Father's arm dropped to his side, and he sat back down.

"Mordechai is a pious and charitable man," Rav Moscovitz said. Seeing his gaze drift away from her and his long pale hand slide in front of his nose and mouth, Hannah realized he knew what he said wasn't true, or at least not the whole truth. "I'll talk to him and the people who saw you on the street. Then I'll come back here. In the meantime, don't speak to anyone."

Father squeezed the arms of his chair so hard his knuckles turned white. "If Mordechai did that to you, we'll deal with him within the community." His voice shook with anger, all the more terrifying because Hannah didn't know if it were directed at her, the butcher, or both of them. That he was even speaking up in Rav Moscovitz's presence... He turned toward Rav Moscovitz. Hannah would never have imagined that he'd look at Rav Moscovitz that way. Apparently Rav Moscovitz hadn't either, as his head jerked back ever so slightly. She wouldn't have noticed that before Mordechai Kaplan had... Now she noticed everything.

"I love you, Hannah." Her father's rage under control; he sounded like he used to when Hannah was a little kid or when he spoke to Rivka. "Try to understand that this is all very complicated. Rav Moscovitz has to deal with it in a way that is best for both you and the community."

No way she'd ever understand; she wouldn't even try.

"While we wait for Rav Moscovitz to return, go to your room and pray," Mommy said, in *her* talking-to-Rivka voice. As if Hannah hadn't prayed enough.

"May I do my schoolwork?"

Hannah hoped she'd draw comfort from her work. She always had, and she tried to believe that *always* included now.

The three adults exchanged glances, unreadable.

"This is very, very serious, Hannah," Father said, green eyes staring at the carpet. "We don't know if you'll be going back to school."

Hannah couldn't breathe. For a horrible moment, she was back on the butcher's tiled, blood-splattered floor.

"The fewer people who know, the better. It will be hard enough to find someone to marry her," Rav Moscovitz said.

Hannah doubled up like she'd been punched in the stomach.

Mommy walked her to the stairs. Out of the men's line of sight, she kissed Hannah on top of her head.

"Do they believe me?" Hannah asked as they went up to the second floor.

"Y-e-s." Three separate syllables. "I do. Your father does. I'm not sure about Rav Moscovitz. But they both know what people saw."

"How could that be more important?"

"Your marriage prospects, your purity. Almost nothing's more important than that."

"But Mommy—"

"If people think the *schvartze* forced himself on you, they'll be more likely to believe it wasn't your fault." *How could it be my fault? Unless... Did I do something, some little thing, to cause it?* "If you blame Mordechai Kaplan, he'll deny it, maybe accuse you of leading him on." Mommy threw up her hands. "I'm sure you did nothing wrong, but—"

"But WHAT!" Hannah yelled, then put her hand over her mouth. She didn't want the men downstairs to hear.

"Some people would believe him, no one would *ever* forget what happened, and some would always think of you as a..."

"A whore?" She'd heard men use that word.

Mommy's head kicked back.

"That *is* the word they'd use, right?" Hannah asked.

Mommy held her stomach as if about to be sick, and maybe she was.

Trembling like she had when...Hannah went to the room she shared with her three younger sisters, who she knew wouldn't be returning that night. People often commented on how beautiful she was with her red hair, big green eyes, and smooth pale skin. Smartest girl in the entire school. None of that mattered anymore. No one would marry her now. Not fair! She'd planned out her whole life.

If she lied like Rav Moscovitz wanted, maybe she could still have a normal life. She had to have faith. Rav Moscovitz and God would work it out. She *had* faith. Didn't she?

Mother came in later, shoulders slumped, body stooped. Even though she'd only had five children, she looked old at thirty-two. Hannah had never noticed before.

Mother sat on her bed and stroked her back.

"I'm sorry I yelled at you when you came home. I was just so scared," Mommy stopped stroking Hannah, hugged herself, then rested her warm hand on Hannah's shoulder. "We'll work this out."

"By lying?"

She waved Hannah's words away. "If you accuse Mordechai Kaplan, it could end up involving the police. People outside the community might hear, and they'd think...it wouldn't be good for us. We don't involve outsiders with our problems." Mommy sighed. "We'll lower our sights. No rabbinical students, but we'll find someone suitable."

Angry or not, Hannah needed her mother's comfort. She

14

hugged her. Thank God Mommy hugged her back.

"Why doesn't anyone care what the butcher—"

"We care very much, Hannah." Very gently Mommy covered Hannah's mouth with her hand. Hannah felt it tremble. "But we must focus on what's most important. Do you think the parents of a good pious boy would want their son to marry a girl who was... This has to be *handled* and kept quiet."

Hannah felt sick. She couldn't tell if Mommy believed the things she was saying. She wasn't sure if anyone but her truly believed what they said.

"Your father will make sure Rav Moscovitz deals with the butcher without damaging the community's reputation...or yours."

"You're sure?"

Hannah looked into her mother's eyes. What she saw caused a stabbing pain behind her eyes.

"One thing before Rav Moscovitz returns. Why didn't you scream when that man put his jacket on you?"

"Mommy! I'd just been—"

A thin wail emerged from her mother's throat.

"How can we explain it without mentioning the butcher, Hannah?"

Too angry to risk a response, Hannah bit her lips. Mother tightened hers to a thin line, the way she did when thinking hard. Hannah's mouth tasted like iron filings. Blood. She must've bitten her lips extra hard.

"We need to come up with something everyone will believe," Mommy said. "So you can start to heal."

Hannah had been brought up to believe that the community strictly followed the teachings of the Torah and the Talmud, the word of God. But what if that weren't true? Then she had nothing, not even hope.

"We've got to get the story straight," Mommy said.

She means crooked.

"I got it! He drugged you." Mommy smiled. "You couldn't help yourself or even scream or fight him off." She stroked

Hannah's cheek. "I'll be right back."

Mommy returned with a hatpin. Shoulders back, her usual perfect posture. She looked younger again.

"Pull up your shirt."

Hannah didn't do it. She wanted to ask what Mommy had in mind but didn't do that either. Mommy lifted her shirt and stabbed her right side.

"Ouch!"

Hannah had yelled because she'd expected the stab to hurt, but it didn't. Mommy swabbed the little wound with an alcohol-soaked cotton ball. Hannah shoved her hand away. Not hard, but she'd never done anything like that since she was little and didn't know better.

"God doesn't want us to lie," Hannah said, voice quivering.

"Oh, so now you know what God wants? When I was your age, I thought—"

"And when did you stop thinking?" Hannah was appalled by what had come out of her mouth and even more appalled by the realization that she'd meant it.

Her mother drew her hand back but dropped it without striking. Without another word, she left the room.

Of course, Hannah would do what Rav Moscovitz told her, but... No, the primary lesson drilled into her head since she'd learned to talk was that there could not be a *but*. In an effort to understand why all this was happening, she tried to remember all the sins she'd committed since *Yom Kippur*, five months ago. All insignificant with two exceptions. She'd read a pornographic book Deborah's bad older sister had slipped her. Reading Emma Goldman's essays was even worse, since Hannah had done it for one of the worst reasons—curiosity, Adam's sin. Were those two sins bad enough for God to punish her this way?

She shouldn't compound the problem by questioning the judgment of God and Rav Moscovitz. She tiptoed into her mother's room.

"I'm sorry for what I said to you. I... Since what happened, everything feels so strange."

Girl

"Of course it does." Mommy looked old again. Her eyes were red. Had she been crying? Hannah wondered what upset her mother more, what had happened to Hannah or Hannah's behavior. She stroked Hannah's cheek. "Rav Moscovitz will return soon. Go back to your room, sweetie."

They again took their places in the living room. "Mordechai says he saw the man grab you," Rav Moscovitz said. "He ran out onto the street, but the man knocked him down. I spoke to the witnesses who saw you walking with the *schvartze*. All say you looked dazed and were staggering."

"He'd drugged her, stabbed her with a needle," Mommy spoke so fast her words ran together. "I'll show you the mark."

Rav Moscovitz raised a long pale hand, no need for that. Good, Hannah didn't have to lie. Not about that anyway.

"You'll stay out of school for a week, then return as if nothing had happened." Rav Moscovitz stroked his beard. "No one will talk about it ever again. Several men from the community will find the *schvartze* and make sure he never comes back."

"Make sure how?" Hannah asked, voice so wobbly she barely recognized it.

"There are many things girls and women ought not to know," Rav Moscovitz said.

Allowing the black man to be hurt or even killed would be a sin for which Hannah could *never* atone.

"What would happen if I told the police what I told you?" she asked, her voice a tremulous whisper. The idea of going to the police wouldn't have entered her head if her mother hadn't mentioned them. She didn't want the nice black man to be hurt.

"You know we don't involve outsiders in our problems," her father said.

Sure she knew; she'd only heard it a million times. *That's how we've survived and stayed together*. Not by lying, though. Not by bearing false witness. Unless they'd done it and didn't tell her.

17

Robert N. Chan

"You wouldn't do that, of course," Rav Moscovitz said.

"*If?*" Hannah asked. *Is there more than one way to make sure he never comes back?*

Three sets of eyes bored into her; but she couldn't stop her mind from running where it wanted to, like little children tearing toward a cliff they didn't see in that pornographic book she shouldn't have read.

"Rav Moscovitz, you know best; but I don't want anything bad to happen to a kind man who only tried to help me."

"*You don't want?*" Father shouted. "What you want doesn't matter." He lowered his voice. "Of course it matters, but the needs of the community and Rav Moscovitz's decisions about what's best for you matter more."

Hannah had never seen her father so volatile, so mercurial. Strange thought: having secretly studied English on her own, she might've been the only one in the room who knew what *volatile* and *mercurial* meant.

"If you don't obey and you tell the police, we will have no choice but to sit *shiva* for you," Rav Moscovitz said.

Both her parents nodded. Nodded! Those nods cut a jagged gash through her insides.

"*Shiva?* Mommy and Daddy, my sisters and brother, my friends, they'd all consider me *dead?*" Her voice squeaked like the mouse her father caught in a trap last Shavuot.

"This is silly, honey," her mother said. "You're not going to disobey Rav Moscovitz."

"But I thought you loved me." She struggled not to cry, not to sound like a stupid little kid.

"Of course we love you, dear, but as Rav Moscovitz said—"

"So you'll keep loving me *if* I lie and let an innocent man get…hurt." Hannah sniffled but didn't cry.

Mommy's head jerked back in shock. Never in a million years would she—or Hannah, for that matter—have imagined she'd speak like that in front of Rav Moscovitz.

"Rav Moscovitz is offering us a way out of our troubles," Father curled his lip like…like the butcher.

18

Hannah bowed her head. What came into her mind wasn't anything from the thousands of hours she'd spent reading Torah. It was from the pornographic book. Holden hated his school because "it's full of phonies, and all you do is study so that you can learn enough to be smart enough to buy a goddam Cadillac some day." Apparently it wasn't only the world of the gentiles that was full of phonies.

"Mordechai Kaplan might do that horrible, horrible thing to other girls," Hannah whispered, literally begging for her life. "Does the community need someone like that more than it needs me?"

Mommy looked at the wall behind Rav Moscovitz, at the engraving of the old city of Jerusalem viewed from the Mount of Olives. Father's lips moved as if he were praying. Rav Moscovitz looked as if steam might come out of his ears any second, but he too didn't make a sound. Anger transformed their faces into the faces of…strangers.

Please, God, help me find a path back. The silence continued. Anger built up inside Hannah. She stopped praying.

"Rav Moscovitz, where is it written that we should lie and bear false witness against our neighbors?" Hannah said in Hebrew, although they'd been speaking Yiddish.

"Don't you *ever* speak like that to Rav Moscovitz!" Her father stepped toward her. His eyes held unshed tears. *Because of what happened to me or because I shamed him in front of Rav Moscovitz?*

"Hannah, I know you didn't mean what you said. You've been through a lot today." The deep formal voice Rav Moscovitz used when addressing the entire congregation. "But you must *never* speak to me with disrespect or presume to know better than me or your parents."

"She's doesn't know what she's saying," Mother said, words running together again. "The drug the *schvartze* injected in her."

"I know *exactly* what I'm saying." Hannah looked directly at Rav Moscovitz for the first time—always before she'd looked at him with her head bent, a sign of respect—and was surprised to

19

see a mean old man's face. "Why is it okay to ignore God's commandments just to protect a…" She didn't know the word in Yiddish or Hebrew. She took a deep breath and said it in English, "To protect a rapist?"

Father slapped her.

She barely felt it.

He pulled his hand back as if he'd touched a hot oven.

Everything in the room came into precise focus, including the three strangers. Hannah and they wanted the same thing—for the world to be the way it was this morning—but that couldn't be. Not with Hannah knowing the community's supposed commitment to the word of God was a lie.

It wasn't just her family casting her aside; it was God too. None of this could be happening without Him. She'd long known a terrible secret—had she been Abraham, she'd have refused God's command to murder his child, Isaac. Maybe God decided this made her unworthy to serve Him, unworthy to be a rabbi's wife, unworthy for *tikkun olam.*

So be it. She knew what she had to do.

"May I please be excused?" she said.

"Of course, dear." Her mother looked pale and ill.

"I shouldn't have hit you," her father whispered, kind and concerned, finally.

"Thank you for coming tonight, Rav Moscovitz. You are a great teacher. Please accept my apology. I'm sorrier than you can imagine. I understand now what it means to be part of a community, *exactly* what it means."

Dry-eyed and calm, she went upstairs. It hurt to walk, but the pain was…of no consequence.

When everyone was asleep, Hannah tiptoed out of her room, carrying nothing since she owned nothing she cared about. She slipped out the back door of the only home she'd ever had.

Like Holden Caulfield leaving Pencey in that pornographic book, she slammed the door behind her and said, "Sleep tight, ya morons."

Girl

II
girl

It hurt to walk. The pain behind her eyes hurt more. She fought off tears. She wouldn't go back and had nowhere forward to go.

She crossed the border of her neighborhood—her former neighborhood. Only five blocks long and five wide, she'd *never* before left it unaccompanied by an adult. Well-kept buildings gave way to tumbledown ones. Loud-talking black-skinned men and women in all manner of dress replaced silent bearded white men wearing long black coats and wide-rimmed black hats. Clean, even sidewalks yielded to cracked, slanted ones, stained with squashed chewing gum resembling grimy nickels and quarters.

Her heart pounded. Breathing became difficult. Mommy and Daddy had told her never to go into this neighborhood, much less alone and never, ever alone at night. She'd be robbed, stabbed, or worse. No one told her what *worse* was, but Mordechai Kaplan had shown her.

She realized she had somewhere to go—away. Away from all she'd known, away from their lies. *Enough with being good. I'll be bad, as bad as can be. Bad like Holden Caulfield, like Emma Goldman. Maybe I'll even be a crack-whore.* She didn't know what that was, but her father spat out the term when talking about *schvartzes* and their sinful ways. She'd fill in the details as she went. She'd write her parents and Rav Moscovitz and tell them all about it; then they'd be sorry.

There had to be a middle ground between being a crack-whore and a *rebbetzin*. She couldn't be a *rebbetzin* and wouldn't be a crack-whore, if only because she didn't know what it was. But she wasn't the middle-ground type. Not with the intensity she'd applied to being first in her school and so good she was almost perfect—except for getting raped and refusing to lie about it.

Girl

The sensible option: go into foster care, get a secular American education, and pursue a regular career. But according to her father, girls in foster care were violated and boys were beaten up just for the fun of it. Social services people were outsiders, meddlers, not to be trusted—like the government, that *schvartze* Mayor Dinkins, and President Bush, who'd told everyone to read his lips, then raised taxes. She didn't want to be sensible, not with life having become so senseless—and anyway they'd probably send her back to her parents.

She had no idea how many blocks or in which direction or directions she'd walked. The past minutes, or hours, were a blank. Her fear had disappeared, but it was frightening that she wasn't frightened. Her anger had disappeared as well. Replaced by...nothing. Now that she thought about it, she realized she hurt all over. The bump on her head throbbed from hitting the butcher's floor. Her stomach cramped and swirled. The place between her legs felt sticky and oozy, even though she'd washed over and over. With every step she felt that awful soreness down there. But she didn't care about the pain.

Knots of people, sitting on stoops or leaning against rusty, bashed-in cars, stopped talking and stared when she walked by. They could see by her long coat, buttoned at her neck, that she didn't belong there. Of course she didn't; she didn't belong anywhere.

"Hey, you see her?" a boy about her age said to another boy who was bouncing a ball against a brick wall and catching it. "She's fucked-up, man. Looks like a zombie or something."

She felt like...she wasn't really there.

The windows had heavy bars across them. Sliding metal grates covered the entrances to shuttered stores, which might've been out of business judging by the many layers of graffiti on walls and doors. An older man pulled down a graffiti-free gate in front of his store and locked it. No sooner had he reached the corner than a pair of kids with spray paint cans ran toward the gate.

I have been a stranger in a strange land. Stranger was the wrong word; the correct translation was *sojourner*. She hadn't known it, but that was what she'd been for fifteen years. What would Rav Moscovitz say if he heard her comparing herself to Moses?

Never again would she be dependent on other people. Never again would she fall for the lie of love. If her parents, Rav Moscovitz, and even God would abandon her, she'd have to be an idiot to think strangers wouldn't do the same when it suited them. According to Emma Goldman, "People have only as much liberty as they have the intelligence to want and the courage to take." Maybe she'd learn courage.

Awful music, the kind her father called *be-bop,* blared from a passing car. She could barely imagine how loud it must have sounded from inside.

She needed food, a place to sleep, a bathroom.

A shoeless, rag-clad homeless man approached her, hand out. She gave him two dollars, all the money she had. The obligation of *tzedakah,* charity, was a fundamental part of Jewish life that she wouldn't give up. Then it hit her; she too was now homeless. How long before she smelled like this man, like she'd gone to the bathroom on herself and hadn't washed in a year? She had to get a job, but no one was allowed to hire her at her age.

Terror rolled over her, scrunching her stomach, short-circuiting her brain, liquefying her legs. She leaned against a building and slowly slid down.

"Girl, you okay?"

A big fat woman ever so gently helped Hannah to her feet. She hated herself for her weakness. No. She couldn't afford to hate herself. She was all she had, all she'd ever have.

"I'm fine. Thank you. I'm..." She forced a smile. "Excuse me, I need to get home."

Standing straight, shoulders back, head high—like her mother had told her to when she'd nag her about her posture—she walked away. Her fear receded.

She returned people's stares. She was done with averting her eyes.

Girl

The idea of being a crack-whore had been silly, but what about being a regular whore? *Whore* was the worst insult the men in her community, her former community, could throw at a woman. That made it sound good. "To the moralist, prostitution does not consist so much in the fact that the woman sells her body, but rather that she sells it out of wedlock," Emma Goldman said. And with her marriage prospects kaput...

A black man in a puffy jacket leaned against a building, his baggy jeans worn so low she could see his underwear. Thick gold chains hung from his neck. His gold-ringed fingers held a skinny misshapen cigarette. The smoke smelled bitter, yet sweet.

Whores had pimps. Sunny, the whore who came to Holden Caulfield's hotel room, had Maurice, a nasty man who punched Holden in the stomach. She'd want a nice pimp, not someone who punched her customers. That would be bad for business. Maybe the man with the saggy jeans would be her pimp. She was having crazy thoughts. Did that mean she'd gone crazy?

"You lost?" He bent down so his face was level with hers. "You shouldn't be wandering alone 'round here at night. Be happy to walk you back to your neighborhood if you like."

Would you like to be my pimp? seemed an inappropriate response.

"Thank you, but I only have a short way to go."

Even the thought of having sex made her want to retch. Being a whore wasn't such a great idea.

The air stank of burning rubber. She stopped under a dark street lamp, its broken remnants crunching beneath her feet. The street looked intimidating and dark. Everything seemed to swirl, making her dizzy. Rivka used to spin until she could no longer stand. She'd never see her again. Pain built behind her eyes. She wanted to cry. She didn't, though.

Three young men leaning against a tenement checked her out, then exchanged looks and nodded. One took a position on her right, another on her left, both close to her. The third stood in front of her, arms crossed. All had tough-guy scowls. As recently as this morning she'd have turned, screamed, and fled. Not

25

anymore. She'd left her fear on the butcher's tile floor.

She looked directly into the bloodshot yellow-rimmed eyes of the man in front of her and said in quiet but firm voice, "Please get out of my way."

He stepped aside.

"Thank you," she said. "Have a lovely evening."

She kept walking. She must've gone in a circle, as she started passing buildings she'd seen before, only now the streets were deserted. She'd never been so tired. She wanted to curl up under the covers on her nice warm bed. She could barely take another step. She'd never make it home even if she tried, wouldn't be able to find the way.

At a garbage-strewn empty lot, she crawled through a hole in the chain-link fence. Jagged bricks, cans, and broken bottles scratched and cut her hands. Squeezing behind a rusted car and a discarded washing machine, she squirmed under part of an old mattress and rested her head on a bald tire. A cloud of black flies swarmed from a rat's corpse. The stench made her gag. She lugged the tire and mattress behind a mound of garbage, stinky but not as awful as the rat. Lying down again, she made sure not to breathe through her nose. There had to be a reason the butcher chose her, why her parents were so willing to sit *shiva* for her, why God had let it happen. Had she been too proud of her heart-shaped face, bow lips, green eyes, and red hair? Had she not averted her eyes sufficiently? Had her scarf not covered all her hair, her coat not been baggy enough?

Closing her eyes, she hugged the tire. Just two nights ago, Rivka had crawled into bed with her after a nightmare. Hannah had wrapped herself around her little sister and told her she'd never let anyone hurt her, not ever. "I love you, Hannah. More than Mommy. More than anyone." Rivka will miss her. Did Rivka do something wrong to deserve never to see her big sister again? Why did Hannah's sin have to affect her?

She saw only shades of gray: light gray clouds and snow, dark gray filth. From the position of the dull gray circle in the

26

sky, it seemed to be around noon. Like a dog abandoned by its owner, she went to the bathroom behind a rusty refrigerator—almost as disgusting as lying down next to the dead rat. Achy, hungry. and filthy, she crawled back through the fence to the street, scratching her hands and knees even more. She resumed her walk toward nowhere.

Snow swirled but, other than in isolated patches, didn't stick. The pure white of the snow couldn't find a home in this filthy gray world. Would there ever be colors again? She continued walking…and walking.

February dusk already setting in, she came to a housing project. A young black man strode back and forth. He wore even more gold chains and rings than her non-pimp, and it looked as if *his* jeans were about to fall off with each loose-limbed stride.

Exhausted, she ducked behind a car mounted on cinderblocks instead of tires. A cold wind howled. Mini-cyclones spiraled old leaves and pieces of trash into menacing funnels. Pigeons flew backwards. Her teeth chattered. She couldn't bear to spend another night outside.

A white guy, seventeen years old or so, walked up to Gold Chains. He had long hair and a luxurious fur-collared shearling coat. He and Gold Chains touched fists and went through a complicated routine. Warm Coat handed something to the young black man, who went inside one of the buildings. Hugging himself as if cold—not that anyone could be cold in that big beautiful coat—Warm Coat paced in a small circle. He lit a cigarette, took a few drags, crushed it out with his foot, then repeated the process several times. Gold Chains returned and handed something to Warm Coat, who hurried off.

Hannah followed, but she wasn't Hannah anymore. She had no idea who she was.

Warm Coat went down the steps to the subway. Not having a token, she ducked under the turnstile. As recently as yesterday afternoon, she'd never have considered doing anything like that. It was kind of fun being bad. She wanted to be worse, a lot worse. She hadn't deserved what had happened to her. Whatever happened to her from now on, she'd deserve. She got onto the train and sat next to him—another thing she'd never have considered doing. She and Warm Coat were the only white people in the car.

She had to find a warm place to sleep, shower, wash her clothes, and eat. In short, she needed money and needed it now. She knew she wasn't thinking straight and that the only idea to occur to her had been as crazy as it was stomach-turning.

"Give me...seventy-two dollars, and you can have sexual intercourse with me."

Seventy-two might be too high, but she could always negotiate down. Four times *chai* seemed a good starting point. According to a traditional Jewish system of assigning numerical value to a word or phrase, the letters of *chai,* the Hebrew word for life, added up to eighteen; thus, eighteen was a spiritual number.

"That's not funny." He looked her up and down. "The way you're dressed...are you a Mormon or Mennonite? Or is this like performance art...for school or something?"

Not funny at all.

"I'm pretty, almost a virgin. It's a *very* good deal for you. In fact, I'm thinking of raising my prices. You just got in under the wire."

He tilted his head, his face a picture of incredulity. She tried another approach.

"Either pay me or I'll tell everyone in the subway car that you have drugs in your pocket."

"Get away from me." He slid to the end of the bench.

She followed. "THIS BOY HAS DRUGS IN HIS POCKET. I JUST SAW HIM BUY THEM."

None of the other passengers even glanced in their direction. He put her hand over her mouth. She bit down.

"Ouch!" He looked at his palm as if it were a foreign object. "I'm sorry I hurt you. I..."

"It's...okay. I...was just startled."

"Really, I... I've had all the *tsuris*—trouble—I can take."

28

Girl

Thinking about the Jobian torrent of *tsuris* she'd suffered through made her voice crack.

"Why, what happened?" He sounded concerned.

Maybe talking would make her start to feel as if it had happened to someone else. She told him, haltingly at first, but then almost as if she were telling Rivka a story. Only now she concentrated on choosing the right English words and speaking without too much of a Yiddisher accent. He leaned forward, eyes wide. She didn't tell him what the butcher had done, just that he'd pulled her into his shop and locked the door. She sped on, before he had the chance to ask a question. When she said *shiva*, her throat constricted so much she couldn't continue. She shook her head.

"It's okay." He sounded like he felt some...empathy—was that the right word? His eyes looked sad.

The subway rumbled on. Neither of them spoke, but he kept staring as if he wanted to say something or wanted her to. She couldn't. She'd used up every English word she knew.

She took off her head scarf, fluffed out her long just-a-little-curly red hair, and smiled like a movie star.

"You're...gorgeous!"

"I was supposed to shave my head and wear a wig after I was married." *I was raped and found out my parents don't love me, but hey, I won't have to shave my head.* "Imagine how good I'll look when the drugs turn you into a mad sex-fiend."

He laughed. Although she didn't know what was funny, she thought she was making progress.

"You're very orthodox?" he asked, words bursting from his mouth like air from a balloon.

"*Haredi* until yesterday."

"Like the crazies in Israel, who stone women and girls for wearing sleeveless shirts or sitting next to men on busses?"

"Wouldn't surprise me." She'd heard about that, but hadn't really believed it, thought the stones had been metaphorical or something. Now, though...

The subway stopped. Some people got on, some off. She and

Warm Coat were still the only white passengers.

Her hands felt damp. She started shaking. Panic, brought on by…nothing. *I can't let myself cry.*

"Please talk to me," she said.

"When you…offered to have sex with me for money, you *were* joking, right?"

"No. I don't know what I'd have done if you'd said 'yes,' but… It's going to be a long time before I feel like being funny."

He made a sad, empathetic sound.

"You do understand that you're too young to be a whore? Anyone having sex with you could be arrested, and you'd go straight to juvie jail."

The train started again. She watched an empty bottle roll across the floor. She needed money, a place to live, food. What was she going to do? She began breathing hard. Tried to control it.

After what might have been a long silence, he said, "My name's Trevor." Getting no reaction, he asked, "What's yours?"

She thought for a minute. It should've been an easy question.

"Call me *girl, small g*." She'd learned from Rav Moscovitz that she was no one special, which was now fine with her.

"Are you going to change it to *woman, small w,* when you get older?" He smiled.

"I don't plan to live that long."

Would Hannah's parents hear about it if she died? What would they say? "Smart of us sitting *shiva* for her when we did. Now we can relax and enjoy ourselves." Not that they were big on joy, but they could pray without interruption while feeling superior to *schvartzes, goys,* less observant Jews, whores, and David Dinkins. Was she not being fair? Let someone else be fair for a change.

The subway crossed under the East River toward Manhattan. A boy and girl sitting across from her kissed and groped each other. Girl studied them. It didn't look all that hard.

Realizing she hadn't spoken for a while, she asked, "Why do you go to a bad neighborhood in Brooklyn to buy drugs?"

Girl

"The guys at school won't sell to me. I posted a sign in the commons bitching about how their stuff has been stepped on so often it's mostly benzocaine and baby aspirin. We had to go to the dean and pretend I'd been goofing on them." He pinched the bridge of his nose. "My shrink says I'm just acting out. Like you, I guess."

A pigeon wandered between the seats. It looked as lost and out of place as girl felt.

"I'm not acting. I'm *transforming*." Girl liked how that sounded. "I'm done with bowing to authority. 'Anarchism stands for the liberation of the human mind from the dominion of religion, the liberation of the human body from the dominion of property, the liberation from the shackles and restraint of government.'"

"Is that a quote from something?"

"Emma Goldman, a distant relative. Maybe I inherited some of her anarchist genes."

"I've heard of her, big on free love, right?" he said. "I've read that whores don't like sex, don't even like men. They have sex with so many people they don't emotionally attach to anyone. It's all...faked."

"I like the not-emotionally-attaching-to-anyone part."

Like was the wrong word. She felt too indifferent to like or not like; but she couldn't have explained that to him...or herself—the self from whom she was becoming increasingly disconnected, as if she were watching it grow smaller from the rear window of a speeding car. Who or what was driving? Would it blow up when it crashed? She hoped so.

"Now you do, but tomorrow? Next week? From what you told me, you were completely different yesterday morning; and you're reacting to a pretty damn traumatic...trauma."

She stared straight ahead at the couple pawing each other. Whatever happened, she'd no longer be Hannah, the nice girl who'd been raped and unloved.

"Where do you go to school?" she asked, two subway stops later.

31

"The Hill School. A fancy private school up on a hill in Riverdale, in the Bronx." His face compressed as if he were mulling over an idea. "My parents are out of town. I'm having people over. Come. Someone's going to be there who might help you."

"I don't want help." She didn't want anything, except to die; and she didn't care enough to do something about that, not yet anyway.

"Everett Talcott, he's the best teacher in my school."

"He's going to a drug party?" Would she ever be anything but a sojourner in a strange land?

"He has befriended female students too well and too often."

"Does that mean he...?" girl rolled her hands.

"He could be fired if he's caught doing it again. Sex with under-aged girls is...Other than that, though, he's a great guy."

Sounds more like a reason why he shouldn't be going to a drug party. Or do I just not understand anything about the world beyond Crown Heights? Apparently I didn't even understand all that much about Crown Heights.

They got off the train at 86th Street and Lexington Avenue. Although it was now dark out, the street hummed with activity. Three lanes of cars raced down the avenue, jockeying for position, running lights. People crossed the street, oblivious to the cars that swerved around them. She and Trevor walked quickly, but faster walkers passed them. She wondered if all those pedestrians and drivers had places they needed to get to or if the point was just to go fast.

She wished she had somewhere *she* wanted to go.

32

III

The Pedagogical Pedophile

Girl chose a chair in the darkest corner of Trevor's family's living room. Across from her a huge spotlit blank canvas hung over a long white leather couch. An equally large painting, also spotlit, consisted entirely of paint drippings and shared a wall with one entirely composed of tiny dots that looked like a cartoon of a woman in a bathtub. A sculpture of welded rusted metal reminded her of the junkyard where she'd spent last night. She'd have thought that people with such a big house could afford fancier art; maybe one of their children made it.

Kids began trickling in, older than her, but it was hard to guess by how much; they seemed so *different.* The room filled with sweet-smelling smoke, *primo weed,* according to Trevor.

He sat next to her, flicked white powder onto a mirror and used the edge of a playing card—a joker—to form it into several straight lines. Then he rolled up a hundred dollar bill. She'd never seen one before but didn't feel right asking to look at it. Using the bill, he inhaled one line of the powder; then he handed the bill and mirror to her.

"No, thank you, I—"

"It'll make you feel better."

If only that were possible.

Covered from neck to wrists to ankles in the only dress Hannah had owned, now stained, torn, and filthy, girl must've looked like someone who'd time-traveled here from another century. The noise level rose. Most guests wore ratty jeans and T-shirts, as if competing to look the most unkempt. They greeted each other, sometimes touching fists and going through complicated gestures like Trevor had with his drug dealer. Ignoring girl, which was fine by her, they passed around the primo weed and snorted the white powder. Girl couldn't tell if the drugs made them feel good, but they sure made them loud.

She bobbed slowly on an unchanging sea of melancholy. Some boys talked to her but made no impression.

Trevor put a large tray of something in front of her. "Thought you might be hungry."

"Yes, thank you...very much." She hadn't eaten since the chicken sandwich Hannah's mother had brought her in her room twenty-four hours earlier. "Smells wonderful"—also a little sickening—"what is it?"

"Mini pigs in a blanket, fresh from the microwave." *Pig?* "It's not kosher but best I could do. The hot dogs are beef."

"It's fine. More than fine, thank you again."

When he left, she whispered, *"Ba-ruch a-tah A-do-nai E-lo-hei-nu Me-lech Ha-o-lam—"* She stopped herself. She wasn't sure she wanted to say *motzi* before eating; and if she weren't sure, she shouldn't do it. She wolfed down the treats like a wild animal, a wolf maybe. Her stomach had been so empty she felt ill even before she finished. Bile fouled her mouth, sour, rotten. Punishment for eating *traif?* Just as likely rape had been punishment for keeping kosher.

She didn't throw up. She took pride in that.

A man appeared in the vaulted living room entranceway. Clad head to foot in black leather, he wore hand-tooled cowboy boots, tight pants with silver medallions sewn into the seams, a vest, and a greatcoat in a style that looked familiar to girl, although she had no idea where she might've seen one like it. All heads turned toward him. Although barely five-seven in his high-heeled boots, he seemed larger than life. The crowd erupted in gleeful greetings and high-fives.

Several minutes later Trevor led him to the corner. "Everett, this is girl."

"Odd name." He flashed a radiant smile.

"You must be a terrific teacher to get away with dressing like that." She hadn't wanted to be rude, but that was all that came to her.

She didn't want to talk to him, didn't want to be there. But she didn't want to be anywhere, and here it was warm and dry.

Girl

There were bathrooms, and there might be more food. So now what? Was she supposed to slap palms and bump fists with him? She extended her hand.

Mr. Talcott didn't so much shake her hand as stroke it. He was the only man who'd ever touched her, other than her father, her pediatrician, and the butcher. His gray eyes locked on girl's green ones, and he flashed a dazzling smile.

A young woman sashayed over, although she carried too much weight in her thighs and hips for a proper sashay. What was the point of the constellation of studs on her right cheek? She kissed Mr. Talcott on the lips which, from what girl could tell, shocked no one.

"Girl, meet Stephanie. Stephanie, girl." Mr. Talcott winked at girl, making her feel like they shared a special secret. She had no idea what it might be and didn't care to know.

"Love the coat, Everett," Stephanie said, not even acknowledging girl. "Whose is it? Ralph Lauren?"

"Looks like what the SS officers wore," girl said, suddenly recalling where she'd seen it.

"It's an *ironic* statement." Having managed to cram more condescension into those few words than girl would have thought possible, Stephanie sat on one of the couches and tapped the space next to her.

Mr. Talcott—his students called him Everett, but she could never use an older man's first name even when just thinking about him—joined Stephanie and motioned for girl to sit on his other side. If she had anywhere else to go, anywhere at all, she'd have left. As she didn't, she paraded in front of him—an awkward-feeling effort to imitate Stephanie—then sat on his right, leaning into him. Her clumsy attempt at seductiveness made her feel creepy, and her physical contact with him made her feel even worse. An image of Rivka cuddling up next to her, when Hannah read to her, caused a sharp pain behind her eyes. Mr. Talcott leaned against her. Stephanie shot her a nasty look.

"How do you know Trevor?" he asked.

Girl took a deep breath, let it out slow.

"*Boring*...I'm going to get high," Stephanie said. "Care to join me, Everett?"

"Maybe later. I'm interested in hearing girl's story." His probing eyes examined girl's face.

Stephanie scowled, then sashayed into the other room.

"Was she one of the girls you...befriended too well?" girl asked.

"So Trevor told you about me? Puts me at a distinct disadvantage. Fair play dictates that to even the odds I hear about you." He faced girl, eyes wide, leaning in, forearms on his thighs.

Could he be flirting with me? Don't be ridiculous.

Maybe if she told it like a story—*The Rape and Betrayal of Hannah*—she'd persuade herself it had happened to Hannah, not her. This would be hard, but she better get used to hard; nothing would ever be easy again. She told him about Hannah's community and parents. Then she said, "As Hannah was walking home from school, the butcher grabbed her, pulled her into the back room, locked the door, and... " Her voice cracked. "I can't...tell the rest."

He put his arm around her.

"I understand," he said, making it sound as if he actually did.

She squirmed away, then in summary form told him about Hannah refusing to lie and her parents being willing to pretend she was dead.

"You should go to the police." Mr. Talcott rested a hand on her forearm. Girl suppressed her instinct to pull it away. "The butcher has to be stopped."

"I... I don't want anything to do with Hannah's family or community..." Any second now she'd start crying and be unable to stop, maybe ever.

Mr. Talcott nudged her to her feet and cradled her face into his neck so no one would see her crying. She let him lead her to another room. He shut the door behind them and turned a knob on the wall, dimming the bright lights that illuminated yet more art. They sat on yet another couch in the now shadowy room.

Trevor's parents' house had more couches than Hannah's parents' house had pieces of furniture. He wiped her face and nose with the hem of his T-shirt. She blinked away the tears, but the room still seemed to be shrouded in mist.

"What are you going to do about your problem?" she asked, hoping he'd talk and she'd bob up from the depths and again float on the Sea of Melancholy—her best option. "Trevor said you'd get fired if you got caught having sex with a student again."

As the words passed her lips, she realized how intrusive her question had been. Having left behind one set of rules and mores and not having learned another, she was socially ignorant. Still she shouldn't be rude.

"I could go to jail for a long time," he said.

"So stop."

"Barely post-pubescent girls turn me on. Older women don't." He didn't seem to mind talking about it. "I can't control my urges. But I've only been intimate with girls I've gotten to know well enough to be sure that my getting involved with them would be good for them."

"One can tell that just by reading Stephanie's facial studs," girl said.

He winced, and girl *really* wished she hadn't said that.

The silence hardened like refrigerated gelatin. Waves of depression roiled the Sea of Melancholy. She focused on finding a harbor to ride out the storm. The one lesson about dealing with men that Hannah's mother had drilled into her was, "Let him talk; you listen." If that would work on promising rabbinical students, no reason it wouldn't work on a teacher who liked under-aged girls. But the only evidence girl had of Hannah's mother's success involved the owner of a small lighting fixture factory who was too quick to raise his hand and too slow to open his heart. Perhaps Hannah's mother should've spoken more when she'd had the chance.

Girl didn't know what she wanted from Mr. Talcott. She knew, though, that she didn't want to take anything she couldn't pay for in some way or another; she'd *never* be dependent on anyone again.

"Okay, my relationships with my students weren't acts of altruism," he said. "The long and *mutual* seduction growing out of their admiration of me as a teacher and mentor was a major part of the appeal."

"Try something new: take me home with you and mentor me 'til I *plotz*." Her boldness astonished her. She imagined her father materializing in front of her and slapping her face, actually felt the sting. "Then send me away when I no longer interest you."

"Turn you out on the street? I couldn't do that."

"I'm already on the street. If I were to stay with you for even a few days, I'd be ahead."

"You're amazingly poised and articulate for someone of your age and limited experience."

If she let Mr. Talcott have *the long and mutual seduction growing out of her admiration of him as a teacher and mentor* he'd said he wanted, she wouldn't be taking charity. She'd just be a…whore. But yuck! Could she do it? She had to know.

She stood and pulled her dress over her head and let it drop to the floor. She fought back the desire to grab it and cover up. She'd thought she'd get away with taking her clothes off in this strange world where none of the rules she'd grown up seemed to apply but…

"Do I look okay?" she asked, even though his wide-eyed, slack-jawed, head-thrust-forward expression had made her question unnecessary. "You don't think my breasts are too big or my waist too little or my *tuchis* too…round and stick-outy?"

Face warm, she held one arm across her chest, the other over her… She quickly put her dress back on.

She tried to pull on the end of her head-scarf. Finding it not there—after taking it off in the subway, she'd thrust it into her coat pocket—she twirled a strand of hair around her finger.

"Maybe we should rejoin the party," girl said, hoping a change of scene might... She didn't know what.

Girl

The living room was less noisy and crowded than when they'd left it. Eyes bloodshot and white powder caked on her right nostril, Stephanie shot them a dirty look.

"You two have fun in there?" she asked, voice wet with condescension.

Trevor joined Stephanie, girl, and Mr. Talcott.

"I guess it's time for me to be on my way," girl said, hoping she'd correctly read Mr. Talcott's reaction to her underwear-clad body. If he wanted to take her with him, now was the time for him to ask. Or was it? She no more understood the rules of this society than she did those of Afghan tribesmen. Actually, from what she'd read, their traditions on treatment of women, dietary restrictions, public modesty, and daily prayer were more similar to what she'd grown up with than those of the people here. Did they even have traditions? She didn't think primo weed counted.

She'd assigned to herself—she and herself having become separate if not quite distinct entities—the task of getting him to make her his *mentee*, but did she want that? She no longer *wanted* anything, except to go back in time and take a different route home from school. Herself seemed to want her to be severely punished for the horrible thing she'd done.

"Where are you going?" Trevor asked.

"God knows."

"You think so?" Mr. Talcott asked.

"How else could everything have become so messed up in a mere 5,571 years?"

"The universe is thirteen and three-quarter billion years old," he said.

But according to the Torah...Whoa! Could that be a fable like the Golem of Prague?

"Proves my point. How vain do you have to be not only to demand that your creations pray to you but also to lie about your age?"

Mr. Talcott laughed.

She blew him a kiss like she'd seen a young woman leaving the party do to Trevor. Then she sashayed out of the room—a slimmer-hipped, improved version of Stephanie's sashay, or so she hoped—and shut the door behind her.

The previously bustling street was now empty except for a cold and censorious wind.

IV
Cold As a Witch's Tit

"Took you long enough." Girl got up from Trevor's stoop, as Mr. Talcott emerged from the front door. "It's cold as a witch's tit out here." She needed to read more pornography, so she'd be able to allude to more than one book and a handful of essays.

"You never doubted I'd take you up on your offer?" Mr. Talcott asked.

"I wasn't brought up to doubt." And now, on the strength of her small and dubious success, she would put aside all doubts, make her choices, and not second-guess.

Mr. Talcott tossed a twenty, for a $5.50 ride, to the driver. Then he scooped her into his arms and lifted her out of the cab. What had she gotten herself into? Would he hurt her like the butcher had?

Still carrying her, he unlocked the front door of a brownstone. He was so strong, she'd never be able to fight him off.

They ascended three flights of squeaky fluorescent-lit stairs. Her heart wouldn't have pounded harder and her breaths wouldn't have come harder and faster if she'd been carrying him up those stairs. When they finally crossed his threshold, and he locked the door behind them, she was so dizzy she thought she'd pass out. At least then she wouldn't feel anything.

He set her down, dropped his coat to the floor, then hugged her. She squirmed away. Her foot caught in a hole in his worn carpet. She struggled to control her breath. She had to calm herself, had to think.

"Wow! You actually live here?" She did an enthusiastic, if inept, pirouette, spinning away from him. "What an apartment!"

Floor to ceiling bookshelves on every wall, piles of books on the floor. She ran her hand along the spines. *If I grow up, I'm going to live alone surrounded by books.* The thought almost made her want to live or at least to survive this encounter.

"After seeing the Trevor family mansion, you think my Upper West Side one-bedroom walk-up is..." He darted forward and picked her up. "Okay, now I'll show you my bed."

"Put me down, please," she said, voice high-pitched. So much for controlling her panic.

He did, but his downcast facial expression and arched eyebrows spelled trouble. Her mind went into overdrive. She could grab a book and smack him with it, but that wouldn't stop him, just make him angry. She reminded herself that this had been her idea. She'd wanted to be a whore.

"What's the syllabus? Picking randomly, we could start here." She pointed to one of the shelves and told herself to speak slower so she wouldn't seem so nervous. "*The Decline and Fall of the Roman Empire, Plutarch's Lives,* the *Aeneid,* sounds exciting. Maybe not if I were to read them on my own, but I'm sure you could make them come alive."

"First things first." He kissed her, mouth open, tongue on her closed lips. Yuck! She pictured the couple she'd studied on the subway. They had their mouths open and leaked quite a bit of saliva.

She took a deep breath through her nose. She'd have to get used to yuck. She parted her lips. He stuck his tongue into her mouth! Too, too yucky. The pigs in her stomach shot out from their blankets and crawled up her throat on filthy, *traif* feet. She pushed back from him.

"You told me what you want: a long and *mutual* seduction growing out of my admiration of you as a teacher and mentor." She had to stop running words together. "So get on with it; start mentoring."

After a moment's hesitation, Mr. Talcott sat in a black leather chair, worn through to the frame at the arms, and assumed a thinking position: elbows on his knees and chin on his interlocked fingers. She presumed she'd see that often, unless he threw her out, deciding he could do without a chaste whore.

Girl

After a long, uncomfortable silence, he said, "I suppose we could do an overview of the intellectual ferment of Periclean Athens and run through Socrates, Plato, and Aristotle, then delve deeper into some of the lesser-known but arguably more profound philosophers, Epicurus, for example, then on to the Romans."

As he spoke, he became progressively more animated. Girl breathed a sigh of relief and, much to her surprise, became caught up in the current of his excitement.

"This is going to be so much fun!" She told herself that she hadn't lied to him. *Fun* was relative and in this case meant *better than being punched or having sex.*

He'd seemed to like it when she undressed at the party, and doing it hadn't been terrible for her. She took a deep breath, then stripped down to her underwear and hopped onto his lap. "I'm fascinated," she said. "Please tell me more."

He launched into a spirited discussion of the first democracy—*dēmokratia*, from *demos*, the people, and *kratia*, power.

After the first few minutes, girl slipped from his lap and took a place at his feet. Thanks to his erudition, enthusiasm, and well-turned phrases, she didn't have to fake her admiring looks. Except to pause for water, which girl fetched from the messy kitchen, he spoke for over an hour. As far as being half-naked, she was glad to be out of that smelly dirty dress.

He yawned, "That's enough for tonight."

"May I clean the kitchen while you sleep?"

"I have a cleaning lady for that."

Girl picked a dust bunny off the floor and held it out for him to examine. "Save your money. I'll do it better."

"Let's go to bed," he said.

Terror cramped her stomach. She hoped it didn't show on her face. If she kept her head, maybe she could find a way out of this.

"What about the long, slow seduction?"

"It's been long enough." He put his arm around her waist and led her to the bedroom.

43

Pain built behind her eyes. *I will not cry. I will not cry. The worst thing has already happened to me. Nothing will hurt me worse, so nothing matters.* She started shaking.

"It's okay, girl." He reached out like he intended to cup her face in his hands. She tilted away from him. "Given what you went through, I was grossly insensitive. I'm very sorry. Take all the time you need."

Tension left her body so fast she felt lightheaded.

Trying to take some small level of control of the situation, she said, "I've got a problem." She bent her head and made a lazy circle on the floor with her toe. Hannah's father had told her she was cute when she did that.

"Talk to me." He sounded concerned.

"It's about Plato. I'm fine with the idea that the information we get by relying on sense experience is constantly changing and therefore intrinsically unreliable. But that this unreliability can be corrected and evaluated only by appealing to unchanging *forms*, which are the basis for all reasoning...." She didn't know how to be a whore, but she knew how to be a great student. Just talking about Plato—in language that sounded erudite even if she'd cribbed it from Mr. Talcott—lifted her spirits. "How can we be sure of these undoubtable principles? Isn't that just a fancy way of saying God created everything?"

He chuckled. "I guess I'll have to assign you some reading."

He *really* enjoyed teaching. Maybe this, whatever *this* was, would work out...for a while.

"Goody!" She clapped her hands. "I was so hoping you'd say that."

Mr. Talcott took several books from the bookshelf. "It's already well past midnight. I don't want you staying up late reading; you'll have all day to read when I'm in school."

"Just 'til two, maybe three, please. I don't need all that much sleep and...I'm so excited." She feared the nightmares sleep would bring.

He gave her a towel and a long, moth-eaten bathrobe and pointed toward the bathroom. When she emerged from the most wonderful shower ever, he'd already made up the couch into a bed.

"Again, I feel terrible about having been so aggressive, given the circumstances of your... If there's any way I can make it up to you..."

There is. You can never ever touch me. "Well...there is one thing." She said, although she thought she might be laying it on too thick. "I feel...greedy and ungrateful just asking, but..."

"You're neither. What would you like?"

"How about a tiny little..." She held her thumb and forefinger close together. "Bedtime lecture on Aristotle's *Metaphysics?*"

He laughed, "Reminds me of Woody Allen's piece, *The Whore of Mensa.*"

"Who's he?"

Girl woke to find Mr. Talcott stroking her hair, muttering something like, "It's okay. You're safe here. It was just a dream."

She moved her head away from his hand and noticed drops of blood on the pillowcase. Apparently she'd bitten her lip during her nightmare. "Sorry about messing up your... and about waking you."

"I was up anyway. A way to convey to a student how to improve his essay came to me. I wanted to write it down before I forgot."

"You're very dedicated."

"A job isn't fun unless you give it all you have." He reached out to stroke her cheek but withdrew his hand when she flinched. "Go back to sleep."

"I'd rather clean the floor, if that's okay."

The next morning Mr. Talcott said, "I don't know what came over me last night. You can't stay here. I need to call your parents and—"

"You don't believe me?" Why should he? She hardly

believed what had happened herself. "Okay, here." She wrote her father's work number on a pad with the Hill School logo, a hill with a rising, or setting, sun.

"It's Sunday."

"He'll be there."

Without saying how, Mr. Talcott told Hannah's father he'd met her.

Girl was close enough to the phone to hear Hannah's father say, "I don't…" A sad, strangled sound emerged from his throat, "Hold on a moment, please." He barely got out the words. "I…have another call." Unlikely since the factory had only one line.

Daddy feels terrible about what he did. He's going to take me back! I won't have to have sex with Mr. Talcott. I'll never have to have sex with anyone!

She heard her father blow his nose and take a big breath.

"I don't have a daughter named Hannah."

Girl covered her mouth to trap the terrible sharp pain inside her. The jagged gash that had cut through her insides—she couldn't pull off telling herself that the gash had only cut Hannah—in her parents' living room reopened, never to close again.

"You mean you did, but now she's dead to you, your family, and your community?" His brows lowered and nose bridge wrinkled, Mr. Talcott spoke slowly, enunciating each word like someone trying to control his anger.

"That's right." Hannah's father hung up.

Mr. Talcott stared at the telephone handset, looking irate and confused as if it had betrayed him.

"So can I stay?" girl asked, voice trembling.

"I should call Social Services."

"Then I'm out of here." She grabbed her coat and headed for the door. Each step was an ordeal as if she'd put on 200 pounds. In fact her anguish weighed at least that much.

"Wait!" He held up his hand. "I guess you're better off here, at least until we can figure out something safer for you than living on the street."

"Thank you." She kissed him on the cheek.

"I still think you should go to the police."

"But I won't." She took several seconds to organize her thoughts. "I need to make a total break with Hannah's world. I don't want to do anything that would replay what happened."

"I know, but—"

"Please, I just can't." She tugged on the sleeve of his plaid, leather elbow-patched jacket.

He sighed, communicating reluctant acquiescence. "If anyone asks, you're my niece, visiting for a few days."

On their fourth day together, girl kissed Mr. Talcott on the lips, open-mouthed. He held her close and rubbed against her fully clothed. Taking cues from his sharp, short breaths, she met his thrusts with ones of her own that seemed to increase his excitement. Over the next few days, the kissing and rubbing became a sort of game. Not one she'd have chosen, but as the oldest sister, Hannah had learned to play games she hadn't chosen and do her best to enjoy them.

She worried about the inevitable. Would it hurt? Would she bleed again? Would she vomit and cry?

When she sensed that kissing and rubbing were no longer sufficient, she suggested they take a bath together. Grinning, he gave her two thumbs-up. She had a special treat planned for him after their bath, something he'd mentioned a few days earlier.

She undressed him and was glad that seeing him naked didn't disgust her. He undressed her. Having worn, during their lessons, skimpy underwear that he'd bought for her at Victoria's Secret, being naked wasn't such a big deal. Nothing was. Virgil had gotten it right in the *Aeneid*: "*Facilis decensus averni.*" The descent into hell is easy.

After she dried him off, she began to softly blow on him, starting at his face and working down.

He laughed. "That tickles."

"But you said…"

47

"That's not a blow job."

"It is in Brooklyn." No, she couldn't pull that off.

Once he finally stopped laughing, he told her how to do it.

Kneeling in front of him on the bath mat, she took several deep breaths, then kissed the tip of his penis. She jerked back. Hand on her head, he gently nudged it down. Appalled as she was to have a penis in her mouth, she wasn't as appalled as she thought she should be. His penis didn't taste like much of anything, and the smell of scented soap was kind of nice. If only she could stop herself from gagging. She could've done without his stroking her hair. Maybe if she got him a teddy bear or a cat, he could pet...

"You don't have to do this," he said.

"Don't interrupt my work."

Eventually she figured out the secret; breathe through your nose.

Afterward her breathing slowed and her shoulder muscles loosened. She realized how tense she'd been. He kissed her. If he didn't care where her mouth had been, why should she?

"I'd like to make love to you tonight," he said after four weeks filled with classical philosophy, epic poems, and Peloponnesian, Punic, and Gallic wars and numerous conversations about the world outside his apartment.

She'd been a prudish whore as long as she could. Last night they'd discussed birth control, and he'd instructed her in the use of condoms. If she were now to return to Hannah's community, she'd be its foremost expert on the subject.

He carried her to the bed, laid her down gently. After kissing and stroking, he slid off her panties and eased himself inside her. She concentrated on her evening's readings from Lucretius: "Such are the heights of wickedness to which men are driven by religion." Everett started going faster, harder. He gripped her tight. She wished it would end, and it did.

"Thank you," she said, referring to his ending it. Her feelings swirled like water going down a drain. Relief from having gotten it over with and its not having been terrible. Anger at Everett for making her do it, even though she knew her circumstances had made her do it. Everett had been nice, gentle, and affectionate. She realized she'd wanted it to hurt…a lot more than the butcher had hurt Hannah, more than anything.

Everett sat at his desk. Seeing him agonize over how to best convey the joy of learning to his students, girl kneaded his shoulders.

"It's wonderful that you care so much." Complimenting him during sex felt disingenuous, but she sincerely admired his dedication and talent. Sometimes his lectures made her tingle with excitement. She was only truly comfortable, however, when alone and focused on a task. If she let her concentration flag, she would be transported to the blood-spattered tile floor or the living room as Hannah's parents turned into strangers. While Everett was at school, girl forced herself to watch an hour of television a day. She'd rather have studied. But as much as she delighted in the western canon, she needed to learn more about contemporary customs and mores. When Everett turned her out, she would need to know how to survive on her own.

Soap operas—where people did stupid, dangerous things without considering the consequences—thrilled her even more than Dante's *Inferno*, which really said something. In one episode a teenager repeatedly cut herself with a razor. A few days later, girl stuck the point of a knife into her arm, not hard or deep but it drew blood. She thought about pulling it down to cut a long swathe. That thought and her tiny stab made her feel relaxed, sort of happy, but frightened. In another episode a customer beat up a whore. Her pimp found her a bloody mess. He shot her full of heroin. She smiled and thanked him, then died. Sometimes when Everett was inside her, her thoughts drifted to that episode. Then she'd bite into his flesh, stimulating him to slam into her and treat her like the whore she'd been from the moment she started exchanging sex for room, board, and an education.

Once a week or so she'd be unable to summon the energy to get out of bed. Everett would respond with gentle encouragement, and she couldn't be bothered to hate him for it. On those days she'd often have crying jags after he left for school. She vowed not to let them last for more than fifteen minutes, but sometimes they went on for hours, leaving her totally spent.

He had told her that none of his prior relationships had lasted for more than a semester. So, under the best of circumstances, their arrangement would end in a matter of months. She would have gained only one marketable skill. She still hoped to come up with a preferable alternative, but whoring offered undeniable advantages. It would be more lucrative and less tedious than other work she could get without a high school degree. She'd be independent and avoid getting sucked into the hurtful lie of love. Hopefully Trevor had been right when he'd said, "Whores don't emotionally attach to anyone."

On their fourth monthaversary, his word, shortly after she'd turned sixteen—her birthday, June 26, 1990, had gone unnoticed by anyone but herself—she heard herself moan when Everett entered her and to her amazement realized that it felt...nice. He kept at it, and she matched his thrusts with her own and...

Nausea and terror slithered through her like a snake, starting *down there* and working its way up. The memory of the rape pressed down on her, making it impossible to breathe. Bile fouled her throat. She buried her head in Everett's neck, writhed in a way he found sexy. After he finished, he wrapped his arms around her. Each of his body hairs scraped her skin, a million sharp tiny tacks.

"My god, Everett, what you do to me, it's more amazing every time," she said, not a lie but... At least she was learning how to talk like a whore.

"Did you—"

"Couldn't you tell?" She said, neither lying nor telling the truth.

She was curious about what an orgasm would feel like but

not so curious that she wanted to have one.

He fell asleep. After what felt like hours, she drifted off.

She awoke at sunrise, sheets tangled, pillow on the floor. Ensconced at his simple desk, Everett was already working his way through a pile of papers discussing the relative merits of the Stoics and the Epicureans. He never let more than three days go by between when students completed a test or handed in an assignment and he returned their work corrected and replete with insightful comments. "If I show respect for their work, they'll respect it too," he'd said.

To celebrate, or rather *commemorate*, their six months together, girl made a chocolate cake. Cupping her cheeks in his hands, Everett stared into her eyes.

"I love you, girl."

She winced as if he'd smacked her. Not fair! She'd aced her test on Immanuel Kant and ached to study the Enlightenment in detail. Maybe he'd admit he hadn't meant it.

"Up to now you've only said that during sex," she said, voice crackling with annoyance. "I was able to disregard it as a passionate...something, like, 'Oh, my God, you've got the world's hottest pussy.'"

"We have fun together, never fight." He kissed the tip of her nose, which he seemed to consider cute. "You're so beautiful, kind, unassuming, thoughtful... You'd make a wonderful mother."

"What?" She couldn't have heard that right.

"One day, I really want children."

"Yes, you've made that clear."

"I didn't mean it that way, and you know it."

"I'll miss you, Everett." She pulled on her undies and T-shirt, picked up her pillow, and started toward the living room couch. "I'll move out in the morning." A tear rolled down her cheek. She didn't want to leave, but she hadn't wanted to be raped, either. She was only sort of equating love and rape.

"I was afraid you'd react this way."

51

Her initial reaction had been purely visceral. Now that she'd had a minute to think about it, though, she knew her response had been the right one. "I love you so much, *bubula,*" Hannah's mother used to say. "I love you, *zeisele* (sweetie), " Hannah's father used to say. Hannah had felt safe, loved, and protected. Then reality made its Faustian proposal: lie and they'll continue to lie to you. If not, you'll be dead to them. Girl never wanted to hear, "I love you," again. If she were ever inclined to give up her soul, it wouldn't be for a lie. She'd fallen for the lie of love once and barely survived the hurt.

But she was comfortable and safe here and was getting an education. She liked living with Everett, to the limited extent she was capable of liking anything, and had nowhere else to go. No! There could be no "buts." She didn't love him and wouldn't pretend she did. To stay with him when he claimed to love her would send a message that her loving him back was a possibility; and if there were anything she was sure of, it was that she would never love him or anyone else, if only because she wouldn't let herself.

"I'll never think of you without feeling a sense of awe," she said.

"This conceit of yours, that you're incapable of love—"

"The conveyers of my genes claimed to love me, but they were willing to treat me as if I were dead. That I'm incapable of love isn't something I *think*," girl said. "It's something I *know*, a fundamental, immutable platonic form." Thanks to the education Everett had given her, she could employ sophisticated concepts when dumping him.

"That's bullshit!" He seemed not to appreciate the results of his fine work.

"If what I went through doesn't lead in a nice rational straight line to my never wanting to be in a relationship supposedly based in love, so be it."

Everett shook his head.

"Don't you get it?" she screamed. "I'm DAMAGED. When we make love, sometimes it's really nice; and we fall asleep in each other's arms. Twenty minutes later I wake up, terrified, soaked in sweat, sick to my stomach. I feel like retching and sometimes do." No reason to tell him about the attacks during sex; let him feel good about his prowess.

His jaw slackened and his head tilted.

"What did you think when you'd wake and find me sleeping on the couch?" she asked. "I don't have night terrors when I sleep alone, only manageable nightmares. The other night I read *La Nausée.* I didn't get what Sartre was up to. The main character's existential nausea seemed pathologically mild. It was like reading *Waiting for Godot.*"

"You never told me." He sounded hurt.

"I'm a whore. I don't share my emotions. As Holden Caulfield said, 'Don't ever tell anybody anything. If you do, you start missing everybody.'"

His lips moved; but he said nothing, perhaps devising counter-arguments and rejecting them because he knew they wouldn't work. He settled for a pained sigh.

Finally he said, "You have no money, nowhere to go."

"I'll figure it out."

"At least stay until you have somewhere to live and a means to support yourself."

Her sigh mirrored his, just a couple octaves higher. He'd even taught her how to sigh.

"I'm not going to let you go until you find a decent place to live." *Let me go?* "For that you'll need money, a bank account, financial references—"

"Just money. I'll work around the other stuff." She hoped. And as to money…an idea came to her.

He rolled his eyes. "Fine, let me give you—"

"No!" She slapped the bed for emphasis.

"Why? Would taking money make you feel like a whore?"

"Someone owes me money. I'll collect it later in the week."

"How much are you owed?" he asked, suspicious.

"There might have to be a pointed negotiation over the amount."

"Would you like me to come with you?"

"No, no. It's not worth your time."

"Why am I getting the feeling that there's more than just a little danger involved?"

"'Cause life's messy?" She yawned to cover doubts she couldn't afford. "I'm so tired, I could sleep in your bed."

V

Shabbat Shalom, Asshole

Two hours before sundown on Friday, women buying food for Sabbath dinner, *aruchat shabbat,* mobbed the butcher shop. Black-cloaked and hooded, girl slipped into the back room. She watched Mordchai Kaplan shoo out his last customer, take off his apron, pull the shade over the glass-paneled front door, and lock it.

"AHHHH!" girl yelled as she jogged from the back room, cleaver held high in her left hand.

The butcher jumped; but by the time she reached him, he'd recovered his bearings. He grabbed her left wrist and bent it back. Girl yelped. The cleaver clattered on the tile floor.

"So, my little Hannah, you've come back for more." His boiled beef eyes brimmed with hate. "Only too happy to oblige."

A kitten-like mewl emerged from girl's throat.

"People wondered what happened to you, but they've moved on to more current gossip." The butcher chuckled, sending a wave rolling through his fat stomach, as it strained against his dirty white shirt. "With no one looking for you because you're considered dead, I'm free to chain you up in the back, so you'll be there whenever and *however* I want you."

His vacant grin indicated how entranced he was by the idea of keeping Hannah as a disposable sex slave. Too bad for him, Hannah no longer existed.

Girl tightened her right hand on the handle of the boning knife concealed under her sleeve. She drove her arm forward and down, slicing through wool trouser, cotton underpants, and butcher's scrotum.

He screamed. His knees buckled. Letting go of her wrist, his hands went to his crotch.

She pulled back, ready for another strike.

"If you'd like to have something to pee out of, shut up and

55

listen." She picked up the cleaver. "I've come to collect what you owe me."

Blood had begun to seep through his hands. She prodded him with the knife, daring him to make a hostile move, even wanting him to.

"What do I owe you?" he asked, voice high and tremulous.

"Everything you have," she said, icy calm. "Get on your knees."

He didn't.

"NOW!"

He knelt. She cut away more of his pants and underwear, exposing his entire genital area. *How had that ugly shriveled thing hurt Hannah so much?*

He grabbed her right hand. With her left, she smacked him on the side of the head with the cleaver. The hollow sound, like a hammer hitting a coconut, made her smile. He released his grip, and she sliced a small piece of flesh from his thigh.

"Touch me again, even by accident, and you'll find your penis up your butt." She spoke quietly, voice devoid of emotion. "Understand?"

He nodded.

"Hold this on the wound and try not to move." She tossed him his apron. "We wouldn't want your balls rolling around the floor. I might be inclined to squash them."

She emptied the cash register.

"Now the safe."

"Don't have one." Girlish whimper.

She again knocked his hands from his crotch, then brought the boning knife to the tip of his penis.

"Good!" An electric jolt of pleasure shot through her. "That means you'll have to pray in the balcony of the synagogue with the other women."

The slightest twitch of her knife hand, and he shrieked like…Hannah had in this same butcher shop. His entire body trembled as if he were shivering. She loved being in total control. *If only sex could be this enjoyable.* She had never loved anything until now. Hannah hadn't loved anything since the tiny droplets of rain hit her face with cold little hellos.

"In the closet," he whispered, his pupils so dilated that black orbs dwarfed his irises.

"Roll over. Stick your fat butt in the air."

He rolled. She cut off the back of his trousers and underclothes.

"Crawl over to the safe. For god's sake no sudden movements. Actually for your sake. God is magnificently indifferent to whether you bleed to death."

While the knife caressed his rectum, he crawled, leaving a ragged trail of blood, like the slime-track of a morbidly obese snail. A wave of nausea started in her stomach and rose up her throat, washing away her earlier ecstasy and leaving repulsion and disgust in its wake. Then a new feeling came over her. No, it wasn't new exactly, but she hadn't felt it since she became girl. She tried to put a name to the feeling. *Yes that's it, I feel alive. I'd been dead. Now, I'm alive—for the moment.*

"Best we keep this whole business between ourselves," she said as he dialed the combination. "Rav Moscovitz told me it would be bad for the community if word of your *proclivities* were to get out."

She smiled. Did he even know what *proclivities* meant?

Stomach hanging down almost to his penis, he pulled at the safe. It didn't open.

"Try again."

Short, sharp stab in his buttocks, or rather his fat, crinkly, sagging ass. A little more blood, no big deal.

"Not that such publicity would matter to me," she said as he turned the knob right, then left, then right again. "No jury would convict, after hearing that I was retaliating for rape. In the world beyond Crown Heights, rape is a serious crime. I might even get a book deal."

He opened the safe and handed her a wad of hundred-dollar bills.

"Also, you probably wouldn't want the IRS to hear about all this green."

He nodded, mouth tight as if nodding took all his concentration.

"*Shabbat Shalom*, asshole. Wish Rav Moscovitz and my family a good *shabbos*. Tell them I'll think of them with every uncircumcised cock I suck."

She walked out into the shimmering, sweltering August heat with $13,000 neatly wrapped in butcher paper with a twine bow.

She felt giddy, joyful, proud, disgusted, sick to her stomach, and relieved. She'd loved the adrenaline rush; getting it by meting out justice had made it morally acceptable. She already wanted to feel that rush again. If only she could without hurting someone else. Unfortunately that left only one person available to hurt. The soap opera where a teenager repeatedly cut herself flashed through her mind, then the one about the whore given a fatal dose. About to live on her own, these desires should have terrified her. Would anything ever terrify her again?

"Here's a month's rent." Girl gave Everett ten hundred-dollar bills. "I figure that's how long it'll take for me to find an apartment."

He handed the money back.

"Please take it," she said. "While I set up my new life, I want us to play on a financially level field."

He shook his head. A negative response, or a reaction to her incomprehensible weirdness? At least he picked up the money, although he appeared to be studying it as if he feared it were counterfeit.

"There's blood on it," he said.

"Blood money. Don't worry about it. It's just butcher's blood."

His eyes bugged. "I'm very worried."

"Not my problem."

He made an all-too-familiar noise indicating extreme exasperation.

"Stay as long as you want," he said. "The longer the better, but I'm not taking your money. You might want to wash the

Girl

blood off your hands and cloak, though. Maybe you'll even tell me how the hell you got this."

"Maybe you'd like to lick it off." She held out her hand, enjoying the faint emotional echo of the butcher's terror.

"Nope."

"Everett, I'm about to be all alone in the world. My choice, but still... You're the only one, other than my parents, who ever told me you loved me. If you turn me down, I'll understand but..." Her voice cracked. *The hell with that.*

"So we'll be lovers for a month; then you'll disappear?" His voice trembled, another echo.

"You're a grown man. You can handle it."

He carried her to his bed, formerly their bed, and slowly, very slowly undressed her. He spent what seemed like hours touching and licking her all over. Finally he slid into her as soft and gentle as a cloud...

She slapped him, then rolled him over and thrust herself onto him hard as she could.

"You want it rough, fine." He rolled her back over and rammed into her, his thrusts angry, brutal.

Her mind fuzzed. Her breaths came hard and fast. Her muscles tightened. All went blank, and then...contractions. Building. Her spine tingled up to her brain and down.

They exploded at the same time with shouts and groans. Both were drenched in tears and other fluids. Mirror image grins. They both laughed. *So that's what an orgasm is. Good. Now I'll know how to fake them.*

Everett cradled her in his arms.

His touch made her skin crawl with thousands of insects that weren't there. Discomfort rolled in like a fog, so thick and wet he must have felt it too. She told him what she'd done to the butcher. The fog lifted, and the emotional weather became overcast with a probability of rain.

"You're heading for trouble, and I am too," he said, "but if you stay with me, our love can save us both."

"You know what the Greek tragedians had to say about fate.

59

We're both doomed. All we can do is make the best of it and go out with a modicum of dignity."

He shook his head.

"I liked what I did to the butcher." Acting of its own volition, her voice dropped to a whisper. "The feeling of power, the risk of getting caught, the freedom to do whatever the hell I wanted to him."

He stared at her, the pedophile seemingly struggling with the teacher/philosopher.

"Not only am I damaged, but also I don't want to heal," she said. "I want my every breath to tell conventional bourgeois morality to fuck itself and the god it rode in on."

"Oh come on!" he yelled. Unusual for him to raise his voice. "You're charitable, willing to sacrifice yourself so an innocent man wouldn't suffer, unwilling to lie, unwilling even to take what you don't pay for."

"Exactly! The opposite of conventional bourgeois morality."

To her annoyance, he didn't even smile at her excellent repartee.

Sadness undercutting his sarcastic tone, he said, "And the award for best Emma Goldman portrayal in 1990 goes to... envelope, please."

He wouldn't acknowledge it, even to himself, but she'd aged out. His professions of love were wishful thinking. She could probably rein in her masochism and desire for danger, but there'd be no point. A pedophile and a young woman who was rapidly growing up were different species. He could pretend otherwise, but girl's pretending days were over.

He'd told her about his earlier dalliances. He'd loved each one in turn; then disillusionment crept in, leading to a gentle, tearful break-up. Blinded by the lie, however, he failed to recognize the pattern. Seeing clearly, girl was not going to let herself be deluded by the lie of love.

Girl turned her attention to finding an apartment, but that left plenty of time and energy to enjoy her lover in most every way imaginable other than actual love. One morning he tied her to the headboard and slapped her repeatedly, stopping only when it became apparent that neither of them were aroused. Their single brutal sexual encounter, satisfying though it was, had been a one-time event. She craved risk and excitement, but not that way.

According to a book Everett had assigned to her, the spring after World War II was declared—before France fell and the Blitz began—had been the most beautiful in living memory. The intensity of the colors of the flowers in the English gardens surpassed anything that came before or after. In Paris *joie de vivre* reached levels not seen before or since. Similarly, at *chez* Everett, weeks zipped by with ineffable sweetness. Everett's feet seemed not to touch the floor. Girl had never imagined that she'd be capable of making anyone so happy just by her presence.

A couple of weeks later, she woke in the middle of the night to find herself wrapped around him. After checking that the sheets and blanket covered him, she listened to his adorable snores and kissed him ever so gently, making sure not to wake him. Then she snuggled against his warm body, timing her breathing to conform to his. That felt wonderful, almost like when Hannah's mommy had hugged her.

With only one choice to make—whether to leave while things were still wonderful or wait until they turned to shit—she redoubled her efforts to find an apartment.

VI

Rebel Without a Pause

Girl had been living with Everett for five weeks since declaring her intention to move. Apartments suitable for entertaining well-heeled customers were ruinously expensive. Moreover, landlords wouldn't even talk to an under-aged applicant, particularly one without a source of income or an adult willing to guarantee the rent.

In response to his nagging about her *needing to get in touch with her feelings*, she said, "In my better moments, I feel almost nothing, barely notice if I'm hot, cold, hungry, or tired. Probably I should regret hurting you, worry about embarking on a dangerous, unhealthy, illegal career, or maybe even be excited about starting a new phase of my life. But I feel nothing."

"Not true. You're often quite emotional."

"I was talking about my *better moments*. When I allow myself to think about what happened to Hannah or never being able to see her parents or siblings again, particularly Rivka, I start crying and can't stop, sometimes for over an hour. Numb is as good as it gets."

"That's typical for rape victims. You're dissociating. Splitting off from yourself is a defense mechanism, not a life skill. You need to get help."

"I don't need help. I'm already very good at dissociating." She smiled; he didn't. "Having sex with a succession of disgusting, degenerate swine should help."

He slammed his hand on the couch, a rare display of anger. "You're so damn..."

"Stubborn? It's part of my upbringing. For hundreds of years, Crusaders, Cossacks, Nazis all tried to wipe out my forebears. We persevered by being stubborn. No reason to stop now, seeing how well it's worked."

"You're heading for—"

Girl

"Lying on the sidewalk in front of the butcher shop, Hannah knew her life had ended. She wished she'd forget what happened and what it had been like to be Hannah. Short of suicide—not that I rule that out—dissociating seems the way to go."

"You've gotten so fucking glib."

"Yes, thank you for that." She stroked his cheek.

He balled up his fists in frustration.

"What was it you said the other day, Everett? Oh, right, 'This world is a comedy to those that think, a tragedy to those that feel.' I bet God's a thinker. He must be laughing his holy ass off."

"Girl!"

She took off her jeans and T-shirt. As always, his eyes went wide. She took her only business suit from the closet. Purchased at a deep discount for her apartment search, it was too short and too tight, which was why she'd chosen it.

"I'm going to look at an apartment. Don't wait up."

"It's eleven o'clock at night."

The one-bedroom apartment on the ground floor of a recently renovated Upper West Side brownstone had sounded ideal in the ad. Half a block from Central Park, near both the Seventh and Eighth Avenue subways, between two crosstown bus lines, and just blocks from the best food shopping in New York, its private entrance meant that customers could come and go free of a doorman's or neighbor's prying eyes. At $2,500 a month, though, the rent seemed steep, especially since she had no way of knowing what she might earn.

An investment banker at Morgan Stanley had bought the building at a distressed price when its owner had gone bankrupt from following the firm's advice. His architect created a palatial home for the banker, complete with a separate garden apartment. Girl and her prospective landlord met in his sterile hyper-designed living room.

He wore his thick black hair slicked back in a way that said, "Look on my works, ye mighty, and despair, for I am H.

63

Connor—call me Charty—Chartwell III." She'd hoped her make-up and too-tight, too-short business suit, with nothing underneath, would make her appear to be at least twenty-one, or sexy enough so he wouldn't care about her age.

"I require first and last months' rent in advance and a two months' damage deposit, in addition to a personal guarantee by whoever will be paying your rent. The guarantee must be supported by net worth and income statements certified by a nationally recognized accounting firm. Alternatively, I'd accept as security a letter of credit from a money-center bank."

"The advance and deposit are fine." Her tongue made a slow transit across her blood-red lips and perfect white teeth. She'd thought doing it would feel weird; but she liked the look on his face, liked having sexual power, wanted more. "The rest isn't going to happen."

He nursed a single-malt scotch but hadn't offered her anything to drink.

"Do you have any idea how hard it is to evict a tenant in New York?" he asked.

"No." Landlord/tenant law hadn't been on Everett's syllabus. "But tell me to leave and I'll be gone like a puff of smoke in a gale." Girl took a joint from her purse and licked it as if it were a skinny penis. She needed to make a good impression in order to subvert his mania for financial security, but she'd do it her way. Her sucking-up days had ended when Hannah left Crown Heights. "Speaking of smoke, mind if I...?

"Not if you share."

His stare fixed on her cleavage. Everett's mind would soften in direct proportion to the hardness of his dick. She hoped that equation held true for his entire gender, or at least extended to Charty. It pleased her that he'd already marked himself as a degenerate. That should make her job easier. She took a hit, held in the smoke, and handed him the joint.

"So who's paying your rent?" He ran his hand along his blue tie adorned with tiny bulldogs and crests featuring the slogans *Lux et Veritas* and סימתו םירוא. *Boola-boola.*

"Me."

"And the source of your money?"

"I'm about to enter the world's oldest profession."

He laughed, spitting out smoke and whiskey.

"As I'll have a separate entrance, you'll have absolute deniability." She smiled in a way that Everett found sexy. "If I get behind in my rent, which I won't, you could call the police and have me hauled away in handcuffs." She marveled at what a tough, sexy bitch she'd transformed herself into. "Maybe, after a hard day of fucking over your customers, you might find it convenient to have me downstairs, so I can do the same to you."

She felt engaged, alive. Not as much as when she sliced the butcher's scrotum but enough…for now.

"Having already invested never mind how much money to ensure a continual stream of premium pussy, I don't need to pay for it. Anyone I bring in here will be on her knees in front of me inside half an hour." His grin communicated that he well knew what he'd said had been offensive but didn't consider her important enough for him to care about the impression he made.

She glanced at her watch, a present from Everett she'd accepted only because he persuaded her she'd need to time her sessions.

"So I've got about sixteen minutes before I succumb. Do you supply the knee pads, or is it BYOKP?"

He smiled. The man had perfect teeth.

"Let me pose a hypothetical," she said. "Let's say I'm living here, and one night I ring your bell when you're entertaining a lady friend. I lost my keys. It's raining and my clothes are soaked, nipples sticking out. You buzz me in and offer me a drink. I politely decline because I'm terrified that I'll lose my inhibitions. Still practicality reigns, and I have to get out of my wet clothes. Next thing I know, my face is buried between your latest conquest's legs."

She hoped Everett's erotic fantasies had an element of male universality. She wanted this apartment more than she'd wanted anything in months.

Robert N. Chan

The corners of his mouth turned up. She was on the right track.

"You dump her because she's a bisexual slut. Then you move on to her best friend, who's lusted after you ever since her pal confided in her about the size of your...house. Once again I'll lose my keys...."

He laughed, but then his laughter stopped so short she practically heard the screech of tires. "If I were to send clients your way, what cut would I get?"

"Whatever I charge them over my usual rate." She took back the joint he'd been hogging. "My mentor told me your set enjoys overpaying for things and bragging about it. So it'd be a win, win, win."

His crooked smile could've indicated anything from enlightenment to indigestion. She took his scotch from his hand, emptied the glass in a gulp, and gave it back to him.

"I could get off on fucking you," he said.

"Any time, but I don't give discounts."

"Even for friends?" He raised his meticulously trimmed eyebrows. He wore a trace of mascara. She made a mental note to ask him for make-up tips.

"Friends would be free, but only because I don't intend to have any."

Wondering if he'd be able to handle it without burning his manicured, clear-polished fingernails, she handed him the joint, now a roach.

"I suspect I'll be able to send a lot of business your way and with my having absolute deniability..."

"Great!" She raised a celebratory fist. "So the rent's $1,500 a month, right?"

"$2,500." His face turned so hard that girl wondered if his earlier smiles and laughter had been an illusion caused by the play of light and shadow. Not that anything could actually *play* in this hyper-designed space. Luckily, the garden apartment hadn't received as much architectural attention.

"That was before we realized the synergies from my living here," she said.

Girl

"You don't really think you can negotiate with an investment banker?" He smiled again and, with his twinkling blue eyes, athletic build, and aura of supreme confidence, he looked downright handsome for a man of his age—he must've been pushing thirty-five.

Didn't he realize they'd been negotiating from the time they'd sat down together?

"I could try," she said in the childlike voice she'd used when Everett wanted her to be prepubescent and terrified by the magnitude of his member.

Not only had she been able to pull that off, but she'd done it without laughing. Halfway through, though, she'd faded out and had little awareness of where she was or what she was doing. Afterwards, though, Everett said she'd played her role perfectly.

She unbuckled Charty's pants and stroked his member. If only Hannah's parents could see her now.

"$2,400," he said when girl lifted her head.

She withdrew her hand. "1,600."

She went back to what she was doing, making sure not to close the sexual deal before they closed the rent deal.

"$2,300, and that's it," he said in a tone that would've been convincing had it not been bracketed by moans. "If I don't make money on referrals, the rent goes back up to $2,500...retroactive."

"$2,000, but to sweeten the deal, I'm yours till you leave for work this morning."

"$2—"

"Don't even think about it, H. Connor." Her hands cupped his scrotum and rapidly increased and decreased the pressure.

"I told you earlier; my friends call me Charty."

"I might give a fuck, but I don't give a crap."

"Fine. Come upstairs to the master bedroom."

"Yes, master."

Everett came to the door, bags under his bloodshot eyes, jaw thrust forward.

67

"Where the hell were you? I was this far from calling the police." Familiar thumb and forefinger gesture with minute separation.

Girl responded with the even more familiar middle-fingered one.

"I'm moving out today."

"What? Where? You can't...shouldn't." His cadence accelerated from confused to desperate. "Let me see the place, help you decide if it's suitable. I'll have a lawyer look at the lease." His tempo wound down to pathetic. "Please, give us more time."

"It's been five weeks."

His lips flapped as if he knew not to say out loud the words coming into his head but couldn't stop himself from forming them in his mouth.

"We'll stay in touch, of course." Everett's forced smile tilted like a painting hung off-center.

"You know it has to be cold turkey, a total break." She flashed back to Rav Moscovitz saying, "We'd have no choice but to sit *shiva* for you," and Hannah's parents nodding like bobble-head dolls. Pain built behind her eyes. Yes, cold kosher turkey.

"But I love..." His voice cracked.

No point in telling him, yet again, if she stayed he'd tire of her in a few months. Maybe all love was self-delusion. Too bad Hannah's parents hadn't seen fit to continue to delude her and themselves.

"I don't want to sound like a broken record," he said, crossing his arms, "but this plan of yours—"

"And with all the other opportunities open to me, a sixteen-year-old girl without a degree. Maybe I should ask Goldman Sachs if they need another M&A partner or see if Mt. Sinai has an opening for an orthopedic surgeon."

He rolled his eyes.

"I have one regret. As much as I tried to pay for everything I took, you gave me so much more than I ever could give you."

Girl

She put a finger to his mouth to stop him from saying something that would embarrass him in retrospect. "If you ever need anything—other than love or companionship—please come to me."

"Come on, girl, you know you want to stay here with me."

"Hannah wanted to stay with her family and devote herself to healing the world. To do that, all she had to do was one tiny little thing: say she'd been assaulted by a homeless man. She couldn't do that anymore than she could've transformed herself into an angel and flown around the room dropping holy turds on their heads."

"There's a huge difference between lying to hurt an innocent man and staying with someone who loves you, whom you could love if only you let yourself."

"Both would require me to be a hypocrite. Whatever else I am, I'm not that."

She could tell how much effort it took for him to pull back his hunched shoulders and manage a nod. This was hard for her too, but easier than it should have been.

She began to pack. Tears streaming down his cheeks, he helped her. Not that she needed help, since everything she owned fit into a supermarket box. She wiped a tear from her cheek.

"Remember, if you ever need anything I can give you…"

And girl was gone.

VII

Niece Work If You Can Get It

Standing alone in her new apartment, girl felt as if she had been transported to another world, one even stranger and more alien than the one she'd left. With bare white walls and white oak- stained floor, the large, empty front room resembled the area where the newly dead waited to be transported to heaven in a movie she'd watched with Everett. The only furniture, a counter with two built-in barstools on each side, divided the room into a kitchen and a living room area. She didn't see a single speck of dust. It was as if the cleaning crew Charty had hired had gone over the entire area with feathers, like Hannah's mother used to do the night before Passover.

No longer the *haredi* girl with every part of her life regimented, no longer Everett's *mentee*, she was totally free. Free to… She looked down at her extended hands, her pale arms, her breasts, her legs, feeling small in the middle of a large, bare white space. Panicked, she sprinted to the door but stopped. Nowhere to go. She turned herself around. From here the space seemed less intimidating.

The only rules she'd have to follow here would be those she'd make herself, and she intended to make precious few. Nothing could be more terrible than what Hannah had gone through. Hannah hadn't survived; but girl would not only survive, she'd thrive…she hoped.

She began laughing and soon was laughing so hard she could no longer stand up.

What now? Perhaps familiarize herself with the neighborhood, buy some food. To celebrate her freedom, she'd make herself the least kosher meal she could think of: pork and shrimp in a cream sauce. But that didn't sound so good, and she didn't know how to make a cream sauce. For that matter she didn't know how to cook pork or shrimp.

70

Girl

An odd ringing sound startled her. There it was again. When she heard knocking, she realized the ring had been her doorbell. She went to the door and stopped, as she had during her earlier panic. The police? Social Services? Everett? Hannah's father? The bell rang again.

She took a deep breath. After looking though the peephole, she opened the door.

"Hi," Charty said, "just wanted to see how you're making out."

"Great," she said without enthusiasm.

"You could use some furniture." *Why didn't I think of that?*

"My decorator could—"

"Wouldn't that be expensive?" she asked, having no clue but... "I haven't had my first customer yet."

How do I go about getting customers? I haven't thought this out very well. Haven't thought it out at all. She pictured Charty, unlocking her door with a master key a few weeks hence, prompted by the stench of her rotting body, after she'd starved to death.

"Ikea."

"What?"

He rolled his eyes. "I'll have my girl take you."

"You have a daughter?"

He smiled. "I pride myself on being politically incorrect."

"I'm sorry; I don't follow."

"I'll tell my assistant to help you."

"I don't need—"

"Yeah, you do."

I sure do. "That would be very nice. Thank you."

I keep saying I want to be independent, to take no help from others and then have to accept help. This will be the last time I allow myself to suffer such humiliation.

"Not a problem. Actually another reason I came down here... I already have two clients for you, both respectable married men, not terribly good-looking; actually it'd be fair to call them trolls, but—"

71

"I don't need good-looking. Send them over."

"You probably need a bed first." He stepped so close to her she could feel his scotch-tainted breath on her forehead. "For all this help, how 'bout a fuck?"

God, no. But as a whore, shouldn't I... Maybe but not quite yet.

"Once I'm all set up and can put a dollar value on your help. You know, best to keep things professional." She wondered if this were how she was supposed to act.

"Right." He smiled. "What are you charging?"

Good question. Some multiple of chai? No.

"$400 per hour seems right," he said. "It's a little on the high side, but no one respects a cheap whore."

"Do they respect expensive ones?"

"Sure. People respect corporate lawyers, and they're the biggest whores in town. They won't fuck you over for less than five figures." She realized she'd see his I'm-so-damn-clever smile quite often.

"Okay, then," she said. "And $500 for my investment-banker-and-lawyer special. That way you can clear $100 on each session."

He laughed. She didn't know why.

"I'll have my girl call you within the hour. She needs to buy some jewelry for my girlfriend-of-the-month; then she's all yours."

"As far as your girl calling me…"

"Got it. I'll have her stop by here and arrange for you to get a phone. You'll need to give the phone company a down payment check and sign—"

"Charty"—embarrassed, she looked down—"I want to keep a low profile, have nothing in my name. Do you think it's possible that…"

His quick intake and release of breath communicated the hugeness of the burden he was about to assume. "I'll deal with it and build the cost of the phone into the rent."

"Thank you. I really appreciate it." She threw her arms

around him, then pulled away.

"You'd better turn out to be a good earner, all the time and effort I'm putting in here."

A week after she moved in, she was pretty well set up. Walking around the Upper West Side alone, everything seemed strange, and... probably would've been exciting, if her emotions hadn't been packed in cotton balls. As it were, she often returned from her walks with a mild headache from the sensory overload.

She'd been eating in fast food places, but, as a major step forward, had just finished a major food, staples, cleaning materials, and condiments shop at a grocery store on Broadway over a dozen blocks from her apartment. There were more convenient alternatives; but she liked the walk and, after comparison shopping, had deemed the store's prices the most reasonable. The crush of people in the narrow aisles and the overwhelming variety of foods and products, however, had made her tense and anxious.

Leaving the store, she started walking uptown and turned to look at the window of a gourmet food shop. The display featured an artful arrangement of cuts of beef. She stopped, stared. Everything began to swirl.

Suddenly she was naked on a cold tiled floor.

"You okay?" asked a woman's voice from somewhere. "Here, lie down."

A pair of hands gently nudged her down. Girl had thought she was already prone, but apparently she'd collapsed onto her butt and had been sitting on the sidewalk.

"It's okay; I'm a doctor." The woman wiped girl's forehead with a handkerchief. "Now raise your legs as high as you can." Arm under girl's knees, she bent her legs upwards.

After no more than a minute, girl sat up, annoyed with herself for having had to accept help from yet another Good Samaritan. The crowd that had gathered began to spin, and the traffic appeared to levitate from the roadway and drift through the air.

"Thank you. I'm fine now."

"You sure?"

"Oh, yes, just a little...dehydration maybe."

Thank god for the cotton balls. As she just learned, when something brushed them aside, the pain could be almost unbearable and that *something* could be almost nothing.

After having had so much sex with Everett, girl had thought that being a whore would be easy, just more of the same. Turned out she had a lot to learn.

When the first of the *trolls* Charty had referred showed up, she answered the door, heart in her throat; she'd sort of hoped he wouldn't show up. After changing several times—luckily she had a limited wardrobe—she'd settled on the lingerie and high heels to which Everett had been partial.

The man wore a business suit, smelled like cologne, was short, overweight, and had an extensive comb-over that was more of a *comb-around*. Sweat glazed his face, due to the Indian summer heat.

"Wow!" he said. He stood in the doorway, looking her up and down, eyes wide.

She took his hand, gently leading him inside and closing the door behind her.

Am I really going to do this? She smiled, hoping her anxiety wouldn't show on her face.

He pulled her close and started kissing her. She parted her lips and inserted her tongue the way Everett liked.

"Nice," he said. "Most...escorts don't French kiss."

"French...?"

"You know, open-mouthed."

"Yes, of course." *Good. Last time I'll do that.*

He disengaged and pulled a wad of cash from his pocket. "Where should I leave the money?"

She pointed to a small table by the front door and made a mental note to insist from now on that customers pay on arrival and that they leave their money there. Would it be bad form to count the money? After she'd done her work, she would ask his advice. The troll had far more experience at this than she.

She took him into the bedroom and began to unbutton his shirt. He pulled her close and kissed her again. This time she brushed her closed lips against his lips, cheeks, and neck. Then...

She felt as if she had left her body and was watching from above, indifferent to what she was seeing.

Next thing she knew, she was lying naked; and the troll was standing by the bed buttoning his shirt, a bit of a struggle given the size of his protruding belly.

"You were terrific," he said. "I hope you enjoyed it as much as I did."

"I'm...new to this. Are there any pointers you could give me? I'd like to be as good as I can be at it."

He sat on the edge of the bed. "How did you get into this...line of work?"

"You're a very sweet man." The sweet stink of cologne accounted for that. "I'd be delighted if you want to see me again."

"I guess you don't want to talk about yourself."

"Not on our first date. What kind of girl do you think I am?" She stood and gave his cheek a playful slap. "But, as I said, any pointers..."

"Well, when you...try not to use your teeth; and if you were a little more responsive, you know, louder, that would be good as well."

"Great. Thank you." She put on a robe. "Would it be bad form to count the money when a customer gives it to me?"

"Do it unobtrusively, like this." He mimed picking the cash off the table, turning his back to her, and flipping through it as he slipped it into a drawer.

She grinned appreciatively.

"You're very nice, genuine," he said. "I'd like to see you again."

Perhaps most men, not just Everett, enjoy teaching and giving

advice, makes them think they're taken seriously, respected.
"I feel the same way about you." And she sort of did. For her
first customer, she could have done a lot worse.

Charty referred so much business to girl that she could
support herself without getting out of bed. Particularly since she
didn't have extravagant tastes, except in one area. She spent
several hours a day walking around the neighborhood, making it
her neighborhood, and buying books, her single extravagance.

As with the extraordinary variety of products available at the
grocery store, she found the variety of books dizzying and
overwhelming. When it came to books, however, she loved the
feeling. She wanted to read everything, to know everything.
She'd close her eyes, spin around, take a few steps, and then
check out the volumes she found herself facing. On her most
recent foray to Shakespeare & Co., her local bookstore, she came
home with volumes on Impressionism, Fauvism, Cubism,
Dadaism, and Post-impressionism. If nothing else, they'd do
wonders for her bookshelf aesthetics. No, she wouldn't let
herself be intimidated. She'd study them and learn. She opened
one at random, Marcel Duchamp's *Fountain*. So that's what a
urinal looks like. She might never buy into Dadaism.

By the end of her second month, she already had two weekly
customers and four who came less frequently. Several men had
referred their friends. At first she'd have a pit in her stomach
before each appointment. Would he be a cop? Would he hurt
her? Would he try to negotiate her fee or even refuse to pay her?
After a few weeks and no bad experiences, however, she realized
that her customers, mostly married and holding high-profile jobs,
had more to lose than she.

Sex with customers quickly evolved into a well-practiced
series of movements, sounds, and responses. Her customers
became as fungible as heads of broccoli to a greengrocer. Not a
perfect analogy since, unlike vegetables, her customers spoke to
her. Regardless of what they said or what roles they claimed they
wanted her to play, a standard response with only minor

modifications satisfied them. After all, not all heads of broccoli were identical either and had stalks of varying lengths, but still Fairway charged the same for each head and had no emotional attachment to what it sold.

Everett had told her to seek therapy for her dissociative episodes, but her customer-induced trances were among the best parts of her day. Suddenly it would be later, she would rejoin her body, and her customer would be dressing, a goofy smile on his face.

More often than not, first-time customers became regulars, so she must've been doing a good job. She took no small satisfaction in having so quickly built a successful business and in providing a service that people seemed to enjoy.

She continued to suffer through nightmares about the butcher and agonizingly pleasant dreams about Hannah's family. Now, though, she no longer had to worry about waking Everett or his comforting her, which made the terror and sadness more manageable. Usually she would get back to sleep after an hour or so of reading, but sometimes the purposelessness of her existence would weigh on her like a 300 pound barbell. She'd tell herself to get up and walk around, eat something, go outside, watch television, but herself would reply that there was no point in any of that. So she'd just lie there feeling empty. Given the enormous psychological damage she, or rather Hannah, had suffered, she had no reason to expect better.

Living in a garden apartment on one of New York's nicer streets and supporting herself by having sex with respectable men six or seven hours a week didn't satisfy her craving for intensity...and danger. She needed something more. But what? She wouldn't let herself fall for the lie of love. God had found her unworthy of *tikkun olam*; and, anyway, the world was beyond healing. She recalled the excitement she'd gotten from soap opera scenes, where drugs destroyed or even killed a character. If something more was out of the question, what about something less? Too bad she didn't know how to go about procuring hard drugs.

Robert N. Chan

The solution arrived from an unlikely source, *The New York Times*. Its piece on a Serbian gang led by a fugitive war criminal provided the name of a bar that operated as their *de facto* headquarters. If only the cops had access to the *Times*, the gang's days would be numbered.

With its splintery wood floors, old beer stink, missing ceiling tiles, and black-and-white TV, The Double Eagle, located in New York's Serbian enclave—Ridgewood, Queens—seemed to exist in the Land That Time Forgot. More likely the place was holding its breath and hoping time wouldn't stumble on it.

Usually when girl went outside, she wore loose jeans and the cape she'd worn when she cut the butcher. Today's costume—short skirt and heels—felt strange.

She sauntered to the bar with a slutty stride. Of the few dozen patrons, only three didn't lock lecherous gazes on her. Skin and eyes tinged yellow, the barflies appeared to be suffering from advanced liver disease. For all she knew, though, they could've been undercover agents.

"Slivovitz, please. Make it a double."

"You got ID?"

"With this bod? You've *got* to be kidding." That awkward stage in life, too young to drink or vote but old enough to turn tricks.

The bartender pointed toward the door.

Girl strutted out. Leaning louchely against the tavern's wall, she took a gulp from the bottle of slivovitz she'd liberated from Charty's well-stocked bar. The corrosive plum brandy scorched her esophagus and began to eat through her stomach lining. A good start. She took another hit. Perhaps a bleeding ulcer could substitute for a heroin overdose.

A handsome young guy with the callused, paint-stained hands of an honest working man approached her.

"You do not look like the kind of person who usually hangs out here." He sounded genuinely concerned. "This not safe area for young woman alone."

Girl

"*Jeb'o ti pas mater.*" In preparation for this meeting, girl had learned a few handy phrases of Serbo-Croatian. Concerned that she hadn't quite pronounced it right, she translated into English, "May a dog fuck your mother."

The man left, without having the courtesy to say goodbye and wish her well.

A wave of reality broke over her. Was she really set on taking a dangerous drug, risking jail and addiction? Maybe, on a subconscious level, she believed she deserved to die. Hannah's parents had so readily agreed to consider her dead; maybe she was worthless. She'd chosen such a generic name for herself that the first letter wasn't even capitalized. That spoke volumes. Mostly she wanted to live but... She'd been serious when she'd told Trevor, "I don't plan to live that long."

Another scalding sip and she decided to return home. But home wasn't *home*. It was an apartment where strange men paid her for sex. Her dissociative episodes, coupled with the all-pervasive emptiness, gave her apartment a creepy aura—akin to that of a public restroom—that never completely went away.

The next person to approach her was a big step up—meaning down—from Mr. Paint-Stained Hands. His shaved head showed off an elaborate tattoo featuring a Siamese twin eagle with heads facing in opposite directions, wings outstretched over four Cyrillic "Cs." According to her research, those letters stood for *Само слога Србина спасава.* "Only unity saves the Serbs."

"Want a hit?" She took a sip of slivovitz, then handed him the bottle.

He followed his ambitious gulp with a barely perceptible wince.

"A little young to be looking for trouble, aren't you?"

"A little ineffectual to give me any, aren't you?" She considered spitting in his face but decided such punctuation might be excessively fatal. "Trouble's the last thing I want. A gram of heroin, a few clean needles, and a little coke would do me just fine."

"How do I know you're not a cop?"

79

"Your tattooist might've gone in too deep. Do I look like a cop, *supak* (asshole)?"

"You look like a TV cop. Real cops aren't that young and hot."

"A cop wouldn't take you into that alley"—she tilted her head—"unzip your pants, and suck your thing into her mouth." *Thing? You're a whore; call it a cock.*

He took a step toward the alley and looked back over his shoulder: *you coming or just talking big?*

Good question. At least she was pretty sure *he* wasn't an undercover agent—not that she knew anything about that sort of thing. In for a penny, in for a pound. She led him around the corner, unzipped his pants, and took him into her mouth. She remained fully engaged, no out-of-body detachment this time. After several seconds, she lifted her head.

"Hey, you're not done." He shoved her head back down.

She jerked away and stood.

"Yeah, I am. I was showing you I'm not a cop, not giving you a freebie."

He pulled back his arm as if to strike her. She grabbed hold of his scrotum.

Oh, no, what did I just do? I must be crazier than I think I am, and that's awfully crazy, emphasis on the awful.

"Your move," she said, hoping she sounded more confident than she felt.

He inspected her arm. "Where do you shoot up?"

"Nowhere yet. I could use some basic instruction."

"You got cash?"

"That and sex." She let go of him. "I charge $400 an hour. If you pay me in drugs, I expect them to be valued at wholesale, not retail."

"I'm Darko." He extended his hand.

"Is that a name or a Croatian curse?" Regretting her comment, girl shook his hand. "What do you do for a living, Darko?"

"Deal smack and fuck people up."

"Cool." She swallowed hard. "Are we going to get high or jabber?"

"You got some mouth on you." He raised his hand, like Hannah's father used to.

"Just kidding around." She smiled. "I'm drawn to hard drugs and risky behavior." She held up her hand. "But not too risky."

She couldn't bring herself to maintain eye contact with him. It wasn't just his dead brown eyes, cruel mouth, and vampiric accent or the way his large ears lay flat against his head, like a wolf in one of Rivka's picture books. His hard, wiry body seemed designed to inflict pain and enjoy it. This was all too real…and scary. Understanding that her desire to hurt herself was a highly neurotic reaction to the rape—an effort to punish herself for something that hadn't been at all her fault—she should have been able to stop herself from doing it. But if things happened the way they should have, Hannah wouldn't have been dragged into the butcher's shop, so *should have* counted for nothing.

"Let's go to my place," he said in a calm, self-assured voice of someone who knew he was totally in control. "For your first time, snort it. If you like it, we can try the needle next time."

"Would you mind coming to my place?" Her voice quivered. She wanted to call the whole thing off, but a terrible inertia carried her forward. "I'm more comfortable there."

"I expect a first-rate fuck."

Before leaving for St. Bart's—wherever or whatever that was—Charty had told girl that if she wanted more bookcases installed, she should call his contractor and make arrangements. Instead she decided to do it herself. Now that she'd drilled holes in the walls, she regretted her impulsiveness. One could only learn so much from reading books and asking advice from hardware store salespeople.

Concentrating on installing the toggle bolts, she hadn't heard the first few rings of the telephone. She picked up the handset just in time to hear the caller hang up. Damn, she'd unplugged the answering machine in order to plug in the drill. Luckily, or perhaps unluckily, the phone immediately rang again.

"Do you have a rug?" a deep male voice asked.

"I'm sorry; I don't buy merchandise over the phone."

"I require an eight-by-ten Persian or Bokhara. It doesn't have to be authentic; a machine-made knockoff will do fine."

"I'm afraid you have the wrong number."

"Is this girl? Charty gave me your number."

"What's this about a rug?"

"I want you to roll me up in it naked. You'll wear high heels, G-string panties, and a long-tailed white man-tailored shirt, and stomp on the rug, then slowly walk back and forth on it."

Would that be any worse than what I usually do? Better, actually, as long as I don't injure him. Still it sounds so...disgusting. I better get used to disgusting.

"I saw some rugs at Ikea that might do the trick. If I recall correctly, they ran about $300 or $400."

"I'll, of course, reimburse you, plus pay for the session and your shopping time. May I come by tomorrow evening, say around six-thirty?"

I could use a pair of boots, so they'll be my expense.

"Sure, I'm looking forward." When she hung up, she stopped looking forward and glanced sideways.

Was she really going to do this? Her mind settled on more mundane issues. Would he pay for the post-session cleaning of the rug?

Bartering drugs for sex, Darko and girl fell into a pattern. They shot heroin, once a month or so, with a cocaine chaser. As foreplay, he bragged about all the people he'd *fucked-up* since he'd last seen her: soaking them with vodka and setting them on fire, using power saws, nail guns, and garbage disposals, filling their orifices with corrosive chemicals. All of which comported with his duties and responsibilities as an enforcer for an ambitious Serbian mobster. Possessing a remarkable work ethic, however, Darko went above and beyond.

Girl

Perhaps cowed by the book-lined surroundings and her relative intellectual sophistication, Darko was well-mannered and respectful. But if she bit or scratched him hard enough to draw meaningful quantities of blood, he'd hit her, which mitigated his otherwise gentlemanly behavior. That he was a sociopath and thus incapable of love made it easier for her to relax with him. His girlfriends who'd become too clingy sometimes made the list of people he bragged about fucking-up. Like many hard-working professionals, he had trouble separating his work from his personal life. Although, ever the gentleman, he stopped short of inflicting injury that resulted in more than a visit to the emergency room.

"How long does it take to get addicted?" she asked him.

"I shoot up every day, and I'm not addicted," he said. "Sorry, joke. Depends on the person, but every day for three days with good stuff and you'll develop a craving."

"And once a month, like we do?" she asked, although they'd already done it twice this month.

"You seem pretty tough. Watch yourself and you'll be okay…if you want to be."

"What does that mean?" Girl knew all too well what he meant, but it pissed her off that he so easily read her.

Girl didn't really like the stuff all that much and hated the feeling the next day. But the risk and self-destructive stupidity gave her a sense of purpose. Or rather an anti-sense-of-purpose, which was almost as good. She preferred the couple of days of disgust that followed her drug-taking to the emptiness and ennui they replaced. Plus she never thought about Hannah's family when high. She did during the self-pity sessions that followed, but she felt like crap with or without those thoughts, so they didn't matter. Thus, her feelings about shooting smack were paradoxical and perplexing—just the way she liked them.

Girl hadn't left her apartment for two days. On the third day, she told herself that she'd stayed inside because of the dank, damp, dreary February weather and that it had nothing to do with it being the anniversary of what had happened to Hannah in similar weather. When her afternoon appointment cancelled, cabin fever and claustrophobia overrode her agoraphobia. She put on her standard outside outfit—dirty canvas sneakers, baggy jeans, loose fisherman's sweater, the hooded black cloak she'd worn for her revenge visit to the butcher, and big dark glasses— and went out for a walk without a set destination.

After meandering, she looked down and saw herself staring at the Citarella window display—a winter scene complete with a frozen pond and a sleigh carefully constructed from sausages and other meat products. After willing herself to stop dissociating, girl rejoined her body and went inside and bought a pork roast. Her purchase wrapped in butcher paper with a twine bow, she emerged from the store feeling triumphant.

Then she headed to Shakespeare & Co. for a cookbook that would tell her how to roast pork and what to do with the leftovers.

The next day she walked eighty blocks in a snowstorm to give an envelope containing $10,000 in cash to the New York City Rescue Mission, a charity for the homeless and others in crisis. However low she sunk, she wasn't going to abandon her commitment to *tzedakah*.

One of her regulars, at $1,200 a shot, took her to parties where he'd introduce her as his niece. She often returned with a business card or two slipped to her by well-groomed, middle-aged men who longed for short-term nieces of their own. She'd never of her own volition have gone to a party or subjected herself to a situation that required socializing. Viewing these excursions as anthropological learning experiences, however, made them educational and even enjoyable, in addition to lucrative. Food wasn't a high priority for her, but she liked the assortment of *hors d'oeuvres* tuxedo-clad waitpersons served from sliver trays. She often found herself chatting with the waitstaff, mostly out-of-work gay actors, who were far more interesting than the guests.

Girl

Six months after her excursion to the Double Eagle, Darko, as he had several times before, set on her coffee table a pair of thin insulin syringes still wrapped in cellophane and two glassine bags, one containing a dull tan powder, the other tiny white crystals. The combined street value of the two was well over a grand. At least, that was what Darko had told her. They didn't intend to use it all, but the lovely still-life—*syringes with bags of dope*—outshone the fresh flowers that usually occupied the spot. She'd shoved aside the birthday card she'd bought herself two weeks earlier when she'd turned seventeen.

"That's a nice rug. Bokhara, right? Is it old?" he asked.

"I've only had it a short time, but it's just gotten a lot of a certain kind of wear and has to be cleaned frequently. Glad you like it. I think it adds needed color to the room."

Girl took the glass shade off the hurricane lamp she'd recently purchased and lit the wick. As Darko had taught her, she mixed about a third of a gram of the tan powder with distilled water in a large metal serving spoon and heated the mixture to a boil. She took a deep sniff of the rising vapor. The fragrance set her heart aflutter and made her palms sweat. What Darko lacked in intellect and moral fiber he made up for in the quality of his drugs. He wrapped his arm with a piece of rubber tubing. She eased a needle into one of his veins and verified the hit by drawing the stopper up until she saw blood. She pushed down the plunger.

"Ahhhh," he said.

Not trusting his fine motor skills, she injected herself. *Ahhhh.* They purred at the base of her skull. Orgasms seemed to ripple through every nerve in her body. She drifted up, or maybe down, until she was simultaneously being born and dying while making love to God just as he said, "Let there be Light." *Mmmm.* It was almost as if she did this for pleasure rather than to make a statement. She opened her eyes in delicious slow motion.

Darko's eyes had rolled back. His breathing, already irregular, became labored. His head wobbled as if his neck could no longer hold it straight, then slowly toppled onto his right shoulder and stayed there at an unnatural angle. He made gurgling sounds. Saliva flowed from the side of his mouth. After a quiet death rattle, he stopped breathing.

Oh, no!

"Don't you *dare* die on me!" she screamed in his ear.

No response.

She shook him: heavy goddamn rag doll.

"Die and I'll send you to Croatia for burial. You hear me? No, of course not."

What did Darko tell me to do if this ever happens? Think. Damn it, think!

In a flash she'd mixed the cocaine with water, cleared the needle, sucked up the mixture, rewrapped his arm, and slid the needle into a vein. She missed. She felt for his pulse. Nothing. Maybe she didn't even have the right spot. For all its virtues, heroin didn't make lifesaving any easier. She tried again to find a vein. Again no blood rose in the barrel. Again. *Finally!* Blood rose confirming the hit. She pushed the plunger. Seconds later he sat up, took several gasping breaths, and grinned.

"Was I…"

"Yeah." She exhaled and felt dizzy and cold. *That was much too close.*

"Well, thanks then." After several deep breaths and a quiet couple of minutes, he wrapped the tubing around her arm. "Here, let me do you."

Impressed by cocaine's miraculous curing ability—a true wonder drug—she made a fist to bring up a vein. He entered her far more gently than he did when they were in bed. She believed that for him, as for her, their sexual relationship was a smokescreen to justify their doing drugs together.

The drug hit her brain. Flowers burst into bloom. Brilliant sprays of color flashed in all four dimensions. Then came a power surge of pure pleasure. She grinned until her grin exceeded the confines of her face and floated off to bring light and love to the world.

Girl

"I think I gave you too much," Darko said from somewhere beyond Mars. "How are you?"

He waved the half-empty bag. Seeing it as half-full, girl waved back.

"High. How are you?" she asked or maybe she didn't. She sent him a semaphore message: *Hello, out there in the asteroid belt.* Where had she learned semaphore language and how to do it without even using those cute flags?

Her heart slammed against her ribcage. Each slam felt like a rotten tomato hitting a wall. Her vision strobed. She jumped up. Sat. Jumped. She twirled on her heels like a bowling pin that refused to go down. Then all went black. No, white. Black.

A hand hit her right cheek, then the wrong one.

"Talk to me, girl."

More slaps, fun.

"I'm calling 911."

"No."

She wondered how she'd gotten to Venus. That noxious cloud cover was a bitch and hot...*oy veh, such heat in all your life you never saw. I'm schvitzing like a rabbi at an auto-da-fé.*

"Please, girl, talk to me."

"Hello. I just lied. Not lied, but I didn't mean it. I..."

"Oh, thank God." He breathed out with a quivering whistle.

"*Yisgadal v'yiskadash sh'mei rabbaw.B'allmaw dee v'raw chir'usei v'yamlich malchusei, b'chayeichon, uv'yomeichon, uv'chayei d'chol beis yisroel, ba'agawlaw u'vizman kawriv, v'imru.*"

"What the...?"

"Mourner's Kaddish. Not exactly thanking God but..."

She looked down and was surprised that her heart wasn't popping out of her chest with each beat. It certainly hurt enough. Too much. If only the room would stop spinning. *Stop the room I want to get off.*

"You scared the shit out of me," Darko pulled her to her feet. "Come, let's walk around the room."

The room continued to spin. Her art—quality reproductions

of Hockney's swimming pool paintings—became a blue blur on jiggling white walls. Looking at it made her nauseous...see-sick, nearly see-nile.

"You'll have to do better than that to make me come."

"I'm sorry, girl. I was too stoned and gave you an overdose; you almost..."

"Almost doesn't count except in horseshit." She stopped walking, turned toward him, and bent to kiss him but missed. "That's great stuff."

She fell on her butt. "Bonk." She grinned.

Ow! Her heart did a triple somersault into a half-gainer and became tangled in a mess of veins and arteries. No more grinning...ever.

"How about a walk in the park?" Darko said. "I want to be sure you're okay before I leave."

"One of my customers likes to watch me put on tottery high heels and crush cockroaches he breeds for that purpose." Her breaths became short, hard, fast, making talking difficult. She metaphorically rose to the challenge but literally fell on her ass. Ouch! "Another has me urinate on him while I read from *Curious George*, but a stroll in the park, that's a new one."

Girl's head ached. Nausea bubbled in her stomach. Her heart alternately kicked like the dangling legs of a hanged man and slowed almost to a stop. Pain shot from her chest to her fingertips, then receded, leaving numbness in its wake. Her vision went in and out, like an Interpol siren. Walking on the wild side was all very well, but sprinting barefooted and blindfolded, maybe not.

VIII
Eggs Two Ways

The next day she went for a long cleansing jog, took a hot bath, ate only fruit and vegetables. She saw only one customer, a septuagenarian who paid to suck her toes and lick her between the legs while she pretended to be asleep, or rather actually was asleep. Later she indulged in a guilty pleasure: reading Spinoza's *Ethics*, better than any drug and far superior to sex. Still, she felt awful—weak, sick, and achy. She wanted more heroin and knew she had to stop using, at least for a while.

The following day, more Spinoza, this time on the chaise in the garden taking long breaks to gaze at the crabapple tree that in mid-July miraculously still retained some of its profusion of bright pink flowers. She worked out with weights and got a massage—a surprisingly emotional experience. She cried with relief as she gave herself over to the comfort and feeling of safety. Soon, though, she felt creepy as the masseuse's ministrations reminded her of what she did for a living. And later...yes! more Spinoza. "All noble things are as difficult as they are rare." Noble things, that's what her life was missing.

For now, though, her only goal was beating the need for heroin. That nagging need coupled with constant pain in her joints, headache, and nausea, gave her a sense of purpose. She didn't intend to stop using hard drugs, but she'd be damned if she'd let them use her.

To add a smidgen of nobility to her life and distract herself from her desire for heroin, she shopped for art for her still too sparsely decorated living room. She didn't want to pay big money for originals—she had no confidence in her ability to distinguish between a good investment and a frippery she'd become tired of in a week. Quality reproductions in good simple frames would do. More Hockney or maybe a Mondrian or a Warhol.

Once she started studying the available art, however, she realized she had become tired of the hard-edged modern décor and didn't want reproductions—even the word "reproduction" gave her the creeps but for very different reasons. She'd previously bought modern art because that was what she'd seen in Trevor's family's and Charty's houses, and she thought her customers would like it. Now she decided her customers already got what they paid for; she wanted art she liked and didn't much care if it appealed to anyone else. She ended up buying a Winslow Homer etching and an 1896 lithograph signed Charles Holroyd.

Walking from her apartment to SoHo, visiting a variety of galleries and art frame stores, and walking back, she covered well over ten miles. Along the way, she distributed thirty twenty-dollar bills to random homeless people. By the time she returned home, her wallet was almost three grand lighter, or rather lighter by the weight of one niece session and two regular sessions.

The next day as she was washing the pan from her ham, tomato, and scallion omelet, her doorbell rang. She should have looked through the peephole or opened the door a crack while the chain remained in place, particularly as she didn't have a session scheduled. Instead she opened it wide, inviting in danger, or as it turned out, Everett and a cute blonde of indeterminate but legal age.

"This is Monika. We're married." They held up their left hands, showing off simple gold bands.

Married? Wow! Seems he was able to change after all. Well...good for him.

"Great news!" Girl kissed both of them on the cheek. "Come on in. May I get you something to drink, smoke, shoot, snort, skin-pop, hold under your tongue, or take in suppository form?"

"We're good," Everett said, preempting Monika, who looked ready for one of each.

Girl sat on a chair. The newlyweds snuggled on the couch. White leather, she'd bought it thinking it was classy as it reminded her of one in Trevor's family's living room. After she'd taken delivery, she noticed that it almost disappeared against the white walls and floor. Also, given the wear it got and the nature of that wear, white hadn't been the most practical choice. Now she noticed a red tomato-like stain on one of the cushions she'd somehow missed.

Stop thinking about the damn couch! Something's not right about this, and it's more than the red stain.

"Wasn't easy finding your address," Everett said.

Must've taken some work to find me. Why did he make the effort? Why now? Presumably there's more to this than their angling for a belated wedding present.

"The deep depression that followed your dumping me brought me to a crisis." He held up a hand. "Don't apologize. It was for the best."

She watered the ficus tree in the corner of the room. A minute ago she'd wondered what brought them here. Now she realized she didn't want to know; she sensed their presence in her living room could be summed up it up in three words: *trouble for me.*

"More than anything else in the world, children we want," Monika said in a heavy Russian accent, "but I can't conceive."

Girl was having her own trouble in that department. She couldn't conceive that this was happening.

"If you'd like money for some sort of *in vitro*, I'd be delighted to help."

She straightened her newly acquired art. *Why am I so tense that I can't sit still?*

"We want your eggs," Everett said.

"My..." Perhaps her drug overdose a few days ago had damaged her hearing.

"Everett says the most extraordinary person you are. The genetic combination of the two of you would be most unbelievable."

"Yes, literally unbelievable." *My eggs?* She wanted to help them but... *My eggs?*

Robert N. Chan

Everett said, "On our last day together, you told me, 'If you ever need anything that I can give you—other than love or companionship—please come to me.' Most people say that kind of thing without meaning it, so I won't hold you to it."

"Pardon my French, but *va te faire enculer, monsieur*."

"And after I go get fucked up the arse?" Everett asked.

The idea of giving them her eggs made her uneasy. Also there was something going on with him that she was missing. She stared at him in the hope that his eyes would be the window to his subconscious, but she felt like she was struggling to assemble a jigsaw puzzle with missing border pieces and no two pieces the same color.

"You have the name of a clinic?"

Everett handed her a packet of information and explained that she'd have to go through a battery of psychological and physiological tests.

She couldn't turn him down. Not only had she offered but also she felt she owed him something, and she *always* paid her debts.

"I don't have a legal existence, don't even have a credit card or a bank account. If they want ID of some sort or…"

"Use Hannah's social security number."

She was surprised she remembered it and that Everett knew she would. She'd always been good with numbers.

"I don't want to ever meet or hear about the kid."

"We would want you to not," Monika said.

"I've been doing drugs," girl said, but her monthly interactions with Darko probably were irrelevant to the issue at hand.

"If there's a problem with your eggs, then it'll be for naught," Everett said, "but that will be the clinic's call."

"And if the kid's hands are permanently frozen in this position?" she raised her middle fingers.

"We will him or her love," Monika said.

Girl shrugged. It required a ton of naiveté to marry a pedophile, or perhaps it was enough to be one of the huddled masses yearning to breathe free.

92

"Okay."

"Yes!" Monika raised a celebratory fist.

Monika and Everett shared a slobbering kiss. He used to be better at it, or at least dryer. Girl popped open a bottle of champagne, undoubtedly a fine brand and excellent vintage, as she'd liberated it from Charty's wine cellar.

IX

Dr. H Makes House Calls

Girl passed the egg-donor tests, even the psychological one—she'd learned from her work how to give answers people wanted to hear, without actually lying. Then she suffered through the medical procedures. In the first phase, *ovarian hyperstimulation*, she received a series of hormonal drugs which they told her caused her ovaries to produce multiple mature eggs during a single menstrual cycle. In the second phase, *egg retrieval*, the doctors removed her mature eggs via *transvaginal ultrasound aspiration*. She didn't want to know what that was and was glad she'd dissociated through it. Given her profession and her emotional devastation from what had happened to Hannah, children were out of the question; and anything having to do with reproduction made her uneasy.

Due to her general good health and desire to exist outside the establishment, she hadn't been to a doctor since she had left Crown Heights. Indeed, she'd never signed any official paper, other than her lease with Charty. Using Hannah's name and social security number made her anxious. Realistically, though, she didn't think using it would expose her to any risk. While Hannah's family had undoubtedly sat *shiva* for her and the community treated her as dead, she was certain they had not filed a death certificate or any other official documents. Given their experience in Poland, they too avoided governmental papers whenever possible. She was super-certain they weren't looking for her.

By the time the procedures had finally ended, the screening, testing, medical appointments, and sitting in waiting rooms had consumed well over seventy hours—more than $28,000 of fucking-and-sucking time. She'd paid off her debt to Everett and then some.

Several times during the following months, she'd thought of

contacting him, but each time decided she didn't want to know what had happened with her eggs.

The clinic had told her she could resume a normal sex life. She hadn't asked about an abnormal one; but after the procedure, she found she had stopped taking on new customers and saw her regulars less regularly. It wasn't a conscious choice; it just happened. Eventually, though, she threw herself back into her work and soon was averaging nine or ten appointments a week again, including two or three multi-hour ones.

Proud of her success, she made a good living, had plenty of free time; and the threat of arrest seemed non-existent as long as she maintained a low profile and only did business with repeat customers or recommendations from them. She liked being an outlaw. Asserting her extraordinary sexual power, she was almost always in control. So much so that she could zone out and get away with it.

In spite of her comfortable income, she spent little on herself beyond her book purchases. She didn't stint, however, when it came to the less fortunate. When she went out, she regularly distributed twenty-dollar bills to the homeless; and she gave far more than that on special occasions. On June 26, 1992, when she turned eighteen, she anonymously delivered an envelope containing $11,664 in cash—two times chai cubed—to the United Jewish Appeal.

Her reading habits evolved over time. For the first year after she had left Everett, she'd read only non-fiction and only that which she deemed *educational.* She'd enjoyed what she read, but now she read fiction too, solely for pleasure.

On a beautiful October afternoon, two years after she'd moved into her apartment, she started *The Grapes of Wrath,* while lying wrapped in a blanket on a chaise lounge in the garden she shared with Charty. She finished it at two the next afternoon, barely aware that she'd gone inside once it had gotten dark and had eaten only two English muffins smeared with herbed goat cheese. Fine by her until she fell asleep that evening during a session with a customer, who left taking his money with him. That night she dreamt she was a nun, devoting herself to helping migrant workers. She woke with a blissful feeling—until she remembered she was a whore scheduled to see a new customer with a half hour to shower, do her hair and make-up, and dress.

The customer had told her over the phone that he was looking for someone whom he could see twice a month or so. Good, she could fit in another regular. Better, he was well-spoken and sounded well-educated. She'd recently been meeting her customers in tight jeans and T-shirts. They seemed to like that she came off as a *normal person,* and she liked that she could pull that off. This guy, though, said he wanted her to *dress like a whore.* No problem there.

Girl answered the door wearing a lacy slip with garters and four-and-a-half inch stiletto heels. She'd painted the soles red so they'd look like Christian Louboutins—who, other than the type of women Charty dated, would pay over $800 for a pair of shoes?

The tall, handsome new customer wore a gray pinstripe suit that must've cost north of three grand. His over-the-shoulder, gold-clasped, black lizard briefcase cost at least that. After looking her up and down, he flashed a Tom Cruise smile.

"Hey, good-looking, come on in." She pulled him gently by the Hermes tie. Closing the door behind him, she kissed him, closed-mouthed. He tongued her neck. She responded in kind, punctuating her licking with a feline purr. The usual out-of-body detachment came over her.

"Mmmm, I want you inside of me," she heard herself whisper in his ear.

"And I want you in this."

Quick and brutal, he pulled a plastic bag over her head and yanked the drawstring tight. The plastic stuck to her mouth and nose.

She tried to knee him between the legs.

96

Girl

He blocked it with a hard muscular thigh and laughed like the butcher had when Hannah had hit him.

The more she tried to breathe, the tighter the bag became.

She pulled the plastic from her face, back-pedaled, and took a swing at him.

He caught her wrist and bent her arm behind her back. Pushing up, he gradually increased the pressure. Forced onto her knees, she struggled, couldn't breathe, tried to fight back the panic, tried to think. Couldn't. Sheer terror.

He taped her wrists together, sat down hard on her back, then loosened the bag. She took deep breaths, screamed.

He sprayed something into the bag, then tightened the strap around her neck. She retched.

Vomit and spray-paint fumes coated her mouth, tongue, throat, and lungs. She was going to die.

She awoke curled up next to the counter that divided the front room into kitchen and living room areas. Her head hurt so much she could barely see. She tried to sit, couldn't. Everything hurt. Paint covered half her face. A cross had been cut into her torso from sternum to belly button and from just under one breast to just under the other. She'd bled all over her rug.

With every wheezing breath, her throat and lungs burned. So dizzy she almost fell, she staggered to the medicine cabinet and taped up her wounded torso, hoping it would heal without scarring. She should've called a doctor, or better yet, gone to the emergency room. She felt too damn awful, and her wound didn't seem all that deep. She could bring herself to do only one thing.

She shot herself up with heroin, the first time without Darko.

Ahhh... She felt safe and warm. No need for doctors. No need for anything. Her brain smiled from inner ear to inner ear and from the all-seeing third eye in the middle of her forehead to the medulla oblongata, *whatever that was.* What a great day this had been.

Later she shot up again. A hundred orgasms. Then bliss.

97

Exhausted, she slid down into depression. She tried to crawl back up, but the slope was too steep and slippery. No problem. Dr. H was there to help. A beam of sunlight from the window in the garden door illuminated her stash. She noted with disinterest that about fourteen hours had passed since her attack. *Mmmm.* Not orgasmic this time, but bliss was fine.

More tired, more depressed, more achy. Dr. H, though, was glad to make a house call. Neither ecstasy nor bliss this time. Just blotto and not all that much of that.

Nighttime and the apartment was dark. Cold slime coated her skin. Every joint throbbed. Even her hair hurt. She couldn't see him but knew the butcher stood near, apron off, pants around his ankles. She covered her ears but still heard his horrible Mephistophelian cackle. What an awful life she had. She'd once wanted to heal the world. Now all she wanted was to shoot up. She coughed and pain shot from her chest to her toes and fingertips.

Her stash and works lay five long steps away. She tried to stand. Her knees buckled. The room spun. She fell on her hip, got up and steadied herself on the counter before resuming her journey. She fell again.

Realizing she had only one positive option—pathetic and humiliating though it was—she crawled to her phone.

"Hi, Darko, I hate to ask this, but could you come over...please?"

"Sure, always up for some smack and a fuck." She could practically hear him grin.

"I've shot up four times in the past twenty-four, or maybe thirty-two, hours." She swallowed. "I feel terrible. I want more. I *really, really* want more. I have to stop, don't know if I can."

"Hang in. I'll be there in twenty minutes."

"You look like crap," Darko said.

"Come in, sit with me, get high if you want." Her head hurt.

Girl

Her throat felt raw. Dr. H would cure her; she needed him.

"You must be awfully low if you called me."

"I started thinking about how lovely it would be to overdose," she whispered, sounding like an old Sony Walkman running out of juice. No, older yet, a 78 rpm record playing at 45.

Knowing nod. At least he didn't judge. He should've judged…and convicted.

"Get yourself a tall glass of ice water and talk to me," he said.

"About what?"

"Start with when you were born and work up to why half your face is blue."

She told him not just about herself but—because she was hazy about her life before she'd moved in with Everett—about Hannah as well.

He listened without interrupting, except for several bathroom breaks during which she suspected he snorted coke. He had the good manners not to do it in front of her, didn't even rub his gums.

"Feeling better?" he asked several hours later.

"A little."

Angry at herself for not doing it earlier, she poured four fingers of slivovitz, added a few ice cubes, and handed the glass to him.

"You're strong, willful. You'll get through this." He rested a hand on her shoulder. "That *tikkun olam* thing, were you really serious about it back when you lived in Brooklyn?"

The Hockneys had become misaligned, but she didn't have the energy to straighten them.

"Hannah was dedicated to healing the world. Compared to her, compared to most everyone, I'm pretty worthless."

"No, you're good people." He reached out as if to cup her face but seemed to think better of it when she jerked back. "You're fair with your customers, make them happy. You give a lot to charity, right?"

"Half my income." She shrugged. "I don't pay taxes, so it's the least I can do."

"The least you can do is zero, like me and most everyone else I deal with." He sipped his drink. "So, this heal-the-world shit? One person at a time or the whole world all at once like Hitler or Lenin?"

"Hannah had huge potential," girl said, ignoring his sarcasm. "She even fantasized about running for congress."

"Oh, please," he laughed.

"No, really. Congresswoman Bella Abzug came from a religious background, not *haredi* but orthodox, and Hannah had been reading Emma Goldman. Her father was always talking about how corrupt the government was, how President Bush had said to read his lips and then raised taxes. It seemed someone should do something to try to change things."

"So this sheltered ultra-orthodox girl—"

"As a rabbi's wife, Hannah would have established a reputation in her community and among the Brooklyn ultra-orthodox and Hassidim. Then she'd have liaised with the minorities, with whom there was a growing friction and a need for someone to bridge the communication gap. She'd planned after that to..." Wistful. Had Hannah accompanied her friends to check out the yeshiva boys that one afternoon, she'd have had a good life. But congress, maybe not. The thought of her now, a drug-taking whore, running for congress almost made girl smile.

"'Idealists foolish enough to throw caution to the winds have advanced mankind and have enriched the world.'"

"The fuck you talking about?"

"Quoting Emma Goldman." Girl waved a dismissive hand. "Hannah's dreams were adolescent arrogance disguised as piety; but as Emma also said, 'When we can't dream any longer, we die.'"

"So, after you were raped and realized your parents didn't love you, you met this Trevor in the subway and—"

"No, no. You're confusing two different people."

"So the relationship between you and Hannah—"

100

Girl

"Please, Darko, one question at a time. You'd asked me about Hannah and *tikkun olam*. Did my answer make sense?"

He gave her a bemused look. Maybe having grown up abroad, he had trouble following what she was saying, not that he ever had before. Girl hoped he wouldn't ask another question about Hannah. The subject made her uncomfortable.

"I was sort of the same way." He shook his glass, making the ice cubes chuckle. "I dreamt of cleansing Serbia of the last Croat and Moslem."

Thinking he was being ironic, but not sure, she smiled.

"After the Nazi-loving scumsuckers killed my father and uncle, I got a dozen of them with a bomb in one of their accursed Popish churches." His eyes became dreamy and his voice heavy with nostalgia. "They marked me for death. Recognizing my talents, Petrović brought me over here in a cargo container, provided me with phony papers and a new identity, and put me on his payroll, fucking up people."

He handed her his glass; she took a few hesitant sips, then handed it back.

"Usually I have a good sense for sussing out trouble; but the guy who attacked me was well-groomed, beautifully dressed, recommended by a gentle...gentleman. I'd let my guard down."

Girl refreshed his drink, although it didn't need refreshing.

"Problem is you don't want to be careful," he said.

She took another sip from his glass. Slivovitz started out esophagus-burning and awful. After a few sips, it continued to be esophagus-burning and awful.

Darko said, "The idea that you and Hannah are two different people...You can't just pretend—"

"I need to shower, re-dress my wounds, remove the paint, and get some sleep." She stood, a little shaky. "Thank you so much for coming."

"I wouldn't be much of a businessman if I let my favorite customer croak herself."

She handed him her drugs. "Keep these."

"See you in a couple weeks," he said with a squint-eyed

101

expression, "or are you done?"

"Make it a month, maybe two."

In the aftermath of the attack, girl was too traumatized to work. So she spent her nineteenth birthday bored, alone, and terrified. She wondered if she'd make it to twenty, not that she cared.

Her earlier pride in her success now seemed delusional. She didn't have a profession but rather a sleazy illegal job. She lived off men who were cheating on their wives or, like her, were incapable of forming loving relationships. The worst thing about that realization was that it changed nothing. She'd continue on, because she had no other way to make a living, no legitimate existence, no degree. She probably could have wrangled her way into school or a job, but sadly she didn't want to put in the effort.

She still felt bound by the obligation of *tzedakah*, charity. She had to make some positive contribution to society, didn't she? So, hearing about a new organization, the Rape Abuse & Incest Network, she sent them $15,000 in cash by Federal Express, a late nineteenth birthday present to herself. Having exhausted her savings, she now had to go back to work.

The paint attack had undermined girl's effort to suppress the emotional damage Hannah had sustained. The butcher and girl's assailant merged into a single malevolent form that starred in her now several-times-a-week nightmares. She dissociated more frequently, and almost anything could set forth an emotional outburst. Her stomach clenched every time a customer rang the doorbell. She kept a can of mace and a knife within reach and feared each customer would be a potential assailant.

One evening a customer flicked on the TV to check the investment news and got an ad in which a mother and a daughter were making a cake. She started crying.

"What's the matter?" the man asked, more annoyed than concerned.

She shook her head. She didn't know.

"You had a rough childhood?"

"No." She looked at her watch. "I'm really sorry, but I've got another appointment soon."

Some days a customer would show up for a scheduled appointment, and she wouldn't have the energy to answer the door. The next day she'd apologize and make it up to him by giving him a free session. While the interludes of depression hurt her business, most of her customers took them in stride. Apparently her competition was even more irresponsible. Also, though she made an effort to be distant and didn't particularly like any of them, most of her customers seemed to like her.

After her attack, she limited her contact with Darko to once a month and never again took hard drugs alone. The realization that neither drugs nor risk-taking would fill her gnawing emptiness added an undertone of despair to everything. She wanted more from life but had no idea what that *more* could entail. She hoped for a clarifying epiphany, even as she believed that such manifestations were as rare as rocking horse shit.

X
Executricks

"I realized something amazing the other day," Darko said as he was about to leave her apartment. "We've been seeing each other for more than four years, and neither of us is dead yet."

"Let's see if we can do even better over the next four." She kissed him open-mouthed but for only a second or two. She stopped because, to her consternation, she liked it.

Four years, really? Yikes! I'm almost twenty-one. Over four years of whoring and what do I have to show for it? A pile of cash, a well-developed professional practice, and a wall of bookcases full of books. Rivka must be almost ten, a big girl. If only Hannah hadn't been raped. Stop! No thinking.

"Sometimes when we're high and fucking"—he looked down as if addressing his Doc Martens—"I think I love you." He ran his hand in front of his mouth. "Sometimes even when we're not high."

Think again, Darko. Sociopaths can't love. Maybe he wasn't a sociopath, just a guy who'd gotten involved in a dirty ethnic war. When he came to the U.S., he got work using the only skills he had. His conscience never seemed to bother him, but as girl had learned from experience with a wide range of customers, every conscience had an off-switch.

"Please, Darko, don't be any stupider than you have to be."

His face torqued red. "Hey, I was just joking."

At least he had the good judgment to lie. Now all girl had to do was believe him.

"Good. See you in a few weeks."

As soon as he left, girl began reading Baudelaire's *Les Fleurs du Mal*. Having only a rudimentary knowledge of the language, she enjoyed the challenge of reading poetry in French. She had a regular customer, a homesick Parisian advertising executive, who spoke to her in his native tongue and gave her lessons over long, lucrative dinners. Although he acted like he believed himself to be a great ladies' man, he was so emotionally crippled that their interactions never crossed the red line separating the professional from the romantic.

A knock on her door only minutes after she had settled into her book, brought on a terrible premonition: Darko returning with an approximately four-year anniversary gift. Yuck. She took a cautious peek through the peephole. An unsmiling business-suited woman on the fatal side of fifty. Well, some lesbian action would be okay. Nowhere near as good as Baudelaire, but it would pay better.

Girl's pleated mesh teddy and five-inch heels had been suitable for Darko. If this new customer wanted something more refined, she'd say so. Girl opened her door. The woman had under one arm a thick brick-colored file folder. Her other arm hung down, hand gently resting on… *Holy shit!*

Hannah's little brother stared up at girl with familiar big green eyes set in an unblinking, unnerving stare. No, of course, it wasn't Isaac. This boy couldn't be more than three; and Hannah's brother would be twelve by now, dressed in black, sideburns grown out into long *payot,* wide-brimmed hat on his head. *But then who is this red-headed little boy, and what the hell is he doing here?* Girl suspected the prune-faced woman hadn't brought him here to observe girl-on-woman sex.

She tried to slam the door. The woman, though, stuck her foot in. Girl had to face the music, discordant and screechy though it would be.

"May I please come in?"

"Who are you?"

"The executrix of the estate of Everett M. Talcott."

Girl felt as if she'd been gut-punched. Unlike when Darko hit her, she didn't like it one bit. Worse, it seemed inappropriate to retaliate physically.

"May I get you… a glass of water or something?" Girl bent down. "A glass of milk for you, maybe?"

Maintaining his *Children of the Village of the Damned*

unblinking stare, the toddler shook his head. The woman sat on a chair. The toddler stood alongside it. Girl struggled for breath. *Maybe executrix of an estate has some legal meaning other than...*

"What happened to Everett?" The strain of trying to keep calm made her voice sound computer-generated.

"Killed in a school shooting in South Carolina."

"He's...dead?" Her throat narrowed and her stomach cramped. Dead? *No!*

The blue-suited woman handed over an envelope addressed to her.

"South Carolina?" girl asked, unable to focus on the more salient issue.

"He'd moved down there after an inappropriate interaction with a Hill School freshman. The school wanted it handled quietly: no lawsuits, no prosecution."

That's how Rav Moscovitz would've dealt with it.

"Some kid came into the school wearing body armor, toting an AK-47. Everyone ran for cover except Mr. Talcott, who tried to save the children. A teacher who kept a gun in his desk started shooting. He missed the boy but killed Mr. Talcott and seriously wounded two students. Turned out the AK-47 was a toy. The child was a student at a neighboring school, trying to get publicity for a video game competition."

The toddler continued to stare.

"Where's Monika?" girl asked. *Everett's dead. No!*

"Who?"

"His wife."

"I'm quite sure he never married." The woman traced her lips with a long thin finger. "His letter explains everything."

"Is that..." Girl pointed toward the toddler. "Your little boy?"

"Oh, no. He's yours."

The boy nodded, "Mommy."

"No one could be that unlucky." She turned to the executrix. "I'm... this is one hell of a mix-up, but I'm sure you'll straighten it out and find the boy a good home."

Girl

The executrix stood. "My job's done here. Well, not quite." She handed the brick-colored file folder to girl. "These are some of Mr. Talcott's personal papers. He wanted you to have them. *Now* my job's done."

"I'm a whore. I work out of a one-bedroom apartment." Girl unfurled her arm to encompass her living room.

"Not my problem. I acknowledge the absurdity, but I'm just the executrix and everything's legal." She sighed, "If you don't want to keep him... I suppose we could help you to arrange for—"

"But... I can't... Really, how could I possibly take care of a child?" Girl felt dizzy. This couldn't be happening.

He could go into foster care where they violated the girls and beat up the boys. Social services people are outsiders, meddlers, not to be trusted.

"You're listed on the birth certificate as his mother. Apparently the child was carried by a surrogate. Papers are all in the file folder."

What a mess. I should've read the papers the clinic had me sign. At the time I was so creeped-out that all I wanted was to dissociate. This boy is not just Everett's child; he's also mine. No.

The little boy hadn't reacted to any of this. Girl barely had. She wanted to wake from this nightmare and find herself alone in her king-sized bed, blackout shades down, a couple thousand dollars left in a neat pile on her night table.

"Has he...had his shots?"

"It's all in the letter. He's got a social security number, everything on the up-and-up. Everett had good counsel, my firm."

"You can't seriously think—"

"I'll leave you two to get to know each other. Oh, you'll need this." She handed girl a disposable diaper.

"Wait!"

The woman headed out the door.

"You forgot someone."

107

The woman kept walking. The little boy continued to stare at girl. She started to hurry toward the door. The boy fell in next to her, taking two wobbly steps for each of hers, equally unsteady but for a different reason.

"Stop, dammit!" girl shouted as the woman reached the sidewalk. "Suck my clit!"

"Suck my clit!" the boy yelled, then looked up at girl and smiled. Having practiced a variety of smiles, girl wondered how he'd managed to pull off such a cute, radiant one.

"Don't get comfortable. You're not staying." Struggling to cage the thoughts flitting around her head like hummingbirds on speed, she recalled that one of her investment banking customers was trying to adopt a baby. "Don't worry. I'll find a good home for you. I know a wonderful couple who'd love to have a little boy just like you."

"Want Daddy." His upper lip quivered.

Girl sighed and plopped down on the couch to read Everett's letter. The boy cuddled up to her and looked over her shoulder, like Rivka used to. *Hannah had wrapped herself around her little sister and told her she'd never let anyone hurt her, not ever.*

"Can you read?"

"I'm three, dumbfuck." He didn't actually call her a "dumbfuck," just implied it.

"You have a name?"

"Epicurus."

"Oh, of course."

"Read," he said.

"I don't think you'll like it."

"I will."

She read out loud:

"If you're reading this, it's too late to hate me."

Painful though it's been for me, I've honored your wish that we not be in touch. Now I write every month and send the letter to my lawyers with instructions that they pass it on to you if something happens to me. It's not that I have a premonition, but I can't stop my obsession with pubescent girls, and there are a lot of armed parents down here. Epi is developing so quickly that I keep revising my letter.

Monika was a paid actress. I still can hardly believe we managed to put one over on you. On a subconscious level, you must have wanted to be deceived. I'd wanted children (no double entendre) all my adult life and couldn't imagine a better mother—in terms of both intellect and character—than you. You disagree and are now cursing me, but you're wrong.

Our son Epi is a wonderful little boy. To his immense good fortune, he resembles you more than me and not just in terms of his appearance. He's brilliant, knows all his colors, his numbers through twenty, and has the vocabulary of a five-year-old. As I write this, he is well into his *tantrum threes*. I'm sure he'll be a handful, but you have beautiful hands and an even more beautiful heart.

I know your first reaction will be blind fury and a determination not to keep him. Before you do that, however, take a minute to recall how you felt when your family turned you away and—

She crumpled the letter up and tossed it toward the fireplace she didn't have. Low blow for Everett to play the Hannah's-family card. Not that her subconscious hadn't already laid that joker on the table face up.

She peeked inside the file folder. The first thing she saw was a gift-wrapped something, marked with a label: "Part of my obsession, I couldn't part with these. My gut tells me they may prove useful one day."

She folded aside a corner of the wrapping: large stack of photos of pubescent girls. On top was one of herself lying naked on his bed, one hand languidly highlighting her then private, now public, parts, the other holding Everett's erect penis. That picture was one of the tamer ones. She rewrapped them and shoved them back into the file, which she intended to burn after extracting any legal documents relating to Epi.

"Black." Epi pointed to her thong panties.

"I'm a drug-abusing whore. I like my life, and I'm not going to change."

"You're my mommy."

She dialed a phone number.

"I'm so sorry, Burt, but I've got to cancel for tonight. I seem to have a baby."

"But last month you weren't even pregnant."

"Yeah, it's a miracle. He'll be gone by tomorrow." The boy's lip quivered. "Maybe not tomorrow but… Call if you want to set something up for next week." She hung up.

"Not going." Epi crossed his arms. "I want Mommy."

"You still going to say that when I stay somewhere else overnight and leave you alone? When I shoot smack? When I have sex with two people at the same time?" She stroked his warm, smooth cheek. She couldn't keep him; it wouldn't be fair to him. "Because I'm not going to change."

Their determined stares met.

Finally she sighed. "I'm sure you won't either, not with your genes." She could no more abandon a child than she could rape a fifteen-year-old girl.

"I make doody."

She slid off his pants and diaper. When the cool air hit him, he peed on her face, which he found hilarious.

"Hey, guys usually pay $500 to do that to me." She cleaned him off and used up her entire supply of diapers. "We're going diaper and food shopping. What kind of food do you like?"

"Carrots and chicken. No cake."

"No surprise there."

"Read."

"Bossy little guy, aren't you?" She picked up the book that lay open on the couch. "*'Fourmillante cité, cité pleine de rêves, Où le spectre en plein jour raccroche le passant! Les mystères partout coulent comme des sèves. Dans les canaux étroits du colosse puissant.'* Happy now?"

She again stroked his perfect little cheek.

"Get this straight, kiddo. Tantrum three's or not, don't even think about throwing a fit. If you have one here, I'm going to tune out and get stoned. There's only room for one troublemaker in our little family, and I got here first."

He stomped his foot. "I got here second."

She wondered if he actually understood.

"Fine, just keep the fits to a minimum. I'll make my *excesses* a little less excessive and try not to die until you're old enough to take care of yourself."

She got dressed.

"All noble things are as difficult as they are rare." Screw you, Spinoza.

"Can you say Spinoza?"

"Pinosa."

"Not bad."

XI

A Cute Myocardial Infarction

Girl wasn't about to get sucked into the bullshit bourgeois
trap of motherhood, but concessions had to be made. Girl no
longer seemed an appropriate name, so she changed it to mom.
Then—not wanting to confuse the little bastard in his coming
struggle with upper and lower case letters—to Mom.

Hanging out with Epi turned out to be so pleasant that she
found herself spending more and more time with him—who'd
have guessed? What might have bothered other people didn't
faze her. She almost liked changing diapers. Plagued by
nightmares, he'd call her at all hours of the night. More often
than not, she'd be up anyway due to her own nightmare or
Hannah's-family dream and be delighted to have company.
She'd read to him, and he'd slip into a restful sleep. Nothing
soothed her more than his rhythmic breathing as he lay next to
her. Still she worried about the frequency and intensity of his bad
dreams. Rivka, Sarah, and Isaac used to wake up screaming, but
not nearly that often.

She told herself that some psychological upset should be
expected, as his father had so abruptly disappeared from his life;
and Epi's nightmares were a phase he'd grow out of. She didn't
quite believe herself and continued to worry.

As she was now screwing for two, Mom raised her rates. She
cut back on her schedule so she could be with Epi for a substantial
portion of the day, including naptimes, mealtimes, and bedtimes.
Once Epi came into her life, crying jags and depression became
luxuries she could no longer afford; and, as if by magic, they
ceased to afflict her. So now whenever she made an appointment,
she kept it, which had a beneficial effect on her business.

Since the paint attack, Mom had derived no pleasure from
her work; but now she realized her job had many virtues for a
single mother: short hours, good money, and she could work

from home. Also it afforded excellent exercise, particularly for the hip flexors and jaw muscles. She even appreciated the change of pace provided by the opportunity to interact with adults, particularly as those interactions were limited in time and scope. Whatever the reason, she began to enjoy her work and to again take satisfaction from doing it well. Her customers responded positively to her increased enthusiasm. Soon business was booming, and she again raised her rates.

A Columbia graduate student in early education took Epi to museums or her apartment most of the time when Mom had appointments, particularly those that might last more than an hour or involve excessive noise. Otherwise in clement weather, Mom instructed him to hang out alone in the garden where she'd set up a miniature playground. In inclement weather, he'd play behind the island that divided the large open front room into a kitchen and a living room area. While she worked, he sometimes played with his toy trucks and dinosaurs there but preferred to work on his letters and numbers, which presented a challenge to a toddler now almost four years old.

Although capable of walking most places they went, Epi preferred the stroller—who wouldn't?

"When are you going to start pushing me?" Mom asked him one spring day.

"When I'm five."

At least he knew his numbers.

As she pushed him down Columbus Avenue toward the Gap to buy him summer clothes, he began crying, for no discernible reason, and thrashing as if his life hung in the balance.

People stared at her, undoubtedly thinking her the world's worst mother; and she feared they might be right.

She took him out of the stroller, held him close, and stroked his back. If anything, he cried harder. He thrashed so vigorously she feared she'd drop him. The only discernible word he spoke through his tears was, "stroller," or rather "troller" as he had trouble with his "st's." Not knowing what else to do, she put him

113

back, strapped him in, and returned to their stroll while his tantrum continued unabated.

Rivka had been calmer, or maybe Hannah at fifteen had been more relaxed around a small child and more confident of her mothering talents. Planning to have at least five kids of her own, Hannah couldn't afford such doubts. Actually Hannah had never had a reason to doubt anything.

A middle-aged man, walking with a scraggly-haired multiply- pierced teenager, smiled at her. "Not to worry; it gets worse. Wait 'til you have to deal with drugs, binge drinking, and homework. You'll look back on these days wistfully."

The teenager rolled his eyes, then bent down to Epi's level and said, "Enough already. Wait until you really have something to cry about, like your dad giving you shit for like no reason at all, except maybe his underwear's too tight."

Epi stopped crying and treated the boy to his lovable grin.

Mom's jaw dropped, "How did you—"

"We're all much harder on our parents than on others," the boy explained. "All my friends' parents are astounded by what a well-mannered freak I am."

"Thank you," Mom said, unable to get over her amazement.

The kid's father beamed at his son.

Mom kissed a customer goodbye, put on a melancholy look, and said, "I already miss you." She wasn't lying, just playing. Almost everyone understood it was a game. She dropped those who didn't and wanted something more than a commercial relationship. She hated their hurt facial expressions and the pain in their voices. Or maybe she just hated that, regardless of their good looks, intelligence, or engaging personalities, none interested her in the slightest. Some complained that she gave them *mixed signals:* avid lovemaking followed by...not much. "Passion without problems. That's what you pay me for," she'd respond, but she was becoming more and more conscious of the innate loneliness of men and hoped Epi would be immune from that affliction.

Girl

She had no one in her life except Epi and most likely never would. She loved him totally. It amazed and gladdened her that she was still capable of love.

As she was about to close the door, Darko materialized. She hadn't seen him for months. Although she sort of missed him, she'd had no intention of exposing Epi to him or taking time away from her son to hang out with Darko.

He had been lurking behind the holly bushes Charty's gardener had recently planted. While Mom tended to the back garden, he employed a gardener for a sixteen square foot patch of dirt. Maybe one couldn't make managing director at Morgan Stanley without demonstrating pathological financial irresponsibility.

"Miss me?" He grinned. "If you didn't miss me, you must've missed our little friends." He held up two bags.

His appearance so stunned her that she didn't have the presence of mind to slam the door. He slid by her. Epi came out from under the counter.

"Epi, please go into the—"

"Whoa, who's this?" Darko stepped toward him. "You have a child. Amazing."

"How do you know he's mine?" Mom stepped between them.

"Just by looking at him. He's a miniature girl."

"I'm a boy." Epi stomped his foot.

Darko chuckled.

"You should go," Mom said.

"Hey, I love kids and they love me."

He bent down so his face was below Epi's eye level.

Epi giggled. "He has writing on his head."

"How old are you?"

"Four and a quarter."

"Oh, so that's why you have a quarter hidden behind your ear," Darko said.

Epi tilted his head, confused. "No, I don't."

Darko pulled one out.

"Hey, where did—"

115

Robert N. Chan

"Gosh, how much money do you keep back there?"

Darko continued to palm coins and pretend to find them behind Epi's ears and under his hair. Soon he had the boy giggling uncontrollably.

"What does he do while you work?" Darko asked.

"Stays out of the way," Mom said. "Like you should." Mom wasn't about to take crap from a sociopath about how she raised her child.

"If you ever need a babysitter—"

"You've *got* to be kidding."

"I'm not a baby!"

Darko again put his face close to Epi's and mimed a careful examination.

"My gosh, you're not." He turned to Mom. "If you ever need a big-boy sitter."

"I don't think so."

"Why not? He's funny." Epi got on the balls of his feet, readying himself to deliver the punch line of his new joke. "Funny- looking."

He broke into a new round of giggles.

"I'll be right back," Darko said.

"Who was that?" Epi asked after Darko left.

Mom shook her head. "He used to be a friend of mine."

"Do you still like him?"

"I'm...confused."

"Why?"

"I'll tell you later." *When I understand it and figure out how to explain it without mentioning heroin or his job of fucking people up.*

Darko returned with two beaten-up decks of cards that he apparently kept in his car, and he proceeded to instruct Epi on how to build card towers. Epi was entranced.

"Take the bags and go into the bedroom," Darko said. "You look like you could use a break."

"Go, Mommy," Epi had never said that before. A good thing that he could separate from her, but she felt a little...hurt.

116

Girl

She didn't shoot up. She took a single snort. *Mmmm.* She had needed a break. No, that was the last thing she needed. She needed Epi, needed to be with him and to make sure no one ever hurt him like Hannah had been hurt.

"We're playing war!" Epi announced when she returned to the living room.

Mom scowled at Darko.

"It's a card game," Epi said, practically glowing with excitement. "Darko's *very* good at it."

Darko broke the ice. Mom's desire for Epi to learn about the real world began to counterbalance her fear of exposing him to bad influences. When Epi was almost five, she even allowed Charty to baby-sit. Initially he liked pretending to his girlfriends that he had a paternal side; but he eventually became quite taken with Epi and often scheduled time to take him to the park to toss around a football, baseball, or Frisbee and sometimes even kept those appointments. Epi enjoyed watching the second game of the 1998 Yankees/Padres World Series from the Morgan Stanley box, even if he did nap through most of the game.

Mom regularly took Epi to the playground. He was overly cautious, afraid to take risks and even feared the swings that didn't provide for him to be strapped in and the big slide which wasn't all that big. Reluctant to play with others, he seemed content in the sandbox by himself. Other kids his age were daredevils and raconteurs. She told herself not to worry. The mothers and caregivers she spoke to, while never letting Epi out of her sight, said the same.

Over their first two years together, Epi developed into a bright and happy child; and his tantrums became mostly a thing of the past, even if his nightmares continued. If anything, he was too quiet, contemplative, and obedient. She read book after book on parenting and continued to worry.

Mom helped a customer tie his tie, not that the graying-at-the-temples corporate lawyer needed help; but she thought he'd appreciate a little pampering, particularly after having just taken a six-inch dildo.

She walked him into the living room.

Epi ran toward Mom from behind the island separating the kitchen from the living room area. On seeing her customer, he stopped short, sneakers with red blinking lights in their soles skidding along the parquet floor.

"Oops!" He covered his mouth.

"Who is… You have a *child* living here?" the customer said, nostrils flaring and upper lip curling as if he'd smelled something foul.

"Uh-oh!" Epi said.

"He's smarter and better adjusted than any kid his age you know."

"I can't believe you and I…with a toddler just a few feet away from us."

"Well, Michael, if you don't believe it, then we're good," Mom said.

"Do you have any idea how psychologically devastating…? I'm calling Social Services."

"Why is he so mad, Mommy?"

"Because he's a self-righteous, hypocritical prig," Mom said, bending down to Epi's level to whisper. She stood, and with her face close to her customer's, said, "Please, no one wants trouble, not me, not my son, not your law firm, not your wife."

"You're threatening me?" His pointed finger trembled with anger. "That's extortion, young lady, a felony in this state."

"This doesn't have to get ugly." She kept her voice calm and her demeanor relaxed. "Stay a while, talk to Epi; then decide if he's well-adjusted."

"Why don't we watch *Lion King*? It's really good. Or Mommy can read us *Harry Potter*. She does all the voices! Wait till you hear her Dumbledore."

"I don't think so." The lawyer weighted his words with enough pomposity, condescension, and disdain for them to plop as they splashed onto the floor.

118

Girl

"Will you at least stay for a drink?" Mom looked at her watch, wondering if she could keep the lawyer there until the previously scheduled arrival of the cavalry.

She poured three fingers of Charty's fourth-best single malt. It had an imposing label and an unpronounceable Scottish name.

"What's your name?" Epi asked. "My name is Epi. It's short for Epicurus. Bet you don't know who he was."

"Fitting...the pursuit of pleasure at all costs."

Epi tilted his head and looked at Mom, who handed the drink to her customer.

"Say what you want about me and my son, but leave Epicurus alone. He wasn't a hedonist. He taught that pleasure and pain are the measures of good and evil, the gods do not reward or punish humans, and the events in the world are based on the motion and interaction of atoms moving in empty space."

Twenty minutes earlier Michael had begged her to shove a dildo up his rectum, then cried like a baby. Now it seemed he was embarrassed. She wished she had the dildo now to ram down his throat.

"And that was 2,500 years ago," Epi said. "That's a *very* long time."

Epi moved his fingers as if counting, his tongue sticking out of the corner of his mouth.

Michael took a sip and sat on the arm of the couch. "You're not going to sweet-talk me."

She'd hoped to do that but now realized her sweet couldn't stand up to his sour. She again glanced at her watch.

"500!" Epi yelled, then looked at Mom, who nodded her approval. "That's assuming I'm five. Mommy says it's okay to round up."

"What's he talking about?"

"2,500 is 500 times my age. Actually much more, 'cause I'm not five yet."

"Yes, you're very smart, but..." The lawyer turned to Mom. "That doesn't mean he hasn't been damaged psychologically."

Finally the doorbell rang. The man blanched, apparently not

119

wanting to be seen here. Unless he was clairvoyant, in which case blanching was the least he should have done.

"Darko, meet Michael," Mom said as she opened the door. "He's threatened to call Social Services. Michael, this is Darko. You'll find his lack of subtlety refreshing."

"I'm leaving," Michael said.

Darko blocked his way. Taller and broader than Darko and face red with fury, the lawyer raised his arms to shove Darko aside. An icy smile formed on Darko's face. His pupils shrank to pinpricks in his dead, brown, unblinking eyes. Feet shoulder length apart, weight on the balls of his feet, he bent his front leg and pushed his rear leg back. Michael dropped his arms to his side.

"Come on, Epi, let's go into the garden," Mom said.

"No, I want to watch."

She picked him up and carried him outside.

When they returned, Michael's shirt was drenched with sweat, the tie Mom had so beautifully tied hung loose and limp, and his face was as red as if he'd had an acute myocardial infarction. His wallet lay next to him on the couch, ID and cards helter-skelter next to the couch. A photo of a woman and one of a child lay on the floor, neat crosses cut into their eyes. A stiletto through the right eye pinned to the floor a picture of a second child.

"You two have a nice talk?" Mom asked.

"We played a fun game of mumblety-peg," Darko said. "He's changed his mind about calling Social Services, right?"

The lawyer nodded.

A year later a man with a shaved head and a four Cyrillic "Cs" tattoo on his neck appeared at her door, five minutes before a customer was due to arrive.

"Darko wanted that I tell you. They nabbed him and wanted him to roll over on us. That would be so very unhealthy for him and everyone he likes." *Have I just been threatened?* "He'll do a

Girl

dime in Attica." The man shrugged. "Occupational hazardous."

"Hazard," Mom corrected, feeling as if the man had kicked her in the gut. "Attica prison, that's near Buffalo, right?"

"He said, 'Do not visit.' Would be bad if cops tie you and him together. You too have occupational hazards, no?"

Epi came out from behind the counter. She shooed him away, as she willed herself not to cry.

Mom hadn't enrolled Epi in preschool or kindergarten. She had told herself he'd learn more from her than in school and that separation would be traumatic for him—it certainly would've been for her. Now with him about to turn six, she had to act. Sending him to public school would mean accepting a government handout. It was bad enough that she used public roads, drank city water, used the sewage system, and benefited from the presence of the fire department and the mixed blessing of the police. So she applied to the only private school she had heard of, the Hill School. Emerging from his interview, Epi gave Mom a double thumbs-up. Then it was her turn.

"Do I pay tuition now or wait for a bill?" she asked after the unpleasant pleasantries.

The Director of Admissions chuckled, then realized Mom hadn't been joking.

"This is a highly competitive process." The director pursed lemon-sucker lips. "We literally have two dozen qualified applicants for every spot."

"Drop the adverb. *We have two dozen qualified applicants for every spot* carries more punch," Mom said. "Now that you've gotten the boilerplate disclosure out of the way, do I pay tuition now or wait for a bill?"

"You will be notified along with other applicant families on March fifteenth." She clipped her words as if annoyed. "*If* he gets in, you'll have to make a down payment to hold his spot."

Mom understood. She made new customers undergo a rigorous screening process, requiring recommendations from friends and other escorts. If her customers believed they risked

121

rejection, she could charge like she was offering an exclusive upscale service.

"Epi practically broke the record on his ERBs. I'm sure he aced the interview."

"He's a smart and charming boy, but..." she said, tone so cold Mom was surprised frost didn't form on the windows. The philodendron on the desk did show signs of freezer burn.

"The Hill School prides itself on its diversity, right? Well, I'm sort of a part-time escort. Bet you don't have many of those on the PTA." Mom regretted her words as soon as they passed her lips.

"We direct our efforts toward remedying the disparities resulting from racial, ethnic, religious, and economic differences, and not toward—"

Left with no choice, Mom dropped the E-bomb, "Everett M. Talcott was Epi's father."

"That name rings a faint bell. Wasn't he..." She seemed to be searching for the appropriate euphemism.

"A world-class pedophile who took advantage of students for more than a decade while the administration looked the other way. He told me about every act of analingus, golden shower, bondage, everything. Better yet he kept a meticulous photographic record, which he bequeathed to me when he died."

Air escaped from the director's mouth in a slow leak.

"I've heard quite enough." She stood.

"Sit!" Not having a rolled-up newspaper with which to smack the woman on the nose, Mom pointed to the chair. "As offended as you seem to be, imagine what the Board of Trustees will say after reading about him in *The New York Times* and seeing that the Director of Admissions had the opportunity to strangle the article in its cradle but didn't lift a manicured finger."

"Are you *threatening* me?" Her face went as white as fresh linen wrapped around a corpse.

"You're not as dumb as you look," Mom said, tone cheery as if she'd given a compliment. "I could have said you're not *nearly* as dumb as you look, but would the adverb have added anything?"

The admissions maven's lips trembled without any words emerging. Mom tried to remember first aid protocol for someone having a stroke. *Baby aspirin maybe? Too bad I don't have a syringe and some blow, that always works.*

"Take your time in deciding how to proceed. The *Times'* *Education Issue* doesn't go to bed for another three weeks. Maybe you'd like to be on the cover? When they're about to snap the picture, maintain the expression you have now, like you've just swallowed an oyster in a month without an "R" in it." Mom dropped her voice to a whisper, "One of my customers is an editor at the *Times*. Suffice it to say that allowing a pedophiliac teacher to run amok in a school is a timely and juicy subject."

The director deflated like a Thanksgiving balloon pierced by an arrow. "Epi is a lovely boy."

"So we're good?" Mom stood. "Once Epi starts school, perhaps we'll meet for tea, crumpets, and clotted cream."

The director shook her head as if she had no idea what to make of Mom, which was weird, given how transparent Mom had acted.

Epi liked school. As the year progressed, however, Mom became increasingly unhappy with the school generally and Epi's teacher, Ms. Morris, in particular. She taught to the middle of the class, grudgingly helped the slower children, and treated the brighter ones as annoyances.

One rainy November day when Mom came to pick up Epi, a stern-faced Ms. Morris met her outside the classroom door and led her down *the trail of tears* to the school psychologist's office.

Dr. Weksler pointed to a chair next to the one where Epi sat, a Jesus-on-the-cross expression on his face.

"We understand that you work from the home." She chewed her nails.

"So Epi and I can spend more time together."

123

"He meets your...clientele?"

"I can't say that I like it, but it has happened. At the school's fund-raising carnival, a member of the board I'd only known as Mr. Anal Plug accidentally bumped into Epi, knocking his nut-and-sugar-free brownie from his hand. I didn't introduce him as a customer, though, and he didn't mention it."

"I hope you're giving this meeting the serious attention it deserves."

"Yes, at least that much." Mom flashed her friendliest smile.

Mom refrained from adjusting the askew silver-framed rainbow flag with interlinked female gender, ♂, symbols or the gilt-framed—*guilt-framed?*—Malcolm-X "By Any Means Necessary" poster.

Dr. Weksler tilted her head toward Ms. Morris, who escorted Epi into the hallway. Mom wondered if Ms. Morris would provide Epi with a blindfold and a final cigarette.

Now able to speak more freely, Dr. Weksler got right to the point, "Ms. Morris asked the children to write a sentence." With the flourish of a prosecutor showing a jury a bloody murder weapon, Dr. Weksler displayed Exhibit A: "I want to kill my self" written in Epi's neat hand.

Mom covered her mouth. The hair on the back of her neck bristled.

"It's generally not school policy to interfere with parenting...methods, but you've made no secret of what you do for a living." Mom thought the shrink was winking at her, then realized she had a nervous tic. "We can't let this go. Epicurus must be enrolled in daily therapy. There are several psychiatrists we can recommend."

Does the school psychologist have a parcel of nervous tics, or am I imagining them to rationalize my selfish desire to hold on to Epi and my terror over what a therapist would say?

"I don't know that he needs—"

"Then you're deluding yourself." Dr. Weksler twirled strands of hair around her fingers. "In fact, it might be time to move him to a more positive and nurturing environment."

Girl

"He's such a happy child," Mom said. *But what about his nightmares? Since turning four, he's almost never had a fit or even an emotional outburst. He doesn't like interacting with children his age and often retreats to an unreachable place inside his mind. All that's perfectly normal, isn't it? My similar symptoms aren't normal, but he'll grow out his. Won't he? Sure, so will I…if I live to be two hundred.*

"To someone who isn't a professional, maybe. To a busy mother who sees what she wants to see, maybe, but…" The psychologist tapped her ragged chewed nails on the incriminating paper.

"Did either of you ask Epi why he wrote this?" Mom asked, her voice high and scratchy as if she'd been punched in the solar plexus, which was how she felt.

"Do we really have to?" Having mastered the art of condescension, Dr. Weksler showcased her talent.

"Please, bring him back in and let's ask him," Mom said, struggling to hide her concern.

Could I lose Epi? No, this isn't about me. Might he have serious emotional problems? 'I want to kill myself'—my God!

After a disparaging shake of her head, the psychologist opened her office door and waved in Ms. Morris and Epi.

"Epicurus, please tell us what you were thinking when you wrote this." Dr. Weksler sounded so much like a Nuremberg prosecutor that Mom expected simultaneous translations into German, Russian, and French.

"That I wanted to make my letters neat and clear and that I didn't know how many 'L's' and 'F's' are in 'self.'"

"What was the assignment?" Mom asked.

"Does that really matter?" Dr. Weksler and Ms. Morris exchanged eye rolls; school would run so much more smoothly if it weren't for the parents and children.

"Ms. Morris told us to make up something and write a sentence about it. When you make up something, it isn't true; and that was the least true thing I could think of, other than 'elephants are minuscule,' but I can't spell 'minuscule.'"

125

Mom fought back tears and laughter. Faces carved in stone, neither Weksler nor Morris reacted in any way. Minds made up, they weren't about to change them, certainly not because of anything as insignificant as the facts.

Back to home-schooling.

Mom pledged to herself that she'd focus all her energy on being a great mother, a great teacher, and a good enough whore so that Epi would never have a material want.

XII

The Talk Every Mother Dreads

Using and improving upon Everett's techniques, Mom was an inspiring teacher. Easy enough, since Epi was an inspired student. They became regulars at the Children's Museum of Manhattan, the American Museum of Natural History, and the Vital Theater Company. Deciding he would benefit from being with other children, she enrolled him in the West Side Soccer League and the JCC-sponsored baseball league. Perhaps because he lacked a parent who could instruct him, he was the worst player, among the least enthusiastic, and the least sociable.

Winter worked out better. Mom and Epi went ice skating a few times a week, great fun. He saw a peewee hockey team and asked to join. Although untalented, he stuck with the sport. Mom flooded the garden on days when the temperature dipped below freezing and set up a net at one end. Epi practiced incessantly. To Mom's surprise Charty sometimes played goalie. He'd played at St. Paul's and Choate, where he'd gone after his father's money had hushed up a cheating scandal.

In spite of her aversion to dealing with the government, Mom complied with New York State Homeschooling Regulations and filed her quarterly reports and annual IHP, individualized home instruction plan. Epi's birth certificate listed his mother as Hannah Levine, so Mom went with that, used Hannah's and Epi's social security numbers and hoped there would be no repercussions, such as a cross-reference with the IRS or the New York Department of Taxation. She made her reports appear sufficiently non-individualized so as not to raise a bureaucratic eyebrow. Although Mom's actual curriculum ignored her IHP and went far beyond the prescribed course studies, Epi did well on the exams required by the state regents. He never met a test he didn't like.

Robert N. Chan

Without any prior conversation between them, a cab driver asked her opinion about whether MSFT or AAPL was the superior investment. She recalled reading that in 1929 Joseph P. Kennedy, after receiving an unsolicited stock tip from a shoeshine boy, realized the market bubble was about to burst and, a few weeks before the crash, sold all the stocks he owned. Now, with the dot-com boom fueling spectacular returns and customers requesting CNBC stock market programs playing in the background during their sessions, she believed another crash was coming. She'd be able to pick up a passable brownstone and renovate it, possibly for as little as a million three. At the rate she was accumulating money, that wouldn't be a problem.

By the time Epi turned nine, the tech bubble had begun to burst. New York real estate prices weakened, but not enough for Mom.

Eight weeks before his eleventh birthday, two planes flew into the Twin Towers. Even as far up as 83rd Street, the stench of burning flesh permeated body and soul. Nightmares of falling buildings plagued Epi and Mom. Customers cancelled, fearing everything from car bombs outside their doors to anthrax in the subways; and others talked about leaving the city. Real estate prices fell. Mom continued to wait.

A criminal investigation focused on Charty's scheme to have a brokerage house pump up tech stocks by putting out glowing research analyses. He'd short them. Then another brokerage firm would publish bearish analyses, sending the stocks into death-spiral. As the Feds closed in, he needed a quick infusion of cash to relocate to Rio de Janeiro. Mom bought the house with eight thousand hundred-dollar bills and opened a bank account in Epi's name, from which she paid all transfer taxes and intended to pay utility bills and real estate taxes.

A hundred grand renovation turned the place into a home rather than a paean to architectural excess. She and Epi moved upstairs, and she used the downstairs apartment as her place of business.

The following year his dedication and hard work paying off,

Girl

Epi made the NYC Cyclones, a competitive travel hockey team sponsored by Chelsea Piers. By season's end he was starting forward and the league's third-highest scorer. He still wasn't a social kid, but he had friends on the team. When it wouldn't interfere with his school work or hockey training regimen, he hung out with them and their school buddies. They seemed to enjoy his company and he theirs.

Mom's customer knocked on her door, right on time. For once it took serious effort for her not to stare when she answered the door. It wasn't her new customer's black hat, long black coat, white shirt with four *tzitzit* hanging from it, and full beard. Rather it was the how-do-I-know-you look on his face.

"Please come in, Jack," she said, using the *nom-de-sex* he'd given when he made the appointment.

Hannah had known him as Yankel, a young accountant who'd worked with her father and had been at *Shabbos* dinner several months before she left. Mom was taller, thinner of face, and—thanks to the regular workouts necessary for someone whose job description required her to look good with her clothes off—better built than Hannah had been fifteen years earlier. Nothing about her pose or manner of dress would make him associate her with Hannah, or so she hoped.

The first thing he said when he took a tentative step across her threshold was, "You look...familiar."

"People say that to me all the time." She gave him her most whorish, least Hannah-like smile. She pivoted to a forty-five degree angle to show off her small waist and ample chest. "May I get you something to drink? Single-malt scotch, perhaps?"

He nodded and followed her. She poured his drink, took his hand—Hannah had never touched the hand of a *haredi* man—and led him to the bedroom.

Dropping his voice to a whisper, he told her what he wanted in revolting detail. She wished his request shocked or surprised her; but, to paraphrase *The Godfather*, this was the life she'd chosen.

129

"You'll be bareheaded in my presence, you scum-sucking kike." She knocked the hat off his head with a vicious swipe. "Get your clothes off!" She slapped him. "NOW, hymie scum!"

He fumbled with his buttons. She pulled off his shirt as hard as she could without tearing it.

"I'll be right back, and you better be naked as a Jew-bird." She slapped his butt.

Seeking a dose of purity, she threw on a robe and went out into the garden where Epi was studying. She wrapped a blanket around him. He kicked it off. Lately he'd begun to rebel at what he viewed as her excessive efforts to tend to his welfare. So cute.

He pointed to the book she'd assigned. "Is this supposed to be serious, or are we supposed to think Holden's a bit off?"

At least he didn't think it was pornography, but she wished he'd had a more positive reaction to one of the books that had shaped her life. Perhaps at twelve he was too young to get it. Maybe she should've made sure that he'd had more interaction with the real world. Increasingly secure and confident in her work life, Mom continued to be insecure about her parenting abilities. Probably natural. Her customers shared with her their concerns about whether they were good fathers. On the other hand, they patronized a whore, so they might have had good reason to worry. If Johns had good reason to be concerned about the quality of their parenting, shouldn't whores be all the more concerned?

"We'll talk about it after I've read your report. I want to know what you think."

"So the reason for this unexpected visit?" He squinched up his face, a pantomime of concentrated thought. "Oh, you want to be sure I don't come in and interrupt your session. Something extra-revolting, no doubt."

"We've got to keep you fed, clothed, and in hockey skates. At the rate you're growing..."

She kissed him on the forehead and went back inside to find her customer standing naked by her bed, head bent and shoulders hunched.

Girl

"On your knees, Shylock." Where was her out-of-body detachment when she really needed it? Most kinks didn't bother her. This one did. "Stick your white flabby Jew-butt in the air."

He obeyed. She hit him with a belt, just hard enough to make a snapping sound.

"Stop, please stop, please, please."

"Jerk yourself off. I'll stop hitting you when you cum all over your fat Jew-stomach." She gave him a bottle of baby oil. "Here's some bacon fat for lubricant."

While he played with himself, she hit him again and again, not even hard enough to make a red mark lasting more than a second or two.

Finally he came with a high-pitched scream.

She handed him his glass. He took small rapid sips of whiskey as she laid his clothes out on the bed and brushed them smooth.

He stared at her even harder than before. Uncharacteristically uncomfortable with her near-nakedness, she put on her robe.

"You have time for a drink and conversation?" she asked.

"Not if it'll cost me more."

"No charge." She refreshed his drink. "Who's this person I remind you of?"

"Her name was Hannah," he said after he got dressed. "She disappeared one night, maybe a dozen years ago. People had seen her with a *schvartze*. Some said she'd gone with him."

"Oh." Mom swallowed hard. "And the black man, what happened to him?"

He had a sip of scotch. "They say he disappeared with her."

"Nobody made him *disappear*?"

He shook his head, meaning "no," he didn't know; or he knew but wouldn't say. He continued to dress and stare.

"Was that in the same community where a kosher butcher… I heard a *rumor* about"—she snapped her fingers as if trying to recall a name—"Mordechai Kaplan, that was the name."

"He was the victim of a hate crime." He gulped his drink and grimaced.

131

"That's terrible. What happened?"

"Six months or so after Hannah disappeared, a gang of young *schvartzes* tortured him at knifepoint. They got away with a thousand bucks in cash and painted, '*Juden raus*, Jews out,' in blood on the wall."

"Only a grand? One would think he'd have more at the end of the week. Maybe a lot more cash would've been hard to explain to the IRS." Ignoring his scowl, she again refreshed his drink. "Strange that a gang of black kids would write in German." She dropped her voice to a whisper. "How did Hannah's parents take her leaving?"

"When they realized she wasn't coming back, they sat *shiva* for her. After that they never spoke of her. Not as I heard, anyway."

But do they think of me? Less than I do them, no doubt. An advantage of having several kids, you can write one off.

"Hannah's siblings?"

"All married with children. Her middle sister lives in Israel," he said after giving her a searching look. "The oldest one married a rabbi. Her brother works in her father's business. The youngest sister, Rivka..." He shook his head. "Her husband lost his job." Another head shake. "She had a difficult delivery and..."

"She and her child...?" Mom's throat clenched.

"Both fine, now, I think; but they had it rough, and the family still has money troubles. Rivka's father-in-law had a stroke and her mother-in-law... Big medical bills with nothing coming in. The community has helped, but it's been one thing after another. People talk; some say they're cursed or..."

"Would you do me a *mitzvah*?"

He squinched up his face. She held up a finger; I'll be right back.

She returned with an envelope, counted out the contents in front of him—fifty hundred-dollar bills—then put them back in the envelope along with a note in Yiddish: "The morning stars sang together, and all the sons of G-d shouted for joy."

132

"Give this to Rivka. Tell her it's from her father; but she can't ever mention it to him, has to pretend he never gave it to her."

He nodded. Then retreated into his own thoughts.

"You...happy doing this?" he asked after a long, sorrowful silence.

"I had a few tough years. Now, though, I'm blessed with a son. A beautiful, wonderful boy."

He stood. "I should be going."

"Thank you for talking to me." She wanted to shake his hand; but now that they were dressed and knew each other, physical contact would be inappropriate.

"Your parents, you think of them?"

"A lot. Miss them, hate them, love them, try not to think of them."

She allowed herself a moment of sadness about the nieces and nephews she'd never see.

"Must've been hard for you." His sympathetic tone made her uncomfortable.

She walked him to the door, started to open it, but stopped. "I'll be right back."

She got Epi. "Epi, this is Yankel, an old friend."

Epi stuck out his hand. "Very nice to meet you."

"Yes, he is beautiful."

"Brilliant, too."

"Mom, don't show me off." He grinned at Yankel. "Single mother, only child. Very nice but complicated."

"I'm sure."

Yankel returned his smile. No surprise. No one could resist that smile.

As Epi approached thirteen, he began to receive invitations to *bar mitzvahs* of his Jewish teammates and their friends and *bat mitzvahs* of their sisters. Even if she had to browbeat him into attending the parties, his popularity gave Mom one less thing to worry about.

"I can't believe it's so late," he said on his return from one of these blowouts at a downtown club. "The music was so loud..." He pounded his palm against the side of his head as if trying to dislodge water from his ear.

"You dance with anyone?"

"Mom," he rolled his gorgeous green eyes, "boys and girls don't dance *together*."

"Like the ultra-orthodox," she said, heavy on the irony.

From the brief flicker in his eyes, she saw he'd understood.

"Anticipating your next question, yes, I talked to some girls; and there were a couple I thought were very nice, even if they all dressed like little sluts."

"You don't like little sluts?" She caused her voice to trill up as it would if she actually had found that extraordinary.

"You're a big slut; that's different. Anyway, you get paid for it."

"So did you have any fun?"

"Actually I did. They had a game room with ping-pong and poker," he said. "I brought you a memento." He handed her a green sweatshirt with a picture of the *bar mitzvah* boy on the front, and on the back a knock-off of the Starbuck's logo with the slogan, "I had Latte fun at Jake's bar mitzvah."

"I'll wear it with pride."

His face became serious. "When you mentioned the *ultra-orthodox*—"

She shook her head. "A failed attempt at humor."

"Remember Yankel, who you introduced as *an old friend*?"

"It's way past your bedtime."

"Always is whenever I ask you about something that happened before you were sixteen."

I really don't want to get into this now. Not ever. She pinched the bridge of her nose. *I suppose now's as bad a time as any.*

She sat on one of the four navy blue leather couches that formed an open-cornered square at one end of the multi-story living room in what had been Charty's house.

"Some things are hard to talk about." Mom patted the place next to her.

Epi sat and she sat cuddled up to him, like he used to when he was little.

"I tell you everything," he said.

"That'll change."

He shook his head. When he broke eye contact, Mom had the feeling something was worrying him that he was reluctant to talk about. Hoping he'd tell her when ready, she refrained from pressing him.

"So?" he said.

"Okay but...as I said, this is very hard for me."

He nodded. His slightly parted lips and softly staring eyes showed deep empathy.

"A girl named Hannah grew up in a very sheltered ultra-orthodox Jewish community in Brooklyn. She believed her family loved her and that they and the community, particularly its leader, a rabbi with the title *Rav*, would always take care of her."

The surprisingly bright light from a full moon shone through the double height windows of the living room—the *great room*, according to the architectural plans.

"This girl was very smart and had red hair and green eyes?" he asked.

Mom nodded. *I wish I could tell this story in first person, but I...can't.*

Epi took her hands in his. "There's nothing you can't tell me."

Mom had been noticing more and more of these role reversals and wasn't sure how she felt about them.

She told him what had happened to Hannah.

"Thank you," he said, eyes wet with unshed tears.

"Do you understand a little better now why I'm like I am?"

"A little, I guess. To me, you're my mother. I love you, and I can't imagine you or our life being any different."

Pain built up behind her eyes. While she didn't understand

135

why, she'd never allowed herself to cry in front of her son.

"There's something I've been meaning to ask you," he said as if he were speaking to the Winslow Homer etching, now outshone by Charty's monumental art. "You've told me that my father was a good man."

"Smartest, nicest, most considerate pedophile I've ever met."

Epi's smile was off-center. "Was that you trying to be funny?"

"I'm not sure."

Now he studied a wall hanging that Charty had claimed to have an impeccable provenance, which Mom had been unable to verify. "Given my background, do you think I'll grow up with a normal healthy attitude toward sex?"

She hated hearing the fear and insecurity in his voice.

"Don't know. I've never met anyone with a normal healthy attitude toward sex. There's a hell of a lot of variety out there; and I'm sure, whatever turns you on, you'll be fine."

Not *sure* of anything when it came to his future, she kissed him on the forehead. They hugged. How could she have been lucky enough to have a child like him?

"I love you, Mom."

Although her every action had communicated her love for him—she hoped—Hannah's parents had so poisoned the phrase that she'd never said, "I love you" to him. Stupid but rather than say it now, she held him closer.

A few days after the United States inaugurated its first black president, Mom came home at 2 a.m. Not that there was any relationship between the two events, one unusual, the other usual. Epi, an early-to-bed-early-to-rise kind of guy, had waited up.

"Good session?" he asked, disapproving tone.

"Nothing special. A threesome with an arrogant neurosurgeon and his two-decades-younger wife. She was hot, though. Women who aren't proud of their bodies usually don't go in for that kind of thing. The men...well, they're also often

136

proud of their bodies but usually with less reason. Would you like to hear the juicy specifics?"

"Drugs?" he asked, tone of unmitigated disdain.

Mom loved everything about him, including teasing him. "Nothing to worry, my dear. Just a little pharmaceutical quality blow and some under-the-table medically prescribed weed," she said, neglecting to mention that she hadn't partaken in either.

She kissed his forehead, something she could now do only if he were sitting and she standing.

"We need to talk," he said.

"Sounds ominous." She felt her smile melt like a burned out candle collapsing on itself. "Is this going to be yet another lecture on how illicit drugs accelerate the aging process in thirty-something women? Give me a minute to roll a joint and drop a molly to put myself in a receptive frame of mind." Due to the cold breeze coming from her son, she failed to reignite her smile. She suppressed a fleeting thought that getting high would help her through this conversation. "May I get you something to lighten the mood?"

"I just had a warm glass of milk, thank you."

"Aren't we serious tonight?"

"One of us is, anyway." The corners of his mouth turned up, and Mom saw a happy twinkle in his lovely green eyes.

"Oh, no!" She sat next to him on the couch. "We're going to have *the talk,* aren't we?"

"It's time. I'm going to be seventeen."

"Okay." All she could do now was be brave or at least try to be.

"I got my SAT results back last week and have been waiting for the appropriate time for us to talk."

"I wondered about that."

"Did you?"

"Does not thinking about it count?"

He handed them to her.

"Sixty off. Could be worse."

"Mom, I got 2340 out of a possible 2400."

"So my math was right." She grinned on the off-chance that he didn't know how proud she was.

"I want to go to college. Not that there's much they can teach me that you couldn't, but the socializing aspect and the value of a degree from a recognized institution…"

"Columbia's only a few subway stops from here and an okay school." She wasn't about to let on that she'd been researching colleges and knew that Columbia ranked fourth on the U.S. News & World Report University Rankings and also knew those rankings were largely bullshit.

"I don't want to stay in New York. I want a broader life experience, meet different kinds of people, get away from—"

"It'd be hard for me to pick up and go somewhere else; after all, my business is here," she said. "Okay, where should we go?"

"Earth to Mom, I'm trying to have a real conversation here."

All too real, she was going to miss him like crazy. "I guess Harvard wouldn't be all that bad; with the Metroliner and the Boston Shuttle, I could practically commute."

He glared at her, but the corners of his mouth again turned up and this time remained there for several seconds. She played the rebel, the bad girl. He played the good boy, the responsible one. Did he understand it was just a game? Well, mostly.

"I was thinking of somewhere smaller and more rural."

"Is this about screwing up the SATs?" she asked, barely concealing a smirk. "You could always take them again."

"I'm within the top quarter of one percent."

"If you want to settle for that…" His glare cut her off. "I gather you already have several places in mind?"

"A Bates alum saw me in the championship game and put the coach in touch with me. All their starting forwards are seniors, and they have a dearth of good underclassmen. I'd have a shot at making the team."

"You're thinking of going to school in a motel?"

"It's in Maine."

"Same thing."

It wasn't as if she didn't know this was coming. His no

longer being with her every day would be hard to bear.

"I'm considering several New England liberal arts schools—Division III—so I'd have a good chance of being able to play."

"Why can't you make the decision on the basis of normal criteria?"

"Availability of quality pussy, access to a variety of hard drugs, and a low legal drinking age?"

"Works for me." She tented her fingers and closed her eyes. "Why do kids these days have to be so damn rebellious? When I was a girl, we respected our parents' opinions on these matters."

He laughed.

"If we're going to spend the next couple weeks looking at schools, I'm going to pack my skates. One more thing, hockey or no hockey, I expect you home for the summer, Thanksgiving, spring, winter breaks. If you prefer, though, I'll visit you and pay for the trip by having sex with your rich classmates."

"That won't be necessary."

He smiled. She hugged him.

"Great work on the SATs."

With Epi leaving in less than a year, as he should, what awaited her? The future looked bleak. Perhaps she'd spice it up with heavy doses of risky behavior.

XIII
Not Without Lubricant

Mom struggled to keep the gnawing empty feeling at bay. It helped that Epi, having started his second semester, seemed to be thriving at college. Like a long-running TV show with declining ratings, she dumped some of her more boring characters. In the hope of bringing in more entertaining ones, she designed a website, with Epi's help, and advertised on the Internet. If anyone on the vice squad had even an eight-year-old's facility with Google, she and almost everyone else in her business would be fucked...or wouldn't.

Most of those who auditioned for the part of regular customer were no more interesting than the old ones, but there were exceptions.

Mom's phone rang. Blocked call, not susceptible to caller ID.

"Hello, Mom? This is Tony Stark."

"Look, *Ironman*, if you feel compelled to make up a *nom de sex* based on a literary reference, you'd be better advised to pick one from somewhere other than a comic book or a schlock movie."

"And you'd be *better advised* not to be a snotty fucking bitch."

"If you're calling to set up an appointment, I'll need a verifiable electronic communication with a telephone number on which I can call you. When you arrive, you'll slip under my door two pieces of picture ID before I let you in."

Before he'd left for school, Epi established a set of procedures to protect her safety. He even installed a security system, including motion-activated video cameras and a panic button. She followed his rules pretty much the way she approached all rules people had attempted to impose upon her and learned how to activate and deactivate the cameras. This guy, though, sounded like a jerk. Didn't matter, he'd hung up.

The next day, when leaving the house, she saw a man waiting on her stoop.

"Excuse me, ma'am." He took off his fedora and held it at his chest. Clean-cut and wearing an ill-fitting black suit, white shirt, and black tie, he looked too old to be a Mormon missionary and too weird to be anything else. With gray-tinged skin, black hair, and pale gray eyes, he seemed to be in black and white while the rest of the world was in color.

"I'm in a bit of a rush," she said. "Come back at a more convenient time, perhaps in the next millennium." She cut around him.

He blocked her way.

"I called you last night. Tony Stark." He held out his hand.

Mom would more likely have shaken a rat crawling out of his sleeve.

Having jogged up the street in three-inch heels, a woman rushed to his side, hair still wet from her shower.

"This is Mary," the ersatz Stark said.

Mary's neck reddened along a line where her make-up ended.

"How did you get my address?" Mom asked.

"Research." Although Mom heard irony the way canines heard dog whistles, Stark's voice communicated only malevolence. "We're here for a threesome."

A small brunette, pretty in a forgettable way, Mary had a nervous bird-like manner. The sun on her face revealed the faded remnants of a bruised cheek, swollen lip, and black eye, along with an attempt to conceal her injuries with several layers of make-up.

"My screening requirements are on my website."

Stark shot a glance at Mary, who handed him something palm-to-palm. He opened his hand, revealing six folded hundred-dollar bills. "Here's our ID, honey-baby."

"Buy Mary something nice with it."

Mary handed Mom a business card proclaiming her to be an audit partner at a big five accounting firm and a driver's license with her picture.

"Please," she whispered.

What the hell was Mary doing with this creep? Not everyone understood the lie of love but still... With Epi, of course, love wasn't a lie but a great Truth. Motherhood was different, though. Too bad it hadn't been different for Hannah's mother. She'd been blinded by other lies. There sure were a lot of those out there.

"Won't you two please come in?"

The man wouldn't be her first sadist and hopefully not her last. Every time she crossed the street in New York, she took her life in her hands; and a hell of a lot more people died in traffic mishaps than were chopped into little pieces by homicidal maniacs. Since her near death-experience almost two decades ago, she'd become better at sussing out danger and keeping customers under control. Also she hoped this encounter would relieve the tedium that afflicted her like a chronic disease.

As a cure for tedium, the event had the potency of half a baby aspirin. Mary seemed to enjoy being with Mom, even if she did fake an orgasm, presumably for Stark's benefit. His chiseled body and acne-scarred back—a telltale sign of steroid abuse—indicated that he could be trouble. As did his tattoos: an American Eagle surrounded by the legend, "A well-regulated militia, being necessary to the security of a free State, the right of the people to keep and bear arms, shall not be infringed," and a silhouette of a couple about to be married over the legend, "Game over." Mom didn't have anything against trouble, but she preferred a more interesting brand. If only she knew what that would be.

Looking forward to offending him with stories about her recent adventures and missing him like crazy, Mom called Epi.

"Mom, my God, we haven't spoken in... Must be almost a week. That's the longest we've ever gone."

"Six days. I must've left you three messages." She tried not to sound angry. Why not? She *was* angry and hurt. Maybe she shouldn't have been. Almost grown, he needed to have his own life. Why the hell did he need *that*? This empty nest crap wasn't for the fainthearted.

"Four actually. I'm sorry but…so much has happened. I've been…" He sounded so excited and happy Mom's anger shriveled like a spent penis. "I made starting forward on the JV."

"That's terrific!" Mom said. "Let me tell you about—"

"I have a girlfriend." She could practically hear him grin, not only from his own happiness but also with joy over announcing it to Mom.

"Whoa! What's—"

"Emmylou. She's from Georgia. Her dad's a—"

"The country, not the state, I hope."

Mom had managed to teach Epi how to properly treat a woman. Quite a trick, given what he'd seen most every day of his life. She smiled, thinking of a comment he'd made when he was eight and had inadvertently walked in on Mom with a customer, "Looks like good exercise, and you get to make such funny noises; but it seems awfully repetitive."

"A snotty suburb of Atlanta. We study together every night." His words practically shimmered with excitement. "She's stayed over the past three nights."

"Whoa!" Mom repeated.

"We remained partially dressed."

"Of course." She rolled her eyes, not that he could see it over the phone.

"It's so nice just being next to each other."

"I'm sure." She hoped her sarcastic tone wouldn't pop his balloon, but if it were to deflate it a little…

"What's new with you?" he asked.

"Nothing compared to all that. Tell me more about Emmylou."

Mom read in the *Times* that Darko's former, and perhaps current, boss Slobodan Petrović was suspected of killing a witness who'd agreed to testify against him. She later read that the wife and two children of the reporter who'd broken the story had died when their house suddenly burst into flames.

She hoped Darko, who should have been out of prison by now, didn't have anything to do with either incident.

Stark came by a few weeks later for a solo. He carried a bag, half-hidden under his jacket. Mom tried not to think about what he had in there. He set down his package, undressed, fastidiously folding and hanging up each item of clothing, and posed. Could he have imagined that the sight of his over-developed body would excite her? His money had already turned her on sufficiently, even if one of his fashion accessories—the shoulder holster he'd hung on the back of her chair under his black suit-jacket—had had the opposite effect. She asked that he shower and used the opportunity to look in his jacket pockets. ID case— Joseph X. Flack. *What's this?* A five-pointed star, with the seal of the United States in the center and a surrounding legend: "United States Marshal."

The bathroom door creaked open.

She jumped.

"Curiosity killed the cat." Face as serious as a canister of sarin gas, he formed his hand into a pistol and pulled the imaginary trigger, "Bang."

"Bang yourself, big boy." Lighthearted smile, although she felt anything but lighthearted.

"I assume you have enough sense to keep my identity confidential."

"I wouldn't have much of a business if my customers couldn't count on my discretion."

"You know, for a fucking whore, you're a fucking cunt."

"Usually goes without saying." She handed him a towel.

He grabbed her shoulder, spinning her around. He slapped her. Her teeth smashed together. Pain shot from her jaw to her toes and the top of head. He wasn't fooling around. She eyed the spot under the edge of her mattress where her knife and mace

144

lay. Curious about what he'd do next, she decided she'd wait to see if he'd hit her again.

"Tonight, cunt, you do what I say." He wiped caked white powder off his nose and rubbed it along his pale gums—even they were colorless. Apparently he'd been entertaining himself in the bathroom. "I'm going to ram ten inches of thick hot man-meat up your ass, lubricated only by your blood; and afterwards if there's any shit on my hog, you'll lick it off."

If his thing was ten inches, she was eleven and a half feet tall. *Why would anyone lie about something so immediately verifiable?*

She yawned. Did she deliberately want to antagonize him? Not deliberately.

"That'll be a grand. Cash up front."

Flack paid the money. Like many things in life, his performance turned out to be less impressive than advertised. Mom managed sufficient screams of pain and anguish to serve as a satisfying soundtrack for his quotidian efforts. When it was over, she even called forth a tear. Thinking about Rivka always did the trick. A thousand bucks for fifteen minutes work; not bad, even when figuring in the cost of the condom and surreptitiously applied lubricant. Mom would have done anal without lubricant only if Flack's government-issued asshole had been the one being penetrated.

He took a gift-wrapped box from his bag. "I got you something," he said, handing it to her while studying his shoes.

Heart pounding with dread, she pulled apart the wrapping—cavorting Christmas elves although it was already late January. A large box of Godiva chocolates.

"Thank you." She kissed him on the cheek. "Want one?" She opened the box and held it out to him.

"You choose first," he said. "I know I come off as an asshole, but once you get to know me—"

"I hope it won't come to that." She popped a dark chocolate-covered cherry into her mouth.

Robert N. Chan

After Mom hadn't seen him for almost eleven years, Darko showed up at her door.

"Let me in," he whispered.

With twitchy eyes and a week's growth of beard, he resembled a rodent. His hair, cut by a barber more sadistic than Flack, covered his tattoo.

Not sure if he could make it on his own, she led him to the couch.

"What are you on?"

"Fear. Petrović's in the midst of one of his purges."

"If the news reports are accurate, his paranoia has grown logarithmically as his power has increased," Mom said.

"That's something of an understatement. Three guys I worked with are dead."

"What can I get you?"

"Water." He rubbed his hands along his face as if he were trying to rid it of tenacious dirt. "May I stay here for a while?"

She didn't want to make Darko's problem with the mob her problem; but he was the closest thing she had to a friend, and he was in trouble.

"Sure."

"I can't pay you."

"Then I can't have sex with you. Otherwise, it's fine."

"I probably couldn't get it up anyway." He gently squeezed her upper arm. "I wouldn't have come here, but I have nowhere else to go."

"Not to worry, you'd do the same thing for me." She pulled her arm away.

"You think?"

"Yeah, I'd force you to."

He chuckled. "You probably would too."

She held out the box of chocolates Flack had given her. He consumed three pieces and then wiped his mouth with his arm, revealing a tattoo of a Croatian flag in a circle with a line through it.

"Maybe it's time you went into another line of work, Darko.

146

Fucking people up is a young man's game."

"What Petrović's retirement plan lacks in generosity, it makes up for in permanence."

"Prison's made you more articulate."

"I plan to stay that way." More face rubbing. "If Petrović continues according to form, this'll blow over in a few weeks. There'll be openings in the organization. I can move into one of them. Despotism augmented by murder, a time-honored management technique."

"Maybe you can be Khrushchev to his Stalin."

"I just want to avoid being Trotsky." He smiled. "I read a lot of history when I was in the joint."

"I'll get some clean sheets and towels. You can have one of the upstairs bedrooms." She handed him a glass of water with three ice cubes. "Stay as long as you like. Just keep out of the way."

"Appreciate it, really." His face went pink. "Thought about you a lot in jail. You try to hide it, but you're good people."

"I make a palatable ham, cheddar, and scallion omelet." She turned toward the kitchen area. "You really ought to consider a new job."

"No problem. I'll do it when you do." He stared at the bookshelves. "Remember when I said I loved you?"

"People say all sorts of ludicrous things when stoned."

"As I started to say earlier, I thought about you a lot—"

"Are you being followed, or to put it less delicately, have you just led a pack of psychopathic killers to my doorstep?"

He shook his head. "I don't think so."

"You *don't think so?*" She thought of how Epi would react to her death, and her stomach cramped; but still she wasn't about to turn Darko away.

"If they knew I was here, we wouldn't still be alive. Patience isn't one of their virtues."

"What are their virtues?"

"Good drug connections and they kill Croats and Bosnians."

She shook her head. "Three rules: no sex, no mention of the

L-word and, if you get me killed, make sure it's quick."

The storm broke two weeks later. Petrović not only welcomed Darko back into the fold but also put him in charge of heroin distribution for Brooklyn. So much for the naysayers' hand-wringing about the end of American upward mobility.

The phone woke Mom, unknown caller from Epi's area code after midnight.

"Mom?"

"Epi, what's wrong?"

"I've been arrested. They're holding me in the police station."

"Oh, my god!" she exclaimed, then relaxed. He must've been joking. Epi in prison, couldn't happen. "What for, attempted littering?"

"Rape and trafficking in child porn."

As electrical jolt shot through her body.

"Don't say anything to anyone." She'd never had a brush with the law, but she knew what to do. "I'll get a car and driver so I can make calls on the way. I'll be there four hours max. A lawyer will follow."

"You didn't even ask—"

"We'll talk when I get there. The lines could be tapped. Whatever it is, we'll deal with it."

"I'm not so sure."

"Sounds like we could use a forensic investigator, someone who'll figure out how you were framed and track down—"

"I wasn't framed."

XIV

An Ice Pick in Her Frontal Lobe

When they met in the police station, Epi told Mom how beautiful, magical his *first time* had been. Although anxious to learn why he was arrested, Mom listened, enraptured. There had been only one problem: the condom slipped, leaked, something. Two problems, actually. Emmylou was the daughter of a Republican congressman, so abortion was out of the question except in cases of rape. Having skipped a couple of grades, she was under the statutory age of consent, if only by a few weeks. Epi had suggested she carry the child to term. He had gladly offered *his hand in marriage*. Emmylou said no way was she losing a semester of school.

"'Grow up, Epi,'" Epi said, repeating what Emmylou had said to him. "'It's just statutory rape; no one gives a shit in this day and age. Where I come from, the only girls still virgins after the age of sixteen are so ugly that people would laugh if they took abstinence pledges.'"

Emmylou was wrong when it came to no one giving a shit about statutory rape. Her father, Clarence Wilson, the Chairman of the House of Representatives Homeland Security Subcommittee, gave such a huge, wet, smelly shit that he'd had the FBI search Epi's computer. It seemed he hadn't known what he wanted them to look for, as long as it would be sufficient for Epi to be transported to Syria for extraordinary rendition. The boy had a Greek name. Greece was near the Middle East. He could be a terrorist.

"That must've been a mind-numbingly boring exercise in futility." Mom hoped her reassuring smile would mask the electrical storm of concern and confusion short-circuiting her brain synapses.

Epi whispered, "Remember my father's photos?"

"The ones in the file that executrix person dropped off along with you?" Mom's stomach fell like an elevator cab with a cut cable. "Didn't I throw them out years ago?"

"They were in a file folder in the attic." His voice sounded as if it came from far away.

"I'm sorry, Epi; it's been a long drive. I'm having trouble following this. What could Everett's ancient papers have to do with—"

"I uploaded the photo of you and sent it to Emmylou."

"Why on earth..." Epi was making about as much sense as...Mom's brain was too fried to come up with a metaphor, or would that be a simile? She hoped the butcher would break through a wall, blood-soaked knives swinging; and then she'd wake up covered in sweat.

"To show Emmylou the resemblance between the two of you."

"E-mailing a body-image that another woman can't live up to is a *crime*?" Like distant thunder, things not making sense to Mom generally signaled worse to come; and, with Epi already in jail...

"Child porn. You were fifteen. There's also using the Internet to persuade a minor to have sex. Along with the photo, I sent a sonnet. It set forth in explicit terms how much I looked forward to the day that she'd be lying on my bed, her hand on my.... Like how you were posed in that picture."

"Putting aside your monumental bad judgment in falling for a Republican named after a country singer, none of that sounds all that bad." Mom clung to her tough girl pose, like someone grasping the skeleton of an umbrella after a storm gust had shredded its canopy. "You'll plead to some minor misdemeanor, sex with a sow or writing poetry without a license, and get off with community service, ten hours of driving the Zamboni to prepare the ice for hockey games, helping unwed mothers cope with their sexual urges, something like that."

Mom's legal analysis turned out to be half-right. Given the closeness of their ages, the DA declined to prosecute for statutory rape.

Girl

She was also half-wrong, and that turned out to be the important half. The United States Attorney for the Northern District of New York, under pressure from Emmylou's father, took an aggressive stance. Not that he'd needed much pushing; child porn charges were a prosecutorial wet dream. With convictions running north of ninety-five percent, the average sentence for possessing child pornography and using the Internet to persuade a child to have sex was 119 months, which made it longer than the average sentences for rape or assault with a deadly weapon.

Once the enormity of Epi's problem sank in, it was as if an ice pick had been shoved into Mom's frontal lobe. She spent as much time with him as the prison rules permitted and worked with the lawyer she'd hired, a former federal prosecutor who seemed to know his way around the criminal justice system, oxymoronic though that phrase might have been. Unable to focus—just as well, as there was nothing she could have done to help—she drifted through the trial preparation, feeling nothing beyond the slow swirl in her stomach and the ever-present pain behind her eyes like she were about to cry.

She had never felt so helpless as she had at the trial. She felt like Hannah had laying naked on the butcher's blood-splattered tile floor. Not that the proceedings were all that complicated. Epi had sent over the Internet a photograph of a naked fifteen-year-old in the midst of a sex act and had used the Internet to try to persuade a minor to have sex. The innocent-looking *victim*, wearing no make-up and dressed like the virginal Christian she pretended to be at home, wept throughout her testimony. Congressman Wilson sat in the gallery, wearing a two thousand dollar suit, never a hair out of place in his gray leonine mane. A stream of business-suited, meticulously-coiffed flunkies came and went, doing his bidding. On breaks he and the judge laughed at each other's jokes. Each time Mom saw their shared hilarity, her stomach cramped.

Because he wanted to control his destiny, Epi, contrary to his attorney's advice, testified in his own behalf. From the jurors' facial expressions and body language, Mom could tell they liked and believed him. During his direct testimony, three of the women smiled at him. Whenever Epi made a point, one of the men nodded, poked his neighbor as if to say, "Told you the boy's innocent." Epi had hit a home run, or rather scored a hat-trick. Mom couldn't have been more proud.

Then came cross-examination.

"Everett Talcott was your father?" The prosecutor paced in front of the witness dock like a caged tiger.

"That's right," Epi said, calm and forthright.

"And Mr. Talcott was the one who'd taken the picture of your mother when she was still practically a child, the one you sent to Ms. Wilson."

One of the previously smiling female jurors gasped.

Epi's lawyer jumped to his feet, "Objection, hearsay."

"Overruled." The judge banged his gavel. "Sit down, counselor, this is just background. I gather no one disputes the origin of the photo."

"I wasn't there, but that's my understanding." Epi retained his confident posture, back straight but not so rigid as to look uncomfortable.

"And he was fired from his job as a teacher at the Hill School because he had raped numerous under-aged girls?" Apparently Epi had told his girlfriend everything about his background, and she'd shared it with the U.S. Attorney.

Epi's lawyer stood to object. The judge, an imposing man with a large head and thick gray hair, motioned for him to sit.

Epi said, "I've been told that he had relationships—"

"You do understand that when a teacher has a sexual *relationship* with a young student, that is *rape*?"

"I do."

Mom worried that Epi's forthrightness looked to the jurors like indifference to the suffering of Everett's victims. Mom tried to appear unconcerned; but with fear cramping her stomach and pinpricking the back of her neck, she might not have succeeded.

"What is your mother's occupation?"

152

"Objection. Irrelevant and highly prejudicial."

Three jurors leaned forward, Epi's lawyer's objection apparently having made them think that he was trying to suppress a key piece of evidence.

"It's borderline, but I'll let the jury hear it," the judge said. "They are fully capable of sorting out the totally relevant from the less so."

"She's a high-end courtesan," Epi said, as proud as if Mom were President.

"Meaning she's a prostitute?"

"Yes."

Mom practically felt hostile stares from the jury box. *So much for their ability to sort out the irrelevant. Lips pressed together, eyes bulging, they look like they might lynch Epi before summations.*

"She's taken heroin and cocaine?"

A formerly friendly juror's jaw dropped.

Epi's lawyer stood. "Objection! Really, Your Honor."

"Just trying to establish the accused's background, Your Honor," the Assistant U.S. Attorney said. "So the jury can understand a little better who he is."

Two formerly bored-looking jurors sat up straight, eyes wide. Anger churned Mom's gut.

"Sustained. Move on, counselor. Even if the defendant's mother was a big-time drug pusher, it would have no relevance to these proceedings."

Mom jumped to her feet. "I'm no such thing!"

"Sit! Now!" The judge banged his gavel.

Mom fell back. She'd made a huge mistake.

"Isn't it a fact that your mother's closest, and maybe only, friend is a gangster who spent ten years in the Attica Correctional Facility on multiple counts of aggravated assault?"

"Sustained." The judge said, even before Epi's attorney had had the chance to object, not that it mattered. The jury had heard it, and they undoubtedly believed it.

It was all Mom could do to restrain herself from jumping out of her seat again and this time trying to strangle the prosecutor. Face reddening, Epi looked like he was about to do the same.

"Oh, Christ, bad apples don't fall far from the tree," one of the male jurors said *sotto voce* to the man next to him. Both men glared at Epi.

"Well, I guess we can all understand how you came to be a sexual predator," the prosecutor said.

"Objection!"

"Sustained. The jury will disregard that last comment."

Like hell they will. Mom felt something inside her die.

"No further questions." The prosecutor pursed his lips and shook his head, communicating his disgust over having to deal with trash like Epi. Several jurors did the same.

The verdict: ten years in the United States Penitentiary, Lewisburg, Pennsylvania, a prison designed to hold some of the most brutal criminals in the country. In addition to a hair-curling list of serial killers and terrorists, the facility had been home to such notorious criminals as Henry Hill, Whitey Bulger, John Gotti, and now Epicurus Talcott.

Mom watched as an armed court officer led her son through the rear door of the courtroom. He turned toward her. They blew each other kisses.

When he disappeared from view, she collapsed. Her lips flapped, unable to form words. The distressed looks on the faces of Epi's lawyer, the courtroom guard, and others who'd come running over made her think she'd had a stroke, not that she cared.

"When does he get out for good behavior?" she asked the lawyer, when she regained the ability to speak.

He sighed. "The Adam Walsh Child Protection and Safety Act allows the Federal Bureau of Prisons to keep inmates incarcerated past their release dates if it appears they'll have 'serious difficulty in refraining from sexually violent conduct or child molestation if released.' A subjective standard, made more so if an influential congressman is looking over the board's shoulders."

Girl

"What chance do we have on appeal?" she asked while watching herself from far away.

"I'll do my best, but in all honesty, virtually none. The judge followed the law. He could have kept a tighter lid on Epi's cross, but he has a lot of leeway. He could've been more lenient, but he didn't commit reversible error. I'm sorry."

"What about that constitutional amendment, you know, cruel and unusual punishment?"

Another sigh.

Hannah—or rather, Mom—couldn't hear his response over the butcher's cacophonous cackle; but she knew all was as hopeless as when Hannah had prayed on the butcher's floor.

Taking to her bed like a character in a Victorian novel, she roused herself only to eat, maintain minimal personal hygiene, and visit the prison. She bothered with hygiene and food because Epi would've noticed a change in her weight or appearance. She now had good reason to take drugs; but, not believing that anything could alleviate her misery, she hadn't had so much as an aspirin since her first jailhouse meeting with Epi. She'd stopped whoring too. The thought of anyone touching her made her feel like vomiting. She didn't want to vomit because that would mean she'd have to again push herself through the excruciating, exhausting effort of eating to keep her weight up.

Darko came by with cocaine and heroin *to cheer her up*, but she sent him away. She didn't want that kind of cheering up, didn't want any kind.

The butcher dragged her naked, kicking and screaming into the back room. He thrust knives through her hands and feet, pinning her to the wall, arms spread, feet together. Hanging by her arms, her bodyweight pulling on her chest, she couldn't breathe. She tried to scream; no sound emerged. So he'd have easier, quicker access, she tried to spread her legs; but with her feet nailed to the wall, she couldn't. While she watched, helpless, he dragged in Epi. "Help me, Mommy; please help me," he begged, over and over, crying like the baby he then turned into. Giggling manically, the butcher dropped his pants. His penis, long, thick, blood-red, and covered with spikes, protruded from under his fat belly. He sneered at her, "What kind of mother are you? Help your son." He rammed himself inside Epi. Blood poured from Epi's mouth. She could see nothing but blood.

She woke screaming.

With nightmares coming nightly, she fought off sleep. Neither fully asleep nor fully awake, hallucinations plagued her: ravenous rats, creepy cockroaches, and big black bloody-taloned bats. Or maybe they were actually there; they were as real as anything else in her life, other than her visits to Epi.

Designed to demean, the prison waiting room featured unadorned, peeling institutional green walls, unergonomic metal folding chairs, and eye-burning fluorescent lighting. Mom took a ticket and filled out a visit request form, using the name *Mom a/k/a Hannah Levine* and Hannah's social security number, transposing digits in what could've been an honest mistake. She then waited with the lowest of lowlifes. She saw plenty of phones and electronic toys but not one book or e-reader. She never used to go anywhere without a book, but now she didn't have one, at least not one she could bear to read without Epi. She hadn't read anything other than the occasional letters on a soup can or cereal box since the trial.

Mom stared blankly at the clock on the wall. The room began to fill. People's names were called. Not hers, though.

Finally she went to the front desk.

"Mind telling me what's going on?"

"Someone will be down to see you shortly."

She had intended to say, "The fuck does that mean, asswipe?" But what came out was, "Please, what does that mean?"

Without even looking up from his female bodybuilder magazine or moving his hand from his crotch, the duty guard pointed in the direction of the seat she'd vacated. Mom shuffled

Girl

back to it, her usual walk now. Time passed. A lot of time.

"Ms., uh, Mom?" said a young, white-coated Latino who looked as if there'd be several years before he would be allowed to vote. "You're Epicurus Talcott's mother?"

"Yes. What's the holdup? I've been sitting here since..." *Oh, no!*

"I'm Doctor Fernandez." He held out a tentative hand.

"*Doctor?*"

"I'm sorry you've had to come out here. They were supposed to contact you earlier. Unfortunately, Epicurus isn't available to see you today."

"How can he be *unavailable*? What, he's on a golf outing?" The squeak in her voice undermined her effort to adopt her tough-girl pose.

"He's in the hospital wing." The doctor avoided eye contact.

"Is he...okay?" she asked, throat so tight she barely got the words out.

"We hope he will be."

"What happened to him?" she asked, voice a trembling whisper.

"When he recovers, we'll remove him from the general population. He should be well enough to see you in a couple of weeks."

It took her a minute before she could speak without shouting.

"Recovers from *what?*"

"He was...violated." The doctor looked at the scuff smudges on his white sneakers.

"Meaning raped?" She saw—actually saw—the butcher toss aside his apron. A searing pain took over her consciousness.

The doctor nodded, lips fused together in a tight unhappy line

The room spun. Her gut exploded. Her vision strobed.

"Please, tell me exactly what happened. Spare no details," Mom heard herself say, in Hannah's yiddisher accent, voice sounding like it came from very far away—Brooklyn in 1990.

"Well, no one has agreed to testify, and the surveillance

157

camera was painted over just before it happened; but we have a pretty good idea of what happened, even if there's nothing we can do about it."

"Go on," Mom said, now entirely in the present and focused.

"You really don't want to hear—"

"No, I don't, but I need to know so I can do my best to help him. Please, doctor."

"Well"—deep breath, slow exhale—"Epi and eight other prisoners were sent to shower, under guard, as is the procedure."

He looked at Mom, "Do you really want to hear this?" She nodded. Another deep breath.

"The guards ran off in response to an emergency call about a fire in the library—a false alarm, as it turned out. Then a white supremacist leader...To give you some idea what kind of person we're talking about, he's got a tattoo on his back of skeletons, holding confederate flags as they march across a smoking battlefield strewn with naked, mutilated black corpses. A banner, 'The South Will Rise Again,' floats overhead."

"And what did this scumbag do?" Mom asked, when the doctor's long pause seemed to signal that he'd said all he thought he'd needed to.

"He said, 'Let's show the rapist what it feels like.' You can guess the rest."

"Please, doctor."

Doctor Fernandez shifted his weigh several times, sighed, then said, "Three men grabbed Epicurus while the leader punched and kicked him. Finally they took turns, two holding him and one doing the act. When they were done, one of them stuck a shank in his side and left him in a pool of blood on the shower floor. As he was leaving, the leader said something that our informer thinks was, 'Congressman Wilson says hello.'"

Wilson!

Mom began to hyperventilate. She envisioned the blood-splattered floor on which it had happened. She struggled to avoid dissociating. *I have to focus*, she told herself. *Have to focus. Have to focus.*

"How the hell?" she shouted, then dropped her voice. "How could this happen?"

"It shouldn't have," he whispered.

"And these Nazi bastards?"

"No one will testify against them. A witness spoke to me under a promise of confidentiality."

"Subpoena him. Or I'll testify about what you told me."

"Which would only get him raped and killed," the doctor said.

Mom struggled to fight back the tide of despair.

"When Epi's removed from the general population?" she asked, voice coming from someone else's mouth, someone very frightened.

"He'll be safer."

"But not safe?" Saying those three words took all her energy.

"We're doing the best we can."

"Bull."

He nodded.

"How is he...mentally?" she asked after a lengthy silence.

"About as can be expected." He bit his lower lip.

"What does that mean?"

"Practically catatonic," he said, so quietly that Mom had to strain to hear and took several seconds to process. "Probably just temporary."

"*Probably?*"

"I'm sorry I can't be more definitive, but all I can say is time will tell." He handed her his card. "Call me in a few days. I'll be able to tell you more."

She had to be strong. Hannah's parents had abandoned Hannah when she was raped. Mom would stand by Epi.

"I want to see him now," Mom said, firm and controlling.

"He won't even recognize you. He's—"

"Practically catatonic, you said that." She stood. "Take me to him."

"Prison rules—"

"Bend them." She fixed him with a hard stare.

159

"I can't let you up there."

"Fine, bring him down here. Put him in a wheelchair if you have to. If he's catatonic, he won't object."

"I'll see what I can do."

"Don't see. Do."

An excruciating hour later, the duty guard called her name. Mom walked through the doors and sat at a visitor's cubicle.

Dr. Fernandez wheeled Epi to the other side of the Plexiglas divider. Bruised, bandaged, unshaven, he stared straight ahead, not a trace of life in his eyes.

Her hand went to her mouth. She snatched it away and as hard as it was for her, forced a smile.

Dr. Fernandez held the telephone handset to Epi's ear.

"Epi, hi." Huge grin.

No response.

"You'll get better; you'll see." Her throat clenched. She willed it not to. "I know what you're going through. I've told you what happened to Hannah when she was fifteen. Let me help, please."

His lips moved…maybe. Was he mouthing "no"?

"Okay, I'll just talk."

She babbled about imaginary appeals and *habeas corpus* motions, told him funny stories about customers, made up a hilarious anecdote about Darko.

His right eye blinked once.

Time for the nuclear option. She opened the book she'd brought, one of seven volumes. She'd read all of them to Epi. He'd read them to her. They'd read them to each other, doing the characters' voices. She began on page one of *Harry Potter and the Sorcerer's Stone*.

She might as well have been reading the telephone directory. She kept reading. Choking back tears, she read until a guard told her it was time to leave.

Epi mumbled some nonsense syllables.

"Epi?" Mom jumped from her seat.

Girl

"Epicurus?" Dr. Fernandez put his ear close to his mouth. "Say that again, please."

Epi repeated what he said.

"Sounds like, '*Omnis cum in tenebris praesertim vita laboret*,'" Dr. Fernandez said. "Does that mean anything to you?"

"'Life is one long struggle in the dark.' It's Lucretius, an epicurean philosopher," she said. *What difference does it make what he said? He spoke!* "Epi."

He waved the guard away, and Dr. Fernandez and Mom tried in vain to coax more words out of Epi.

"I'm sorry," Dr. Fernandez said. "I'll be in touch, I promise. Could be he'll be better in a week or two."

"And if not?"

"Medical science is just scratching the surface when it comes to the human mind." He looked down at the shell of a person that used to be Epi, then back at Mom. "I'm hopeful."

Unable to speak without breaking down, Mom nodded her thanks.

As the doctor wheeled Epi away, Mom blew him a kiss. Epi's eyes moved to get a final peek at her.

When he was out of sight, she gave way to tears. So much for being there for Epi. There was nothing, absolutely nothing, she could do to help him.

Mom trudged down a corridor, past security, and ultimately to the visitors parking lot. It wasn't all that long in distance, but shuffling along like an arthritic octogenarian made it take a while. So helpless. So hopeless. She tripped on a curb and too out of it even to stick out her hands to block her fall, landed face-first in a muddy puddle.

Eventually fury overrode misery. Soaked and shivering, she got to her feet.

Distant rain shafts and dark clouds stood out in high definition. A cold wind ruffled her hair. She'd had no idea what the weather had been when she arrived, but she knew that now everything had changed.

161

There were plenty of people at whom she could direct her anger, but she chose the closest, herself. How could she have allowed herself to fritter away time on the self-indulgent luxury of depression?

She had a job to do. She had to get Epi out of prison.

She called her most odious customer from her car.

XV
Catching Flack

"What the fuck?" Flack whispered over the phone. Someone must've been in the room with him. "How did you get...? Oh, right, you went through my pockets, pissed the shit out of me. Don't call me on this number. Don't *ever* call on *any* number. I'll call you if interested. Not that that's likely; this town is full of whores—"

"I'm terribly sorry to intrude, but this is an emergency." The diffident voice in which Mom had been speaking for weeks now felt alien and took effort. "Please, I need a favor."

"Even better reason not to call. I don't give a shit about your emergencies," he shouted, apparently now too angry to care about being overheard. "And as for doing *you* a favor? You've got to be out of your fucking mind."

"Please, I'm desperate." She made her voice crack. "I thought that as a government employee, you'd have at least a modicum of compassion." *If I can make him believe that, he'll believe anything.*

"You thought wrong."

"Please, at least listen."

"You got sixty seconds."

"It's about my best customer. She's a Victoria's Secret model, tightest body, firmest natural double D's you've ever seen. She's bisexual, *loves* sex, and she always has this astounding blow. If your nose starts to drip, God hands you a Kleenex wrapped in gold leaf. I won't bore you with the details because I know you're busy. Here's my problem: she's coming over this afternoon, wants me to set up a threesome. She's incredibly hot but so damn particular, insists the man be tattooed, well-built, and hung. As if that weren't hard enough to find on short notice, she likes it rough. Flack, please, if you know someone who might be interested... Obviously there'd be no charge."

Robert N. Chan

"When's this happening?"

"Four o'clock, but... hey, really truly sorry to have bothered you. Don't know what got into me. I'll never violate your privacy again."

She disconnected.

Her phone rang.

"I'll be there, maybe not four but definitely by four-thirty."

"Thank you! I owe you big time. I'll try to keep her busy."

She made a slurping sound.

Mom answered the door, talcum smudged on each nostril.

"I better not be too late," Flack said, through heaving breaths. A saddle of sweat soaked his rumpled shirt. "Wasn't easy to get away. Traffic was a bitch."

"So was my customer. Sorry." Mom ran her hand slowly up his crotch. "I'll do my best to make it up to you. Victoria, that's actually her name..." Mom rubbed her gums, then giggled as if she were high. "We were so turned on to each other we couldn't wait another nanosecond. Her body... I was wet to the knees just looking at her, and..."

"Fuck!"

"Yes, of course, but first may I..."

She got on her knees in front of him and undid his zipper with her teeth. Taking him in her mouth, she thought she'd retch. She hadn't had physical contact with anyone since Epi's arrest. Blessedly she faded out and watched herself with disinterest as she went through the motions like a drinking bird.

Once she had him going, she whispered, "I want to make it up to you. Do some blow; then, if it'll turn you on, slap me around. When I beg you to stop, ignore me. Slap me. Force yourself on me from behind...." When she finished giving him the details, Mom pushed a button by her bed to activate the security system Epi had set up.

"I don't need to pay you, right?" Flack said when they were done with the first round, and she wiped away the fake tears.

164

"Just with a favor. Actually, it would be more of a favor for you than for me."

His pectorals and trapeziums tensed visibly. She massaged his shoulders and muscular acne-scared back.

"The marshals are in charge of witness protection, right?"

"Yeah." Flack pronounced the word as if it had three syllables.

"And they work closely with law enforcement?"

"Not sure I like where this is going." He ran his tongue over his gums. "I had a nice time, but don't even think I'll let you anywhere near my work life."

"I have a son. A lovely boy, straight-A student, star hockey player." She was so focused on what she was doing that her reference to Epi didn't cause more than an emotional blip. "He's doing ten years at Lewisburg for…" Now she had to struggle to keep her voice steady. "Nothing, actually."

"Yeah, everyone in there's innocent. Just ask 'em."

"He was… He's in the hospital. When he recovers, they'll move him to protective custody but…"

"Lewisburg's the asshole of the federal prison system," Flack said, finally sounding sympathetic. "Why's he in maximum security?"

She told him.

"Child porn's the flavor of the week. If he'd just killed someone, he'd have gotten off easier." He sighed, "No politician's going to stick up for sex offenders. They're all too busy tripping all over themselves to get a monument erected to Martin Luther Fucking King to do anything that makes sense." He smiled, pleased with his political profundity. "Point is, nothing I can do for him, even if I wanted to stick my dick out."

"I have information law enforcement would be very interested in." Mom paused for effect but saw only boredom in Flack's face as he looked around the room with growing disinterest. "There's a Serbian gang that's taken over the drug business around here."

"Slobodan Petrović's crew. What of it?"

165

"I know the guy who runs all his drug distribution for Brooklyn," she said, dropping her voice to add import.

"He won't talk. They're more afraid of Petrović than they are of us, with good reason. A DEA agent, sort of a friend of mine, had a plan to infiltrate them. He and two others are missing and presumed dead. All that's turned up are portions of several organs, removed with a serrated knife, while the agents were still alive...no anesthesia, lots of salt and lye."

"What could you get for me in exchange for testimony that would convict Petrović?"

"A funeral oration." He smiled at his own cleverness. "I understand that you want to help your son, but you're in way over your head here. *Way* over."

"If I come through, can you get my son, me, and my friend into witness protection?"

"It'd take every bit of suck I got; and, when your scheme failed, I'd be fucked right up the ol' chocolate highway."

Mom took a second to enjoy the image. "So you could if you really wanted to?"

"I'm sure as hell not going to find out."

Mom had expected the conversation to have gone as it had. People say, "You never know," but she almost always did.

She got out of bed. "Excuse me a few minutes. When I come back, let's see if I can get you excited enough for another go." She wiggled her bare ass in his face.

"I hope the delay gave you a chance to recharge your batteries," she said on her return. "Shall we start by watching porn? I'm starring in a new video. I'd love to get your opinion."

She turned on the TV, hit play, and snuggled up next to him. On screen Flack snorted cocaine, told her he was going to take her up the ass, and when she begged him not to, slapped her hard.

"WHAT THE FUCK? That makes it look like I did coke, then raped you."

"You know, you're right." The video looked great except

that his gray skin tone, light-gray eyes, and black hair made it look like he'd been shot in black-and-white, while she and her bedroom had been shot in color. "If that ever got into the hands of the tight asses in the Department of Justice or MSNBC... Well, I did tell you I intended to *really* fuck you."

"You bitch!" He pulled his arm back.

"Uh-huh," she shook a finger. "Bad idea with the camera running and all. Use your words."

His body shook with fury. "You invited me over here on a lie and—"

"Oh, yeah, I really took advantage of you. Gave you coke, let you take me up my butt, then offered you a deal that could make your entire career."

"Let me have the tape." He held out his hand, palm up. "NOW!"

"No can do. It's automatically sent to a secure location, and any attempt to fiddle with it sets off the panic button." She stepped toward the corner of the bed, so her knife and mace would be within reach if she needed them. "Epi installed the system before he left for college and intentionally made it difficult for me to tamper with."

His face turned lobster-red. Finally now that there was some color...

"I let the word out in the prison, and it won't be ten minutes before your son's dead."

"I let the word out to my friend in Petrović's gang, and you won't live long enough to do that," she said, ignoring the spasm of pain that had shrunk her stomach to the size of a cherry pit and then blew it up to the size of a beach ball. "It would seem *very* long to you, though." She was about to describe how Edward II died from a hot poker being shoved up his ass but decided this might not be the time for historical references. "Let's put the blackmail talk behind us and resume this discussion in the spirit of mutual respect that has been the hallmark of our friendship. What if I were to do a drug deal with Petrović—himself, not one of his minions—and record the transaction?"

167

Robert N. Chan

"What if you stop watching TV cop shows, so you'll still be alive next time I want to fuck you?"

He'd want to have sex with me after what I just did to him? After all these years, I still don't understand men. The only sane one I know is doing ten years in Lewisburg.

"I entrapped you and you're smarter than the average bear."

But the average chimpanzee? Maybe not.

"The three dead DEA guys had an idea along the same line as yours, and they actually knew what they were doing."

"If I try and fail, it's no skin off your ass; but if you were to have a hand in bringing Petrović down, it'd be a feather in your dick, right?" *Not my best lines. At least the camera's off.*

"What makes you think you can pull this off?"

"I'm highly motivated, I have a friend on the inside who owes me big time, and—"

"Stop right there. There's no way you'll persuade—"

"To sweeten the deal, I'll arrange for the video I just showed you to disappear if I die by Petrović's hand."

After a long silence, he said, "I'll nose around, see if there's interest."

"You'll do more than that."

She pushed *play* on the remote and turned up the sound track, so her begging him not to violate her came through loud and clear. She zoomed in on the anguished expression on her face, the hand-shaped red mark from where he'd hit her, and finally the tears rolling down her cheeks. Then she zoomed out again so he could see him enter her as she screamed in pain and protest.

"If that *ever* gets out, you're dead." He stabbed a finger into her sternum. "Don't fuck with me."

"I like fucking with you, even more than I like sucking your big beautiful cock." She blew him a wet kiss.

"Fine, I'll push for it, but that video better disappear." With shoulders hunched and muscles slack, he looked smaller.

The next day Flack called.

"Maybe we can work something out. I'll need to meet with

168

you and your friend. If I have confidence that he's for real and there's a plan there that has some chance of success... But remember what I said about that video disappearing."

Now all she had to do was persuade Darko to risk his life on a plan that would most likely result in a slow painful death. How hard could that be?

XVI

Psychopathy Loves Company

In the two-story great room, with its dramatic spiral staircase, floor to ceiling windows, brightly colored rugs, wall hangings that Charty had purchased at inflated prices from people as venal as him, and the *fin de siècle* paintings by obscure artists whom Mom was partial to, she laid out two fat lines of Darko's coke and handed him a rolled-up Ben Franklin. After he hoovered up the white powder, she explained what she wanted.

"*Bog Te Jebo* (may god fuck you)!" he said.

"He already has, but let's not dwell on the past."

Darko handed her the snorting tube. She shook her head and set out another pair of parallel lines.

"This is a great opportunity," she said. "You've been wanting to get out for years, a fresh start."

"I'm now the Serbian equivalent of a made man."

"Which means you have the life expectancy of a suicidal fruit fly. It's just a matter of time before Petrović's paranoia resurfaces, and he institutes another purge. We can get away, start a new life."

"You and me together?" A crease appeared between his bushy eyebrows.

She nodded, although that hadn't been part of her plan.

"That's almost appealing," he said.

"Epi's been in Lewisburg for three weeks." Her voice became raspy. "He's already been shanked and gang raped. He almost bled out. He's catatonic...."

"He's a good kid. I always liked him." Darko's expression softened. "When I was in Attica, I had friends inside. Still almost didn't make it through. If I thought there was any chance of success—"

"Darko, I need you."

"I'd like to help but…"

170

Girl

She brought over a couple feet of rubber tubing, a serving spoon, and a bottle of distilled water. She mixed and heated one hit of heroin.

"Darko, please help me."

"Not a chance." Mom tied his arm. "You think I'm a sociopath because I fuck people up? Compared to Petrović, I'm a cherub. Anyone I've hurt for him, it was an act of charity. He'd have done far worse."

"That's why we can do a deal. Law enforcement wants to put him away." She pulled out the plunger, sucking in the mixture, then cleared the needle with a couple taps of her fingernail. "For Epi."

He shook his head. "You're not having any?"

"I've lost my taste for the stuff."

Was there anything worse than waiting for Epi to recover? *If* he recovered. Maybe heroin would dull the ache of waiting and not knowing... No.

"Drugs are the place you go 'when no one else will take you in,'" he said, a telltale sparkle in his usually dead eyes.

He must really care for her if he were reading Robert Frost. Maybe there still was a chance that she wouldn't have to do something terrible to get him to cooperate.

"Petrović won't meet with you. Believe me, that's a good thing. He's not a people person."

"Neither am I, but life's all about stretching one's capabilities. Explain that to him." She shot him up.

His eyes closed, his head leaned back, and a stupid smile took up residence on his face. Mom struggled through a few pages of *Fear and Trembling*. Although she agreed with Kierkegaard that "Life can only be understood backwards; but it must be lived forwards," she had trouble concentrating. Before Epi's arrest, she'd have pushed herself, but now she closed the book. At least she was reading again.

"Remember what we were talking about?" she asked, when Darko opened his eyes.

"Stupid idea, Mom."

Robert N. Chan

"Man up, Darko. He's just a guy, for chrissake."

"Nothing about him is for Christ's sake. I've worked for him for almost twenty years—since he brought me over here after the Nazi-ass-licking Croats marked me for execution—actually met him only four times. Each time I wished I hadn't. *Fucking terrifying*, and I don't scare easy." He looked around as if to make sure no one else was in the room and dropped his voice to a whisper. "Once I actually shat myself. Now I deal with his senior management, which is fine with me."

"Here." She tossed him a bottle of massage oil and a couple tissues. "Finish yourself off. I've got stuff to do."

"Hey, don't be mad. It's for your own good…not that I could set up such a meet even if I wanted to."

"I've been mad since you were humping explosives in Serbia. And when I need you to tell me what's for my good, I'll be even worse off than I am now. But, just for the record, I damn well know what I'm doing is nuts. If I had any other way…"

"This is not a *way*. It's a suicide mission."

"If you can't set up a one-on-one with him and me, then we'll do it together. Tell him I want five kilos of smack." She took a small pinch from his bag and snorted it. Mmmm, maybe she should have shot up with him. "This same stuff, uncut, but I need to meet him."

"Why?"

"Tell him I'll want to do a big deal soon after, a *real big one*; and I only trust people I actually see and talk to."

He shook his head, "Not gonna happen."

While he stroked his monkey, she left for the bathroom.

Sitting on the edge of the tub, she pleaded with herself not to go through with her plan. She had no problem with risking her own life when Epi's hung in the balance, but to risk Darko's on such a long shot? *I'll give him one more chance, but after that… I have to do whatever I can to save Epi.* She felt sick to her stomach, hated herself; but she was going to go do it. Maybe she was the true sociopath. No reason why they both couldn't be. Psychopathy loves company.

172

Girl

When she returned, Darko was already half-dressed.

"I'd help you if I thought there was any chance—"

"Please, Darko, I'm begging you." She got down on her knees, hands together, head bent. "The entire time I've known you, I've never really asked for anything from you. I took you in when you were in trouble."

He shook his head.

"I wish I didn't have to force you." She took a deep breath. "You okay to walk to your car?"

"You do know I'm only trying to stop you from getting yourself killed?" he said.

Yes, I know that all too well.

"Where are you parked?"

He squinched up his face at the odd conversational turn. "Two blocks down the street, just off Amsterdam. Why?"

He seemed to be having trouble putting his shirt buttons into the appropriate holes. She helped him. At least he wasn't going to drive in that condition.

She closed the door behind him. To stiffen her resolve, she thought about Epi. Then she called 911.

"There's a man walking west on Eighty-Third Street. He's now a few houses in from Central Park West. He's going to his car, a cherry red BMW with black detailing, parked near Amsterdam. He's carrying an ounce of heroin, an ounce of cocaine, and a syringe. About five-foot-nine, a hundred and seventy pounds, with a tattoo of the Serbian national symbol on the top of his shaved head."

She called Flack, "Darko's on board."

"Really?"

"Practically." She told him what she'd done.

"You're insane."

"You going to set up the meeting or start a psychological diagnosis practice?"

She thought of what a sweet, moral, optimistic girl Hannah had been and allowed herself a short self-indulgent cry.

"Darko, I'm so sorry," she said to no one.

173

XVII
God Is with Us

Mom now had no income, big legal fees, and the possibility that she might need significant amounts of money in a hurry. So she sold the house—with all its furniture and her beloved art collection—to one of her customers for all cash, at a deep discount, forging Epi's name on the transfer documents. Within two weeks, she'd moved back into the downstairs apartment on a two-month lease from the new owner. Giving up the home in which she and Epi had lived so happily made hardly a blip on her emotional radar screen. Suspended over an abyss deeper and darker than any she'd ever known, she focused on putting one hesitant foot ahead of the other, as she negotiated the frayed tightrope of her scheme to get Epi out of prison.

"You fucking bitch! I'm gonna fucking kill you!"

Manacled, Darko leaned across the bolted-to-the-floor metal table.

"Don't be tiresome, Darko. I told you you were going to help me. Unfortunately, you needed more persuading. How's that my fault?"

She smiled as if she meant it, and she was so into her role she might actually have. Most everyone she knew had a nearly infinite capacity for self-righteousness. She should have had at least some, which she could call on in a pinch; and her current situation was pinching so hard she could barely breathe.

"I said it was for your own good. I should've told you to go ahead, then told them you were working for the cops."

"But you didn't, and your selflessness inspired me to do something for *your* own good."

He tried to raise his arms, perhaps to strangle her. The chains clinked menacingly.

"I'm looking at *twenty years* here, you fucking—"

"Not to worry; I got your back," she said, more or less sticking to the script she'd gone over with the cops and Feds who were watching behind the one-way glass. "We pull this off, and you go right into witness protection."

"You're nuts." Due to his restraints, he had to bend forward to bury his head in his hands. "You have no idea what these people are capable of."

"Petrović's teetering on the edge," Mom said, acutely aware of her own teetering. "All he needs is a little push. He's killing federal agents, which means he's desperate. They'll get him. Only question is, Are we going to reap the benefits, or are you going down with him?"

"Leave me the fuck out of your looney tunes idea. And get the fuck out of here. I can't fucking stand looking at you."

Understood. She couldn't stand looking at herself.

"Between your drug habit, your avocation of fucking people up, and your connection to an erratic psychopath, you had a date with the mortuary. Luckily, I broke it for you."

"Yeah, lucky."

"Please, Darko, I'm begging you; don't make me do anything else to convince you. I'd hate to, I don't know…get word out via law enforcement that you're about to rat on Petrović."

"He'd never believe—"

"Really? His paranoia's cured? I'd have thought that even if he had the tiniest doubt about your trustworthiness, he'd fuck you up, if only to serve as an example for others."

She sat back. He struggled against his restraints. He shifted in his chair, frowned, squirmed.

"Enough, Darko. You in? Or out, which is to say in for twenty years?"

Darko stared at her. She stared back. He broke eye contact. "How the fuck?"

"I've got a customer who's in the U.S. Marshal Service. He says if we bring in Petrović, they'll let Epi out; and the three of us will go right into witness protection."

175

His eyebrows knitted. "I'd think you'd be smart enough never to trust a cop."

"I've got a video of him snorting blow, slapping me around, and taking me up the ass while I scream in protest," she whispered, so those listening couldn't hear.

Darko shook his head. "You're some piece of work."

"We can leave all this behind, start over. More than once, you've claimed you love me, and—"

"I fucking fell for you, asshole move that was."

"We do have a certain sexual chemistry." She recalled, from the science she'd learned to teach it to Epi, that certain elements didn't react with each other; and the noble gasses didn't react with anything. So non-reaction was chemistry, wasn't it?

He grinned. "We do, don't we?"

"Set up a meet." She shot him a hard look.

Long silence in which she could almost hear the screech of rusted gears in his head.

"He's always looking to move weight. If you had big money connections..."

"When Petrović checks me out, he'll see I've got quite the up-scale practice. That and nothing else. My Internet footprint is the size of a newborn's. To the government and pretty much everyone else, I barely exist. *But* I can show evidence"—she punctuated with a finger point—"of my connections to malefactors of great wealth who are looking to hedge their hedge-fund businesses. According to documents I can make available, they've pledged eight figures in cash to front me."

"For real?" His eyes went wide.

She wiggled her hand. "Realish... enough to impress the hell out of him. I've got a wide range of customers with a wide range of talents and financial means. Most like me enough to do me a favor or two, particularly if I blackmail them into it. The documents will be unimpeachable, and I have enough ready cash to establish my legitimacy." She dropped her voice, "I sold my house."

Darko's fury receded to the point where it merely skulked in the background. He might at any time turn on her. Her 911 call, though, had probably increased his respect for her. Vicious dogs cringe before abusive masters. The trick would be to convince him to bite on her command and not Petrović's. She'd have to be more terrifying than a psychopathic war criminal turned drug lord. How hard could that be?

"I still think trusting a cop—"

"Pulling this off will make him look good to his superiors. Pulling a fast one on me wouldn't be in his best interests."

"Fine," he said, after wriggling like a fish on a line. "Get me out of here."

"I'll post your bail this afternoon, all half million bucks. That'll get attention. Tell Petrović I've got connections in the highest levels of the northeastern establishment, the baby-boomers and generation-Xers who did drugs in college and miss it—a market he hasn't been able to crack. With decrepitude and boredom stalking them, they want to experiment with the harder stuff. As I learned from whoring, they like paying top dollar and bragging to their friends about how much they spend to get the best. They're afraid of dealing with mobsters, but a classy woman with a brownstone off Central Park West... They don't need to know I'm now just a tenant. Transfer papers are yet to be filed. Tell him I only do business with people I meet face-to-face."

"Don't even think about wearing a wire."

"A recording device and miniature video camera in my shoe. Two minutes on line and I found dozens of tiny hidden recording devices."

He rolled his eyes. "And now, playing the part of Miss Moneypenny..."

"Q's the one with gadgets."

"Who's the one who gets tortured and killed?"

"That would be you, if you don't go along with me here." She gave him a look so cold he got goose bumps. "I'm willing to sacrifice anything, take any risk, to get Epi out of prison."

"I'm not quite so committed."

177

"That's why I'm motivating you."

She hated herself for what she was doing to him and could only hope she'd be able to make it right.

"Don't you get it? Mom, you're dealing with people who'll—"

"All I need from Petrović is a meeting where money and drugs change hands and—"

"Not talking about him." His stare stuck her like a sharpened stake. "There may be no honor among thieves, but there's a fuckload less on the other side. Crooks know they're crooks. The Feds think they're on the side of God. As I said, I read lots of history when I was in the can; and I read more on the can. One thing comes through loud and clear: worst shit in the world is done by people who think they got God on their side. You know what the Nazi soldiers had on their belt buckles? *'Gott mit uns,* God is with us.' These fuckers have on their coins, 'In God we trust.' Same shit."

"Maybe, but I've got no choice, and neither do you."

"Petrović won't meet you. He does everything through his people."

She walked the circumference of the table, thinking about what he'd said.

"How about if I do a relatively small deal, say a quarter kilo of smack, 750 grams of blow? Whatever a hundred grand will get me. I do it with your Manhattan counterpart, then let word out that I want a really big deal; but my financial backers insist I meet the guy I'm dealing with."

He winced as if a cop had shined a flashlight in his eyes.

"I want something in writing from the marshals and the DEA," he said.

"We'll meet with them tomorrow."

After Mom posted Darko's bail with cash, Darko, Flack, Mom, and a Department of Justice lawyer met. The lawyer handed out a document on DOJ letterhead.

"Explain it to me," Darko said.

178

Girl

The lawyer started to speak, but Darko cut him off.

"Not you, her." He pointed at Mom.

After reading it twice, she said, "Looks good. We provide evidence of Petrović doing a major drug deal or committing some other serious felony—"

"Like him killing us?" Darko said.

"And if we agree to testify against him and his crew, Epi gets out of jail, his record is expunged, all charges against you are dropped, and we all go into witness protection."

"I encourage you to have a lawyer look it over," the attorney said.

"We're allergic to them," Darko said.

Sitting in a black SUV, Mom bought $100,000 worth of pure heroin and cocaine from Darko's Manhattan counterpart.

The man in the driver's seat wore a cheap black suit and a black turtleneck, as did the bigger, smellier cheese in the back. The driver took her bag of cash, handed her a similar bag, and began counting her money.

"Taste." He pointed to his bag. "Then take and go."

She snorted a fingernail's worth of the smack, rubbed some on her gums, and wondered, yet again, why she'd given up drugs. She did the same with the blow and wondered some more.

"If I turn this over in a week, I want to do ten times this amount; but I need to deal directly with Petrović."

The driver grunted. The man in back toyed with a length of wire. Mom had never seen a garrote but knew he wasn't making a cat's cradle.

"Tell him if he wants to expand into an untapped market, he'll meet with me. I'm offering to pay big money and shoulder all the risks. Tell him."

"No one tell Slobodan nothing."

"I don't ask messenger boys for their opinions." At least she'd refrained from correcting his grammar.

He shrugged.

Deep breath. Radiate confidence, faked confidence will do.

179

Robert N. Chan

"Don't shrug your shoulders at me," she said. "*Jebem te dok ti oci ne ispadnu a posle zato sto su ti ispale.* 'I'll fuck your ass off until your eyes fall out;' and after, I'll do it again because they fell out."

The driver went for his gun.

She went for her pocketbook and pulled out a sheaf of papers.

"Give this to your boss..., please."

He pointed to the door.

She met the DEA agent in the back of a van, where he was carrying out some sort of surveillance and sipping vodka from a Poland Springs water bottle. He wore his headphones like a crown of thorns.

"Amazing," he said on hearing her report. He listened to the audio from her shoe recorder and declared it to be "as clear as a bell." He called the video from her glasses "fair."

"Any interest in grabbing some dinner tonight?" he asked, voice trilling up.

"No," she said, considering him too insignificant to insult. "I've got drugs to sell."

She picked up the drugs.

"Hey, that's evidence."

"It's also seed corn for the big harvest."

He pinched the bridge of his nose, then handed her a form.

"Fill this out and take half."

Outside the van a Turnerish sunset painted the city pink. Coming from somewhere in the distance, a saxophone note floated through her.

Mom didn't want to have sex with customers. All she wanted was to see Epi. If she had her way, she'd get stoned and stay that way until she could see him. But, as Hannah's father had so eloquently put it, "What you want doesn't matter."

She went back into whoring full throttle, making it known to her customers that she could supply them with high quality drugs

180

Girl

and assuring them they'd face no risk dealing with her since she'd paid off all the right people. Motivated by the promise of a piece of the action, her customers told their friends and acquaintances. Nothing like being in a business that created its own demand and was also under government protection; it was like being an oil company.

Dr. Fernandez advised her by email that Epi had been released from the hospital and removed from the general prison population. Mom poured herself a glass of wine and called him to find out when she could visit.

She felt his sigh at the base of her spine.

"I'm sorry."

"But in your email you said…"

Seconds ticked by in silence.

"Dr. Fernandez?"

"He was attacked again," he whispered as if even he hadn't wanted to hear what he'd said.

"I thought he was in protective custody." Her voice shook with anger.

"The guards intervened but…"

"So he's not hurt?"

"Physically he's…if it were just a question of his wounds… Psychologically, he's…not reacting well."

"What exactly does *not reacting well* mean?"

The doctor sighed again.

Mom waited. Hurricane-force winds buffeted her. The tightrope swayed and several of its strands snapped. The abyss below glowed blue and stank of burning sulphur. The cable, though, held…for now.

"He's regressed. He stays curled in a corner of his cell. He soils himself because he lacks the energy to walk or crawl the few feet to the toilet. Guards were dragging him to the cafeteria at mealtimes, but he wouldn't eat. Last night he lost consciousness. We moved him back to the prison hospital. He's hooked to a colostomy bag, being fed and hydrated intravenously."

181

She squeezed the glass so tight it shattered.

"If I see him, maybe I can help bring him around."

She pulled shards of glass from her hand and tossed them into the wastebasket. The blood dripping onto the kitchen floor seemed to come from someone else's hand, that of a fifteen-year-old girl, and the blood-splattered tiled floor... She suppressed the thought but only at the cost of letting several more tightrope strands snap.

If she hadn't known it already, the call would have convinced her that she could have one and only one priority: getting Epi out of prison. For the first time in two decades, she felt like praying. Not that prayer had done Hannah much good.

"Let me try something else first," Dr. Fernandez said. "I told him you want to visit, but the warden won't allow it until he starts tending to his bodily needs. Perhaps that will motivate him. Please, just give us a few days."

Mom felt like one of Epi's wind-up toys that he used to make march over the edge of the kitchen/living-room island—again and again.

"Is there some way he can be released on compassionate leave or something?" Her voice cracked. "At least moved to a minimum security prison?"

"I wish. Apparently someone in Washington's made your son a special project, and the guy running for senate in this state is campaigning on a platform of getting tough on sex offenders."

"What's he asking for, castration?"

"Among other things," he said.

She could barely suppress her fury at Emmylou's father, the candidate, and by extension all politicians who climb the ladder of power on the backs of the poor, disadvantaged, and powerless. But she knew she couldn't afford anger. For now she had to put all her energy into one thing: getting Epi out of there.

Or die trying.

XVIII
Swelling Like a Tick on Dracula

Epi shuffled to the visiting station like an arthritic octogenarian—like Mom during her post-conviction depression, only he was also limping. Pain shot through Mom with every step he took. Worry lines creased his forehead, and his eyes seemed to focus on a spot somewhere in the distance, or rather nowhere. Epi put his palm on the Plexiglas divider. Mom did the same. She could almost feel his warmth through the barrier and was sure he felt hers. He started crying. Her entire body wanted to cry. Precious minutes ticked by. She stared at him through a tear-blurred fog. Both of them forced smiles. He appeared to break up into multiple images, an infinite regression seen through parallel mirrors. She began chattering about hockey. He listened, a weak but genuine smile on his face.

She stopped talking, took a deep breath.

"Epi." She looked into his beautiful green eyes. "I don't want to lie to you and can't tell you the truth." A long shot at best, she didn't want to mention her witness protection plan.

"Can you be a little more mysterious?" He sniffed in. "I'm afraid I almost understood that."

"I'm working on something. I might be able to get you out of here. I'm sorry, but I can't tell you any more than that."

"If this involves any risk to you, I don't want you to do it."

A guard started in their direction, then turned toward a pregnant girl, of no more than sixteen, being shouted at by a middle-aged prisoner with a swastika tattooed on his neck and three teardrops below his right eye.

"Whatever possessed you to think that I'd be in danger?" Mom forced a smile.

His eyes narrowed, studying her. She flashed back on how six-year-old Epi's tongue used to stick out of the corner of his mouth when he concentrated.

"I love you, Mom," he said.

She let his love wash over her, a purifying wave. An unpleasant realization caused an undertow. Hannah's parents had so poisoned the phrase that she'd never said, "I love you" to him. Damn them. No, bless them. If it hadn't been for them, she'd never have had Epi. Even with her current troubles, she'd been blessed. "Blessed art thou, O Lord our God, King *of the* universe"...*the hell with that.*

She was about to tell him she loved him when the guard announced that their time was up. She couldn't say the words in the presence of an intruder.

"I'm going to get you out of here," she whispered.

Mom met Darko in an Amsterdam Avenue bar crowded with drunk college kids sporting phony IDs. His face was bruised and puffy, his eyes swollen almost closed; and his nose looked as if it had been pulled off and put back crooked. Mom's face hurt just looking at him. He coughed blood into a napkin. He had a bandaged stump where the last two joints of his left pinkie used to be.

"My god, what happened to you?"

"Slobodan's going to check you out. If he's comfortable with what he finds, he'll meet with the two of us." He coughed up more blood. Lifting his bandaged hand, he said, "This is their way of saying you better not be fucking around. Went light on me, thanks to my years of loyal service. If you'd been there, they'd have cut off your left tit."

I did this, even if it weren't my fists that pounded him. She restrained herself from lightly kissing his wounds.

"But that makes no sense. You were only a messenger."

She flashed back to the visit from Petrović's henchman. They already knew about her relationship to Darko. She shouldn't have involved him.

"Not making sense makes them more terrifying."

She faked a smile. "You going to thank me for bailing you out now or wait until later?"

184

"It's on my things-to-do list, right after killing you for turning me in."

She went to the bar and got him a double Bushmills and a Perrier with lime for herself.

On her return she rested her hand on his. "When are we doing it?"

"*If* he agrees to do it, it'll be within a couple weeks, give or take."

The muscles in her lower back contracted, causing alternating sharp and dull pain.

"Earlier would be better." She bit her lip. "I don't know how long Epi can last in there. Emmylou's father has targeted him."

He looked at the tabletop.

"I already lost one finger, don't want to lose another."

"Try the phone, Darko."

An odd look came over his face. "I never know with you. Am I crazy, or are we actually friends?"

"Both. You're pretty much my best friend. Pathetic."

"Bathetic," he said. "I've been building my vocabulary, in case we do end up together."

"That's…" To her surprise she didn't feel like responding with a put-down. "Nice." Gently, mindful of his injuries, she rested her hand on his.

He was a decent person, the nicest sociopath she'd ever met, far nicer to her than she deserved. It would be a lovely gesture not to get him killed.

Mom called Flack.

"We hope to be able to complete our end of the deal within a week. I'm calling to make sure you'll be ready on your end."

After an excruciating silence, he said, "Mom, I'm working like a Trojan here to put your deal together."

"I thought my deal was *together*. The Department of Justice signed off on it."

"Yes, of course. Just details…*mechanics*."

That last word hit her like a sucker punch.

Robert N. Chan

"Details make me wet. When can I see them in writing?"

She took a deep breath. It wasn't easy maintaining her usual line of banter, but stepping out of character would be a sign of weakness that Flack might pick up on.

"Love it," he said. "I deal with the world's worst scumbags, and they don't trust *me*."

"Funny, I feel the same way." Having started to tremble, she had to get off the phone. "I'll see you and the DOJ shyster at noon tomorrow, Central Park, Bethesda Fountain. I trust that by then, you'll have all wrinkles ironed smooth."

She felt like she was falling down an elevator shaft.

She got a text from Dr. Fernandez containing a number on which she could call within the next hour. Epi would be with him.

After three failed attempts due to her trembling fingers, she got through.

"Dr. Fernandez, what happened?" her voice shook with panic. *When I talk to Epi, I'll have to calm myself...somehow.*

"Epi had been doing better; then last night he woke to find a half-dozen rats in his cell, all with body parts bitten off...by human teeth."

Her stomach clenched. "Is he...."

"When I told him he could talk to you, he rallied somewhat but... he's here. I'll put him on."

"Wait, first, how could that have happened?"

"Seems a guard was bribed. There'll be an investigation."

"Which I assume will find nothing?"

He sighed.

Next thing she heard was Epi bawling. She hadn't heard him cry like than since he was seven and poured boiling water on himself while trying to make her tea as part of a surprise breakfast in bed.

"Mommy..." Heaving breaths.

"I'm here, Epi."

"When you said"—he sniffled; she had an all too clear picture of him struggling to regain his composure—"you might

186

be able to get me out of here?"

"Maybe as soon as a week. Hang in there."

"I…" He began whimpering.

The sound cut into her.

"The rats … must've been terrible." She barely avoided whimpering herself.

"They were alive, squeaking…pitiful. They just wanted to die. I knew just how they felt." A horrible, high-pitched caterwaul emerged from his throat. "I had to kill each of them, stomping on them to take them out of their misery."

"You'll get through this…somehow." Her voice trembled.

The butcher cackled. Congressman Clarence Wilson did the same.

Mom met Darko at the Bethesda Fountain fifteen minutes before noon. Fog and drizzle made it impossible to see more than a few feet. In the gray swirl and total silence, they seemed to be the only people in a post-apocalyptic world.

"Petrović heard about you bailing me out, checked your financial docs, your Internet persona, your reviews on the whore evaluation websites," Darko said. "He's willing to meet."

He paused, waiting for a reaction. Mom, though, had trouble focusing on…anything. Agonizing about Epi, she hadn't slept more than the few minutes it took to have a nightmare about rats chewing off his flesh while she watched. She'd gone through so much trouble to get here, so much angst over what she did to Darko, and now…

"Good work," she said finally. "When?"

"He'll give us forty-five minutes' notice. We'll be picked up somewhere and driven blindfolded somewhere else." Darko lit a cigarette and took a deep drag. "Whether he wants to do a deal or kill both of us because he's onto you, I can't say."

"I've got to get Epi out of there ASAP."

"Petrović works on Serbian time. If we try to make him comply with our schedule, it'll push every paranoid button he's got."

She took one of his hands in both of hers. He seemed to swell like a tick on Dracula.

"Soon, Darko, please."

Somehow they ended up in an embrace. Head tucked into his warm tattooed neck, she allowed herself a few tears, then pushed away.

"Thank you for being such a good friend."

He flushed. "Wasn't entirely voluntary."

"Nothing ever is."

They looked into each other's eyes.

"Flack should be here any minute," she said, breaking eye contact.

Darko rested a hand on her thigh and looked into her eyes. "You know I..."

"Yes, but let's not talk about it."

She liked Darko, a lot, not that it mattered. They waited in silence. The drizzle, now becoming a light rain, didn't bother her; but Darko started to shiver. Mom put his hands in hers and rubbed, careful not to press the wound from his missing pinkie joints. Then she blew on them, like she used to when she'd skate with little Epi and they'd stayed out too long because of his joy at being on the ice. The pain behind her eyes was hard to bear.

Wearing gray shades and his standard black-and-white Mormon missionary/Blues Brothers outfit, Flack materialized out of the swirling fog ten minutes late, a long ten minutes.

"Here's the revised deal." Face frozen in a part smile, part grimace as if he'd had a bad facelift, he handed copies to both of them. Mom read it while Darko stared into the mist.

"YOU PIECE OF SHIT!" Mom screamed. "Epi doesn't get witness protection."

Darko's nostrils flared.

"He's a convicted child-pornster." Flack held his arms out, palms up, the picture of innocence. "You have any idea what the women's groups would do if they heard—"

"I know what our deal was."

"They pulled rank on me." Smarmy smile. "He raped a

188

congressman's daughter. Not just any congressman but Clarence fucking Wilson, head of the Homeland Security Subcommittee, who's a lock to become senator."

"Epi didn't rape anyone."

"Wilson thinks he did. Also, child porn's akin to murder these days. Pornsters don't have the lobby the NRA's got." He paused for a chuckle he didn't get. "With it all, I got your son a damn good deal."

"Our deal is he goes into witness protection with me," she said, even as she knew that wasn't going to happen.

"He'll be moved to Allenwood; that's one of those country club prisons. With the wimps they got in there, if anyone gets raped, he'll be the one doing it; and he'll get some great stock tips along the way. He'll be released in no more than a year and out on parole." The corners of his mouth started to turn up, then turned down as if he realized there was nothing to smile about. "I fought as hard as I could, probably lost myself a long-deserved promotion; but I got Epi sixty-five grand to help him set up his new life. I won't kid you, though; the parole terms will be rough."

Flack wrapped his thin black tie around his middle finger, then unwrapped it. Mom and Darko waited.

"You won't be allowed to see or communicate with him."

"I…" Mom's throat narrowed so severely that she couldn't complete the sentence.

"Standard terms in any witness protection deal. It's for a damn good reason. Any communication with him would put you *and him* in danger from the Serbs."

"Just disappear from his life?" She bit her lip hard.

"The prison will tell him you died."

"I'll tell him."

"That might not be so convincing," Darko said.

"I can't ever contact him again?" Her voice cracked.

"You wouldn't be able to if he got killed in prison or if Petrović killed you. Not seeing him again is the only sure thing."

Too overwhelmed to know or care who had said that or even

whether she'd said it to herself, she glared at Flack. Despite the cold, sweat formed on his forehead.

"I did my best, I really did, almost got myself canned," he said. "The son of a bitch practically owns the Homeland Security Subcommittee, and they own us."

After an angry silence, Darko asked, "Will Epi be on the sex offender registries?"

"Can't be helped."

Darko glared at Flack, who glared back. They looked as if they were about to paw the earth, lower their heads, and charge at each other.

"I'm not doing it on those terms," Mom said.

"In that case Darko serves twenty years, you go down for dealing smack, and Epi...well, you know."

"Wait, dealing? I only did that because—"

"We had a deal that you now seem unwilling to go through with."

"Because you—"

"The DOJ lawyers tell me that if we both breach, it's as if there was no deal. We have you on tape buying a large quantity of heroin. You've seen what happens when a powerful congressman gets behind a criminal prosecution. It's not like in the movies where justice triumphs." He grimaced. "I don't like this any more than you do."

Darko caught Mom's eye and tilted his head toward Flack, to ask if he should kill him or at least *fuck him up*. She wanted him to, but what she wanted didn't matter. Stupid, stupid, stupid buying drugs without a firm deal in place. But, she reminded herself, she'd had a deal and had little reason not to trust the Department of Justice. She heard herself snicker at her naiveté.

"Where are you sending us?" Darko asked.

"For your own protection, you'll learn that after you testify."

"This just gets better and better, right, Mom?"

"If I die in the interim?"

"Paragraph Sixteen B. Once you get the shit on Petrović, if you die for any reason except suicide, your son gets his transfer, his parole, and the money." Flack puffed out his over-developed chest, proud of his and his government's generosity. "Understand this is an ongoing obligation. If you live, we'll need you to testify, not just against Petrović but his whole organization."

"Seems I called this one just right," Darko said.

"Piece of shit that you are, you come out of this pretty fucking great." Flack shot Darko a hostile look. "You skate on serious felony charges and get a new life you can fuck up at your leisure."

"When does Epi get out of Lewisburg?" Mom asked.

Flack turned the page of the agreement and pointed to a paragraph. "Right after you do the deal with Petrović, assuming we get usable audio."

"If Petrović kills me before I get the chance to testify, I want Epi to get his transfer, parole, and money."

Flack nodded.

"In writing, Flack."

"Sure, but…"

"Now."

He sent an email. They waited. His phone beeped.

He showed her. "DOJ will follow up with a signed addendum."

"What do I get?" Darko asked.

"More than you fucking deserve."

"I'll need cash to help me *fuck up my new life at my leisure.*"

"Ten Gs if you testify and verify the usable audio."

Darko stood. "See you guys around."

"Walk out of here and—"

One quick move, and Darko was holding a knife to Flack's eyeball.

"And what will you do, *jeb emti dupa?*"

"Buttfucker," Mom translated, feeling a touch of pride over her mastery of Serbo-Croatian curses. "Darko, go along with this; and Flack promises you'll go to a good place with thirty-five K in your pocket."

191

Robert N. Chan

"In writing, signed," Darko said.

"Get this psycho off me."

Mom liked hearing the tremor in Flack's voice. While the two of them remained frozen in position, she scrolled through the saved videos on her phone.

"Back off, Darko; there's something I want him to see with both eyes."

She turned her phone toward Flack, displaying the video of him doing coke and anally raping her.

"You're threatening me? Actually threatening me?"

"If you'd prefer, Darko can extract your right eyeball; and we'll all part as friends."

"That I have to spend my life dealing with scumbags like you two." He shook his head in disgust.

"I know just how you feel. *I* actually had to suck the cock of a federal marshal."

Darko laughed.

"Okay, just to close the deal, twenty if you get usable material on Petrović, and we'll throw in an additional five each time you testify," Flack said. "That's the limit of my authority."

"When do I say goodbye to my son?" Mom asked.

"There's a visiting day tomorrow." Flack smiled again. "Hey, you'll go to a nice place. I promise." *Nice would be if Darko kicked Flack's teeth in.* Flack's smile faded. "One more thing: I get that video back and all copies."

"After Epi's transfer." *I didn't say how long after.* "Oh, and one more thing. In that country club place, he gets five hours a week of ice time."

"What?" Flack slapped his ears as if to punish them for hearing wrong, then started laughing. "That was a joke, right?"

"Guards will take him to a rink." Mom stared at Flack in a way that let him know she meant it.

"I'll manage to do that...somehow."

"Mom and I go to the same place, right?" Darko asked.

"If you're referring to the afterlife, yes. Otherwise, no," Flack said. Darko fingered his knife. "Nothing I can do about it.

192

Girl

We separate material witnesses…for the obvious reason."

"*Yebem ti drzshavoo*," Darko said.

"Fuck the government," Mom translated. "If we pull this off, Darko, we'll both be better off than we are now."

"Seems like we're all stuck with this." Darko blew out air through closed lips. "Thanks to Mom."

"Now you better bring in Petrović. My ass is on the line because of how I stretched for you shitbags."

"That'll motivate us," Mom said. "We'd hate to make you look bad."

XIX
To Really Want to Cause Pain—to Enjoy it

"You feeling better?" Mom asked on her final prison visit, the last time she'd see her son—ever.

"Healing." Epi smiled with only a slight wince; his facial bruises had healed somewhat. "Between boredom and depression, I don't feel much of anything. Given the alternatives that's about as good as I can hope for. The nightmares since the rat thing"—he bit his upper lip, took in a deep breath, and exhaled slowly—"I suppose they'll stop at some point."

She had to tell him goodbye. God, this was hard.

"To tell you the truth, you don't look great," he said as the silence was about to become uncomfortable.

"Tell me the truth about something else." She forced a smile and waited for him to speak.

"Can you believe that piece of crap Wilson is about to be elected senator?"

"Shit rises to the top," she said, grateful for the reprieve, even if it would last only a few minutes.

"Emmylou visited the other day."

"*Really*? What was that like?"

"She's engaged to a right-wing talk show host twice her age. Already planning her run for her father's seat, she thinks she can spin having been raped and forced to get an abortion as a political positive, a way to get the women's vote."

"Glad everything turned out so well for her." Mom wanted to spit.

She realized she hadn't heard Epi say so much at once since he'd gone to prison, and she gave him a genuine smile.

"She said she was sorry, hoped I'd understand, didn't know her father would go so crazy. She says I should be happy for her, that she turned it all to her advantage." He tried to smile. "One thing I *am* happy about. I'd never had call to use the phrase 'fucking cunt' before. Finally I got to say it, in an appropriate context no less."

She smiled. "It's like—"

"You've got to do the voice," he said, sounding as excited as when he was five and she read him the newly released *Harry Potter and the Sorcerer's Stone;* or when he was fifteen and he read her the newly released *Harry Potter and the Deathly Hallows.* "Harry tried to use the killing curse on Bellatrix, and she taunted him." He unfurled his arm.

"'Never used an unforgivable curse before, have you, boy?'" Mom said in her Bellatrix Lestrange voice. "'You need to mean them. You need to really want to cause pain—to enjoy *it*.'" Mom smiled again; but as soon as they'd shared the moment, her most serious face returned. "Don't try to take revenge, Epi. From here on in, try to think positively."

"What if I'm positive I can destroy the son of a bitch's career and his daughter's as well? I don't want them dead, just disgraced and in a place like this, for a long time."

"Depends on whether you can get away with it, I suppose." Shouldn't she discourage such madness? How could he take on a U.S. Senator?

"Might get to the point that I don't care."

"Hope not," Mom said.

It was unimaginable that they'd never speak again.

"I don't want *you* trying to take them on." Epi pointed at her. He started out a bossy little guy. The bossy part hadn't changed all that much.

"Me?" Mom held her arms to her side, palms up. The picture of innocence.

"Promise me."

She nodded. But maybe someday…

More silence. Their last precious seconds together ticking away.

"Maybe you should run for congress," he said in the deadpan voice that she could never entirely see through.

"Sure, they could use a whore in there…broaden the representation."

195

"They already have plenty. What they could use is an honest and competent one." He smiled. "You've shown the ability to satisfy your constituents' desires and work intimately with people of all political persuasions."

His all-too-obvious attempt to break the ice had succeeded only in scattering icebergs in the path of the conversation she needed to initiate.

She took a deep breath, let it out slow.

"If everything works out, I'll be able to get you transferred to a minimum security prison and your sentence reduced to one year."

"Really?" Epi pumped a celebratory fist.

"It's not as good as I'd hoped. Your parole will last another nine years. You'll be a registered sex offender. You won't be allowed to leave the city without permission, which will be damn hard to get, won't be permitted to live within twenty-five hundred feet of a school or playground."

"That's...almost half a mile. Most everywhere is within a half mile of a school or playground."

"Some Brooklyn neighborhoods comply." She hated that she'd failed to get him into witness protection.

"Minimum security and reduced sentence, those are big plusses." He held up a hand. "But, Mom, remember what I said last time about you not taking any risks? Our call the other night"—he looked down—"I was a little hysterical. I'm better now."

Even with his bruises, he was a beautiful child, skin otherwise unmarked, red hair practically shimmering in the ugly fluorescent light, green eyes wide and innocent. How could anyone who'd been raped still be so innocent? At least he hadn't been betrayed by his family. Although with what she was about to tell him, it might seem that way. It seemed that way to her.

"Also, I can get you about sixty-five grand. You'll need every bit of that, given your parole conditions and the virtual impossibility of getting a job."

"The house has to be worth—"

196

Girl

"I had to sell it." She bit her lip. "Long story."

His jaw dropped. "You sold our—"

"There are things I'm not allowed to tell you. Please don't even try to guess. I should make up something that makes sense, but that would mean lying to you. I won't. Certainly not now with this being our last..." Her voice cracked. "I love you, Epi. You're the best thing that ever happened to me; nothing else came close."

She started crying.

"I love you," she said again through choking sobs.

His head kicked back.

"Never seen you cry before." He sniffled. "You've never actually said, 'I love you.'"

"After what happened to Hannah, I lost my taste for the phrase." She dropped her voice and said more to herself than to Epi, "Not quite sure why her experience affected me so."

He gave her an inexplicably incredulous look. "Mom, it's because—"

"Then there's my profession. I trained myself to shut down emotionally, seems that spilled over into my non-professional life. I wish it hadn't, but..." She took another deep breath, "I hope you never doubted my love."

"Not for a nanosecond. You're the best. The best mother, best teacher, best friend," his voice cracked.

She fought back her tears.

"Allenwood, the prison I think I can get you transferred to, is one of those so-called country clubs." She tried to put a happy lilt to her voice, "You'll meet a much better class of crook."

"It'll be like hanging out with Charty." He got the happy lilt almost right.

She closed her eyes for a few seconds, letting the waves of love wash over her. She felt almost clean.

"I'm pushing to get you five hours a week ice time."

He laughed, actually laughed. Apparently he thought she was joking. Be a nice surprise when it turned out to be true...*if* it turned out to be true.

197

She again touched her palm to the Plexiglas divider. He did the same on the other side.

"It almost feels as if we're actually touching," Mom said.

He nodded.

"I...came to say goodbye."

"Wait a minute. What?"

"Part of the deal I made."

"What sort of deal?"

She'd been squeezing her hands, fingers interlinked, so tightly that they'd become an ugly patchwork of blue and white.

"Any effort by either of us to communicate could be fatal for both of us."

Tears streamed down his face. He wiped his eyes. More tears. She probably shouldn't have told Epi even this much—he'd hear *witness protection* between the lines—but how could she not have?

"I'm glad we at least had the chance to say goodbye," he finally said, sounding as if he were being strangled.

Mom began crying uncontrollably, not that she had any desire to control it. She wished she could stay there forever, crying and touching Epi through a quarter-inch of Plexiglas. Hardly the best moment of her life; but whatever happened, it would be the best between now and when she died.

"If all goes well, they'll tell you I died from an accidental overdose and didn't suffer."

He opened his mouth to speak, but she put a finger to her lips.

"Goodbye, my darling. Never forget that I love you. I'll always love you."

They put their hands on the Plexiglas, and she was sure she could feel his fingers through it.

There was nothing more to say. She'd cast all the die life had given her, coming up with a streak of sevens before crapping out. Because she'd let Everett trick her into giving up her eggs, her life had been worthwhile, better than worthwhile, blessed, better than she'd had any right to expect after what had happened to Hannah.

XX

Eyes Like Piss Holes in Snow

"You sure you want to do this?" Darko asked.

"No, let's just forget it, go to prison, and let Epi continue to be raped, shanked."

It appeared that he'd tried to shrug, but his shoulders were so tense it came out as a grotesque twitch.

A black SUV with tinted windows pulled in front of the American Museum of Natural History, where Mom and Darko waited in the midst of a screaming scrum of school children and their two on-the-verge-of-nervous-breakdown teachers. The SUV's back door opened and they got in, carrying Fairway shopping bags, actual lettuce covering the metaphorical lettuce beneath. The driver, a man with a shaved head wearing a black suit and a black turtleneck, handed them strips of cloth, also black. Apparently with these guys black was the new black. The similarly dressed thug on the passenger side indicated, with the muzzle of an automatic pistol, that they should put the strips over their eyes and tie them in back.

"Possible you've seen a few too many movies?" Mom asked.

Breath coming in fierce little hydraulic gulps, Darko whispered, "You *really* don't want to fuck with these guys."

"I don't know, the one with the bushy Stalin moustache is kind of hot."

The man pointed his gun at her forehead.

"*Da Bog da gledao svoja pluca u tegli sa formalinom.*" She turned to Darko, now an interesting shade of lilac, "I tried to say, 'May god give you to watch your own lung in a jar.' Did I get that right? It's bad form to mangle other people's languages."

The thug poked her with his handgun. She put the blindfold on over her clunky glasses.

"So what now? You spin me around, give me a pin, and I get to stick one of you donkeys in the ass? Or your asses in... Oh, never mind."

She told herself that coming off unconcerned might work for her, but her barely maintained jocular tone failed to insulate her from the terrifying reality. Maybe because the last line had flopped on the floor like a newly hooked trout. More likely, though, because she faced the probability of being tortured and killed. At least Epi would get moved to Allenwood and released—if the Justice Department honored its promise.

They drove. Mom hated the blindfold. Her heart pounded. Sweat pinpricked the back of her neck. She couldn't breathe. Panic from the lack of air trumped all other fears. She focused on breathing slowly while she pictured Epi's facial expression when he scored his first goal for the NYC Cyclones. That made her feel a little better...until she remembered she'd never see him again.

From the sound of the wheels, they were passing over a bridge, probably the Queensborough since they didn't slow to pay a toll or use an E-Z Pass. How could they only be at 59th Street? She couldn't stand this.

But she had to.

Finally the car stopped. The door opened. "Out," one of the fungible thugs said. Still blindfolded, they got out of the car and shuffled along a pebbled path. They climbed five stone steps and stopped. After a clank of tumblers, an opening door scratched a flat note. She stepped inside. Something Mom guessed was an assault rifle—certainly an upgrade from the pistols they'd had in the car—slapped her ass, directing her forward, then to her right. Shuffling footsteps and macho stomps communicated that Darko and the two thugs were with her. A stab to her gut directed her to stop.

"Off blindfolds." A deep voice.

Looking down to avoid the light, painfully bright even with her thick tinted glasses, Mom blinked several times at the white-stained oak parquet floor. She lifted her head. She, Darko, and the two war criminals stood in a large sunlit living room under-furnished with a pair of chintz-covered couches and several mismatched folding chairs set around a card table. A thin line of smoke rose from a cigarette, balanced on the lip of a can of Diet Coke. A flag—three horizontal bands, red on the top, blue in the middle, and white on the bottom—hung from a wall, along with several Byzantine icons. The oversized triple-paned windows revealed a well-tended English garden and dense privet hedges that didn't quite conceal the electrified fence behind them. They were on the ground floor of a starter suburban mansion, similar to one in which she'd serviced an ovoid Fortune 500 executive and his wheelchair-bound wife.

Another deep voice barked a command, a single word rendered incomprehensible by the man's heavy accent. Mom glanced at Darko, who responded with a syncopated headshake. The thug who'd first spoken shoved his weapon into Darko's gut and raised it, popping his shirt buttons. He repeated his earlier command, which, after that helpful illustration, Mom understood as "Strip."

Mouth set in a taut little dash, Darko did as told as quickly as his shaking hands and Petorvic's inconsiderate removal of the last two joints of his pinky would allow. Mom complied slowly and sensuously, as if auditioning for a new customer.

"Take off shoes." The man pointed his gun to assist her navigation though the stormy sea of his accent.

"No way. The heels make my legs look longer and sexier." She rolled her eyes. "Okay, fine." She stepped out of them. "See? Now I bet you're sorry you asked." She put them back on.

Darko glared at her, then looked away so quickly she feared he'd lose his eyelashes. Despite her efforts at self-control, her upper lip began trembling and her skin goosebumped. Looking down on herself, she appeared shrunken and terrified. She willed herself not to dissociate—not now, please—and all she felt was an overwhelming desire to flee.

An assault weapon pointed at her glasses, then withdrew. Apparently the war criminal manqué had lost interest in the game.

The mobsters performed far less intrusive body-cavity searches than those to which her professional life had accustomed her.

Robert N. Chan

"When you're done sniffing around my public parts, you think maybe I can meet your boss and do some business?"

Darko's expressions changed like random songs on an iPod shuffle.

The thugs tossed aside the lettuce and emptied the Fairway shopping bags. Wrapped packets, each containing one hundred hundred-dollar bills, tumbled to the floor. After counting the money, they replaced it as neatly as they'd found it, then handed one bag to Darko and the other to Mom. Perhaps in their home country it was considered demeaning to tote bags of cash.

The hitherto silent thug slapped her ass with his gun. "Walk."

Darko shuffled as if being led to the gallows. Although terror chewed her stomach walls like swarms of termites, Mom sauntered like a model on a catwalk. The thus-far-silent thug ogled her. The other stood straight and stiff like a Buckingham Palace guard. She turned her head toward him and ran her tongue slowly along her lips. He didn't react.

They entered an ornate wood-paneled room. The ceiling was painted with a fair copy of Botticelli's *Primavera*. A large dragon-patterned Chinese rug extended from beneath a huge Victorian partners' desk. A smaller rug, parallel to the larger one, looked like a shoddy copy; maybe that meant it was worth more. Other than rolling one of her customers up in one and stomping on it, she had had as little experience with rugs as she did with assault weapons.

The man behind the desk, Petrović presumably, didn't bother to look up from his paperwork. Mom hadn't thought that big-time drug dealing was a paper-intensive business. Closer inspection, though, revealed that he was struggling with a Sudoku.

"Put a nine in that box and a six in the one just below it," she said.

His two factotums took their places at either side of the desk, their automatic weapons held in ready position. Their eyes seemed confused. Should they stare at Mom's breasts or her

202

Girl

shaved pudenda? It was as if they'd never seen a high-priced whore naked before. They didn't look at Darko, apparently having seen plenty of naked sociopaths with tattoos referencing the motherland.

Mom tried to clear her mind as she stood straight, stomach in, chest out, hips facing the thug who'd stared at her and shoulders and chest facing Petrović.

Puzzle completed, he glanced up.

His suit, black as a hearse, looked more expensive and better tailored than those of his lackeys. With his crisp white shirt, quietly patterned silk tie, and slicked-back black hair, he could have passed for a successful investment banker, except for his deep-set yellow eyes, which resembled piss holes in snow. He trained his gaze first on Darko until Darko shivered as if cold, then on Mom, who responded with a wide whorish smile.

"Yes, we had a very pleasant trip here. Thank you for asking," Mom said. "But I have a regrettably busy schedule, so may we please get down to business and save the more cinematic excesses for our next get-together?"

"Sit," Petrović said, voice smooth as Charty's most over-priced blended scotch.

Before Mom could comment on the absence of chairs, a man with a tubercular sunken chest and hollow cheeks rushed in carrying two and set one behind Darko and one behind Mom.

"Darko, Mom, allow me to introduce you to Miloje, one of my oldest friends." Dracula accent.

Head bowed like an oft-beaten dog, Miloje stepped onto the cheap-looking rug.

Petrović took a pistol from his drawer and shot him. A red hole opened in his gut as he dropped onto the cheap-looking rug. Two other black-clad guards marched in with parade-ground precision, wrapped his soon-to-be lifeless body in the rug, and carried him off.

"Simple up-front demonstrations save everyone from subsequent unpleasant misunderstandings."

Bile scorched Mom's throat and filled her mouth. She kept

her lips tight. Her heart pounded in her ears. Terror took control of her breathing. In an effort to regain a measure of equilibrium, she conjured up the image of girl slicing a boning knife through the butcher's scrotum. She flashed her best whore's smile, something she'd trained herself to do under every conceivable emotional condition. She couldn't afford to let this psychopath see her fear.

She yanked an unreactive Darko into a standing position.

"Let's go."

His jaw dropped open wide enough to take a tangerine…or a spring-loaded BDSM mouth gag.

"Do you understand where we are?" he whispered. "What the hell are you—"

She kneed him in the balls, and as he folded, grabbed his ears, pulled down, and jammed her knee into his chin. He fell in a modified fetal position, approximately where Miloje had dropped.

"I sympathize with how you feel about your friend," she said to Petrović, tone calm and conversational. "I'm very fond of Darko; but, as I explained to your factotums—factoti?—I'm not a gun person, so my demonstrations are more hand-to-hand."

Darko's eyes fluttered, and a thin line of saliva trickled down his bottom lip. Given his previous injuries, it was hard to tell how badly she had hurt him—far less than it appeared, as Mom had made sure that his thigh would absorb most of the blow from her knee.

From the corner of her eye, she noticed the admirer-thug staring mouth agape as if she'd been served on the half shell. A hard-on pressed against his trousers, and his assault rifle drooped at his side. She grabbed the muzzle and shoved the stock into his face. After a satisfying *crack*, she handed the gun back.

"Maybe I should be more open-minded about guns."

The other thug, who had been momentarily stunned, pointed his assault rifle and looked to his boss for instructions. With an economic movement of his open palm, Petrović directed him to lower his weapon.

Girl

Mom sat as demurely as she could, considering that she had her legs spread.

"Would you mind terribly if we stop this whose-is-bigger stuff and get down to business?"

Petrović smiled which, given the condition of his teeth, he shouldn't have done. Mom refrained from asking whether the last dentist willing to work on his mouth had been deported or shot.

"You have an enviably small electronic footprint, and with certain notable exceptions"—Petrović tilted his head toward Darko, who seemed to be having trouble climbing back into his chair—"an upscale clientele."

"Affluent, bored baby-boomers, nostalgic for the good old days. A market thus far untouched by your efforts."

"I see no evidence that you can move the quantity you seem to be talking about."

"That's my problem. All you should care about are two things. First, that I can pay for it, and those blue-paper-band-wrapped packets of Ben Franklins demonstrate that I can. Second, that there's no blowback in your direction, and your *simple up-front demonstration* communicated that crossing you would be deleterious to my health."

He nodded. The thugs took the bags of cash. She slapped their hands.

"Not quite yet. I'd like to see the product and take a random taste."

Petrović nodded again. One of the lackeys left and returned with bags bearing a drawing of a tacking sailboat and the words *Cape Cod Yat* Club—nice touch in spite of the misspelling—and containing bricks of well-wrapped powder. China white, to her untrained eye. She chose one at random and handed it to Darko.

"Be Slobo's guest."

He sampled more than strictly necessary, then nodded his approval. His loopy expression confirmed his nod.

Mom stood. "I look forward to further meetings."

"Pity though it is, you and I will have no further direct

communications. This was a special accommodation, the sort few have lived through."

"That's a shame, but Darko is perfectly—well, sufficiently—capable of dealing with your flunkies on future transactions."

Blindfolded and dressed again, Mom and Darko were driven back to where they'd been picked up. They then took a cab to a garage in Long Island City. The cavernous space was empty except for several U.S. Post Office trucks. A quartet of shorthaired, bulked-up uniformed postal workers milled about, watching them from the corners of their eyes. Mom and Darko stood at a small side door marked *Electrical equipment do not enter.* The door slid open, and they walked into a large windowless room, undecorated and under-furnished with a delaminating conference table, a half dozen mismatched chairs, a pot of coffee going sour on a hot plate, and a carton of Styrofoam cups. Flack and three government-issued types in cheap suits sat around the table, looking as if they wanted to shoot someone.

Mom handed Flack the audio recording shoes and video glasses. A scraggly man with a plaid shirt and long uneven sideburns emerged from a side door Mom hadn't noticed, took the shoes and glasses, and receded from where he'd come. Flack gave her a pair of pink flip-flops. She began talking nonstop like an excited ten-year-old just returned from her first day at school, telling all assembled about Petrović's piss eyes and how she'd barely been able to control her terror when he shot Miloje. Darko didn't speak.

As soon as she stopped talking, sat down, drained and exhausted.

Flack stood. "Time to go."

The others stood as well.

Mom hugged Darko.

"Best of luck to you. I'm sorry this has to be goodbye."

"Me too," he said, eyes wet with unshed tears.

Flack and one of the men escorted her out, while the two others left with Darko.

"Where are we going?"

"Your place. We'll help you pack; then it's off to a safe house."

He'd actually said *safe house,* a term she'd never expected to hear in real life. But was this real life or, as she feared, a slow and dreary existence neither real life nor real death but a barely real purgatory? She recalled the gnawing emptiness that had enveloped her before Epi. At least then she'd had drugs and work.

Now life would be what she made it. That didn't sound good. She practically heard the butcher cackle, as Flack and his partner walked her to a dirty gray Ford Taurus.

XXI

Too Depressed to Kill Herself

Witness Protection installed her in a rear-facing third-floor apartment in Hoboken, New Jersey, while they made arrangements for the longer term. They set up a small but adequate gym in the basement, and agents got her whatever food and books she requested; but she wasn't permitted to leave the building. Not that she had anywhere she wanted to go.

"You're lucky," Flack said. "Most everyone dreams of having the opportunity to start afresh, free of old mistakes. This is the first day of the rest of your life."

Great, life begins in Hoboken with a chipped linoleum floor, paintings of cats playing with twine on the walls, and a jackass spouting platitudes.

"Hey, Anna—your new name, Anna Able—I know I've given you plenty of reason to dislike me: my sexual kinks, your deal changing, even though I fought like a tiger to get you all I could. Anyway, I like you and want us to be friends."

Anna Able? Unintended irony perhaps.

"I'm not big on friendship."

"As I said, this is a new beginning." Grinning, he looked almost likable.

She tried to picture a worthwhile new beginning—the Epicurean ideal of living self-sufficiently, surrounded by friends, striving to attain a happy and tranquil life characterized by *ataraxia*, freedom from fear, and *aponia*, the absence of pain. But her mind's eye could only see an empty charcoal gray expanse.

"Hungry?" he asked. "How 'bout if I go out and get us sandwiches and a few beers?"

She shrugged, unable to conjure up sufficient enthusiasm for a verbal response even as she recognized he was making an effort to be nice.

Girl

A recurring nightmare plagued her. The butcher, Hannah's father, or even Flack raping Epi while she, nailed to a wall, watched. Flack gave her a bottle of Ambien. They blocked her dreams, but she stopped taking them after a few nights. Those nightmares were her only connection to Epi.

"The tapes you gave us were just what we needed," Flack said two days into her Hoboken confinement. "Epi's being transported to Allenwood as we speak."

"How's he doing?"

"Seems pleased to be moved," Flack said. "I'm looking out for him like I promised. We've arranged for a grief counselor to help him deal with your passing."

"Fuck the counselor—not literally, Flack—just give him skates, a stick, and a puck, and get him out on the ice."

"You doing okay?" he asked, sounding as if he actually cared.

She shrugged.

The DEA arrested Petrović and several of his top lieutenants. According to Flack, Witness Protection relocated Darko to a pleasant Sunbelt city, sent him to a technical school, and introduced him to another protected person "prettier, smarter, and nicer" than the piece of shit deserves; but hell, I know you have an inexplicable soft spot for him. So I went the distance."

"Is there something you can take for your delusions of adequacy?" Mom asked.

Witness Protection set up Anna Able in a small Ikea-furnished house in Choctaw, Tennessee, a college town in one of the poorest, reddest-necked counties in the country. Other than the college, the only cultural attraction was over fifty miles away, a museum celebrating the 6,000-year history of the universe. They'd considered replicating the Ark but lacked the intellectual capacity to pull that off. How long's a cubit? *Too snide? Yeah, tough. Let me watch Epi play hockey just one more time, and I'll give up snide as easily as I kicked heroin.*

209

Robert N. Chan

The rolling hills and mountains that hadn't been strip-mined and the narrow valleys that weren't littered with trailers, rusting automobiles, and ancient appliances had a spectacular natural beauty that outshone Central Park, the only other hunk of nature she had to compare them to.

A widow whose abusive husband had drunk himself to death, Anna Able had exiled herself to hill country to write a fictionalized memoir. Flack took great pride in contributing its title: *Sunny Uplands, Next Stop.*

"It fucking better not contain one word of truth," he said.

"Not to worry; I'm not writing it."

"One thing that should make you happy. As part of my official duties, I'll be visiting often." He grinned. "Need to make sure you stay sexually satisfied."

"Please don't."

Every day she checked the National Sex Offender Registry. In four months Epi's name appeared, meaning he'd been released from Allenwood ahead of schedule. Flack reported that he'd found a place to live in an industrial slum not far from the Brooklyn/Queens border. Creeping yuppification might mean he'd have to move to an even more dilapidated area, perhaps in a pestilential swamp—or rather *wetland.*

For at least twelve hours a day, sometimes more, Anna dozed, periodically waking to find her pillow wet with tears and sweat from a nightmare. She would count until she fell back asleep, sometimes getting as high as 10,000. In her waking hours, she'd walk the circumference of her small living room, look in the refrigerator on the off chance that something appealing had materialized, then sit for a while. Repeat. Repeat. She never imagined that a minute could be so long. And an hour… Had the earth stopped revolving?

She'd achieved her only goal, getting Epi out of prison. Now what? A job? Why? She still had money from the sale of her house, and with her living rent free and spending on almost nothing beyond modest food and gas, it would last for years. People seemed to like sex, and love had inspired innumerable poems, books, and acts of idiocy. Even the idea of a romantic relationship seemed preposterous, however; and what if she didn't dissociate while having sex? Yuck! Like any other game of chance, money had made sex more interesting; and it hadn't been all that interesting then. Having stopped playing for money, doing it for pleasure seemed as absurd as a New Jersey Turnpike employee collecting tolls free of charge. She could try to make friends with...someone. She missed Darko, and he hadn't even been such a close friend. She could do without missing anyone else. Hannah had had a bunch of friends, lot of good they did her. Therapy? The thought of talking about what had happened to Hannah made her skin crawl even more than the thought of having sex.

Every three days or so she went grocery shopping in her Witness-Protection-supplied five-year-old Ford Fiesta—the only times she bothered to venture out of the house. People wouldn't make eye contact, although they seemed convivial with their own kind. The locals apparently thought she had a connection to the college, a reasonable assumption since she wasn't obese and had all her teeth. Those in the college community seemed to think she wasn't one of them because they didn't know her. All fine with her.

Except nothing was fine with her. Camus had dubbed suicide the "only truly serious philosophical question," but she was too depressed to wrestle with anything truly serious. Too depressed to kill herself didn't sound so hot.

Finally an idea: she'd devote herself to learning Latin and Ancient Greek, so she could read the classics in their original. After a frenzy of Internet research, she ordered half a dozen books from Amazon. When they arrived, however, she'd already lost interest and couldn't bring herself to open the carton.

"So, Flack, anything new on Epi?" Anna asked, as he crossed her threshold on an *official visit*.

He handed her a large box of chocolates and a basket of carefully selected goodies from Citarella and Zabar's, gourmet food stores in her old neighborhood.

"He's jogging, a route that avoids schools or playgrounds. I arranged to cross paths with him. Without telling him who I was, I pointed out a parking lot that's deserted on weekends and put the idea in his head of flooding it and skating on it."

"Thank you." She bit her lip to stop it from trembling. "I wish he could go to a rink."

"Way ahead of you, I suggested that to his parole officer." He took off his shirt and flexed his overdeveloped muscles. "She's checking whether there's a time without kids being there. I'll follow up."

"I wish he had a social life."

Flack dropped his pants.

Anna reminded herself that he'd gone way beyond his official duties, periodically checking on Epi and wrangling concessions from his parole officer such as access to the local library. She wondered why it bothered her to feel like a whore. She began to undress, apparently not fast enough for him. He tore off her clothes, picked her up, and threw her onto the bed. Blessedly she dissociated and the rest was a blur—gray like Flack.

As soon as he ejaculated, Anna locked herself in the bathroom. She hoped Flack would get the hint and go. But when she emerged, he hadn't moved. A customer had told Mom, "Men don't pay women to have sex with them; they pay them to leave as soon as the sex ends." Anna wondered how much Flack would charge to leave.

"You need to get a job," he said. "If you were happy doing what you were doing, I might push my superiors not to care but…"

"My contract doesn't require me to be happy. Anyway, I've reached the depressionable age, and my depression is very dear to me."

"Protectees often experience an initial period of despair. Get a prescription for Prozac."

"I'm too depressed to care. Good break for you, as I wouldn't give in to your sexual demands if I felt better about myself."

He snickered. Lucky for them both she didn't have a boning knife within reach.

Dialing back her anger, she said, "Any shrink who'd live around here should have her own head examined."

"There are some good how-to books that—"

"I'd need a why-to book," she said. "Flack, I know I'm circling the drain; but face it, there's no way to replace the plug."

"You're required to stay alive to testify."

"So if I kill myself, you'll have a slam-dunk suit against my estate."

"They'd pull Epi's parole and with a little political interference from Senator Wilson, he'd go back to Lewisburg."

"Got it," she said. "Now please go."

"I'm sorry if it seemed like I forced myself on you."

She shrugged.

"I like you and want things to be good for you; no, more than good—terrific."

She shrugged again.

Anna's depression mutated into an intense sensation of emptiness. She felt cored out from the inside and surrounded by an oily chill that sealed her off from all pleasure and suffocated her pleasant memories. She couldn't endure this; yet she had to for Epi's sake.

She had to fill the aching void inside her. Hannah had her family and her dream of *tikkun olam*. Girl had her rebellion, the excitement of making a new life, and drugs. Mom had Epi. Anna had nothing—not even the prospect of suicide.

A woman is locked in a room, buried deep underground, with no windows or doors and a limited supply of oxygen. How does she get out?

213

XXII

Van Gogh's Ear for Music

Hoping to enlist endorphins to battle her death wish, Anna took up jogging. The unpleasantness of pushing herself to the point of pain and beyond passed the time. After seven weeks, she had her distance up to ten kilometers, over six miles. Her route took her uphill past a derelict factory, across unused railroad tracks, and by a decrepit trailer park, then downhill through an abandoned farm well on its way to becoming second-growth woods, and finally into winter-brown fields. If she started early enough, she'd see little traffic and no people.

Then another jogger homed in on her like a cold-seeking missile. The woman, probably in her mid-thirties, rightfully proud of her long legs and trim body, wore a college T-shirt and shorts regardless of the weather. Whenever she'd see Anna, she'd run alongside, tossing out sunny bromides and trying to entrap her into conversation. Anna thought the woman's excessive attention would have felt creepy even to a normal person who wasn't in witness protection. She considered changing her route, but like so much she thought about doing, didn't get around to it.

A crisp clear morning with a spectacular sunrise and happily chirping birds. Within five minutes Anna saw deer, an opossum, a porcupine, and a skunk, a real-life Disney cartoon except the opossum was road kill...as was the skunk.

As she neared the crest of the first major hill, a mud-spattered pick-up truck with a rifle, shotgun, and assault weapon mounted on a rear window gun rack slowed to her jogging speed. The driver, who wore a scarlet baseball cap imprinted with the symbol of a fist and raised middle finger, leaned out the passenger-side window.

"Now that you're all hot and wet..." He opened the door of

his truck. "Get in; we'll make some productive use of your...lubrication."

She flipped him the bird, then wondered if it had been such a great idea to antagonize someone with three lethal weapons so close at hand.

He sped off, leaving a streak of black rubber.

Upon clearing the hill, Anna saw an auburn ponytail bobbing over a telltale orange Whitney-Frick College T-shirt.

She spun around, but the truck came around for another pass. That couldn't be good.

As she sprinted by Ms. College T-shirt, Anna said, "Asshole in a pick-up truck coming this way."

The woman increased her speed to match Anna's.

"Hi! I hoped I'd run into you today!" The woman's grin practically burned Anna's retinas. "Having someone to run with makes the miles fly by, particularly on such a scrumptious day!" If the English language hadn't already had an exclamation point, this woman would have had to invent it.

"Can't talk. Doing speed work."

"How fun!" she said, accompanied by a girlish hair flip, only partially successful as sweat had plastered strands to her face.

The truck pulled up alongside them.

"Hey, babes, let me show you a better way to keep in shape. If those college faggots were doing you right, you sure as shit wouldn't be out here sweating your pretty little asses at seven in the morning."

"*Idi u tri...*" Anna stopped herself. This wasn't the time for Serbian curses and "Go back to your mom's vagina" only worked well in Serbo-Croatian.

"Pick on someone of your own intellect," the other runner said. "There's a pig farm back the other way."

Anna smiled.

The hillbilly seemed less appreciative. "You need a lesson in down-home fucking courtesy, and I'm just the man to give it to you."

Having been hassled by him or some other redneck before—all big, unshaven lugs were starting to look alike—Anna came prepared. She reached into her pocket and tossed a handful of large tacks in front of his truck.

"Time for some speed work," she said to the other runner.

Anna heard a pop. Then a scream. "Stop! Hey, I said, stop, you snotty fucking college bitches!" She looked behind her to see the huge red-faced fellow grab his shotgun. A sporting man, he'd chosen the least lethal weapon in his arsenal.

A shot went off, presumably aimed over their heads.

"This way," the woman said, as she took a hard right into the woods and onto a path Anna hadn't noticed.

Anna followed.

"I don't have my phone with me," the woman said. "Maybe you should call 911."

"I don't have a phone. Makes it easier not to communicate with people."

The woman laughed, a two-note descending peal like a door chime.

"I'm Elizabeth." Without breaking stride, she held out her hand.

Anna left the woman's hand extended like a section of a washed-out bridge.

They followed the muddy course of a dry stream. The concentration required to keep their footing precluded conversation.

Back on more even terrain, Elizabeth said, "With your looks, the men must be falling all over themselves just to—"

"Just a minute ago I almost had a shotgun wedding."

Three-note laugh, the last note awkward and nervous.

The path now snaked through dense, dark second-growth woods. Elizabeth continued chatting throughout, but the crunching of dead leaves gave Anna an excuse not to listen.

"That was a fun adventure!" Elizabeth said when they emerged onto a road. "It's funny; I don't even know your name."

"Anna."

"So, Anna, what kind of work do you do? Are you married? Single? Involved?"

"I'm a little disoriented with all our twists and turns," Anna said. "To get back to my starting point at the base of the hill, I turn left, away from the campus?"

Elizabeth nodded. "I'll call the police about the stalker when I get home. Not that they'll do a damn thing, but maybe when they fish our corpses out of the river..."

Anna obliged her with a ten-watt smile.

"What was that you started to say to the jerk in the truck?" Elizabeth asked.

"Nothing really. A friend taught me some Serbo-Croatian curses and..." *What the hell possessed me to say that?*

"There is no such thing as *Serbo-Croatian*," Elizabeth said, surprising undertone of anger. "It's Serbian or Croatian. Two separate languages." Her smile looked forced and her eyes still glared. "Or so I'm told."

They slowed to a walk and Anna concentrated on her breath to dispel the uneasy feeling in her gut, which she blamed on an overactive imagination.

"Maybe we can...meet up again?" Elizabeth brushed a hair out of her face. "Ever run in Nathan Bedford Forrest Park? Recently renamed Bedford Forest, after a college protest. It's wonderful! Has some nice climbs and even a gorgeous gorge, complete with a waterfall! I can swing by your place tomorrow morning. Shall we say around seven? Just tell me where you live."

"Thanks, but I can figure it out myself." As a protectee, Anna ought to be concerned when a far-too-nosy stranger asked for her address.

Elizabeth bit her upper lip like little Epi had when Mom told him she'd be away overnight.

"I suppose we could meet somewhere," Anna said, surprising herself.

"Great! The corner of Hog Hollow Road and Route Thirty at 7:15?"

"Okay."

A smile lit up Elizabeth's face.

When Anna got home, the cored-out feeling and oily chill returned. She realized that running with Elizabeth had

217

temporarily filled the emptiness. Well, as Galsworthy said, "Life calls the tune; we dance." Too bad her life had Van Gogh's ear for music.

She checked on Epi via the National Sexual Offender Registry and looked up his address on Google Maps. He still lived in a dreary industrial area whose sole virtue lay in its location, more than 2,500 feet from a school or playground. No surprise. She'd checked just the day before. Whenever she looked, she felt a pain behind her eyes. Sometimes she fought back tears; sometimes she encouraged them. As a condition of his parole, he wasn't permitted to use the Internet; but she was sure he'd come up with a way to get around that. She could probably devise a way to communicate with him that wouldn't be detected by Witness Protection. According to the *Times*, however, there'd been a spike in drug-related killings in New York. The Balkan names of the victims confirmed that even with Petrović in the slammer, the Serbian gang continued to be active. They had nothing to link her to Epi, and she wasn't about to give them anything.

Anna felt awkward seeing Elizabeth the next day. They started jogging, and the awkwardness matched stride with them. They behaved as if they'd had drunken sex the night before and woken up in bed together, embarrassed. Not that this had ever happened to Mom. It probably had to Anna, though, given her unfortunate marriage to a drunk.

Soon, however, Elizabeth began talking non-stop. Anna let her mind drift…. Brilliant, beautiful Epi, bursting with potential, now a parolee and registered sex offender. How could she not have been able to make a better life for him? Pain built behind her eyes.

"What's the matter?" Elizabeth asked.

"Nothing. My eyes tend to tear in the cold. Oh, yesterday you asked about my social status. I never answered." Hearing herself run words together, she slowed her cadence. She felt the uncharacteristic urge to engage Elizabeth in conversation, better

218

than wallowing in self-pity about Epi. "I'm a widow. My husband drank himself to death."

"I'm sorry."

"Trust me, it was no loss. For me, it's as if he never existed."

Anna smiled. "Tell me about yourself."

"I'm ABD—"

"Oh, my god!" Anna covered her mouth. "I'm so sorry."

Elizabeth laughed. "It means—"

"*All but dissertation* for your doctorate. My attempt at humor. I'm not used to being social."

They jumped aside as a passing truck loaded with hogs sprayed a rooster tail of water. "My husband Jason is a history professor," Elizabeth said. "We have a twelve-year-old girl, something I wouldn't wish on anyone."

I wish I could talk about Epi to someone who'd listen and hold me while I cry.

They entered Bedford Forest and began a steep uphill climb on a narrow dirt path up a hill through dense woods. The woods fell away, revealing a surprise view of rolling green fields, a river white with rapids, and distant mountains tinged blue by the haze. Tiny, like something little Epi might've made out of brick-and-slate-colored Legos, Whitney-Frick College spread out along a valley on one side. On the other the fields gave way to woods. Waves of forested hills with only the occasional strip-mining scar seemed to go on forever. Going downhill and back through the woods, Anna and Elizabeth reached the river.

Although her thighs burned and she had a stitch in her side, Anna didn't want the run to end. She'd enjoyed talking to Elizabeth—first time she'd enjoyed anything in quite a while. Also, she realized, the only way she could create a fulfilling life here in Dogpatch U.S.A. would be via the college community. Elizabeth could lead the way, like Virgil leading Dante through hell.

"You were right; the park's fabulous," Anna said, noting that Mom would never have said that, certainly not with such an upbeat tone. "And so was…I enjoyed talking to you. I'm glad we did this."

"So tomorrow?"

"Maybe we should take a break for a few days. I just… to so quickly have become actual running *partners*…I'm not that kind of girl."

"I get it." Elizabeth studied the bark on a nearby tree.

The sting of hurting someone else's feelings wouldn't have stuck Mom so painfully. Perhaps on becoming Anna, she'd changed more than her name.

"Well, I don't. So maybe tomorrow when we meet to run, you'll explain it to me."

Elizabeth's smile again illuminated her face, but seconds later the lights went out. "You have any friends here?"

"Besides you, my next closest acquaintance is the guy in the pick-up truck."

"That must be awful."

"Not at all," Anna said. "It's… awful describes it quite well, actually."

"Saturday night there's a cocktail party, mostly history faculty but a smattering of interesting people too, and you can meet Jason. Come by our place at six for the pre."

"The…?"

"College term. At fraternity and school-sponsored parties, drinking is strictly limited, so the kids get smashed beforehand. They call it the *pre-game* or just *pre*. The resulting binge-drinking has given rise to a new verb: EMT. As in, 'She EMT-ed last night.' Saturday night stomach pumping is big business at the college health service. The faculty doesn't binge, so I used the term facetiously."

Anna wondered if Epi had ever had a drink at a school party.

"As I was saying before I took off on that tangent, come over and we'll go to the party together."

"Lovely of you to invite me, but…" What about Elizabeth's weird anger when Anna had said "Serbo-Croatian," rather than "Serbian"? Anna decided to throw caution to the wind, but was it a cyclone? "Okay, fine, give me your address."

XXIII
The Beast

Anna didn't know what one wore to a hill country academic cocktail party; but the short skirt, fishnet stockings, four-inch heels, and tight V-neck blouse she'd worn when playing the role of niece wasn't it. For one thing, she was old enough to play the lascivious aunt. She'd taken few clothes with her when she'd left New York and had done little to replenish her wardrobe since. Having procrastinated, there now wasn't time to order online. Her choices: slutty niece outfit, running sweats, jeans and T-shirt, or a sequined something she'd purchased in town that would look right for an appearance on *Grand Ole Opry* a decade ago.

The obvious solution: tell Elizabeth she'd come down with the bubonic plague. But Anna didn't have a telephone and didn't know Elizabeth's phone number or even her last name. She could stand them up; but neither Hannah, nor girl, nor Mom would ever do that. As for Anna—the new improved Anna—she wanted to go even if only a little more than she wanted to open the box from Amazon and work her way through Ovid's *Metamorphoses*.

So on with the slutty niece outfit and hope for the best or at least something better than the worst.

A man opened the door in response to the bang of the horseshoe-shaped brass door knocker.

"Whoa... I mean, you must be Anna. Please come in; I'm Jason."

He looked professorial in a Brooks Brothers sort of way, right down to the graying at the temples, brown corduroys, and the sort of tweed jacket that went with a pipe and a phlegmatic spirit. When he smiled, he was downright handsome. Anna thought she saw the tops of four Cyrillic "C's" peek out from the

221

button-down collar of his blue micro-checked shirt; but it could have been dirt, a birthmark, or even an illusion.

He led her through a foyer, lined with family photos, into a comfortable living room.

"What can I get you to drink?"

"Club soda, if you have it. Otherwise tap water." The tap water in these parts had a disagreeable sulphurous aftertaste, likely the result of the proximity to hell.

Elizabeth came running from another room while putting on earrings. She wore a little black dress, perfect for the occasion.

"Anna! I'm so glad you came!" She kissed Anna on both cheeks.

"Elizabeth, didn't you tell me this was a costume party with everyone dressing like sluts?"

"You look fabulous. If you've got it, flaunt it." Elizabeth led Anna to a couch. Jason brought over a martini for Elizabeth, a whiskey for himself, and Anna's club soda with a slice of lime stuck with a cutlass-shaped plastic toothpick.

"I advise against attempting to experience this evening sober," he said.

"Her husband was an alcoholic," Elizabeth said *sotto voce.*

"Sorry."

"Don't be," Anna said. "I have a history of risky behavior. Once I even walked into town wearing an Obama T-shirt."

Elizabeth laughed harder than the comment merited.

"So, Jason, who should we introduce her to?"

"Guess I'm taken."

"Don't look so disappointed, asshole." Elizabeth hadn't actually said *asshole,* just implied it.

"What about Tobin?"

Elizabeth responded with a double thumbs-up. Anna contemplated bungee jumping without the bungee or perhaps following Billie Joe McAllister off the Tallahatchie Bridge. It couldn't be too far from here.

"He's a rising star in the history department," Jason said. "Just published a groundbreaking paper, and he's started an

222

Girl

interdisciplinary course that's the hottest thing in the college. Just be sure you avoid—"

"The Beast," Elizabeth said. "Christ, is *he* going to be there?"

"He'll crash," Jason said. "After the lawsuit, they'll be too cowed to toss him out."

"Who's—"

"Robert Kahn, an obnoxious reactionary history professor who got tenure via litigation," Jason said. "His case came up before the local wing-nut judge, who practically created a constitutional right to be a flaming asshole. Just to stick it to the college, as our local politicians so love to do."

"You'll smell him before he gets close enough to paw your breasts." Elizabeth rested her hand on Anna's knee. "He's opposed to personal hygiene on religious grounds."

"What religion?" Anna moved her leg from under Elizabeth's hand. Apparently that martini hadn't been Elizabeth's first drink of the evening. Perhaps there'd been a pre-pre.

"Last week, in a freshman lecture, he claimed to be a follower of Ba'al," Jason said.

"Like the biblical Jezebel?" Anna asked. "Child sacrifice and all?"

"He claimed Ba'al got a bad rap," Jason said. "Something about history being written by the winners."

Elizabeth looked at her watch. "We should get going."

"Anna Able, meet Frederick Tobin," Jason said, within minutes of their arrival. "Now touch gloves, go to your corners, and come out fighting at the bell."

Jason drifted off leaving Anna stranded with the tall professor, who looked like Hollywood's version of the ideal presidential candidate—Rick Perry after a brain transplant—except for the pink ribbon and pink triangle lapel pin. He reeked of self-confidence, charisma, and…*could that barely detectable odor be sex appeal?*

"I heard you just published a groundbreaking paper," Anna said. "Is it all tractors and backhoes or does it cover garden tools as well?"

"I don't know that it's quite as fascinating and important as people say." Tobin's self-satisfied smile indicated that he thought it more fascinating and important than people said and that Anna's attempt at humor had been neither.

"I understand you've designed an interdisciplinary course that's the hottest thing on campus."

"*Historicizing Whiteness: The Making of White People in America.*" Pride seemed to waft from every pore and enough to go before the fall but also to accompany all four seasons. "Whiteness is a concept employed to describe how Caucasians dominate and oppress people of color. We examine how European immigrants transform into American white people. We investigate the idea of *whiteness* as an economic, cultural, historical, and political construct that has become the most fearsome means of oppression the world has ever seen."

"But haven't white people also made significant positive contributions?" Anna asked. "Some of our greatest presidents have been white, and many of the words in our language spring from the culture of white people. Such as, oh I don't know, *many, of, the,* and *words.*"

"I gather you're not part of the college community."

Anna hadn't heard so much condescension and disdain so succinctly compressed since Mom's corporate lawyer customer had told Epi he wasn't interested in watching *The Lion King.*

Tobin sailed on. "We go on field trips to the state capital to observe the legislature in session and to the Creation Museum and Piggy's to observe the dimmer end of the white spectrum in its natural habitat, where the troops of oppression are bred. Their ignorance is truly breathtaking, but maybe that's just because we're laughing so hard we can barely breathe." Tobin emitted a single truncated giggle to underline his cleverness.

Anna flashed back to the jokes she'd made to herself about the locals' obesity and the condition of their teeth and her

224

Girl

references to the town as Dogpatch, U.S.A., the fictional location of the *Li'l Abner* comic strip. Shame pierced her conscience like the fangs of a water moccasin. Abandoning Hannah's childhood goal of helping to heal the world was one thing, but to make the world worse with prejudice...

"I need to freshen my club soda with something stronger, maybe a slice of lime."

Coalesced into clumps, the guests were attractive, thin, and well-dressed—with one notable exception. Even from a distance, she felt the gaze of the exception: a short, solidly built, bald man leaning against a wall, surrounded by a semi-circular no man's land in the otherwise crowded room. If Tobin could've been cast as a presidential candidate, this man would've been the assassin. He stood out like the star of an old movie. Lit more brightly than the supporting players, he appeared to be larger and brighter than life and about to strut across a stage set created just for him. He took a long drag from a cigarette—no one else in the room was smoking—and strode toward Anna.

In a minor panic she scanned the room, then to her relief saw Jason packed into a professorial scrum. Under threat of the approaching Beast—she had no doubt about the identity of the man heading in her direction—Anna squeezed in next to him.

Jason introduced her around. The conversation turned to bellyaching about history department politics and gossip about people she didn't know. The ambient volume rose on an incoming tide of alcohol, and she tried to recall why she'd wanted to develop a social life. Having resumed his wall-leaning, the Beast ground out his cigarette and lit a fat spliff.

Oh, no! Seeing a peril far more dangerous than the Beast, she tugged on Jason's sleeve. "Who's that guy in the tight Italian suit?"

"A visiting professor from Columbia. Why?"

Because he was a customer of mine who'd suck on my stiletto heels while I read Beowulf *to him.*

"I think I'll head home. I'm fighting off a bug of some sort. Lovely of you and Elizabeth to invite me."

225

"Loved meeting you. Please stay in touch."

"For sure," she said and meant it.

Keeping her back to her former customer, Anna made her way toward the exit. She caught a whiff of marijuana. Then an arm slithered around her waist. She removed it with perhaps excessive force.

"I've been waiting all evening for a chance to talk to you. I'm Robert Kahn, a/k/a the Beast."

"I've heard."

"Anything amusing?"

"Feigned obnoxiousness is never amusing. It's got to come from the heart. You have to really mean it and feel it."

Her comment drew a smile, a rather appealing one at that.

"Allow me to take you away from all this." He pulled at one of the few locks of mouse-colored hair that clung to his scalp like flowers fighting for life on weathered rock.

His crazy-blue almost violet eyes held too much: warmth, intelligence, and something dangerous. A touch of mischief at the corners of his mouth seemed to say, "Hey, I'm just kidding. Nothing here is worth taking seriously." Perhaps Anna had had too much club soda.

The high-heel-and-Grendel fetishist started in their direction and seemed to be trying to recall who she was.

"Okay." She took the Beast's hand—*paw?*—and headed toward the exit.

"My place is less than a mile from here," he said when they got outside.

The air had an invigorating chill, not to be confused with the oily chill that had receded. "Good to know. I'm heading home."

"I'll come with."

"I'd rather jump into a full bathtub while holding a toaster oven."

"May I watch?" His eyes went wide with exaggerated excitement. At least Anna hoped it was exaggerated. "Having pissed off so many self-important self-righteous jerks, there's got to be something interesting about me, right?"

"No."

"Let's have dinner."

"You're asking me out on a *date*?"

"Why not? The beauty and the beast motif appears in the literature of so many disparate cultures, there must be something primal and satisfying about it."

"The satisfaction comes when the hero slays the beast, then rides off with the beauty." Speaking more to herself than to him, she said, "I've never been on a date."

"Try it; you might like it."

"That's the theory that got me to this party."

Her former customer emerged from the house. "Mom!"

"Poor guy's so drunk he thinks his mother's here." Turning her back to the doorway, Anna put her arm around Kahn's broad shoulders. "Maybe I should practice dating on someone I have no interest in."

She liked his smile.

Kahn approached a chartreuse Cadillac. The meticulously cared-for relic from the big fin era had a big bushy raccoon tail tied to the antenna and vanity plates: GREATKAHN.

Her former customer lurched toward them.

Anna fumbled for her car keys. Kahn opened the passenger-side door of the Cadillac. "Come on in; I promise you'll have a good time."

"And if you renege on your promise?"

"I promise I'd never do that. "He smiled and his amazing eyes twinkled. "If you don't enjoy the evening, I'll pay for your time at...let's say—"

"$600 per hour."

"For $600 I could get two of the best whores in town for the whole night and still have enough left over for dinner and intoxicants."

"Have a good time." She put her hand on the door latch but realized she couldn't make it to her car without confronting the fetishist. "Okay, just be on your worst behavior."

"Where would you like to go?" he asked when she got into

his car. Associating with the Beast would hamstring Anna's efforts to infiltrate the college community. But it was time she got out and did something, and Kahn appeared to be sufficiently entertaining that she might have a good time talking to him. Good times had been too rare lately to pass up.

"Pick the place. The only decision I care to make is not to put out."

"Because it's our first date?"

"Because it's our last."

XXIV

The Wrong Way Down a One-Way Street in Crazy Town

Kahn claimed Piggy's Smoke Shack—the destination of one of Tobin's field trips—was the best restaurant in the area and dismissed the ones frequented by the college crowd: "I don't go in for all that health-food bullshit."

From the outside, the place looked like several interconnected barns that hadn't been painted since before the Spanish-American War. The interior, big enough to assemble 747s, retained the barn ambiance with bales of hay serving as random substitutes for chairs. A live pig rooted in one corner. "One of the patrons, looking for a lost contact lens," Kahn said.

A blond hostess, her only imperfection a single missing tooth that somehow made her all the more sexy, led them to a table. They passed groups of leering drunks, who became hostile when Kahn flipped them the bird or in one case mimed mooning a table of three-hundred pounders.

"You trying to get us into a fight?" Anna asked.

"Not to worry; we're all friends here, and the bartenders have shotguns. When things get too rowdy, they shoot off a couple rounds. Management has nothing against fights *per se*, but fisticuffs have a deleterious effect on the furniture."

"This just gets better and better," she said, echoing Darko's words when Flack began changing their deal.

The hostess started to pull out a chair for Anna, then lost interest and left them to pull out their own fucking chairs.

"They have Red Dog on tap. Tastes like piss and sauerkraut, but upside down the logo looks like Batman eating out Catwoman," he said. "Best way to kill the taste is alternating gulps of the stuff with shots of their homemade firewater, one hundred and fifty proof. Goes down like battery acid, but you no longer care about the quality of the beer."

229

"You go ahead." *My beautiful Epi a registered sex offender not allowed to live anyplace decent enough to have a school within a half-mile. How could I have let that happen? Maybe I could use a drink...or ten.* "Okay, order a large pitcher and a couple mason jars of the moonshine; but if you drive into a tree on the way home, make sure it's fatal. I don't want to be wheelchair-bound." *If I died that way, Witness Protection wouldn't pull Epi's parole.*

Kahn gave their order to a waitress—younger than Epi and dressed even sluttier than Anna— who seemed offended that she had to interrupt her texting to deal with the bullshit of serving customers.

"I don't even know your name," he said when the waitress flounced off.

Anna considered telling him she'd rather keep it that way but instead told him her name.

"Tell me about Anna." He leaned forward, resting his chin on interlinked fingers.

"She doesn't like talking about herself." She smiled—not much of one—but at least it wasn't whorish. "So why do you make such an effort to be obnoxious?"

"Look where obnoxiousness has gotten me," Kahn said. "I'm having dinner with the hottest woman at the party."

The waitress plopped down their drinks, spilling some. Tipping the table with one hand—so she could continue texting with the other—she caused the spill to cascade onto the already wet floor. She left it to her customers to grab hold of the sliding jars and pitcher.

"Please bring us a couple glasses," Kahn said, drawing a hostile look.

"How did you manage to alienate the entire academic community?" Anna asked after the waitress left.

"It started with my book, *Their Finest Hour*, which praised the civilizing influence of the British Empire and quoted from primary sources that contained forbidden words such as *wog* and *nigger*."

"I seem to recall...didn't Sharpton or someone of his ilk...?"

Girl

"To my delight, the Rev led a protest in front of my publisher's building, as if I should have changed the words people actually used. That got me thousands of bucks' worth of primetime vilification on MSNBC." Kahn sat up straight and puffed out his broad chest. "Spike Lee jumped in, along with a bunch of rappers no one ever heard of. Best of all, the *New York Times* accused me of 'resurrecting long-dead ghosts of hatred, snobbishness, and bigotry.' Never mind that ghosts can't be resurrected because they don't die, or that neither the op-ed author nor any of the protestors had bothered to read anything more than the deliberately provocative reviewers' packages I sent them." He grinned. "My book outsold everything else written by the department that year—everything put together. Tobin was beside himself, and two Tobins are worse than one."

He chugged some rot-gut out of the jar, and Anna did the same—not *quite* as bad as battery acid. She could be wrong; she'd never drunk battery acid.

The waitress slammed down two glasses and looked disappointed that they didn't shatter. When Epi arrived on the scene, Mom bought plastic shatterproof plates and glasses. He still ate off them up to the time he left for college.

"A tip…to insure proper service." Kahn handed her something palm to palm.

The waitress unfolded a small envelope, looked inside, and grinned.

"We good for the evening?" Kahn asked.

"Couldn't be better." She kissed him, tongue sliding over his closed lips.

"Bring us some ribs, fries, anything that's really greasy."

"On its way, baby."

"Was that coke?" Anna asked.

"What kind of asshole do you think I am?"

"Trying to figure that out."

"It was Oxy, hillbilly heroin, better than money around here."

"You have one thing in common with the college community—your condescension."

231

His head turned as if slapped. "I play ball, fish, or hunt with half the guys in this place. They're beaten-down exploited proletariat, like my parents. It's a love-hate relationship, like I had with my parents; but these guys only hit me when they're drunk. College types confuse uneducated with stupid. Whatever these people are, they're not stupid, just so fucked they don't know what to do beside cling to the past and hope for the best. The average person in this place gives a far greater percentage of his income to charity—typically through his church—than the academics do. They look out for their neighbors and help each other through their shit, not like…" He waved a hand. "Sorry about the rant."

Sounds almost like the community Hannah grew up in but with a nicer, more charismatic Jewish guy playing the role of Messiah. Although, in fairness, Rav Moscovitz had less of a nepotistic advantage.

Anna swallowed some beer. "This really is bad."

He lifted his mason jar. She touched hers to it. She was enjoying herself. The jury was still out on whether she was enjoying him.

"So the college fired you because of your book?" she asked, tone communicating incredulity.

"Oh, no, that was just the first step. I sealed my fate with the administration when I came out in favor of lightening up on sex offenders." Perhaps misinterpreting Anna's grimace from the sudden sharp pain in her gut, he said, "I'm not talking about rape, but some so-called sex crimes harm no one. Anyone who says anything like that in polite society these days might as well be advocating cannibalism."

Whoa! Does he really believe that, or does he know about Epi?

"You okay?" Kahn leaned forward, blue-violet eyes damp with empathy.

Just in time to save her, the waitress returned with a huge platter of ribs.

"They smell wonderful," Anna said.

"Best in the mountains, Honey," the waitress said.

232

Girl

"Why do I get the feeling that you're depressed?" Kahn asked after the waitress left.

She took a shot of moonshine and washed it down with several gulps of awful beer, determined to continue until it started tasting good or ate a hole through her liver.

"Anna, I… Okay, I'm an intrusive jerk, guilty as charged." He rested a hand on hers. "But I'm drawn to you."

She neglected to pull her hand away.

"Any reason beyond my supposedly being the hottest woman at the party?"

He pulled a rib off with his hands and began munching, barbecue sauce smearing across his face, making him look like a feral child. Anna did the same, perhaps to the same effect.

"Delicious," she said with her mouth full and sauce adhering to her lips.

"Have you tried drugs, an SSRI or SNRI?"

She leaned over to him, smiling. "*Jebo ti konj sa krvavim kurcem sestru na majcinom grobu a ti to kao invalid gledao, dabog dao!*" Though she expected him to be mystified, he laughed so uproariously that the people around them turned to look.

"She just said," he explained to everyone within earshot, "'May a horse with a bloody dick fuck your sister on your mother's grave while you watch as an invalid, and God make it so!' In Serbo-Croatian no less."

Anna curtsied to their seemingly baffled but amused neighbors. Not a smart idea to speak Serbo-Croatian in public—or *Serbian* as Anna, and no doubt Petrović, would have called it. Someone might get the right idea. It was only once she sat down that suspicion tore at her gut.

"How do you happen to know Serbo-Croatian?" she asked.

"Just some of the curses. I had a Croatian research assistant who didn't react well to my innocent affectionate gestures."

"Probably just cultural differences," Anna said, sarcasm as thick as the barbecue sauce.

"I'm sorry, Anna. My question about anti-depressants was inappropriate."

He might have been an asshole, but he was an empathetic and sensitive asshole.

"This conversation is like driving the wrong way down a one-way street in Crazy Town."

He laughed. "We seem to bring out the best in each other, by which I mean the worst."

She liked making him laugh.

"These days there's such a fine line between best and worst."

He laughed again, the unselfconscious belly laugh of someone comfortable with who he was.

"On the house." The waitress set down another pitcher of beer and two more jars of moonshine. Suddenly her mouth formed into an "O," and she scurried away, as if fleeing the scene of a fatal accident.

A shadow fell over the table. Anna looked up to see an angry giant of a man, wearing a scarlet raised-middle-finger cap.

"You the bitch who threw tacks under my tires?"

Anna stood. Even with her heels, the guy had six inches on her.

The place suddenly went silent.

Kahn pushed his chair back. With a Petrović-like movement of her open palm, she conveyed, *Sit, I've got this.* He sat.

This is a problem, but no reason to get him hurt as well as me.

"You deserved it." Anna stare locked on the giant's.

Screeches from chairs being pushed back sounded loud in the otherwise quiet room. Several dozen pairs of eyes trained on the two combatants.

"You got one big set of balls on you," the behemoth said.

"And you got a clit the size of a shriveled split pea," Anna said, drawing hoots and guffaws from the growing audience.

"Watch yourself, bitch." His threatening finger was as large as most cocks.

She shoved him, hard. "Don't make me hurt you, shitkicker."

Raucous laughter.

The brute, now red-faced, looked more confused than combative. Was he really going to beat the crap out of a woman half his size with half the town watching?

234

Girl

"This ain't over." He turned.

"Then where you going, shitkicker?" Anna shot him one of her better whorish smiles. "Join us for a beer or five."

"You really think I'd drink with *you*?" His tone was disparaging and dismissive; but after his stare traveled up and down her body, his eyes became approving and inclusive.

"Maybe I'll have to sweeten the deal by throwing in a couple tabs of Oxy, but sure." An even more whorish smile. "Hey, come on. I love the hat." She gave the brim an affectionate tug.

"Well, in that case…"

A waitress in a tight "Check out my tits" T-shirt brought over a chair. "Another round?"

Kahn held up two fingers.

While Anna got pleasantly plastered, the two men discussed hunting, football, and who you shoot first when the commies in Washington try to take away your guns. Several drinks later the story of how Anna flattened the big man's tires after he'd done nothing more than call her a *snotty fucking college bitch* had become a hilarious tale of conflicting cultural norms. The man— who'd now acquired the affectionate nickname *Shitkicker*— conceded that the word *college* had been inappropriate, given her situation, but balked when Anna demanded her tacks back.

"You hunt?" Shitkicker asked her.

"If I ever wanted to kill an animal, I'd chase it down and bite open its jugular. Weapons are for pussies." The return of her old bravado hit the pleasure center of her brain like a shot of cocaine.

Her former adversary stood and addressed the room, "I asked the girl if she ever hunted, and you got to hear what she said. Stand up, girl."

After a moment of alcohol-induced confusion in which she thought Shitkicker had learned her old name, Anna repeated her comment for the crowd.

"I'd like it if we became friends," Anna said at least two hours later while she and Kahn walked around the Piggy's parking lot, and he chugged his second double coffee.

235

Robert N. Chan

"I'm not good at committed relationships."

"There's a shocker."

A fingernail moon cast a spectral light.

"I'd be delighted, though, to be your fuck-buddy."

"You writing a follow-up book?" She fished his car keys from his pocket. "Another encomium to snobbishness and bigotry?"

"Ach!" He shook his head. "I've been struggling through volume two of *Their Finest Hour.*"

"Why the struggle?"

"I can't seem to... I need a research assistant." He grabbed for his keys, missing them by a foot. "My previous assistant was a history major with a creative writing minor. Her edits and additions pushed the manuscript up another couple of levels. I can't seem to replace her."

Kahn took her hand in his.

She took a deep breath. "Play your cards right, and I'll take the job."

"You'd probably be good at it." He laughed, presumably to communicate that he knew she hadn't been serious.

"Let's call a cab."

Anna removed her hand from his grip and picked up the pace, leaning into a cold wind that seemed to impede them when they walked into it but not assist them when it blew at their backs.

"It'd take them an hour to get here, and the driver would be in far worse shape than me." He held out his hand, palm up, demanding the return of his keys. Anna ignored him. "So admit it; you had a good time."

"Worst date I've ever had."

"But also the best?"

"That too." There being no remote button on his keys to his antique car, Anna inserted the key into the lock of the driver-side door. "I'm driving. You're riding shotgun."

"You've had as much as I have." He slurred his words.

"Not to worry; I'll drive as fast as I can to expose us to

236

danger for the least amount of time."

Anna drove his car back to where she'd left hers when she'd driven to the party.

"Follow me to my place," she said as she got out of Kahn's car.

She was drunk enough that the idea of having sex with him didn't make her skin crawl. She'd dissociate so sex with Kahn would be pretty much nothing one way or the other for her; but for reasons she didn't care to understand, she wanted to impress him with something she knew she was good at. Anyway, that was what one did after an enjoyable date, wasn't it?

"I don't think so. I hope this doesn't sound as stupid to you as it does to me; but I like you, and I want our relationship to develop more before we make love."

She laughed, "You're a ridiculous person."

"I'm flattered that you've paid enough attention to realize that."

He got out of the car, and they stood close. Anna wanted to reopen a conversation he'd shut earlier but bafflingly couldn't get up the courage.

He kissed her on the tip of her nose and turned to leave.

"Wait," she said.

He turned back. "What?"

She shook her head.

"If there's something you want to say...? Whatever it is, believe me, it's fine."

"Thank you but... I can't be the one to ask...again."

"Okay, when I figure out the question, I'll return with the answer."

XXV

More Kinks Than an Old Garden Hose

Anna woke feeling like a leprous rodent died in her mouth, a tiny steel-stamping mill was going full tilt in her brain, and her stomach was a toxic waste dump. However, neither snow nor rain nor heat nor hangover would stay her from the swift completion of her appointed rounds.

When she returned from her run, she found Kahn perched on her doorstep, clear-eyed and grinning.

"I figured out what you wanted me to ask." He got on his knees and took her hand in his, "Anna, will you be my research assistant and editor?"

"I'd be delighted." She helped him to his feet and kissed him on the forehead.

While she showered and changed, Kahn sprawled out on her couch as if he lived there, reading the most recent issue of the *Economist*.

They traversed the long hallway on the second floor of the Admin Building, the ugliest on campus. An architecture major who'd flunked out and gone on to be a bond trader had made a huge donation to the college on the condition that it build the building according to the plans he'd drawn for his failing senior project. Anna kept an eye out for her former customer.

Kahn bade her enter his office, soon to be their office. An emaciated brown-skinned boy in a white loincloth sat cross-legged operating a large fan.

"Meet Kim."

To her relief Kim was a mechanical model rather than a real *punkah-wallah*. Not bothering to suppress his pride, Kahn pointed out the faded regimental colors the 24th Sikh regiment had carried at Lucknow in 1848 and those of the 95th (Derbyshire) Regiment of Foot.

238

"I've tried to recreate the atmosphere of an officers' mess at the height of the Raj," he said.

"And to ensure that no one in the history department with an eye toward furthering his or her career will dare darken these already crepuscular doors."

"If it's okay with you, we'll work across from each other." He unfurled his arm toward a large Victorian partners' desk eerily similar to Petrović's. The rug, though, appeared to be Indian in origin and free of identifiable bloodstains. "May I get you a gin and tonic? I make it with real quinine. Stuff really works. Haven't had malaria in years."

"No, thanks."

While he went through a pile of papers on his desk, Anna turned on her computer, reset the security settings, and checked Google maps and the National Sex Offender Registry. No change.

Having received no instructions from him, she asked, "Where would you like me to start?"

"I'll email you a partial list of primary sources for a chapter on the British prohibition of the rite of *suttee*. That's—"

"Widows were expected to throw themselves on their husbands' burning funeral pyres."

Anna looked forward to learning about something in great depth. She could've done without the mechanical *punkah-wallah*; but she liked Kahn's childish compulsion to offend, if only because it was so similar to her own.

"Understand, I'm not a fan of imperialism," she said, "don't much like government in general."

"The only fan is over there." He tilted his head toward Kim. "My interest begins and ends with the truth."

"In the middle, though, you devote considerable energy to playing the obnoxious reactionary."

"Sells books." He shrugged. "At least I know I'm playing. Unlike Tobin and the rest of the politically correctors who think they walk with God even as they deny his existence."

"One can take not taking oneself seriously too seriously."

239

"Ahh, you've had that experience too." He grinned.

"It's later than I thought," Kahn said sometime after sunset. "Let's grab dinner and drink to excess."

"I'd prefer to keep working." Anna's fingers continued to race across the keyboard. "I've hit a pleasant stride." She hadn't thought about anything but her work. Now that he'd interrupted her, however, she realized that the ache of emptiness had gone into remission.

"You know what they say about all work and no play, Anna."

"One of the many examples of *they* being full of it," she said. "As I used to tell...a friend, all work is meaningless; but, unless you blow it off entirely, it's more fun to do it well than half-assed." It had taken all her self-control not to sigh when she'd referenced Epi.

Appearing to settle in for a long conversation, Kahn sat on the corner of the desk, legs crossed, revealing cobalt blue socks with crimson red polka dots.

"Please go. Let me work."

Due to her long, intense hours and her daily jogs with Elizabeth, she'd begun to lose weight. Noticing—annoyingly, Kahn noticed most everything—he insisted that he cook her dinner several times a week. Although an erotic undercurrent ebbed and flowed through their rapidly developing friendship, they'd yet to even kiss. Not that she wanted to but...

"Beef Wellington! Kahn, if you're trying to impress me, you're doing one hell of a job," Anna said, after they'd been working together for a couple months.

"Fattening you up for the kill." There was more than a dollop of truth in that. He specialized in recipes that required ample quantities of butter, heavy cream, and other ingredients the medical establishment condemned. Kahn said he intended to live long enough for the "hypocrats" to anoint cholesterol as the key to longevity.

Girl

"I wonder why I'm so comfortable with you," Anna said. "I even let you serve me. I never used to let people do things for me."

"Not a big mystery." He poured a glass of wine for each of them from a bottle he'd opened the night before. For all his talk about drinking to excess, they rarely consumed more than a single glass each. "You know I like you. We give each other all the space we could want."

"I don't even act out with you."

"Why would you bother?" he said. "You know I wouldn't give a shit."

They touched glasses, took simultaneous sips, and exchanged smiles.

"Are you as comfortable in your skin as you seem to be?" Anna asked.

"Pretty much. I wish you were."

"What's that mean?" She punctuated her statement with a scowl, even though she was too relaxed to feel scowly.

"Your silence about your past."

Anna longed to tell him about Epi, but a slip of the tongue could be fatal for Epi; and the thought of dropping her emotional drawbridge—any more than she had—terrified her.

"You see how that piece of shit Patterson continues to push for castration for all sex offenders?" she asked.

"Now that he's replaced his asshole buddy Wilson as chairputz of the House Homeland Security sub-committee, he thinks he's hot shit. Even I'm embarrassed that he's our congressman, and I don't embarrass easy." Kahn shook his head, then smiled at Anna. "Seamless change of subject; good job."

He set out small plates of string beans with shallots. For him vegetables were a garnish.

"Kahn…" She rested a hand on his. "I'm amazed how quickly we've become friends, but there are things about my past I intend to keep private."

"Like pretty much everything, except for your bullshit about being the widow of an alcoholic and moving here to write a novel."

241

"Hey, what makes you think it's not true?" She so pugnaciously thrust her face forward that the next step would've been to bite off a piece of his nose, something she was loath to do as she liked it the way it was. "What about your bullshit?"

He dismissed her accusation with a hearty laugh. She tried to feel annoyed but couldn't. Other than saying he'd wanted to be her fuck-buddy, he'd been appallingly honest. She didn't want to reference that one dishonesty for fear he'd think she actually wanted such a relationship. This friend stuff wasn't as easy as it looked from the outside. No wonder she'd avoided it for so long.

"No problem," he said. "When they come to arrest you for being an enemy agent or a serial killer, I'm better off having deniability."

She again touched her glass to his. His boyish smile, warm enough to defrost a pot roast, brought a twinkle to his otherworldly blue-violet eyes. In the time they'd been working together, the short bald predator from the cocktail party had transformed into a compact well-built man of boundless energy whose smooth head contained a marvelous brain. She might even have tried to seduce him, if it weren't for the fact that for her, sex would always be something she did to earn a living, neither a portal to intimacy nor a source of pleasure.

When called to New York to testify in connection with the arrest of one of Petrović's thugs whom she'd seen at his house— Anna had made up a story about a sick aunt and Kahn had the good manners to act like he believed her—Flack told her Epi's continued safety required that she engage in a threesome with him and a buxom newly blond FBI agent. "I've told her all about you, and she can't wait to eat you." He magnanimously offered to supply the cocaine. Anna went along with his offer primarily because of Epi but partly out of curiosity over how a return to her old life would feel.

She went through the motions, faking a few orgasms so expertly that even she wasn't sure if she actually came. The cocaine was like the return of a beloved after a long harrowing

Girl

voyage. *Hello, bad boy!* She couldn't get to sleep afterwards without the Secobarbital and two Ambiens Flack filched from his girlfriend's bag. She woke up feeling dirty, depressed, and disgusted. *Sorry, old friend, we've drifted apart.*

Flack kissed the blonde goodbye. As soon as the door closed behind her, he undressed and again folded his clothes neatly on the back of the chair.

"Hate the way she takes so long to move her butt in the morning." He stroked Anna's breasts.

She knocked his hands away. "It's over, Flack."

"Come on, Anna. You loved it last night."

She reminded herself that he was her sole connection to her son. "How's Epi doing?"

"As a special accommodation to my favorite protectee, I've been checking on him. He's figured out how to get on the Internet without anyone knowing, anyone but me that is. He's been secretly hacking. Seems he's compiling a dossier on Wilson. Can't believe that shitbag actually made it to the Senate. Of course, going on the Internet is a violation of Epi's parole, not that I'd drop a dime on him, with you and me being such good friends." His smile reminded Anna that when chimpanzees smile, it's a sign of aggression. "Not to worry; I'll visit you every now and then to renew our friendship."

"Don't bother."

"Anna. I've got a serious girlfriend. I'll just come around often enough to make sure your pipes still function." He stroked her cheek, making her cringe. "Come on. You know I like you. I'm sorry if it sounded like a threat."

"*If?*"

"Hey, I know what turns you on." He struck a bodybuilder pose. "You've got more kinks than an old garden hose."

She needed Flack. He was her only means of finding out about Epi and helping him, but... "I've had it with being sexually exploited."

"Anna, really." He chuckled. "You're a whore, for chrissake."

243

Robert N. Chan

"Not anymore." She caught him in her laser stare. "Remember how much I liked Darko?"

"Never understood what you saw in that scumbag."

"Remember what I did to him when he refused to help me with Epi?"

"Whoa, baby, are *you* threatening *me*?" His smile transmogrified into a nasty grimace.

"I told you how I feel. I trust I won't have to tell you again."

"One more time for the road."

"No."

He slapped her face. "I said 'one more time.'"

"And I said 'no.'"

He hit her again. "Remember all I've done for Epi…and all I could do."

She let him take her, although she remained stiff and unresponsive. She told herself she did it for Epi's well-being. That was a big part of it, but the darker part was to solidify her dislike of Flack. From time to time she'd been grateful to him for helping Epi. Now they'd be irreconcilable enemies. One day she'd balance the ledger, as girl had with the butcher, but perhaps not in such a hands-on way.

While waiting under protective guard to testify, she saw Darko.

"I still think about you, particularly when I'm putting it to my girlfriend," he said.

"Thanks for sharing. How you doing?"

"Good. I'm into auto repair. The Marshal's Service sent me to school when they realized I wasn't qualified to do anything except what I'd been doing. They got me in a small city in the southwest. I have a house and a girlfriend. The house is a shithole, and she's a pain in the butt but no more than most. All in all, I'm happy you rescued me from my old life. You?"

"I miss Epi, worry about him all the time. I seem to see murderous Serbs everywhere. Otherwise, I'm doing great."

"Keeping it wet?"

Girl

"I've entered a nunnery of the mind, devoted to serving the god of history."

"Glad to see you've lost none of your strangeness."

"You too." She took his hand and smiled, feeling buoyant. "It's really nice to see you and hear you're doing well."

He tilted his head. "Irony-free sincerity? You've changed more than your name." He returned her smile. "It's really nice to see you too and to hear you're doing well."

She looked forward to going home. Home? *Hmmm.* She hadn't felt as if she had a home since Epi left for college.

XXVI
Profiles in Cowardice

Spurred on by the publicity package Kahn created, liberals excoriated *Their Finest Hour Volume II;* and MSNBC talking heads competed to see who could express the most outrage. Never ones to avoid a pointless confrontation, Fox News lauded the book. Those who'd actually read the pre-publication copies—a group unrepresented by personnel from either network—praised its scholarship, the easy elegance of its style, and evenhandedness.

With his in-class comments gleefully quoted, Kahn became a campus icon, the beloved curmudgeon some loved to hate. He beat out Tobin in elections on Facebook for the most popular teacher and the most disliked.

Rumors of the depraved goings-on between Kahn and his sexy assistant/coauthor so enhanced his image that they found themselves fending off multiple dinner party invitations. They hung out at Piggy's once a week. Anna enjoyed the locals' raucous sense of humor, and to her surprise she and Shitkicker became friends. She continued to run with Elizabeth, and Anna and Kahn had dinner with Elizabeth and Jason from time to time. With the help of ample quantities of wine, they got along fine even if the political arguments sometimes became heated enough to result in broken glassware. The *Beowulf* fetishist returned to Columbia, and she no longer feared that every new person she met might be a murderous Serb. All in all, her life was as good as it could be, considering that she'd never see Epi again and that she'd always be traumatized by what had happened to Hannah.

"So, Anna, what should we write next?" Kahn asked, as they settled on the couch after dinner at his place. "On the strength of *Volume I*'s sales, *Volume II*'s advance notices, and the controversy I've begun to stir up, we can wheedle a hefty advance from the publisher for anything that sounds credible."

He poured them each a glass of port.

When she realized he was waiting for her to make a suggestion, she said, "Well...we *could* call for the dissolution of the Republican Party and for a fiscally conservative, socially liberal, and pro-science one to rise from its ashes. Given the damage the party's inflicting on itself and with congressmen like our Mason Patterson..."

Other than Senator Wilson, she disliked Patterson more than anyone she'd never met. His political association with Wilson and his bill to castrate sex offenders...

As Kahn was a lifelong Republican, Anna was surprised he didn't immediately nix her suggestion. Instead he sipped his port and stroked his chin.

Finally he said, "If we put it into historical perspective and gave it an international focus..."

She grinned. He never ceased to amaze her.

"I've got a great title—*Profiles in Cowardice*," she said.

After more sipping and stroking, Kahn said, "What if we were to discuss political chickenshitedness generally but primarily focus on the collapse of the Whigs in the United States, the Liberal Party in Great Britain, and the Social Democratic Party in pre-Hitler Germany? The final chapter could be your clarion call."

"That would be...terrific," Anna said.

"I'll talk to the publisher in the morning. If they give us an advance, I'm in."

She hugged him but quickly disengaged, hoping she hadn't given him the wrong idea, or would it be the right one?

After a four-month hiatus, Flack called to say he was coming to town "to discuss significant new developments." He told Anna to meet him in his motel room. She told him to make it the Holiday Inn bar.

He ordered a double Courvoisier when she arrived.

"It's on your tab since you suggested the place," he said. "I

247

got you a present." He handed her a new iPhone. "It's tricked out to be untraceable. I set the GPS chip to show random movements around Chicago. You'll never see a phone bill."

When she didn't take it, he placed it on the bar in front of her.

"First, the good news," he said, seemingly indifferent to her hostile silence. "Epi's skating twice a week, ten-thirty to noon."

"Great! What else?"

"He's still obsessed with Senator Wilson." Flack shifted on his stool. *Why is he so uncomfortable?* "I happen to run into him every few weeks when he's jogging. Lately he's seemed happier. Maybe he's come to terms with his parole restrictions and being a registered sex offender."

He'd only be happy if he were working on something that interested him. Wilson? Sounds like trouble. What can I do to help him?

She tried to smile. "Appreciate you doing what you can for him."

"Now the better news: my girlfriend will be here this evening."

"The buxom, unnatural blond FBI agent?"

"Christ on a stick, Anna, that was months ago. This one's a different buxom blonde. She's a DEA agent, hot but in need of loosening up."

The bartender set down Flack's cognac and Anna's club soda. Flack was as predictable as...every man she'd known, other than Kahn. That didn't make her any less angry at Flack, but Anna had anticipated this situation.

"Well, you're just the guy to do it," Anna said. "Are there any *significant new developments* not involving your dick that we need to discuss before your big date?"

"Anna, you owe me."

He twisted his swizzle stick, then untwisted it. *Could it be something about Epi that's making him uncomfortable?*

"Have you forgotten our discussion from the last time?" Anna loosened her grip on her glass for fear she'd shatter it.

248

Girl

"Come on. I know women don't say what they mean. I've seen how you get off on girl-on-girl action, and I know how much you want Epi to be okay."

Anna wanted to kill him. Instead she reached into her jacket pocket and pushed the button.

"Tell me what you want me to do," she asked as if all the fight had gone out of her.

"Come to our room precisely at 9:00, wearing five-inch fuck-me heels, a leather miniskirt, and a leather vest with nothing underneath and pretend you're startled. Say the hotel gave you our key. I'll have her so turned on that she won't think about how the story doesn't hold together. Thinking's not her strong point." His mouth puckered like a cat's anus. "You'll apologize. I'll offer you a line for the road. One thing will lead to another; and over the course of the evening, you'll turn her into a full-fledged, card-carrying dyke."

"Flack, you know I don't want to do that."

"Brought up as a good Catholic girl, she pretends to be little-miss-goody-toes, but a few flicks of your tongue in the right place and..." He took an excited little sip. "I started her out by putting blow on the tip of my dick, then on my tongue before I kissed her. Finally I told her that, as a DEA agent, she needed to know what it was like so she could talk the talk. Now she does it whenever we're together, then fucks like a thousand-dollar-a-night whore."

Anna reached into her jacket pocket and pressed rewind.

"I'm not doing it." She stood.

"Hey!" He pointed a finger at her. It took all her self-restraint not to grab it and try to break it off. "I stuck my neck out for you, got Epi wads of cash, got you placed in a college town. You have any idea the shitholes we usually stick people in? Hick towns with a collective IQ of *maybe* 120. The locals even *suspect* you of believing in evolution, they'd burn you at the stake, if only the art of fire making hadn't passed out of their mental tool kits." Flack emptied his glass and held it up for the bartender. "This shit goes down nice. Make it a triple this time."

249

"He's had enough." Anna snatched the glass. "My drug and threesome days are over, Flack. I'm involved with…just as friends but…"

"We don't want you involved with anyone, not with all the shit that's going down."

She didn't ask what *shit* was *going down*. She cared only about Epi; and she thought—hoped—she'd be able to keep Flack in line on that front.

He got the bartender's attention. "I'll have a whiskey, house brand. You can put it on my tab."

She stepped toward the door. "If you have to check on me again, do it by phone or email." Realizing she didn't own a phone, she reluctantly shoved into her pocket the one Flack had given her.

"You step out of here and—"

She took her recording device from her jacket pocket, pushed a button, and out came Flack's voice describing his threesome plans.

"You …you fucking recorded our conversation." Flack's face contorted until it became as ugly as his soul. "Use that and—"

"Forgive me, Flack, for I have sinned. I lied to you when we made our deal." She hung her head. "I still have the video I made of you snorting blow and raping me. For now it's mutually assured destruction."

"Elmo's dead."

"Sorry to hear that. How's Big Bird taking it?"

"Darko's witness protection name."

"Oh." She collapsed onto the barstool.

Wait, why should I believe him?

"How?"

"He'd been tortured, third degree burns over much of his body, electricity to the genitals, the works."

"Oh, god!" Anna struggled for breath. *No, can't be true. The jackass is pulling a number on me.*

He handed her his phone, displaying a picture of Darko's

250

face, half of it recognizable, half of it hamburger.

Covering her mouth with a napkin, she ran to the ladies room. She retched, cried briefly, knowing she wouldn't stop if she let go, and cleaned up. Then she returned to the bar, still sick and dizzy.

"How did they find him?"

"He sent an email from an Internet café to his mother of all people. I didn't even know he had one." Flack shook his head. "They arrested the Petrović thug with the Stalin moustache, the one who got away last time. We need you to testify about your earlier meeting. It'll be in about eight weeks, give or take."

"I'll keep up my end of the deal, so long as your end stays in your pants."

"We have reason to believe your cover's been blown."

"Unblow it. To lose one dead protectee may be regarded as a misfortune; to lose both looks like carelessness." Hard as she tried, she couldn't banish the image of Darko from her mind.

"They've been circulating your photo. We intercepted a text describing you as "serving the god of history." *Damn, my comment to Darko. They must've tortured him for a long time to get him to reveal that. I can only hope he didn't tell them about Epi.* "They're looking for you with all they have. You're insane not to be worried."

"Actually I am worried," she said. "Not being much of a worrier, I didn't quite notice the feeling; it's like a pit in the stomach, right? But no matter, I'm staying put."

Am I making a big mistake? That photograph of Darko. I can't think straight.

Flack's quick intake and release of breath communicated effort and disappointment. The trials of Job were nothing compared to what Anna was putting him through.

"I'll make a call." He stood, swayed, and seemed about to tip over. Anna refrained from shoving him.

"Fine, your funeral," Flack said upon his return. "We'll videotape your testimony tomorrow morning at the FBI's

Nashville offices. If you're not still alive come the trial, we'll use the video. The scumbag's lawyers will be there to cross-examine. You'll be behind a barrier, and your face will be blurred on the video. We'll do our best to protect you, but…"

Would Darko even have a funeral? It took all her self-control to avoid tearing up in front of Flack.

"I wish you'd listen to reason," he said. "My superiors don't think you're safe here, and I agree."

"Listening to reason isn't my thing."

Anna sat trembling in her car in the Holiday Inn parking lot. In a very real sense, Darko had given his life for her and Epi. She wanted to cry but couldn't. She started to take out her phone to call Flack for the name and address of Darko's live-in girlfriend but realized she couldn't attend the funeral or even send flowers. "You were a good man, Darko," she said out loud. "A good friend. I'm glad I knew you."

Damn it! She couldn't even tell Kahn.

XXVII

Locked in a Cold Cell with a Bottle of Hate

Anna dealt with her misery over Darko by throwing herself into *Profiles in Cowardice*. Risk or no risk, she couldn't leave Kahn in the lurch. Once finished, she'd have Flack arrange a new identity for her.

Kahn groaned, interrupting her concentration.

"What's the matter?"

"A story in the *Times*. This kid had been sentenced to a decade in maximum security." His voice shook with outrage. "All he'd done was email his girlfriend a picture of an under-aged girl having sex. He got an early parole, but you wouldn't believe the terms they…"

Just a coincidence; it has to be someone else, has to be someone else, has to be.

Kahn had stopped talking and was staring at her, his face stamped with concern.

"Continue, please," her voice squeaked through her straw-thin throat.

"He wrote a long letter to the *Times,* setting forth the details of a senator's interference with the justice system, not just how the dirtbag had royally screwed *him* but also the asshole's favors to friends, paybacks… He supported every allegation with hard evidence. The kid must've been researching for months, hacking into computers, the works." Kahn pointed to his computer screen. "This is the first of three articles, front page *New York Times*, a major exposé."

"That's good, right?" someone said. As it wasn't Kahn and no one else was in the room, Anna assumed it had been her. Not that she expected her words to be heard over the drumbeat of her heart.

"In order to draw attention to the issue and to the scumsucker's atrocities, the kid killed himself. That got the

253

Times to assign their top investigative reporter."

A sound like a cat being run over by a motorbike shot from Anna's throat. She staggered to Kahn's side of the desk. A pointless act because her vision was too blurred to make out words on his screen.

"What was the boy's name?" Her voice sounded computer generated.

"Epicurus." Quiet chuckle. "If I had that name, I'd off myself too."

She hit him in the face. Hard, closed fist. Then dropped to the floor bawling, as if she'd been the one who'd been hit.

"What is it?" Holding a tissue to his nose, he got down next to her. "Talk to me."

She kept crying. He stroked her back.

"Whatever it is, I'm here for you."

He took the tissue away from his face and moved closer. Blood dripped onto the floor. He pulled her unresisting body into a sitting position, eased her head onto his shoulder, and stroked her hair. He had the good sense not to say anything. Finally she ran out of tears.

"Who was he to you, Anna?" Kahn asked.

She shook her head.

"You once told me you had a son."

She pulled back. "I never said that."

"I guess I guessed."

"You're such a scumbag!"

"There's a shocker." He stroked her wet cheeks.

"Leave me alone."

He carried her to his car.

"I'm taking you to my place. You'll stay there until you recover."

"I don't want—"

"I don't care."

She allowed him to set her in the passenger seat. He cancelled his classes for the next week: death in the family.

Epi was dead. Her life had been a waste.

Girl

Kahn carried her over the threshold and deposited her on his bed. He undressed her, got her into his pajamas, and covered her with a duvet.

"You want to help me? Spend the next few days shooting me up with smack. When it looks as if I might've overdosed, revive me with coke and make lust to me. When you're done, lick me until you're ready to go again."

"Fine," he said as if her request couldn't have been more reasonable. "Take this in the meantime." He handed her a bottle of gin. "Come with me while I score. I don't want to leave you alone."

Her hands shook too much to open the bottle. He did it for her. She took a few big gulps. It felt like hot sandpaper scraping her esophagus, worse in her stomach. She'd always hated the medicinal taste of gin. She had more. He wiped her mouth for her. She drank. In one quick move he got his trashcan under her before she vomited; not much came out. She gargled with gin, then swallowed. She swayed and took another gulp. She hiccupped and felt dizzy.

"Did he suffer?"

Kahn didn't respond. Anna fixed him with a hard stare.

"His homemade bomb brought down the vacant factory building where he lived. The police found scraps of his clothing, bits of DNA, but no actual body parts"—Kahn dropped his voice—"other than a fingertip and part of an earlobe. It must have been quick for him. I'm sorry."

The next hit of gin went down easier.

With the aid of Viagra, Kahn had great staying power. Also he knew how to find a vein and administer not quite fatal doses of drugs. He even kept his mouth shut except to sexually minister to her. If it weren't for the deadening effect of the drugs and what had happened to Epi, the sex might have been pleasurable. Under other circumstances she might've enjoyed the brief drug reprise, as well. Now the best feeling she could hope for was blotto, and thanks to Kahn, she got that.

After a couple of days, he almost ruined everything by

255

asking how she was doing. She considered telling him to fuck himself or walking out but going with the third option, she said, "Locked in a cold cell with a bottle of hate."

"At least you can still turn a phrase."

"Does it bother you to be locked out?"

"I'm delighted to be able to push sustenance under the door."

A tiny bubble of clarity rose through the haze of drugs and misery.

"You love me. Goddammit, you do." She glared at him. "Don't deny it; you *love* me."

"Desperately and passionately, almost from the moment we met and more and more each day. Never thought I was capable of a grand passion, but there you are."

"That's stupid."

"Wouldn't do it otherwise."

She considered walking out but kissed him instead.

"I did that to see how my pussy tastes in your mouth."

"And?"

"Can't tell. I need another taste." She kissed him again, even as she wondered why she was doing it. "Could be worse."

"Let's get you dressed." He pulled her to her feet. "We're going to your place to get your stuff. You're moving in here."

"Why?"

"If you're going to overdose, I don't want you to die alone."

"The drugs were an interlude. I'm done with them," she said. "I'm overreacting like a prima donna."

"Hard to overreact to your child's death."

"We hadn't spoken or seen each other in years." She started crying again, then sniffled in. Kahn handed her a tissue. "I pretty much knew he'd do something like this. I'm sort of proud that he pulled it off, although I sure wish he didn't have to die in the process, even if he hated living as a convicted sex offender."

"One piece of good news. Wilson's about to be indicted for improper influence and a fistful of related felonies, including money laundering. His daughter's going down too. Seems she was the laundress."

256

Girl

Kahn set his iPad in front of her and clicked on a video.

The congressman's daughter stood on a flag-draped stage. A sign behind her: "Welcome to the National Police and Troopers Association Convention."

"When I was a sixteen-year-old virgin, an older man raped me. Now in a classic case of blaming the victim, this child-porn addicted animal wrote a letter to that liberal rag The *New York Times*. I'm fully confident that none of you God-fearing Americans are going to believe—"

Two dark-suited, clean-cut men walked on stage. A man, presumably the candidate's manager, stepped between them and her. One of the men showed him a badge. He stepped aside. The senator's daughter glared at them.

"Emmylou Wilson, you are under arrest on multiple counts of money laundering. You have the right—"

"I'm in the middle of a speech." Face torquing red, she cast a brittle grin to her now silent audience then turned back to the man with the badge. "Sit down! When I'm done here, you may talk to my lawyer—"

"…to remain silent. If you can't afford a lawyer—"

"You're making a big mistake, boy." Too bad the agent she addressed wasn't Afro-American. "Do you know who my father is?"

"Yes, ma'am. He's being arrested as we speak."

"*Arrested?*" she screeched. "You and the liberal establishment you support aren't going to get away with—"

"Last night we offered for you to come in and give yourself up quietly." The agent stepped within a couple feet of her. "Now there's just one remaining question: are you coming with us, or do we need to cuff you?"

Her face, now purple with rage, and eyes so wide it looked as if her eyeballs were about to pop out from her head, she screamed, "I told you to sit down!"

Isolated boos and hisses from the audience.

The agent pulled out a set of handcuffs. She slapped them away. Not the smartest thing to do before an assembly of lawmen.

"Hands behind your back." The hitherto silent agent, who *was* Afro-American, said. "Now!"

She turned around. They cuffed her and led her offstage to a round of applause. Anna smiled, something minutes ago she thought she'd never do again.

"That's great...terrific actually. At least Epi got what he wanted."

"Tell me everything," Kahn said as he shut off his iPad.

"I can't."

"Please, Anna, not that again."

"Damn!"

"What?"

She shook her head. "I'm so selfish, self-indulgent, thoughtless."

"Anna!"

"By letting you take me in, I've put your life in danger."

"Maybe it's true what they say about cocaine and heroin messing with people's heads."

She stood. "I'm going to take a shower. While I'm in there, get rid of all the drugs, except what you want to keep for your own pleasure. Then we'll talk."

Wearing Kahn's terrycloth robe, Anna emerged from the bathroom, hair turbaned in a towel. She found him perched vulture-like on a corner of their bed.

"There's quite a lot you don't know," she said. "I wouldn't be doing you any favors by telling you."

"I don't want any."

"This could get you killed."

"Good opening line." He lit a cigarette. "Captured my attention."

She talked for hours without Kahn interrupting. She told him about Hannah, girl, Everett, Mom, Epi, Darko, Flack, *tikkun olam*, whoring, drug abusing, drug dealing, witness protection, everything she remembered and more as it came to her. When she finished, he rested his chin on the tips of his tented fingers.

She did the same. He assumed her cross-legged sitting position, sort of—his knees didn't bend as well as hers. Their gazes met. She laughed.

"Feel better?" he asked.

"Not sure how I feel or how I felt; but, quite obviously, I've got to be moving on. Flack will resettle me, and I'll build yet another new life...I suppose." *Or a new death. With Epi gone, suicide is an option.*

"I don't think we should move," he said.

"*We?*"

"That's right."

He hugged her. Felt good. It'd been a long time since she'd been well and truly hugged. She lingered but finally squirmed away.

"Please, Kahn, you know I couldn't expose you to—"

"Correct. It's *my* life. Only I have the right to decide when or how I'm going to risk it, and I've decided. You probably never realized, as I don't make quite the show of it you do, but I'm as stubborn as you are." He stubbed out his third cigarette.

"Need I reiterate what they did to Darko before they killed him?"

"I could handle that a whole lot easier than losing you."

"That's the most melodramatic line I've ever heard."

"Really? I'd think that with all those soap operas you watched when living with that pedophile..." He again hugged her. "I couldn't have been more sincere."

She again enjoyed his embrace and again squirmed away. She stared, speechless.

"So how are you doing with that chapter on British and French cowardice?" he asked.

Almost knocked over by the wave of affection she felt for the man and for his having changed the subject, she grinned. The only way she'd be able to get through Epi's death would be to throw herself completely into something, and the only such something available was her work. No, she had to let Flack move her.

"Nothing that hasn't been written about thousands of times before, but it makes the point."

"What was it that Churchill said in his address to the House of Commons when Chamberlain returned from Munich?" He sounded too casual and too curious to be either.

"He said that Britain and France had to choose between war and dishonor. They chose dishonor. They will have war." Her annoyance with herself for letting him suck her into this line of thought caused the wave to recede, leaving behind a barren rock-strewn beach. As much as she pretended otherwise, she knew there'd soon be another wave...and another. "I never liked the Socratic Method and always hated being manipulated."

"The stuff you told me about Flack pissed me off," he said.

"Yeah, so?"

"Hiding never works, not for people like us anyway. We 'take arms against the sea of troubles.'"

"'And by opposing, end them: to die, to sleep no more'?" she said. "Where you going with this?"

"With you."

"Well, I'm going to the office," she said to her surprise. A few minutes earlier, she'd been about to let Flack move her. Now she was staying until they completed their book. As for taking arms...she had no idea.

"You coming?" She stood. "Or you going to continue to sit there, fingers tented, trying to devise new ways to lure me into doing what you think I should?"

"You know the first thing about you that blew me away?" Kahn asked, while they walked to campus.

"My legs in that mini-skirt?"

"The way you stood up to Shitkicker, not only backed him down but also made him your friend."

"Smoke and mirrors. Did you really think he'd beat up a woman half his size with half the town watching?"

He grinned. To show she was onto him, Anna drew back her arm, but instead of slapping him, kissed him.

"Your mouth tastes of tobacco smoke with an undertone of sex."

"What do you intend to do about it?" he asked.

"Kiss the taste away."

While they necked at the entrance to the campus, a trio of passing students shouted encouragement. By the time Kahn and Anna disengaged, more were staring at them.

"With all this crapola about your being in love with me," Anna said, "I might sort of be starting to feel a similar way about you, unless it's neediness resulting from my recent loss."

He took her hand, and they continued walking toward their office.

"You understand, I hope, that even if I could give myself to you emotionally—and the jury's still out on that—I certainly won't be able to until I come to terms with Epi's death, even though we've been virtually dead to each other for some time now," she said, although that might not have been true.

"And your other demons as well."

She shot him a hard look. "My other—"

"Quite obviously, you still haven't successfully dealt with being raped and let down by your family."

"You mean, Hannah…" She shook her head. It was time to give up on that one. Actually that time had long since passed. It was about time she acknowledged it.

"Also you need to get back to your calling."

She squinched up her face. Kahn was a wonderful man, but that didn't mean he couldn't be full of shit.

"*Tikkun olam,*" he said, as if stating the obvious.

"Our drug and sex interlude only put a temporary Band-Aid on a gaping wound," she said. *But could he be on to something?*

"However long it takes," he said. "I've waited forty-eight years."

She didn't know how to deal with the intense pleasure she felt—as if she were simultaneously being born and dying, while making love to God as he said, "Let there be light," and reading to little Epi as he cuddled against her. It had taken eighteen years

261

for her to tell Epi she loved him. Too bad it was unlikely that she'd have another eighteen ahead of her to tell Kahn and keep telling him.

They kissed some more. When they broke for air, she experienced a moment of clarity.

"So taking arms against a sea of troubles means striking back at Flack and standing up to the Serbs?"

He nodded.

"Well, okay, something definitive has to be done about all this lovey-dovey shit, and what could be more definitive than a Serbian bullet?"

"Wouldn't any nationality of bullet do?"

"I might just do what you're suggesting," she said, "if only to demonstrate what a stupid idea it is."

"Good."

"And after that?" she asked.

"We'll figure it out," he said, and she knew they would.

"You seem to know what you're getting into," she said, a last- ditch effort to kill the mood.

"No. I just don't care."

"Until death do us part?" she said, her tone a sarcastic spit in the face.

"That's right," he said, his sincerity a protective shield.

XXVIII

This Thing Depends on Me

Kahn entered her gently, too gently for her taste; but, as Anna didn't dissociate or become sick to her stomach when with him, she had no desire to give instructions. This time, though, it was starting to seem different. Following a rhythm unique to them, they slowed their tempo, then sped up. Now they thrust into each other, hard, powerful, almost brutal, as if they were striving to meld into a single *überperson*.

Her mind fuzzed. Her breath came hard and fast. Her muscles tightened. Her mind went blank, and then...contractions. Building. Her spine tingled up to the roof of her skull, then down and then... *Mmmm*. She and Kahn exploded at the same time with shouts and groans.

"Wow!" she said, she had no idea how much later, as time had warped and wobbled—in quite a lovely way.

"You can say that again."

"Wow!"

They both laughed as if she'd been extraordinarily clever.

"That was the first time you really came with me," he said.

"No...no. When you gave me oral sex, while I was stoned, I...many times," she said but felt confused. "But this was...much more intense. I..."

He looked at her questioningly. She put a finger to his lips, then closed her eyes, letting her mind drift before offering a further explanation.

"I got so good at faking orgasms, the line blurred between the faked and the real. This was the first time I truly let myself go, let myself enjoy it."

He kissed the tip of her nose, something Everett used to do and considered endearing; but when Kahn did it, it actually was.

"You fucking stud, you. You made a whore come."

He laughed.

They lay entwined, neither inclined to move.

"Better to have loved and been killed than never to have loved at all," she said.

"I'm having second thoughts about—"

"My *getting back to my calling*?" Her sarcasm rang false.

She closed her eyes again. Clarity built up force inside her like a sneeze long in coming.

"*Davar zeh talui bi,*'" she said, in a voice that didn't quite sound like her own. It sounded more like…perhaps a several octave higher version of one she'd heard while lying on the sidewalk in front of the butcher's shop.

Kahn's head tilted, slit-eyed. His fearful look was insufficiently fearful.

"'This thing depends on me.' It's what Moses said after he talked God out of annihilating the Israelites for worshipping the golden calf. God had told him to descend from Mt. Sinai—his people had lost their way. Moses realized he must *take responsibility for* his people, not stand above them but be one of them and guide them," she said. "I've been a sojourner in a strange land. It's time I came home."

Kahn stroked her cheek.

"I had a vision last night about what I ought to do if the Serbs don't kill me," she said. "I didn't want to tell you until I'd thought it through."

"A *vision* as in a bush that burns but is not consumed?" Kahn's sarcasm also rang false. Worry lines creased his forehead.

She sat up and took both his hands in hers. "More like when God commanded a peasant girl, who could neither ride nor fight, to lead an army to lift the siege of Orleans."

The sound of a laugh died in his mouth. "You do know the story of Joan of Arc is at least as much legend as fact?"

"A damn powerful one. It helped win the Hundred Years' War and legitimize the French monarchy for almost 400 years."

"Please don't tell me you're conversing with God."

"It's a thought experiment that feels like it's directed by

something beyond myself." She put on his bathrobe and sat on the bed within his reach.

"If you wear a suit of armor and carry a banner with a figure of Our Lady, you'd get quite a bit of publicity. But, confined to a loony bin, you'd be even more vulnerable to the Serbs."

"Epi died to destroy Wilson and his vaginal wart of a daughter," Anna said. "His asshole buddy Patterson is almost as bad. I want to fight Patterson and all the other morally bankrupt sons of bitches who trample on human rights, deny science, muck up the works with pointless regulations, and think economics is the art of aiding the rich at the expense of the poor. Hannah believed she'd been put on earth to help repair the world. You were right when you said I felt empty for much of my life because I rejected my calling." She took a deep, fortifying breath. "Once one starts to compare herself to Moses, pretensions of modesty drown in the Red Sea of arrogance. I'm toying with the idea of running for Congress." *There, I said it.*

Kahn stroked his chin. Anna waited for him to speak.

"Patterson is two hundred pounds of shit with a bad toupee. Since he played such a prominent part in shutting down the government and threatening to make the country default, he's been polling poorly but—"

"He's on the wrong side of most every issue and continually thwarts his constituents' interests." All wound up now, Anna felt like she were giving a campaign speech. She liked the feeling. And if she were to concentrate on something to distract herself from Epi… No, she was done with distracting herself. She would *consecrate* herself to healing the part of the world in which providence had placed her. "*Someone* has to try to change things around here. I was brought up to distrust government and with good reason. It hasn't been all that trustworthy lately. But staying on the sidelines doesn't qualify as taking arms against a sea of troubles."

Kahn's face twisted as if he'd suffered a sudden attack of Bell's palsy, presumably the result of the strain of appearing credulous, his own damn fault for starting her down this path. He had to know that she wasn't the middle ground sort.

"You think a godless Yankee Jew whore would stand a chance?"

"According to Emma Goldman, 'When we can't dream any longer we die.' If an army of feudal knights and lords would follow a peasant girl..."

"If."

"Let's get dressed, go to the office. We've got writing to do." She began to dress. "I'm still mulling it over. Just months ago I avoided all human contact. Now, with your help, I've busted out from my cocoon. Hard to tell where I'll go when I spread my wings and fly. Maybe my entire life has been a struggle to bust out."

"Take me with you." He got off the bed.

"Whatever I do, wherever I go, you better be there." She pointed a commanding finger. "Let's let the thoughts percolate while we finish *Profiles in Cowardice*."

More sensible would be to leave here with Kahn and devote herself to building a relationship with him, developing friendships, and healing. But sensible wasn't her thing. She'd been sleepwalking for too long. Now, fully awake, she was as hungry for action as a she-bear after a long, cold winter's hibernation.

"I didn't mean to discourage you," Kahn said while making dinner that evening. "Whatever you decide to do, I'm with you."

"If there's a chance I could make a credible run for Congress..."

"You can do whatever you put your mind to." He poured heavy cream into the sorrel and a white wine base that had been simmering in the sauce pan. "Barring a fatal bullet, the campaign would be fun. I've always preferred the preposterous to the mundane." The corners of his mouth turned down. "Please don't die, though."

"I've been trying to kill myself on and off since I was fifteen, haven't succeeded yet."

266

"That's not as comforting as you think."

"As Gary Gilmore said before the firing squad blew him to hell, '*Let's do it.*'"

"I'm with you, Anna." He hugged her.

She pushed away. They looked at each other for what felt like a long time but might've been just an instant. An intense something passed between them.

"I'm not Anna anymore." She cupped his face in her hands. "Call me Hannah and help me try to heal the world... Please."

XXIX

Cool As a Cryogenic Cucumber

While Hannah concentrated on completing *Profiles in Cowardice*, Kahn pushed his promotional genius to new limits. He engaged student tech-wizards to enhance Hannah's video and audio recordings of Flack. The YouTube video of a federal marshal doing cocaine and anally raping a protectee—her face hidden by a cascade of red hair, but her tight slim body and round butt in full display—got a half-million hits in twenty-four hours. The audio recording of Flack trying to extort Anna to do a threesome made the list of top-hundred downloads of the week, only twenty-eight spots below Psy's failed effort to recapture his barely remembered *Gangnam Style* success. Flack's arrest made headline news.

The media's speculation about the identity of the mystery woman at the center of the *Witness Protection Scandal* began to build. "She's living in a small town in the southeast," perhaps Appalachia, Fox News revealed, based on a credible source. MSNBC excoriated them for endangering the life of a courageous woman who'd had the guts to come forward and fight sexual exploitation. Fox countered with a story that she'd been a prostitute. *Per se* evidence that she'd been sexually exploited, proclaimed a fighting mad Rachel Maddow. Another leak and Rush Limbaugh declared, "I'd like to be exploited by being paid six or seven hundred bucks an hour to lie down and spread my legs." Rachel hinted that she might pay that if she got to use a studded dildo on him sans lubricant.

"Last chance. Are you still set on this?" Kahn asked, a week before the date they'd chosen for the public revelation of her identity.

"I'm terrified, but I'm done hiding, thanks to you," she said. "I'm about to become a minor celebrity. Hopefully the Serbs will realize that the public outrage from killing me would bring unwanted attention from law enforcement."

Arms around each other's waists, they walked along a dirt path planted on one side with primrose lilies in their full yellow glory and on the other with lovely lavender lilacs. Hannah breathed in... "Ahhh! To be in love on this perfect early spring day... It would be a shame to die."

"Or it might inspire them to demonstrate that no one is beyond their reach," Kahn said.

She kissed his cheek. She liked doing that.

"To quote your friend Winnie Churchill, 'What is our aim? I can answer with one word: Victory—victory at all costs, victory in spite of all terror, victory however long and hard the road may be; for without victory there is no survival.'" She held up her arms, making V-for-victory signs with her fingers.

Kahn shook his head, his exasperation reminding her of Everett.

"Have you always been such a foolhardy pain in the ass, or do I bring out the worst in you?"

"You've been a moderating influence." She kissed the tip of his nose. "I was once willing to die just to avoid boredom. Now I require a cause."

"What if you emerge from the closet on TV? *The Rachel Maddow Show* might bite. Rachel's already into the story. At least in a television studio, we can protect you. As for running for Congress... Exposing yourself so publicly to danger does seem, well, asking for it."

"We're doing it at Piggy's, and I'm running. If I get killed, use your PR genius to make me a martyr to...whatever you want."

"Okay, till death do us part."

They hugged.

A few days later, Kahn showed Hannah the poster that teams of students would tack on every barnside and storefront in the county.

Robert N. Chan
OPEN BAR! NO COVER!
Sunday night Piggy's @ 7
The biggest announcement since the state seceded from the Union.
You've seen her story on YouTube. Now see her face and meet her in person.
The star of the Witness Protection Scandal Reveals Her Identity and...
MUCH MUCH MORE

"Kudos to the photo enhancers. Even with my face hidden, I look pretty hot. The picture alone should pack in a certain segment."

With chairs and hay bales arranged auditorium-style and a rostrum at one end, Piggy's housed its second largest crowd ever. The blue ribbon went to Super Bowl XLV when a local boy played on one of the Steelers' special teams. The stink of tobacco, old beer, and moonshine added notes to the testosterone-infused body odor from the mostly male audience. The posters and YouTube had done their job. Now it was Hannah's turn.

She stood alone at the podium, wearing a black pantsuit that wouldn't have looked as good on Hilary Clinton or Michelle Bachmann.

"A former whore, drug abuser, informer, and protected witness. A mother who lost her only son to injustice. I'm going to be your representative to Congress."

Laughter and catcalls.

"In the months to come, I'll be knocking on your doors; and I hope you'll show me some of your famous hospitality." A tsunami of hoots and jeers. "After we talk, you'll realize I'm one of the smartest and hardest-working people you know. It'll dawn on you that it would be good to have me on your side. I'll be a giant step up from the lying hypocrite who's represented you for three decades while he grew rich, and most of you slipped further into poverty."

270

Outraged murmurs, not that she'd expected better.

"Calm down and listen, or the bar will close before it opens."

That quieted them.

"My message is so simple that even a hillbilly can understand it: VOTE YOUR OWN INTERESTS, NOT YOUR CONGRESSMAN'S!

"This congressional district has the fourth-highest unemployment rate in the nation, the second-lowest longevity, the smallest percentage of people who've gone to a doctor or dentist in the past year, fifth highest divorce rate, fourth highest percentage of out-of-wedlock births, third highest percentage of illegal abortions, sixth highest murder rate, lowest percentage of college graduates, and the most meth and Oxy use per person."

"Let's hear it for us!" someone shouted, inviting a chorus of rebel yells.

"Thirty years ago you were doing better in each category. Then you sent Mason Patterson to Congress. Now he's one of the richest men in the county, not that he's here much. He prefers to hang out with his lobbyist cronies in his Georgetown townhouse or his Palm Beach villa."

Murmurs.

"You there, in the overalls." Hannah pointed. "Tell me what he's done to help with jobs around here?"

"He ain't done dick, ma'am."

"Correct. Give that man a jar of whiskey.

"Can anyone here name one thing—one single thing—Patterson's done to help balance the budget, cut red tape, or reduce welfare for the big corporations and the super-rich?"

Silence.

"You in the middle there. Do you have your hand raised, or were you thinking of scratching your butt and got confused along the way?" Hannah feared she might've gone too far, but the laughter persuaded her otherwise.

A huge man stood. He had a shaved head, goatee, and a T-shirt with the slogan, "Here's a real stimulus package," and an arrow pointing to his crotch. Hannah smiled, as if she expected a welcoming comment.

"So, whore, you gonna finance your campaign by taking us all on?"

"If you could afford to pay my rates, back when I was a whore, you wouldn't need me to represent you."

That drew hoots, mostly favorable. Not that that mattered much. Hannah intended to win the war on the ground, house-to-house, trailer-to-trailer, sun-up to midnight.

A shaved-headed man in a black suit and turtleneck stood.

"*Samo Sloga Srbina Spasava.*" He pointed a pistol.

Some in the crowd screamed; others ducked for cover. Those that hadn't seen the gunmen saw their neighbors react. Panic visibly spread through the crowd like a wave at a football game, only in reverse.

Hannah stepped from behind the podium, hand on one thrust-out hip—she'd show the voters that she wouldn't flinch under fire, or she'd die trying.

A scarlet raised-middle-finger baseball cap rose from the crowd. The man wearing it lifted his arm. Light glinted off *his* handgun.

A deafening report.

A red hole replaced the Serb's left eye.

Chaos. People dove for cover.

"Nice shot, Shitkicker," Hannah said, cool as a cryogenic cucumber.

Silence, as if everyone had stopped breathing.

"Did I neglect to mention that there's a gang of Serbian drug dealers trying to kill me?" Hannah's voice was so soft that the crowd had to quiet to hear her.

A smattering of nervous laughter. Faces peeked from under chairs and behind bales of hay.

"We have enough time for maybe one more question, a song, and a few drinks before law enforcement locks this place down as a crime scene."

"I got a question," said an obese man wearing a T-shirt with a red cross and the slogan, "Orgasm donor." "Wanna get shitfaced and come huntin' with us tomorrow?"

"Sure, as long as you promise not to get so drunk you shoot someone who might vote for me." Big grin. "So what say we close with a song? One written by an English abolitionist more than eighty years before rich slaveholders from the flatlands suckered your forebears into dying for them. Never mind that your forefathers were too poor to own slaves and couldn't have cared less about so-called states' rights."

Kahn had suggested the song. Hannah had her doubts.

"How the fuck would we know the words to some limey abolitionist song?" one of the few women in the crowd called out.

"If you don't know the words, hum the tune or shut up. I'm going to sing."

Not so good at carrying a tune, Hannah counted on others to join in.

"Amazing Grace, how sweet the sound..." She strode through the crowd, shaking hands. By the time she got to "I once was lost but now am found," most everyone was singing. A start.

She believed, or maybe just hoped, that no one wanted a representative as dumb and clueless as they deep-down feared they were. Whatever Hannah was, she wasn't dumb; and at long last she was no longer clueless. She'd been blind but now...

Getting in touch with her inner monomania, Hannah transformed herself into a people person. Exuding unconventional but inexorable charm, she showed up at every gathering of more than a dozen people and visited well over a thousand homes and trailers. Many others were visited by Kahn; Elizabeth, Hannah's campaign manager for the college community; or Shitkicker, her local campaign manager and a celebrity in his own right for putting one in the Serb's eye at fifty feet. At most visits, people invited friends and neighbors. Having permeated even this benighted corner of America, social media multiplied the favorable impressions.

At public gatherings, an armed militia, self-christened

273

Hannah's Horde, protected her. Their "She's with Us" T-shirts featured a photo of Hannah in tight bare-midriff army camouflage, standing in front of an American flag with a bald eagle perched on her left shoulder. A Browning BAR Stalker deer-hunting rifle braced on her right hip emitted a muzzle flash.

In a press release issued from Washington, Patterson complained of "voter intimidation." Hannah counter-complained of "the chickenhearted congressman who couldn't inspire loyalty if his constituents' lives depended on it—which they do." She always referred to her opponent as *"congressman,"* never mentioned his name. Kahn's market research found that *"congressman"* had more negative connotations than *"scumsucker," "whore,"* or even *"New Yorker."*

Stories about her coolness under fire and her appearance at Piggy's, where she'd declared, "If I ever wanted to kill anyone but a human, I'd chase it down and bite open its jugular," grew with the telling.

Hannah showed up uninvited at a PTA meeting called to promote abstinence pledges.

"Oh, look who's graced us with her presence," the chairwoman said. "Come on, girls, let's give her our undivided attention. We might hear a sob story about how she was forced to be a whore but found Jesus and is all pure and repentant."

"I don't do repentance, and I'm about as pure as the strip-mining sludge being held back by that leaky dam up in Benson Hollow." Hannah strode to the high school auditorium stage and took the microphone from the stunned woman. "That dam will burst in the next big flood. Some of your kids will get very sick as a result. If that's what you want, vote for your congressman, who's fought every appropriations bill for the EPA or the Army Corps of Engineers." Eyes rolled and brows concentrated on knitting. "Most of you remember what happened when the Thompson Creek Dam broke through three years ago."

Kahn had told her she lagged way behind her opponent with local women, and she had to confront the problem head-on. He also claimed people respected her for sticking to what she believed in. Given the hostile vibes from this audience, she wasn't so sure.

A stick-thin, stone-faced woman in a long gingham dress that wouldn't have looked out of place at an 1890's Grange gathering, stepped to the front of the stage. The now silent audience gave her their rapt attention, something they hadn't done for Hannah or the chairwoman. The woman's haunted eyes called to mind Walker Evans' depression photos. She seemed more apparition than human, the timeless manifestation of America's white rural female poor.

Hannah braced herself for a diatribe.

"I'm votin' for her and any of you who consider yourselves my friends will do the same and tell your friends to vote for her too." Deep scratchy voice of unshakable authority, like an Old Testament prophet's. "Thank you for coming, Miss Hannah; but now kindly leave us, so we can get back to the purpose of this here meeting."

People bent their heads as if in prayer.

When she visited the woman later that week, Hannah learned she'd lost her twin boys to an infection likely caused by a sludge spill. Patterson, her second cousin, hadn't gone to the funeral or even sent a condolence note.

"When you meet him in hell, kindly spit on him for me," the woman said.

The first poll of likely voters: Hannah eighteen percent, undecided twenty percent, and Patterson sixty-two percent.

"If you want to quit, no one would blame you," Kahn said.

"So far only one person has tried to kill me, so we're already doing better than we thought."

He smiled. "You're enjoying this, aren't you?"

"Immensely, but I won't be happy if I lose or get shot."

"Both of which seem likely."

"Not to me," she said, even though she knew the Serbs wouldn't give up.

"I don't mean to be negative. I just—"

"I get it. You care about me and you're concerned." She kissed the tip of his nose. "I don't mean to be so repulsively positive about everything, but sunny optimism has always been an essential part of Hannah's personality."

XXX
Shabbat Shalom

Kahn's fiercely loyal students volunteered *en masse* to work on the campaign. Dozens took a semester off. They went into the high schools and found their counterparts who yearned to believe in something new. The local kids had been brought up to resent the college kids; but now that the college kids had come to them, they found inspiration in the message: help heal the world. The high schoolers inspired the middle schoolers who looked up to them.

Soon swarming hordes of smiling kids seemed to be everywhere, knocking on doors, putting up posters, and using social media with a facility that astounded everyone over twenty-five. At Hannah's rallies, they dressed in white and hummed "Amazing Grace," providing angelic background music. Oldsters were unimpressed—at first.

The sign in front of the Valley Baptist Church, whose pastor was one of Kahn's hunting buddies, read, "Let the little children come to me and do not forbid them; for of such is the kingdom of heaven." The following Sunday the pastor of Calvary Baptist Church blessed the white-clad *Children's Crusade*. Never mind that the actual Children's Crusade had been one of history's more horrific events. He concluded, "As these children instinctively understand, it is an *abomination* to pervert Our Savior's words of loving-kindness to aid the rich, oppress the poor, and foment hatred."

Hannah rose to thirty-two percent in the polls.

"I must admit that my idea of expropriating 'Amazing Grace' was pure genius," Kahn said. "I'm amazed, though, that they're actually falling for it."

Hannah put a finger to his lips. "Jesus embodied *tikkun olam*."

"You going to take up the cross now?"

277

Robert N. Chan

"I'm taking a couple days off from the campaign to go to Brooklyn for *shabbos*."

"Oh, can I come!" His *Mephistophelean* grin.

"If you stifle your instinct to offend."

"Can I come anyway?"

Kahn dropped Hannah off a few blocks from the synagogue. She walked the rest of the way out of respect for the prohibition against driving on the Sabbath. Wearing a head scarf and a modest dress, she gazed at the sidewalk but could feel the stares of the bearded men she passed. As she climbed the stairs to the balcony of the neo-Romanesque building and looked down on the black-hatted crowd, old words came to mind: *Ma tovu ohalekha Ya'akov, mishk'notekha Yisra'el.* How lovely are your tents, O Jacob, your dwelling places, O Israel.

On the balcony the women's stares were more intense than the men's had been, and their whispers sounded like the beating of dozens of crows' wings. No one made eye contact with her. A space opened next to a gray-haired woman, sitting next to a pretty woman of about thirty and her three girls, who ranged in age from three to thirteen. Hannah felt... she wasn't sure what she felt—some combination of anger, regret, and affection—but whatever it was, a lot of it swirled inside her. Hannah's middle sister, Sarah, and four girls whom Hannah assumed were her daughters, were sitting at the other end of the balcony seemingly oblivious to Hannah's presence.

"*Shabbat shalom*, Rivka," Hannah said.

It seemed to Hannah that the cavernous space had never been so silent for so long, although in actual fact the silence probably didn't last for more than a few seconds.

"*Shabbat shalom*, Hannah. Thank you so much for your help when I needed—"

"I'm sorry. I don't know what you're talking about."

Mother stared straight ahead toward the Torah ark, the *Aron Kodesh*, as if the service had already started.

"Mommy," Rivka fixed her mother with a hard stare.

278

Girl

After another long silence, Mother stood, hesitated, and eyes damp, motioned for Hannah to come closer. When she did, Mother hugged her. Hannah couldn't see through the fog of her tears.

"Please come to *shabbos* dinner," Rivka said.

Mother shot Rivka her slit-eyed look, still all-too-familiar after all these years. She turned it on Hannah, then back to Rivka. Finally she sighed and nodded her submission.

"Understand, though, your father won't—"

"I'd be delighted to come. May I bring my fiancée? Actually, I haven't gotten around to telling him that we're going to be married but..."

"Is he Jewish?" Mother placed her hand on the balcony wall, bracing for the anticipated blow.

"He loves me with all his heart and treats me better than I deserve." Hannah kept the edge out of her voice.

Rivka elbowed her mother, who, with a quick intake and release of breath, communicated pained acquiescence.

"Perhaps your father will enjoy lecturing him on his godless ways."

Rivka grinned.

"I've heard the men whispering about you. They say you were a whore and running for congress," a pretty girl of about thirteen said, drawing nasty looks from her mother and grandmother. "They say it's a stunt, and you don't have a chance."

"Meet my ill-mannered, precocious daughter Rakel," Rivka unfurled her arm.

Facing away from Rakel's mother and grandmother, so as not to scratch at old scabs, Hannah whispered, "Whenever *they* say anything, they're usually wrong, no matter who the *they* are."

Rakel motioned for Hannah to come closer, and Hannah brought her ear to her niece's mouth. "'The most violent element in society is ignorance,'" Rakel whispered. "Do you know who said that? She was a distant relative of ours."

Hannah nodded, trying not to break out into full cry.

The house in which Hannah had happily spent the first fifteen years of her life now seemed claustrophobic, dark, and forbidding. As soon as she and Kahn walked through the door, Rivka and her five children surrounded them, peppering them with excited questions. Rivka called over her tall, thin, pasty-faced husband, Aaron; but he didn't seem to hear her. Mother cut off the conversation by abruptly calling them to sit down for dinner. To Hannah's disappointment, but not her surprise, neither her brother Isaac nor her sister Sarah were at dinner. "They chose not to come," her mother said. Hannah's other sister, Rebekah, lived in Israel.

Rakel and her siblings were relegated to a children's table, much to Rakel's undisguised annoyance.

Neither Aaron nor Hannah's father—now bald, his beard gray, and his face deeply lined—acknowledged Hannah's existence. Treating him as an honored guest, they let Kahn cut the *challah*. He obliged them with a flawless recitation of *motzi*, not that he understood the words of the blessing over the bread. The three men became engaged in an animated discussion of politics. Kahn spoke of his support for Israel, his distaste for government sticking its unclean hands into matters within the sphere of religion, and his disgust with the decay in morals as shown by the widespread use of birth control and the casual resort to abortion. They accommodated him by speaking English. Avoiding any contact—even eye contact—with Hannah, he too acted as if she didn't exist.

Hannah told herself not to be angry at Kahn, who, after all, was doing what she'd claimed she wanted. As for her father, and even Aaron, she shouldn't have expected different. What was the point of confronting them? If they couldn't appreciate the huge gesture she'd made by coming here... She shouldn't have expected better, but she had hoped...

Mother and Rivka filled Hannah in on the doings of her siblings, nieces, and nephews; but the conversation lacked warmth and emotional connection. Maybe when Hannah got Rivka alone... But did it have to be that way?

She would never achieve reconciliation with her parents or even closure. To have taken a break from the campaign for this. She began whispering progressively more creative Serbian curses. She'd take her leave before dessert and coffee, polite but firm. No, there'd be no reason to be firm. No one would object. Aaron and her father might ask Kahn to stay. Not that he would. Although the way he laughed at their tired old jokes and pretended amazement at the perceptiveness and relevance of their Talmudic references, she couldn't even be sure of that.

A knock on the front door—no one would ring the bell on *Shabbos*. Hannah's parents exchanged confused looks. *Sarah and Isaac had changed their minds and brought their families!* Kahn's mouth curved into a mischievous grin. With a seigniorial flick of his wrist, Hannah's father directed his wife to answer the door.

She got up from the table, walking with a pained arthritic gate. The front door squeaked open. Then a muffled scream, as if she were having a heart attack.

Aaron and Hannah's father pushed back from the table, their chairs scraping the floor. Before they'd taken a step toward the door, they heard Hannah's mother say, "Oh... What a surprise. Yes, please come in. We have a *guest*...two guests... I couldn't not invite...didn't know you would be... We're honored, of course."

Footsteps, one set a series of pained, nervous shuffles, the other self-assured strides. Rav Moscovitz, not Sarah or Isaac, appeared in the dining room. He hadn't aged since Hannah had last seen him. Indeed, he seemed taller and stouter. Everyone snapped to attention, as if a general had just entered an officers' mess.

"Ahh, Hannah, so lovely to see you again." Welcoming grin. "My father very much regretted the circumstances of your leaving and admired your moral courage."

"Oh, Jacob, hi." Hannah put a hand over her mouth. She'd

once dreamed of marrying this man, the son of the Rav Moscovitz she'd known. "I guess you're now Rav Moscovitz. Congratulations on having succeeded to your father's position"—not that there was much doubt that he would—"Very nice to see you too."

Hannah was certain that the Rav Moscovitz who'd wanted her to lie had never regretted anything and had had as little use for Hannah's moral courage as he did for a ham, cheese, and mayo sandwich.

"I'm delighted that you've come back to us, if only for a short visit." He shot Hannah's father a sharp look. "I know your family is overwhelmed with joy over being able to spend this blessed *Shabbos* with you."

Hannah's mother offered him her chair.

"I regret I must be going." He shook his head, highlighting the depth of his regret. "I don't want to interrupt this joyous reunion any more than I already have. My intention was just to greet Hannah and wish her well. Hannah, I hope we have a chance to chat at length one day."

Chat? "I'd like that very much, Rav Moscovitz."

When her father and Aaron walked Rav Moscovitz to the door, she whispered in Kahn's ear, "WTF?"

"I accosted him in the street after *shul*, while you were upstairs talking to Rivka and Rakel. I explained how much better it would be for the community if it had a friend in congress, rather than an enemy."

"An enemy? I'd never—"

"Of course not, but how could he know?"

"Hannah, darling," Father said on his return to the dining room, a welcoming grin splashed across his face, "I enjoyed talking to your betrothed, but now I'd love to hear all about how you came to be down south running for Congress."

"I've no reason to discuss anything with Rav Moscovitz's unthinking puppets."

Her mother sucked in air. Father stepped forward, and for a second Hannah thought he was about to strike her. Rivka looked at her plate. Hands interlinked in front of him, Kahn half closed his eyes and practiced deep breathing. Out of the corner of her eye, Hannah saw Rakel cover her mouth to hide a smile.

Aaron said, "Hannah, you have to understand—"

"I understand all too well. I was the one who was wronged, and I reached out. That was more than I should've had to do." Hannah was tired of being angry. In addition to her negative feelings about them, she still felt affection for her parents, damn it. But too much time had gone by; and, as her father had said, what she wanted didn't matter. "Mother, thank you for dinner. Rakel, Rivka, please stay in touch."

She stepped toward the door. Kahn stood.

Mother opened her mouth. Father raised a hand to silence her.

"She's right. I was wrong," he said, voice choked with emotion. "I've spent twenty-five years regretting what I did. And I shouldn't have needed Rav Moscovitz's permission to say so."

Hannah had never heard him admit he was wrong, but still...

"He sometimes calls your name in his sleep," Mother said.

Hannah tried to picture that, but tears fogged even her mind's eye.

"Hannah, can you forgive an old man? Please. I may be an unthinking puppet, but I'm not an unfeeling one. At least now that I've reached the age of regret." He looked old and sad.

"I don't know," Hannah had trouble speaking. "Maybe if you'd hug me."

He did. Her tears came in a steady flow.

Hannah and Kahn hurried down the Nashville International Airport jetway. After sitting two hours on the tarmac at LaGuardia due to a landing-gear problem, they arrived late for a fundraising appearance at Vanderbilt University. By the time they left the secure area, they'd reached jogging speed.

Shots rang out.

Kahn fell. Hannah dropped on top of him.

Running, screaming people. Chaos.

283

More shots. Automatic weapon fire.

A pair of strong hands under her armpits.

A man in a bulletproof vest with "FBI" stenciled on it in yellow lifted her to her feet. Kahn stood. He looked shaken but waved off help. A cordon of armed men formed around them.

"Kahn, you okay?"

"Yes, I…" A bullet had gone through his sleeve. He had a ugly looking red abrasion on his arm. "I think I fell in reaction to… Are you alright?"

"Just a little shaken…but not stirred." She turned to her FBI savior—if that was even what he was. "What's happening?"

"We're taking you to safety, ma'am. We can talk there."

Hannah's heart pounded. Her vision went in and out like an Interpol siren. She saw at least three men down, blood pooling around them. One had a black turtleneck and a shaved head. Another wore an "I ♥ Nashville" T-shirt and had a Serbian tattoo on his shaved head. A long black wig lay at his side. The third she recognized as one of the thugs who had helped carry the dying Miloje out of Petrović's office.

Down a hallway through a door marked, "Emergency Personnel Only" and down another hallway into a windowless room with a conference table and six chairs. A distinguished looking middle-aged black man with military bearing stood at parade rest at the head of the table.

"Ms. Levine, Mr. Kahn, I'm glad you're safe." He had the calm voice of an airline pilot. "I'm Assistant Director William Jackson of the Federal Bureau of Investigation. Please sit."

"What just happened?" Kahn asked, sitting, his face wet with sweat, a little blood on his sleeve.

"We intercepted this." The assistant director handed him a tablet, showing an email that set forth Hannah's schedule for the week, their LGA to BNA Delta Airlines flight highlighted in bold.

"We believe this was sent by a Patterson staffer to one of Slobodan Petrović's associates."

Hannah sucked in air.

Kahn asked, "Did Patterson—"

"We're investigating. You two are the only people outside of the Bureau who have seen this. After much discussion, we decided to give you a choice. You have the right to go public with this, but we'd prefer to conduct our investigation in secrecy. We believe that would give us the best chance of connecting the dots. Maybe they will lead to the congressman, maybe not. But, as I said, it's your choice."

"You'll win if we go public," Kahn said. "With the mistrust of Washington, everyone will believe Patterson sanctioned his staffer's email, knew about it, or at the least had made it a point not to know. You'll be a congresswoman, be able to try to heal the world. It's a no-brainer."

"I'll win anyway," Hannah said, heart still pounding.

"Honey, you still trail by a large margin." Kahn rested a hand on her thigh. "There's no way the investigation will conclude before the election."

He looked at Jackson, who nodded.

"I'll wipe the floor with him at the debate."

"The debate comes pretty late in the game. Most people will already have made up their minds."

"They made up their minds before the campaign started. My job's to change their minds. If I can't, I don't deserve to win."

Kahn shook his head. "An investigation in the public eye, with the press looking into every corner, might be more effective. No offense meant, Assistant Director, but Patterson *is* head of the House Homeland Security Sub-Committee."

"None taken. As I said, your choice."

Hannah tented her fingers as she sized up the man. She trusted him but didn't have much faith in her initial read on people.

"Assistant Director Jackson, you're convinced that the best chance of arriving at the truth is if we stay mum?" she asked.

"Yes, ma'am."

Kahn let out an exasperated wheeze. "Really, Hannah, you can't be considering—"

Robert N. Chan

"I'm not *considering* anything. We've got people waiting for us, Kahn." She stood. "May we leave now, Assistant Director?"

"Of course. The area has been cleared of hostiles."

As they approached the limo provided by Vanderbilt, a woman shoved a microphone in her face. Two TV camerapeople aimed their weapons at her. Other reporters closed in.

"Ms. Levine, do you have a statement?"

"Sure do. It's wonderful to be back home again, breathing the sweet Tennessee air. Yet another beautiful country day, partly sunny with a chance of raining lead. Keeps me on my toes." She flashed her now habitual grin. "I'd love to hang out with you and talk about the issues, but we're already running late."

A surreptitiously recorded video surfaced from a Georgetown cocktail party at which a supporter asked Congressman Patterson why he wasn't in his district campaigning. Voice loud and unsteady from alcohol, he said, "Dumb crackers may still be a little pissed-off about our shutting down the government, but they ain't voting for no Jew York whore, even if she is a piece of ass."

"Let's get up some money, so we can all fuck her," someone said off-camera. "We'll make it back from fucking over your constituents."

The congressman responded with two thumbs-up and a series of hip thrusts. Everyone laughed.

No one laughed at Piggy's when Kahn showed them the video.

When it went viral, Hannah moved within thirteen percentage points of the congressman—five-point margin of error.

Now when news commentators referred to Patterson's campaign, they did so as part of an epithet: "Congressman Patterson's troubled campaign" or "The Tennessee congressman's scandal-plagued campaign."

286

Kahn began to get optimistic.

Hannah cautioned him. "A thirteen-point loss is no better than a forty-point one."

The audience filed into the high school gym, the second largest public space in the district. The largest, Piggy's, had disqualified itself as a venue for the debate when it put up a poster depicting Patterson trying to wriggle through the eye of a needle. Having arrayed themselves along one wall, Patterson's sky-blue robed choir serenaded the new arrivals, "Give me that old time religion, Give me that old time religion, Give me that old time religion, It's good enough for me."

Patterson and Hannah took their places behind their podiums. Patterson raised his arms as if about to give a benediction. His choir went silent. With his toupee coiffed to resemble a full head of natural black hair and wearing a charcoal gray suit, white shirt, and red tie, he looked every inch a congressman. In a short statement the moderator explained the rules Kahn had worked out with Patterson's Chief of Staff—there were none.

Patterson spoke first: "The media has been doing their darnedest to smear me; but you, my dear friends, have known me since I was this high"—hand a foot off the floor—"and you know that, for over thirty years, I have worked night and day for you. My gorgeous young opponent makes many seductive promises, a skill she honed dealing with her rich New York City clientele in her former business. I'm not qualified to do what she did for a living." He paused for laughter and got plenty. "But what experience does Miss Levine have that qualifies her for my job?" His jabbing finger punctuated each word. "Yes, I know, these days some people think experience in politics is a negative; but like any profession, the longer you do it, the better you get at it. If you don't know how to get things done in Washington, you can't get them done."

"Amen, to that," a woman shouted. Many applauded.

"I'm not here to criticize my undoubtedly well-intentioned

287

opponent; but, let's be honest with each other here, moral character counts for a lot. Someone who would sell her body, use and deal heroin and cocaine… Is that really the kind of person you want representing you?"

More "Amens," and "Give me that old time religion, it's good enough for me. It was good for Paul and Silas, it was good for Paul and Silas…" Dozens of hands clapped to the beat.

Hannah's turn: "It's a shame that, in the more than three decades that the congressman has suckled on the public teat, he's had so few accomplishments that all he can do now is launch personal attacks." Hannah shook her head as if it were a *damn* shame. "The question, Congressman, is whether it's worse that years ago I had sex for money, like some claim Mary Magdalene did, or that you continue to screw over your constituents, so you can glom onto yet more power, prestige, *and* money." Hannah stepped from behind the podium, hand on one thrust-out hip— her now iconic pose. "I ask you whether it's worse that I've taken illegal drugs or that you've enabled so many of your constituents to ruin their lives with meth and oxy while you deprived them of access to medical care."

Applause, but less than that Patterson had received.

"*ENABLED*? You've now gone too far, young lady. My record of opposing illegal drugs is second to none. Many of you in this room have heard me quote our savior, 'Your body is the temple of the Holy Spirit—' First Corinthians, chapter six, verse nineteen. That you'd even make such an accusation…" He shook his head, too shocked and dismayed to continue.

"Jasper McCoy, Beauregard Crowe, Jim Bob Crowder, Dewey Hatfield. Who here knows what they all have in common, other than being some of the congressman's largest contributors?"

Many hands went up. The undertone of murmurs grew louder. Hannah didn't know if that was good or bad.

She pointed to a tattooed man wearing a Confederate flag T-shirt.

"Drug dealers, ma'am."

Girl

"If everyone in this room knows who they are, why are they still in business? Perhaps it has something to do with the federal prosecutors your congressman has had appointed. Does a congressman supported by drug money, who refers to his constituents as *dumb crackers*, have the right to spout off about moral character? At least I've acknowledged my youthful mistakes and long ago stopped making them."

Several amens and more than a smattering of applause.

"Outrageous!" Patterson pounded the podium.

"Not nearly as outrageous as your depriving the children of this district of medical care, the opportunity to get a decent education and, most importantly, of hope."

Face red with indignation, and not the righteous kind, Patterson screamed, "Another outrageous—"

"Do I need to read off the names of the huge drug and insurance companies who've helped to rake in cash without government interference, and who in turn made you rich in exchange for your ... ?"

"My marijuana initiative is the toughest—"

"It's been a financial bonanza for you, Congressman," Hannah said, cool under fire as usual. "Since neither big pharma nor the local drug pushers want marijuana to be legal, they're happy to buy your support; but would someone of good moral character put his support up for sale to the highest bidder?" *Am I going too far?*

Patterson's forced smile contrasted with the parallel strain lines in his forehead and made him look like he suffered from a Botox overdose. He ran a hand through his carefully tousled toupee.

"Us good folks down here don't need no Yankee carpetbagger telling us how to live our lives."

"I understand why you might think that, given how little time you've spent in the district in the past two decades, but now that you're here, look around. We sure as hell need something, and we aren't getting it from you."

Patterson screamed, "I'm not going to stand here and listen to you curse in front of God-fearing women and children!"

289

"Then sit." To highlight the contrast between her and her opponent, Hannah dropped her voice, so people had to strain to hear her. "Jesus spoke in plain, simple language that everyone understood, even if it got under the skin of highfalutin' rich people like you, congressman. While I'm not so presumptuous as to compare myself to him, I intend to speak as plainly as he did."

Children's Crusade singing "Amazing Grace" drowned out his response. Many in the audience, arms linked, joined in. The larger men in Hannah's Horde carried her off stage on their shoulders while her adversary's lips flapped, and his face turned the color of Shitkicker's hat.

Hannah didn't know if she won as convincingly as the final demonstration would've indicated; but the visuals were on her side, and there was, she hoped, a sizable TV audience.

The last poll before the election showed Hannah trailing by six percentage points. ·

The election night crowd that gathered outside the Whitney-Frick College Administration Building reeked of pessimism. Although not yet ready to declare for Patterson, with less than ten percent of the votes counted, Fox News had labeled him the probable winner.

"Great campaign! Really great," Elizabeth hugged Hannah. "It was a privilege to be a part of it."

"No progressive candidate has ever come this close to winning here since FDR," Jason added.

"CNBC has us too close to call," Hannah said.

Arm around her waist, Kahn remained uncharacteristically silent.

"You carried the town and the college people. The rural votes come in later," Jason said. "But win or lose, you were amazing. I really mean it."

"I'm only amazing if I win." Hannah smiled her now habitual smile, but she couldn't stop her stomach from churning.

She mounted the steps leading to the building's monumental entrance.

Girl

"I thank you all for your help. You're the best. I'm off to Piggy's. You're all invited. Win or lose, it'll be an opportunity to drink. Their beer tastes like urine with overtones of sauerkraut, and their homemade firewater goes down like battery acid; but after a few sips, you no longer care about the quality of the beer."

That drew laughter and applause.

Several cars full of college people followed her. Most had never set foot in Piggy's and had never imagined that they would.

Hannah had never heard Piggy's so quiet. CNBC still listed the results as too close to call, but Fox had just declared for Patterson.

"It all comes down to the hillbillies," Kahn said. "They've always gone big for Patterson, but..."

With little better to do, the bartenders stared at the TV monitors.

People milled about.

Rebel yells. CNBC labeled Hannah the probable winner! Kahn squeezed her hand.

"I fear that's just in response to Fox," Jason said, appearing by her side. "The networks still have it too close to call."

"Elizabeth, Jason, you came! Never thought I'd see you in this place."

"First time for everything!" Instead of her usual cornea-burning smile, Elizabeth's expression tilted and shifted like a drunk on a balance beam. "You were right about the beer and moonshine."

"All these hill...*rural folks*, they're here for you?" Jason sounded incredulous.

"The beer and moonshine were a big part of the draw."

ABC: "With twenty percent of votes counted, Patterson up by 1,800." Chorus of groans. CBS: "Patterson the probable winner." Silence.

"Come on, everyone," Kahn shouted, standing on a bale of

291

hay, "don't hold back. Drinks are on us."

The TV anchors reported on other races. Even though the alcohol consumption increased, the crowd stayed glum.

Hannah made the rounds, talking to people, her campaign grin unaffected by the tension. She liked these people. Much to her surprise, she realized that, like the pre-rape Hannah, she liked most people.

Deafening noise. Piggy's shook. *Was that a bomb?*

No, but...*What just happened?*

A pair of strong hands grabbed her waist. Next thing she knew she was on Shitkicker's shoulders, and a mason jar of moonshine was being shoved at her. Confused, she looked down at Kahn.

"Fox just moved you into the win column. They're predicting that you'll get fifty-three percent. CNBC has moved you up to fifty-seven."

After Hannah passed out at her victory party, Kahn carried her to his car. She didn't even stir. While she slept, he drove.

"Wh... whoa, I've been asleep." Hannah yawned and stretched. "I feel...groggy. I must've slept for four, five hours. More...sun's rising already."

"More like fourteen," Kahn said. "It's setting,"

"Every joint in my body hurts...including my head. Didn't know my head was a joint. Never sleep in a car. Wait, you said fourteen... Where the hell are we?"

"Near Buffalo, about to cross the border."

"New York, *that* Buffalo?" She rubbed her eyes." Did I do something so terrible last night that we have to leave the country? Didn't I win?"

"I thought you could use a break."

"Isn't it enough that my joints hurt? Do we have to break them as well?"

"We're going on a Canadian vacation. It'll be fun."

"I'm going to close my eyes for a bit." She yawned. "Maybe, when I open them, things will make more sense."

"Where are we now? Place looks like a dump. With all due respect, Kahn, next time we take a vacation, I'll plan it."

"Hamilton, Ontario. See that big curved building?" He pointed. "That's Copps Coliseum, known as *The Dog Pound*, home ice of the Hamilton Bulldogs."

"Never heard of them." She shook her head. "You sure know how to show a girl a good time. Couldn't we have gone in the other direction? Maybe take in a live sex show in Juárez or Tijuana? At least we'd be warm."

"We've got great seats, center ice, first row, right behind the penalty box."

"I feel like I'm in the penalty box." His words began to sink in. *Could Kahn really be that insensitive?* "Kahn, I could do without a hockey game, thank you. Do they have any movie theaters?"

"Hey, took mucho work to set this up. Your candidacy got a lot of attention in the media. Someone on the team wants to meet you. He sent us free tickets."

"He could've come down to us. I'd have bought him all he could eat at Piggy's."

"He's not free to come to the U.S." Kahn pulled into a parking lot. "Turns out the team's been plagued by injuries; the entire first-string line is out."

"This just gets better and better," she said, quoting Darko.

The players skated onto the ice as their names were called.

"Playing right wing, Luc Hannahsson."

The player turned toward Hannah, grinned, and blew her a kiss. Pressure built up behind her eyes.

"Luc?" she managed to choke out.

Acting on instinct, without conscious thought, she was about to vault into the penalty box before Kahn restrained her.

She turned toward Kahn, not knowing if she were going to kiss him, hit him, or faint.

"What the…" The rink swirled; her knees buckled. She was

293

dreaming, had to be. She fell back into her seat, which felt totally real. "He looks just like... Yes, of course it's him. H-h-how? What?"

"Short for Lucretius," Kahn said calm, grinning. "After the explosion, he crossed the border and established a new identity."

"But—"

"As I told you, the investigators found no major body parts," Kahn said. "It seems the rumors of his death were exaggerated. He left behind some DNA tokens, sacrificed a finger joint and part of an earlobe, then skedaddled. As you can see, he's alive and well. As a parole violator, he's on the lam. We're having dinner after the game. He'll tell you all about it."

"He looks terrific," Hannah said, tears of joy streaming down her face.

At the conclusion of the game, Kahn led her through a door marked, "No admission" and down a flight of stairs. At another door, he flashed a press pass, earning them admission to the locker room.

Still wearing his skates, Luc ran toward Hannah and threw his arms around her.

A player hooted.

"You want to improve your image, you have to suck up to the press," Luc said.

"Lucretius?" Hannah asked. "You couldn't do better than that?"

He grinned. "Hey, everybody. Meet my mom. She used to be a whore; now she's a congresswoman. She'll probably be President one day. I'll be First Fugitive."

"Until I pardon you."